The REST *of* HER LIFE

ALSO BY LAURA MORIARTY

The Center of Everything

The REST of HER LIFE

LAURA MORIARTY

HYPERION

New York

Library of Congress Cataloging-in-Publication Data has been applied for.

ISBN 978-1-4013-0271-9

Hyperion books are available for special promotions and premiums. For details contact Michael Rentas, Assistant Director, Inventory Operations, Hyperion, 77 West 66th Street, 12th floor, New York, New York 10023, or call 212-456-0133.

Design by Nicola Ferguson

FIRST EDITION

10 9 8 7 6 5 4 3 2 1

To Carolyn Doty and Bud Hirsch,
who cheered so many on.

The REST of HER LIFE

Chapter 1

SEVERAL TIMES THAT SUMMER, Leigh further tormented herself by considering all the ways the accident might never have happened. She thought of the stray dog, and how its presence had, in a sense, decided everything. If there had been no dog, there would have been no accident. If the dog would have stayed home where it belonged, if it would have had a more responsible owner, if it wouldn't have dug under a fence or slipped through an open door, it would not have followed some scent this way and that until it ended up in the middle of Commerce Street at that particular time on that particular afternoon. Leigh's daughter would most likely have driven home without incident, and Bethany Cleese would still be alive.

But the dog had been there, standing on the raised median of Commerce, and maybe enjoying its freedom, though Kara later said that it was panting hard when she saw it. It was warm out, the middle of the afternoon of the last day of school. Kara, being a senior, had already been out for a week, but she and Willow had gone back to the high school to pick up their graduation gowns. On the way home, they stopped at the Sonic drive-thru, and when they pulled back onto Commerce, they noticed the dog as it started to step off the median. They watched, cringing, as the dog moved past screeching tires until it reached the other side of the street. Kara, who volunteered Sundays at the animal shelter, who on her twelfth birthday asked her parents to take the money they were going to spend on her presents and instead buy food for the shelter's animals, couldn't just drive away. She pulled into the parking lot of Raymond's Liquor, where she and Willow got out of the car, crouched low, and held out their still-warm fries to lure the dog away from traffic, into their arms, and eventually, the Suburban that Gary, not Leigh, had allowed Kara to start driving around town as soon as she'd gotten her license.

So really, Leigh often thought, any small change in detail might have altered the horrible outcome. If the stray would have been a different breed of dog, not so friendly, more skittish, it wouldn't have come to the girls, and Kara would not have been so distracted when she pulled back out of the lot. Willow later told the police that they were both laughing, trying to keep the dog in the backseat when they heard the dull thud that turned out to be the sound of the car striking another girl hard enough to kill her. But Leigh knew there had been other distractions: Kara had been on the phone— she'd admitted that from the start. Leigh imagined the girls had the radio turned up as well, though she never asked if this were true. Leigh was a mother capable of tact and sympathy. She tried. She was always trying. Sometimes, however, despite her best efforts, she apparently said the wrong things.

When she imagined the interior of the Suburban in those final moments, she pictured the dog as a terrier mix, tan, for some reason, like Benji. Leigh never actually saw the dog. She didn't even know about the dog and its involvement in the accident until much later, even though when the accident happened, she was just seven blocks away, teaching eighth grade English at the junior high, as she had been almost every school day for more than a decade. She was seven blocks away, and she had no idea it had happened. Just after the ambulance arrived, Kara used her cell phone to call her father's office on campus. Gary wasn't there, but the call had gone back to the English Department, and the secretary, hearing the distress in the caller's voice, had tracked him down in a faculty meeting on a different floor. Gary told Leigh later that when he got on the phone, he didn't recognize their daughter's voice. She was crying hard, and it sounded as if she were shivering, which, he remembered thinking, made no sense on such a warm day. When he finally understood, he gave the phone to the secretary and ran across the neatly trimmed lawns of campus to the parking lot in his tie and jacket. He had not run so far and so quickly for many years, and when he finally got to his car, he had to stand still for a moment to catch his breath, his hand pressed hard against his heart.

All this happened around three in the afternoon. Leigh remembered hearing the sirens, and she felt the worry she always did, but it was the vague worry she associated with other people's losses, other people's children. She didn't know the sirens had anything to do with her life until she arrived home hours later, her students' final exams rolled under one arm. She had been slightly irritated. Someone had overturned the recycling bin in the mudroom, and she almost slipped on a stray aluminum can. Catching herself, she looked up and saw her husband and her daughter in the living room. They were on the couch, sitting very close to each other in a way that made her think of couples she sometimes saw in trucks, the man driving, the woman in the middle where an armrest should be. She'd made a clicking sound with her tongue, loud enough for them to hear. They had just left the cans sitting there for her to pick up. But then she walked closer, and she knew something was wrong. Gary had his arm around Kara's shoulders, and his other arm held her hands down against her knees. She couldn't see Kara's face, just a tangled mass of dark blond hair. She could see Gary's face, strained with effort, his eyeglasses crooked on his nose. And Justin, Justin was there too. He sat on the floor, his lunch bag and backpack by his feet, looking up at Leigh as if the three of them had been stranded there together for days, and she was the long awaited help that had finally arrived.

"What's going on?"

No one answered, and she felt the first tick of dread. But they were all there, her husband, her son, and her daughter. So nothing so terrible could have happened. She glanced through the picture window. The Suburban wasn't in the driveway.

"What happened? The car?" There may have been a hint of righteousness in her tone. She had been against letting Kara drive the Suburban to school. It was Gary's old car, seven years old with a dented fender, but when Leigh was in high school, she'd taken the bus. There was nothing wrong with the bus.

Kara said nothing, squinting up at her mother as if she were a too bright light. Maybe it was only later that she decided this, but the way Leigh remembered it, the very moment their eyes met, even before she knew what had happened, she had the impression that something about her daughter's face had changed in a permanent way. Kara's posture was usually so good, but she sat hunched forward on the couch, and she looked young and small next to Gary. Her eyes had that luminous, silvery glaze they took on when she'd been crying, and they moved from the floor to the ceiling to the wall in quick, jerky movements. She looked like a dying bird, Leigh thought, a fledgling kicked out of the nest.

Leigh ducked to meet her gaze, but couldn't catch it.

"What?" she said again, the *t* sound coming out hard. She looked at Gary, but he, too, said nothing. Leigh felt herself getting angry. They had already formed their alliance, Leigh thought. They would not admit she had been right about the car.

"There was an accident," Gary said, and Leigh understood by the tone of his voice that the Suburban was not the concern. She let herself fall into an armchair, her keys jingling in her hand. Her key

chain had a large, pink heart attached to the rings—it was sentimental and cheap looking, nothing she would have purchased for herself.
But it had been a gift from Justin last Christmas, so she had dutifully
clipped it to her keys. As Gary talked, Leigh saw that Kara had
scratch marks on each cheek. Gary was holding her hands down, she
realized. She looked at Kara's polished, pink nails, and turned the
metal heart in her hand.

"Kara was driving. She hit someone in a crosswalk. A girl."

Kara's eyes moved in his direction, then back to the floor. Leigh
held her breath. Gary's eyes were shiny behind his glasses, and just
by that, perhaps, Leigh should have known. They'd been married
for twenty years, and she'd seen him cry exactly twice—when he
first learned his mother had cancer, and again on the night she died.

"What happened? What happened to the girl?"

He closed his eyes briefly. When he opened them, he looked
away, as if he had answered her question.

"Gary. What?"

"She died," he said. He sounded annoyed, as if she were pester-
ing him about something obvious.

Leigh glanced through the kitchen and the mudroom to the door
she'd just come in. Two minutes earlier, she'd pulled into the garage
on a sunny afternoon, another school year over, U2 playing on the
radio. She'd been worried about Mr. Tork and the PTA. Before she
got out of the car, she'd looked in the rearview mirror and considered that she had been skinny and fleshless her whole life and this
was probably why her face was aging so quickly. These things—the
PTA, wrinkles—had been her concerns.

"Who?" she asked.

"Another high school student."

She braced herself. "Who? What was the name?"

Gary frowned. He loosened his tie, unbuttoned two buttons. His
shirt was stained with sweat beneath his armpits.

"Bethany Cleese."

They both flinched. Kara had spoken, and her voice sounded unfamiliar, low and gravelly, like an old man's. Leigh made a quick, pushing movement with her hands, but an image of Bethany came to her at once, the way she had looked in Leigh's eighth grade class, her dark hair pulled back in a ponytail, sitting at her desk in the front of the room. Leigh had had so many students over the years, and it was hard to remember the quiet ones. But last year, she'd bumped into Bethany and her mother at the grocery store. The mother had a different last name, something Leigh couldn't remember, and she'd had dyed blond hair, yellowy and flat under the grocery store's fluorescent lights. She'd apologized for never making it to parent-teacher conferences. She'd been working in the evenings then, she explained, but she'd very much wanted to meet the teacher her daughter had liked so much. Bethany had looked embarrassed, Leigh remembered, her large brown eyes cast downward. But the mother kept talking, pushing her shopping cart back and forth as if there were a sleeping child inside. She'd started her own cleaning business, she said, and now she could be at home with her daughter in the evenings. Business was going well.

Leigh had nodded enthusiastically, thinking she wished she could convey that it wasn't necessary to explain all this: Bethany had been out of her classroom for a year, and she realized many parents worked evenings. But then the mother reached into a compartment of her purse and handed Leigh a card. She had room for another client, she said. The rates were low, the service fantastic. Bethany made a quiet growling sound and turned away for a moment, but then they both smiled at Leigh, looking at her with their matching dark eyes. Later, when Leigh caught sight of them in the produce aisle, Bethany had her head close to her mother's shoulder, and the mother was laughing at something she'd said.

Leigh had thrown the phone number away. She and Gary might

have been able to afford a cleaning, maybe once a month, but Bethany's mother, even with her bleached hair, had seemed like such a neat and tidy person, with her clipped coupons and her organized purse. Leigh would have been embarrassed, knowing how bad her house could get.

Now, sitting stunned in the armchair and holding the metal heart key chain, she could recall Bethany's mother perfectly, her snub nose, her high thin brows. Leigh wondered if she knew yet, and if so, how the news had been delivered. She pictured her doubling over, shaking her head. She would hate them. She would hate Kara. Leigh looked at her daughter. Gary had pulled her hands away from her knees, and Leigh could see the half-moon marks her nails had left in her skin. She'd started going to a tanning booth just before the prom, and the skin around the marks was golden.

"Oh honey," she said, and at that moment she was speaking for all of them, for Kara, for Bethany and her mother, for Justin, and for Gary, who looked so miserable and hot. He had pale skin that burned easily, and the afternoon light coming through the window was strong and bright. Leigh stood up and pulled the curtain shut, then sat on the armrest next to Kara, reaching behind her so her hand grazed Gary's side. Her knees touched Justin's small back, and for a moment, she felt stronger, knowing they were all four physically connected. It was as if she'd been activated, a lamp plugged into a socket. But then Kara stiffened, and Leigh was certain she seemed to pull away from her, leaning a little closer to her father.

"They just...let her come home with you?" Leigh heard her own voice, so uncertain. She didn't know what to say. "What did the police..."

Gary leaned forward. "She wasn't drunk. It was an accident."

Leigh shook her head. That wasn't what she'd meant. She touched Kara's arm. Her fingers looked pale against her daughter's tanned skin. "Were you... She was in the crosswalk? You're sure?"

Kara shrugged. "I didn't see her."

"Why not?"

She asked this as gently as she could. But she needed to know. Everyone else knew what had happened, but she was just learning. The information would all come to her secondhand. She would never know as much as she should.

"Did she ... Did she run out?"

"I don't know." Kara looked up at her mother, her gray eyes wide and bright. "I can't tell you. I don't know, okay? I don't know why I didn't see her. I just didn't."

Leigh drew back. They were both mad at her. It was this same old hurt, she thought, feeling selfish and stupid, that brought the first tears to her eyes. She should be crying for Bethany, or not at all. She swallowed, shook her head, and stood up.

"I'm going to make you a sandwich," she said. She didn't look back. She didn't want to hear yes or no. She would find out the details from Gary later. But when she got to the entryway of the kitchen, she turned around and looked at them once again. Gary's arm was still around Kara's shoulders, and it rested there in a natural, easy-looking way. Kara was turned toward him, her cheek pressed against his chest. Leigh stared for a moment, holding her breath. Her whole life, she'd blurred sadness with anger. She knew this about herself. She was aware. But it was still hard to tell when this blurring was a fault.

She walked back into the living room and coughed twice. Gary and Justin both looked up, and Leigh nodded her head toward the kitchen. When Justin started to rise, she raised her palm. At twelve years old, he could understand subtle gestures, but Gary, the one she actually wanted to stand, stared at her dumbly from the couch. She moved her head again and bulged her eyes. When Gary stood, she ducked back into the kitchen. She turned on the dishwasher. There was a bag of sliced bread on the counter, but she took a loaf out of the freezer, pulled out two slices, and put them in the micro-wave. She went to the sink and turned on the faucet.

"What are you doing?" Gary always had to duck a little as he passed into the kitchen, the white frame grazing the top of his head. He liked to joke that it was the frame that was taking his hair off, a little more every year. She took his arm and pulled him to her. "I'm making noise so she can't hear." She'd intended to whisper, but it came out as a hiss. "My God. Tell me what happened."

He nodded, readjusting his glasses, and she saw how exhausted he looked. She could smell the dried sweat on his shirt. It was then he told her about running across the campus lawn, how his heart had pounded, how it had seemed to take forever to drive across town. When he got there, he'd found Kara in the backseat of the sheriff's car, lying on her side, her arms covering her face. She'd called him "Daddy," he said. She hadn't done that in years.

"Why didn't you call me?"

He blinked. For a moment, he seemed not to know. "I tried. I tried right away, as soon as I got the call. It was after three, so I called your cell. You didn't answer. I tried again from the car."

And then she remembered. Her phone had rung when she was talking with Jim Tork. The meeting had been tense—Jim Tork did not want his son reading *The Great Gatsby* in Leigh's eighth grade English class the following year because—Mr. Tork had counted off each reason on a long, thin finger—the story was inordinately de-pressing; it held up a decadent lifestyle as something to aspire to; it narrated adultery as if it were commonplace; and more than one character casually took the Lord's name in vain. He was also upset about the Flannery O'Connor story, and the memoir by Tobias Wolff. He'd looked at all the stories on Leigh's reading list, he said. The common thread, as far as he could tell, was that they were all depressing.

Mr. Tork had an elegant face, Leigh considered, with a Roman nose and tragic-looking eyes, the outer edges drooping. He was handsome, and he had a deep, confident voice. While he talked, she'd nodded with an earnest expression and thought about how with a face like that, under different circumstances, he might have been a famous actor. Had he been born in a different part of the country, or reared by different parents, she might have encountered him only on the big screen, with a better haircut and an expensive suit, half smiling for the camera. The moment she realized she wasn't listening to the real Mr. Tork of Danby, Kansas, who had a very bad haircut, and who was wearing a polo shirt buttoned to the top button and not smiling even a little, she'd reprimanded herself and refocused her attention. She had to at least appear sensitive to his concerns; he could get other parents behind him. So when her cell phone rang, she'd reached into her purse and switched it off without even looking at the number.

She walked past Gary to the counter and opened her purse, rifling through its contents until she found her phone. He watched her flip it open and touch several buttons, scanning the screen.

"What are you doing? Leigh, I'm telling you, I tried to call. You don't bel—" He stopped, realizing.

Leigh stared at the screen. He reached for her shoulder, but she pulled away.

"She probably thought she couldn't get ahold of you," he said. "Honey. She was out of her mind. She wasn't thinking."

"You could have called the office. They would have sent someone to my room."

"There wasn't time." He looked at the sink, at the water rushing out of the faucet and into the drain. "I needed to stay right with her. They were already asking her questions. They were interviewing Willow."

"Why?"

"She was in the car. She was in the car with Kara."

Leigh shook her head. She had pictured Kara in the car alone. This was how it would be, she realized. She would remain unclear on the details. She would never know as much as he did.

Gary took off his glasses and rubbed his eyes with his thumb and forefinger. He looked old, Leigh thought. He'd always had a long, narrow face, but now his skin appeared heavy, weighted down, sagging from the bones of his cheeks. "They'd already given her a Breathalyzer test, but they were looking at her carefully, asking her questions. Someone was searching the car. There was a crowd of people watching. A couple different people taking pictures."

"Did you see her? Did you see Bethany?"

He frowned as if she had said something hostile. "She was covered up." He glanced to the side, over her shoulder. "I saw where she fell."

"Was her mother there?"

He seemed confused. "No."

She looked away again. The refrigerator was covered with small mementos of their life—an invitation to Justin's upcoming recital, a receipt for dry cleaning that Leigh had failed to pick up for more than two months, a picture of Gary dressed up as a vampire so he could answer the door on Halloween. There was the small newspaper article reporting that Leigh had won a state award for her work with disabled students. And just to the right of this, somehow more eye-catching than anything else, was a picture of Kara clipped from the newspaper a year earlier, an amazing color shot of her on the soccer field just after she'd maneuvered the ball away from another girl. Her long right leg was extended, muscles flexed, and the ball was at the tip of her toe. The picture was still held in place by four words from the poetry magnet kit Leigh had purchased on a whim: LOVELY GIRL KICKS WELL. Gary had cut out the picture, but it was Leigh who had arranged the words while talking on the phone with her sister one day. She hadn't really thought about it. The words fit, though. Kara was lovely in the picture, all youth and strength, her ponytail flying high behind her.

The timer on the microwave dinged. Leigh and Gary looked at it as if it had interrupted.

"She was in the crosswalk?" Leigh asked. This question mattered, she thought. She would keep asking it until someone answered her.

Gary lowered his eyes. "Not by then. She'd fallen by the curb. There was blood there. They were measuring it." He frowned, pointing at the kitchen floor. "The distance to the tires."

Leigh balanced herself against the counter. She pictured Bethany again, her dark eyes, her slow smile, the curve of her cheek reflecting light from the classroom window.

She looked up at Gary. "So what happens now?"

"They said they would do a report. It'll go to the municipal court, and then maybe the district attorney."

"She'll be arrested?"

"I don't see why. It was an accident, Leigh."

"Yes, but..." She shook her head, trying to think. "Even with accidents, you know this, if she was careless..."

He put his hand over his mouth. "I don't know. They didn't say. They kept the Suburban, but they let me bring her home." He leaned back and peered through the entryway. She stood on her toes to look over his shoulder. In the living room, Justin had moved up on the couch next to Kara, his cheek pressed against her shoulder. She patted his hand absently, staring out the window of the opposite wall.

"I gave her some Valium just before you came in," Gary whispered. "I had some left over from my surgery." He rubbed his eyes beneath his glasses again. "We'll need to call a lawyer," he said.

They stared at each other for several seconds, and then he turned and walked back into the living room. Leigh stood where she was. The bread in the microwave was overcooked and hard. She threw both slices in the garbage, then took eight new slices out of the bag, laying them out on the counter.

When the phone rang, Gary walked quickly back into the kitchen.

"Don't answer it," he said. "We shouldn't talk to anyone yet."

Leigh looked at him. His jaw was set, and she could see he was still breathing heavily. He rarely spoke in such a commanding tone. She pictured the garage door lowering, the bridge of a moat drawn up.

The machine picked up the call. They heard the outgoing message, Kara and Justin singing their rhyme:

The Churchills are not at home.
If we were, we'd run for the phone.
But we're not, so wait for the tone.
Unless you're a telemarketer—in that case, leave us alone.

There were a few seconds of laughter, followed by the jarring *beep*, and then the soothing but imploring voice of Eva Greb rose up out of the machine.

"Leigh? Hello? Anyone? Oh my God. I just heard. Willow is so upset. She's worried about Kara. We'll be home all night. Just call as soon as you can.... I'll come right over with anything you need. Call tonight. I'll stay up late. I just want to make sure..."

Gary shook his head. "We can't talk to anyone yet." He kept his eyes locked on Leigh's. "You understand? Anyone. Especially not her."

ONLY JUSTIN ATE HIS sandwich. He took small, soundless bites, his napkin folded neatly in his lap. Leigh pulled back the curtain again. It was early evening now, and the dim square of light from the picture window had moved from the couch to the floor. Kara's eyes looked small, her lids heavy. She'd taken off her hoop earrings, and she was shaking them in a cupped hand as if they were a pair of dice.

The phone kept ringing. A reporter from *The Danby Chronicle* left her name and number. Willow called next, her airy, high voice so quiet it was difficult to hear. At seven, Eva called again. "Just checking to see if you all are home yet. Both Willow and I are worried. I might swing by later. Just call me when you can. I'll be up late."

Leigh didn't look at Gary. She went back to the table, picked up her sandwich, and set it down. Moments later, the phone rang again.

"Hello? Hello? Hello? This is Ed-na Cas-tle."

There was a long pause. Justin looked at his mother, and they almost smiled at each other.

"I am calling for Jus-tin Churchill," the voice said carefully, as if testing a microphone. "We thought he was coming by tonight so we could sing. We're all down here waiting. We were all looking forward to having him play."

They listened to the dial tone. Gary, who was sitting on the piano bench now, smiled. "You can go if you like," he told Justin. "Just don't talk about it, okay? Don't say anything about your sister or the accident."

"I don't have to go," Justin offered. "I can call them and tell them I'm sick." There was resignation in his voice, concern in his expression. He wanted to do his part. He'd long finished his sandwich, but he was still sitting at the table.

"Go ahead," his sister said, and again, both Leigh and Gary were startled by her voice, the new lowness of it. She sounded like a completely different person. Her brow was furrowed, as if it required great effort for her to speak, and her shoulders appeared concave, folded in. "Go on, Justin. It's okay. You can't help by staying here."

He looked at his mother. Leigh nodded, and he stood with his empty plate. "You'll drive me?"

She almost nodded again, but stopped herself. She always drove him. She drove him everywhere, to the nursing home, to the video store, to the grocery store for his special requests. Normally, she didn't mind. But Gary had already gotten his time alone with Kara on this terrible night. Leigh deserved hers. There was something ridiculous and petty about worrying about this now, at a time like this, but on a deeper, more crucial level, Leigh also believed something—or someone, maybe Gary—was always cutting her off from her daughter in a subtle but strong way. She looked at Gary.

"Can you take him? I'd like to stay here."

She asked this lightly, as if he might have expected the request. But there was a pause after she spoke, and during the silence, Leigh felt her own discomfort, and saw it reflected in the eyes of everyone else in the room.

"Sure," Gary said, and his voice was lighter still. But for several seconds, he and Justin only stared at each other as if they were both unsure of how to proceed. Justin pointed to the piano bench his father was still sitting on. "I need to get my music," he said. "It's in there." Gary stood up, feeling his pockets for his keys. Leigh felt a heavy dread move across her chest, but she said nothing. Once they left, she and Kara would be alone, and she would be able to say something right and useful, to show Kara that though she ached for Bethany and her mother, she would stand with her and love her through it all. The words would come to her. She would say them in the right way. She would just say what she felt.

BUT AS SOON AS they heard Gary's car leave the garage, Kara stood up and said she was going to bed. Leigh hadn't gotten even a word out.

"Are you..." Leigh followed Kara to the stairway. "Honey? Are you okay?"

"No." Her tone made Leigh think of how Gary had sounded earlier, pestered by a ridiculous question. She managed the first few steps, holding on to the banister as if the ground were moving beneath her.

"You should eat something," Leigh said.

Kara turned and gave her a look of such disdain that if such a horrible thing had not just happened, Leigh might have spoken to her sharply. Kara's eyes were strikingly similar to Leigh's, and so when Leigh looked at her daughter, she sometimes had the disconcerting sensation of staring into the face of her younger self. But Kara, at eighteen, was already several inches taller than Leigh, and her gaze could also seem condescending, as if she were observing her mother not just from a physical height, but a moral one, with equal parts humor and pity.

Or maybe Leigh was imagining that. It didn't matter, she thought. She shouldn't be thinking of herself now.

"If you want to talk...," she called up.

Apparently, Kara did not. She continued her climb, holding the rail as if she needed it for support, and Leigh was left by herself in the dark living room, the windows backlit in dusk. She sat on the arm of the couch and gazed out the window. She could not feel sorry for herself. Somewhere, not far away, on this warm spring evening with the lilacs in bloom, Bethany Cleese's mother was taking in the news that her child was gone forever. Leigh tried to concentrate on this, as if feeling the pain of it were some penance, something she could do to help.

But the image that appeared and then stayed in her mind was of her own daughter, at a particular moment when she was very young. She'd just gotten off the school bus, and she was running up the driveway in cotton tights and tennis shoes to meet Leigh with outstretched arms. Leigh could still see her crooked-toothed smile, pre-braces, and that burst of love in her eerily familiar eyes as she'd jumped up into her mother's embrace. They'd started out so well together, she and her little girl; but now, sitting in her darkening living room by herself, she thought of something she'd read in a magazine once, something Jackie Kennedy had said: "If you bungle raising your children, I don't think whatever else you do matters very much." Leigh had liked that quote when she'd first read it. She had grown up sure she would always be on the good side of those words, a good mother, certain and smug.

But on this lovely spring evening so many years later, the same words felt like a damnation. Despite her best intentions, apparently, she'd somehow bungled raising her daughter. Now that Kara had bungled too, it was true—nothing else seemed to matter.

Chapter 2

BEFORE THE ACCIDENT, IT was Justin whom Leigh worried about. For the most part, she worried secretly, self-consciously, even around Gary, for she knew her fears might be misunderstood. She knew she should just feel grateful to have two healthy children, and aside from all that, in some deep, emotional way that had little to do with reason, she'd always thought of Justin, especially, as a gift she didn't quite deserve. He seemed almost otherworldly to her sometimes, with his dark eyes and pale skin, his body so bony and light.

It was the rest of the world she would change if she could, nothing about Justin himself.

She loved his sense of humor. Even when he was very young, he liked to thumb through Gary's *New Yorker*s and read the cartoons—his favorite was a drawing of a cat giving a ride to a mouse in a wagon to some unknown destination. Another mouse stood in the foreground shouting, *"For God's sake, think! Why is he being so nice to you?"* Justin had showed the cartoon to Leigh, and when he read the caption, he did a high, squeaky voice for the mouse. For some reason, his timing maybe, her mood, this struck her as unbearably funny; she laughed so hard coffee came out of her nose. After that it became a shared joke between them, something he might shout down the driveway when Gary and Leigh went out for dinner. He didn't overdo it. He had good timing and, for a child, a surprising sense of restraint. Leigh wondered if he would be a comic genius—already he was dissatisfied with the worn-out jokes of many sitcoms.

"Same old same old, hardee har," he'd say, rolling his eyes away from the television. "Why are they laughing?" he asked Leigh once, referring to the studio audience. "It's not funny. Are they paying the people to laugh?" She could tell by his face that the question was in earnest. She told him she was pretty sure the laughter was prerecorded. The people had been laughing at something else, she said, and then they played it again for the show he was watching now. Justin had seemed distressed by this answer. "That's wrong," he'd said, looking solemnly at the screen. "They shouldn't do that."

His ethical streak was wide and strong. Leigh assumed he'd gotten it from Gary. Once, her son, nine at the time, had caught her calling in sick to work when she wasn't sick at all—a film was playing at an art house in Kansas City, and Leigh had wanted to take the day off and drive in to go see it. She was on the phone with the school secretary, faking a cough and a hoarse voice, when Justin wandered into her bedroom. He was already dressed, his favorite red shirt tucked too tightly into his jeans. She waved him away, but he remained where he was, staring at her with a worried expression. They were alone in the house. Gary was already on campus, and Kara had left early for a student council meeting.

After she hung up, he looked at her with no accusation, just concern. "You're sick?" he asked.

She nodded and coughed again. She'd already put on lipstick, and she watched his eyes move over her mouth. She glanced at her watch. He would be on the bus in fifteen minutes. "I might just stay home and rest today," she'd said, rubbing her lips together. And then he'd leaned forward and gently pressed his palm against her forehead, as she had done so many times to him when he'd had a fever or a cough. The moment she felt the warmth of his hand, a surge of guilt moved through her. She tugged the shirt out of his jeans and smoothed it down over his belt loops. He was so good. She knew that. She wished he could be more deceptive, a little less naïve, if only to protect himself.

She guessed he knew what he was up against, or what he would be up against soon: they lived in a small, football-crazed town that made it clear, in so many ways, that it had no use for boys like him. He did not like contact sports. He had slender ankles and wrists, and his body was thin, his chest an indent between his shoulders. On weekends or summer evenings, when other grade school boys went to baseball practice or to arcades or to movies about things blowing up, Justin went to the Blue Stem Retirement Home, where he played accompaniment to a trio of octogenarians who sang harmony songs from World War II. That would have all been fine, if Leigh thought he'd had a choice. But she suspected—no, she knew—that these old women were her son's only friends. She had driven by his school on her lunch break many times and seen him walking along the outer fence by himself in a way that made her think of prison movies. He kept his hands in his pockets, his chin lifted, his eyes staring up at the sky. The other children moved about in large and small clumps, playing hopscotch and jump rope and soccer and kickball. They looked like children, not prisoners, and the difference between them and her own child stabbed hard into Leigh's worried heart.

And that was at the neighborhood grade school near the college, where the children had grown up together, and many of their parents knew Leigh and Gary. Next year, Justin would go to the junior high where Leigh taught, the big river fed by five elementary schools. For eleven years, Leigh had supervised the courtyard every Tuesday and Thursday at lunch. She had broken up fights and tilted back bloody noses, and she couldn't imagine Justin there, grist for the mill. Her son still seemed so small to her, so young.

Gary must have been worried all along as well. One evening when they were in bed, he announced, for no clear reason, that Justin would be fine if he could just learn a sport. He didn't need to be a star player, Gary said, as if Leigh had argued the point, but learning the basics of, say, basketball, would give him confidence and a way to interact with other boys. Gary had played basketball in his high school days—he'd won a scholarship to Rice, in fact, though he'd lost it in the first year after injuring his back. By the time Kara was born, he only watched the game on television— Leigh couldn't remember ever seeing him even dribble a ball.

But when Justin started fifth grade, Gary got out the ladder and his screwdriver and installed a hoop and net above the center of the garage. Every day after dinner that autumn, he and Justin would change into shorts and T-shirts and go out to the driveway with the ball. The leaves of the big sycamore hadn't fallen yet, so there was still shade in the driveway, and the evening breeze was cool. Through the open windows, Leigh would hear her husband's patient, encouraging voice and the thumps of the ball on the pavement. *Almost had it that time, J. That was better. Try to do it with one hand.* It all sounded promising. But when she got up and looked out the window, she usually saw Gary loping down the driveway after the ball, and Justin panting by the garage, hunched forward and squinting at his father. Gary would throw the ball gently, but Justin often turned as if warding off a blow, and the ball would land behind him in the flower bed, or bounce sadly against the fence into the grass.

But her son rarely complained. He hardly ever spoke, Leigh noticed. He would only nod to show he'd understood his father's suggestions, and then try once again to steal the ball, to dribble up the driveway without tripping. He took shot after shot, his thin arms raised over his head, his lovely face still with concentration. Watching him from the window, Leigh felt a surge of unaccountable and overwhelming love. She wished she could be invisible for a moment. She would go outside, put her hands around Justin's waist, and without his knowing, lift him high enough so he could easily drop the ball into the hoop.

KARA WOULD SOMETIMES GO out to the driveway with them. She didn't shoot while Gary and Justin were outside, but she would cheer Justin on, and run down the driveway after the ball so Gary could catch his breath. "You up for a game, love?" Gary would ask. Kara always refused, tossing the ball back to him. Later, after Gary had come in to take a shower and Justin had gone back to his room, the house would be quiet enough for Leigh to notice the occasional thumping of the basketball in the darkening driveway. Straining to see out the window, she would see Kara practicing layups and free throws, moving in and out of the oval of light from the dim bulb in the garage. Just before Kara made a shot, Leigh was often struck by how much her daughter resembled her son when their expressions were the same—all determination and focus. But there was a difference—for Kara, the ball regularly sailed through the hoop, and Leigh would catch the quick, satisfied smile on her daughter's face that she rarely saw on her son's.

Leigh didn't let Kara know she was watching. Kara didn't want her to watch when she played—she'd made that clear. Once, Leigh had called to her through the window and asked if she had done her homework. "Did it," Kara answered, her eyes trained on the hoop, the ball still in her hands, her body crouched like a small animal going still until a danger passed. Then Leigh walked away from the window and heard the ball bouncing again.

By the end of October, Kara was regularly making shots from the far end of the driveway. After Justin was in bed, Gary would sometimes go back out to the garage with two mugs of hot chocolate and watch her through the open door. By then, the central heat was on and the windows were closed, but when Leigh graded papers in the dining room, she could hear them talking, and his occasional applause.

Leigh had known Gary would be a good father; it was, perhaps, what had drawn her to him, not quite subconsciously—she clearly remembered thinking it when they were first dating. She loved him, of course, aside from all that. If they had not been able to have children, she would have still counted herself fortunate to spend her days with a man so even-tempered, so thoughtful, so morally and ethically bound. She'd told him this once, trying to be nice, and ended up hurting his feelings. "You sound pragmatic," he'd said. And then he'd shaken his head and laughed it off. At the time, she was pregnant with Kara, ready to burst, but when he stepped toward her, he put his hand on her cheek, not her belly.

"I loved you as soon as I saw you," he said. "I loved you almost the moment I saw your face."

In response, Leigh had squinted at him for a long time. He looked so earnest. But she was not exactly Helen of Troy. She was small-eyed and too thin; even when pregnant, she didn't look voluptuous. There was nothing soft or lush about her. When she pointed all this out to Gary, he didn't argue. "I don't mean beauty," he'd said, gazing at her in a way that made it clear he was considering the concept and not her feelings. "I mean your force." He'd made fists with both hands and touched each of her shoulders lightly. "I could see it. Your force. Your will. I just wanted to be around it."

He'd written a poem about her when he was in grad school, back when they were still just dating. He was shy when he showed it to her—he knew how to teach literature, he cautioned; writing it was entirely different. He was taking a poetry writing class as an easy elective, a pleasant distraction from his doctoral studies, and it had made him insecure and miserable—the instructor kept making him rewrite his poems, to try again, to *resee* his initial visions. Leigh could give no help. She read poetry, but she read poetry she understood, and Gary's poems were full of allusions to Greek mythology that made her feel both tired and ignorant.

But she loved the poem he wrote for her, the poem about the weed. It wasn't a good poem, technically speaking. His instructor had given him a C– on it, with *I know more is inside you!* etched across the top of the page in her scraggly (and, Leigh thought, narcissistic) script. The instructor could go to hell, as far as Leigh was concerned. Gary had written a poem about a weed he once saw growing out of asphalt on a bridge in Boston. It sprouted "without soil / pushing its green, through hard rock / up toward the loving sun."

He never revised the poem. There was not, he told his poetry instructor, more inside him. He would keep his C–, and he would keep the poem the way it was—sappy, perhaps, sentimental, with an easy image that no doubt had been used before. But his poem, his sappy image, had made his smart, serious new girlfriend put her head on his shoulder and tell him she'd never felt so understood.

WHEN KARA WAS SIX, maybe seven, she'd had a white shirt with an iron-on butterfly that she'd loved. She asked Leigh to wash the shirt for picture day, and Leigh had forgotten. The oversight was understandable—Leigh had recently given birth to Justin, who was having trouble nursing, so she was a little behind on the laundry. But when Kara woke that morning and learned she would have to wear something else, she'd cried as if someone had slapped her. Leigh was sympathetic at first. She offered to let her wear her silver chain necklace, and to fix her hair in French braids. Kara allowed this, but she continued to cry. Leigh pulled her into the bathroom to find a comb and elastics, trying to ignore not only Justin's but also Kara's steady wails, congratulating herself for being patient and understanding, pulling the comb as gently as she could through the mass of blond hair, as she knew Kara had a tender scalp. Kara's cries turned into steady sniffs, and the whole situation might have just died down, but something about the sniffing, especially, struck Leigh as comical. She smiled to herself, forgetting that she was standing in front of a mirror.

"It's not funny," her daughter said quietly, her gray eyes luminous and steady on her mother's reflection. "It's what I wanted." The sniffing had stopped, but she looked so hurt, so incredibly wounded, that more than a decade later, Leigh would ask herself if that one silly moment was the germination of the trouble between them. Perhaps all the difficulties of pregnancy, childbirth, and mothering in the early years wouldn't matter—after all that work, you could permanently alienate your child by simply laughing at her at the wrong time.

But if Kara had really been fragile enough to let that moment stay with her, she seemed to grow up healthy enough, well loved by her teachers and peers. When she was in grade school, Leigh never would have driven by to find her daughter walking the perimeter of the school grounds alone. She would be lucky to catch sight of her at all. From the very start, Kara had been at the center of that whirl of children, a magnetic nucleus impossible to see from the outside. She was naturally athletic, good at everything she tried. She got invited to slumber parties, and when she had them, every girl who was invited came. In junior high, they had to limit the number of phone calls she could take in a night.

Kara was dating before she got to high school. The boys who came to the house were somewhat varied—there had been a wrestler with an overly strong handshake, a shy boy who kept his hands in his pockets the entire time, and a really cute short one— Leigh's favorite—who hadn't had a car but walked several miles to the house so he and Kara could walk some more. These boys were each at least a year older than Kara, but they had all shared a nervous, ingratiating way of acting in front of Leigh and Gary that made Kara seem older and more confident in comparison. The wrestler called Gary "sir" and told Leigh he'd loved having her as a teacher, though Leigh didn't remember him as a student. Even the shy one had cleared his throat and said he liked their house. Leigh had been nice to each of them, but the whole ritual struck her as tedious and contrived, as if they were all acting out parts for some television sitcom, life imitating art that had never imitated real life in the first place. She didn't remember boys from her own adolescence acting so solicitous. She didn't remember anyone coming to the door, and it made her wonder if this behavior was not just for television but truly the mating behavior of adolescents in the mid- to upper-middle classes.

But it wasn't that. The boy without the car lived by the meat-packing plant with just his mother, and remembering this, Leigh could only guess that maybe the reason these boys were so polite was because they really liked Kara, and they didn't want to mess things up.

It surprised her, her daughter's success with boys. She felt guilty for her surprise, and she knew that most mothers would say and even think just the opposite. So she never announced her surprise aloud. But secretly, she marveled when Kara was asked to Homecoming and Prom every year without fail. Daughter or not, there was a fact to contend with: Kara wasn't a great beauty. She wasn't ugly. Leigh was quick to point this out, even in the privacy of her own mind. Her daughter had a mane of thick, gold hair, and her body was long and lean from all the running and the sports. When she was fifteen, out of nowhere, two perfectly sized breasts appeared high on her chest, and she started wearing T-shirts that fit close to her frame. But her gray eyes were small, and her chin jutted forward a little too much, giving her a masculine look from some angles. She looked, in fact, much the way Leigh had as a teenager, only taller. She'd gotten Gary's height.

Leigh chided herself for thinking like this, for being so reductive and shallow. It was certainly possible that high school boys could be drawn to a girl for reasons other than looks. And Kara had other things going for her. She was a good athlete. Gary had gotten her started with soccer, back when she was seven or eight. He coached the intramural team one summer, and he went to all her practices and games. She ran track in the spring. And she was smart, of course, and ambitious. She was interested in politics. She was president of the Spanish Club—she'd purposefully made friends with Mexican students and encouraged them to correct her pronunciations. She'd been selected as a National Merit Scholar her senior year. By that March, she'd received acceptance letters and scholarship offers from three out of the four schools she'd applied to. Two were in New England, and over spring break, Kara and Gary had flown to Boston and toured each school. It was supposed to have been a family vacation—they'd purchased four airline tickets. But two days before the departure date, Justin came down with a bad flu. Gary offered to be the one to stay home with him, but Leigh pointed out the obvious—Gary knew his way around Boston. Leigh, who had spent almost her entire life living in various small towns, would get lost just trying to get the rental car out of the lot at Logan Airport.

That was the argument Leigh made, anyway, and it was enough to convince Gary. So she did not have to give all the reasons she knew she shouldn't be the one to go to New England with Kara. She did not have to come out and say she knew she would be much better at caring for her son, measuring out medicine and heating up soup, than she would be at chauffeuring her daughter from one expensive college to another. For really, it was not the idea of driving in Boston that intimidated Leigh so much as the idea of delivering her daughter into a world of options she herself knew nothing about.

WHEN KARA AND GARY returned from New England, they spent several evenings together at the dining room table, looking over course catalogs and leafy photo spreads of the highly selective campuses competing for her favor. Leigh knew he wanted her to choose Rice, because Texas was close, and, she suspected, because he'd gotten his undergraduate degree at Rice. But those nights at the dining room table, he only listened as their daughter talked, nodding respectfully as she went over the advantages and disadvantages of each college. This one had the best political science program. This one would let her spend two semesters in Madrid. This one had an exchange program with a school in Costa Rica. Leigh watched from the kitchen, her forearms resting on the countertop. The sadness she was feeling, she decided, was for Kara, for the sense of having already lost her. The arrival of the college catalogs made their impending separation seem real and imminent, and Leigh had the sense that she'd run out of time without accomplishing a task she couldn't quite name, failing them both in some important way.

This sense of failure surprised Leigh. When she was growing up, she had always known she would be a mother, and not just any mother, but a good one. She would be the kind of mother a child—a daughter, especially—could come to for advice or understanding. She'd had it all planned out. Before Kara was even born, Leigh had imagined entire conversations she would have with her teenage daughter. Unlike Leigh's own mother, Leigh would be sensitive and caring. She would ask questions and listen to the answers. She would show her daughter respect, and therefore, she assumed, her daughter would respect her, and her gently imparted wisdom. There would be none of her own mother's old tricks, turning the conversation back to herself so the daughter had to do all the listening.

But reality proved her naïve. By the time Kara was a teenager, she seemed to neither need nor want her mother's wisdom. Maybe she didn't think it existed. A perfect example was Leigh's pathetic attempt to talk with Kara about sex. Kara was in tenth grade, and she had just started to date Eric Vorkamp. Leigh knew enough to worry. She'd had Eric in her class years earlier, and even then, he'd been good-looking and deep voiced, with stubble on his cheeks—and the subject of one very vulgar poem written in a female hand on one of the wooden desks of her classroom. One morning, she had turned a corner in the corridor to find him making out with a girl on a radiator—as Leigh passed, she could actually see the outline of Eric Vorkamp's tongue in the girl's cheek. When Eric opened his eyes, Leigh held his gaze, but she had been the one to look away first. That was when he was fourteen. By the time he started dating Kara, he was a senior, and he looked like a grown man, with dark hair on his arms, almost as tall as Gary. Friday nights, he picked Kara up in his mother's maroon minivan. He was as polite and attentive to Leigh and Gary as the others, and before they left, they announced plans to go to movies or restaurants, maybe a school dance or a game. But Leigh remembered how easy it had been to lie about these things when no one was paying attention. As soon as they pulled out of the driveway, she could hear the minivan's stereo turned loud, and she knew her daughter could be on her way to anywhere.

She considered several options. She could follow them in the car some evening, or, on a night Kara told her she and Eric were going to a movie, she could wait outside the theater to see if they really came out. It would be dark. They wouldn't see her, even if they were really where they said they would be. But both these ideas seemed obsessive, not something a normal mother would do. And Gary would never approve. "We should trust her until she gives us a reason not to," he liked to say. "And she hasn't given us a reason yet."

He said this as if it were impenetrable logic, but it made Leigh think of a story her own mother had told her once. *I should have known your father was going to screw around on me,* she once told Leigh and her sister. *"When we first got together, you know, I told him I wasn't a jealous person. I told him, 'Maybe cause nobody's ever cheated on me.' You know what he says to me, girls? He says, 'How do you know?' He says it with this little smile. Gives me chills now, to think about it. Guess I needed to be hit on the head a little harder."*

"How would we know if she's deceitful?" Leigh asked Gary once. He was adjusting his tie in the master bathroom mirror, and he stopped, turned around, and looked at her like she was insane. Leigh smoothed her hair down, looking beyond him to her own reflection. She hadn't brushed her hair yet that morning, and her curls coiled out in all directions. "I'm just saying we don't know," she added. "That's a rational point, Gary. If she's a good liar, we wouldn't know if she's deceitful or not."

He turned back to the mirror, still watching her in its reflection. It was hard to tell if he was amused or worried. He smiled a lot, so with him, both emotions looked the same.

She stepped forward, resting her chin on his shoulder. "When I was her age, I lied about where I went sometimes. And no one knew."

"Well." He gave her cheek a gentle pat, his fingers only grazing her cheek. "She's not you."

TECHNICALLY, IT WASN'T AN insult. But for the rest of the day, in her car, in her classroom, when she was making copies in the teachers' lounge, Leigh moved about with a vague, wounded feeling, a general dissatisfaction with herself. She shouldn't have told Gary she lied sometimes, she decided. It wasn't entirely accurate, and it put her in a bad light. She hadn't really lied—the truth was, really, that when she was Kara's age, no one asked her where she went when she went out at night.

But that wasn't even the issue, Leigh considered. She had distracted herself. Bringing herself and her own adolescence up had derailed the conversation from her real concern, which was that Kara was at the age when she might start having sex, which meant she could end up sick or pregnant or, at the very least, betrayed and hurt.

She decided to face the problem head-on. She and Kara would just have to talk.

She knocked on Kara's bedroom door that evening. She waited for an answer before she opened the door, but when Kara saw her, she still looked slightly annoyed. She was sitting Indian style in the middle of her bed, her trigonometry book open in her lap. She wore eyeglasses, as she did whenever she studied. Her glasses were wire-rimmed, elegant-looking; whenever Leigh saw her daughter in them, she thought of actresses who wore glasses for certain roles to make them look smart or serious. But Kara really needed the glasses sometimes. Leigh had taken her to the optometrist herself.

"Do you have a minute?" she asked. She felt as if she were intruding, disturbing things, though she still hovered in the doorway. Kara's room was the cleanest in the house. She made her bed before she left for school each morning, the pillows arranged so that it looked like a bed in a catalog. Her clothes hung neatly in her closet, organized according to season. She liked to do her own laundry—Leigh had a habit of leaving things in the dryer until they got wrinkled again.

Kara leaned forward to turn off her stereo. Leigh could see the muscles move in her lean arm.

"I just kind of wanted"—Leigh fluttered her hand as if she were waving—"to uh, to just talk." In her rehearsal of this conversation, she had not been nervous. She had imagined what she would sound like, and the voice she had heard in her head sounded warm and full of concern. But now she felt clumsy. She closed the door and sat on the foot of the bed. She smiled at Kara. Kara smiled back. But it wasn't a real smile, Leigh thought. It was a patient smile, the smile of a shop girl waiting on an irritating customer, impenetrably polite.

"I just wanted to talk with you a little. About Eric."

And there it was, Leigh thought, the amused look. The patient smile was still there, but one of her daughter's arched eyebrows rose just over the frames of her glasses.

"He seems nice," Leigh offered.

"Yeah. He is. He's nice."

"I know he's really popular. I mean, at least he was when I had him in class." She waited. Nothing. "He still is, right?" She gave Kara a knowing look. "A lot of girls liked him, I remember. He's popular. With girls."

"I guess."

Leigh hated that phrase. Using it was the tactic of someone trying hard not to communicate. She didn't allow it from her students. "What do you mean, 'you guess'? Is he or isn't he, Kara? I'm trying to talk with you."

Kara rolled her lips in. The smile was gone, and now she seemed guarded, uncertain. "Well, I don't really think of people in those terms."

Leigh put her face in her hands.

"I just like him because he's nice."

"Great. Great." Leigh looked up again. She would persevere. And fail. "That's good. That's what matters."

They nodded at each other somberly.

"By the popular thing, I just meant . . . I know he's older, and a lot of other girls probably like him, and well, what I mean is, what I wanted to ask you about was, I wonder if you might feel sort of... pressured."

Kara stared at her blankly. Leigh glanced over her shoulder, as if someone helpful might be waiting there with a cue card. But she saw only Kara's posters—the rock star with a diamond in her navel, the beautiful volleyball player with the long hair. The summer that Kara was ten, Leigh had let her pick her favorite color out of a paint sampler, and though she'd chosen an odd shade of red, Leigh had painted Kara's entire room that shade while she was away at summer camp. She'd bought her a matching bedspread. She'd bought wooden letters to spell out her name over the bookshelf. She'd done all this over the course of two weeks while Justin was napping. When Kara came home from camp, she'd said, "Wow!" and "Thanks!" But she'd also squinted her eyes up at the walls and said the color looked different than the way it had looked in the sampler. Leigh tried not to take it too hard. But over the years, Kara had put up more and more posters, and now Leigh could hardly see the red walls at all.

"I just remember that when I was your age, I always felt"—she focused on the navel of the rock star—"lucky to have a boyfriend, or not even a boyfriend, just any guy paying attention to me."

Kara's right eyebrow now lowered itself so it was parallel with the silver frames of her glasses. "That's sad," she said.

Leigh shook her head. "No. That's not what I mean. I'm not trying to get you to feel sorry for me." She laughed, and it came out high-pitched and strained. "I mean I remember maybe doing things I maybe wasn't ready for, um, or thinking I should do them, I mean, because I thought I was lucky to get someone's attention, and I didn't want to lose it."

It was then that Kara took off her glasses and peered into her mother's eyes. This was a gesture Leigh associated with therapists. Leigh had never been to a therapist, but when she saw them portrayed on television, they were often doing what her daughter was doing now, biting softly on the earpiece of a pair of glasses and looking at a babbler in a thoughtful, analytical sort of way.

"Are you talking about sex?"

Leigh narrowed her eyes. "Yes." She'd thought that was obvious.

"Oh my God." It was hard to read Kara's expression now. Her eyes were wide, her full lips parted and slightly curled in a way that implied a combination of many emotions: sympathy, surprise, disbelief. It had not been Leigh's goal to inspire any of these.

"That's really, really sad," she added.

"We're not talking about me," Leigh said. There were vacuum tracks on the beige carpet, and she smoothed over the edges of one with her shoe.

"Okay."

"I'm talking about you. I'm worried that you're dating a senior, and I'm worried that you're having sex, or that you're thinking about it."

"I'm not."

Leigh frowned. She had expected this answer, but she'd imagined Kara saying it with more conviction. More outrage. Kara's voice was neutral, rational. She sounded a lot like Gary.

"Okay. Good. Okay." Leigh stood up and walked toward the wall with the posters, and then walked back to the bed. She had to tread carefully here. "But I'm worried you might feel pressured soon. You know, you might feel like other girls like him, and you want to hang on to him—"

Kara shook her head slowly. "I don't really think like that."

"Good," Leigh said. "That's great. That's good to hear."

"I mean, I guess I think he's pretty lucky too."

"Great." Leigh didn't know where to stand. She moved to the door and shifted her weight. "That's exactly right."

Kara leaned back on her hands. "When I do have sex, it'll be because I want to."

Leigh took a step back. "What?"

"I said, 'When I do have sex, it'll be because I want to.'" She'd raised her voice. She really thought her mother just hadn't heard her. "It would be for me, not for him."

"Well." Leigh sat on the foot of the bed again, her palms pressed together between her knees. Her daughter was talking with her about sex. She was being open with her. That was good. But there was something so final in her tone. She wasn't asking for any input. "I hope you'll hold off on that for a while. There's no rush. A lot of problems come with it, you know. Things you don't need to worry about right now. You can get sick, all kinds of diseases. You can get pregnant."

The amused look returned. "I know."

Leigh stood up quickly. It was such a joke. It hadn't been such a joke for Leigh's sister. Their mother never would have tried to talk to them like this, so respectfully, so caring. And if she would have ever tried, Leigh would have been grateful. She certainly wouldn't have laughed. She touched the doorknob and turned around. "I don't know what you think is so funny." She was surprised by the volume of her own voice. She tried to quiet it. "I came in here to have a serious conversation with you. I came in to tell you that I hope you're not having sex. But if you are, then I hope you'll let me talk to you about birth control and about... and about condoms."

Kara remained silent. Her knees were tucked beneath her chin, and she had her arms wrapped around her legs as if she were cold.

"Okay?" Leigh tried again. She had both hands extended, a conciliatory gesture. "I hope you will. I wanted to talk to you about this because I worry about you. I just don't want anything bad to happen to you."

Kara nodded. She'd put her glasses back on, and her face had lost any trace of amusement, sympathy, or surprise; all that remained was disbelief.

Chapter 3

THE NIGHT OF THE accident, after Kara had gone upstairs, Leigh sat at her kitchen table and tried to think of words she could write that would not inflict any further pain on Bethany Cleese's mother. She had always preferred writing over speaking, especially in difficult situations. Many times, when she was having a high-stakes conversation—when she was arguing with Gary, when she was explaining a failing grade to a student or a student's parent, or, lately, almost any time she was just trying to talk with Kara—she wished for the luxury of time that she had while writing, the allowance for second thoughts and better judgments.

But on this night, sitting in her quiet house, her daughter weeping or sleeping upstairs in a Valium-induced haze, Leigh sat staring at several pieces of used stationery, and suspected that no matter how much time she had to write this letter, she would never find the right words.

I am so sorry about what happened to Bethany. As you know, I was her teacher several years ago, and she was such a lovely

I know I cannot comprehend the sadness you are feeling right now. Please know that both Kara and I are thinking

Please know our family is thinking

We feel terrible. Kara is so sorry. I am so sorry. I am a mother too. We would do anything to reach back in time and pull your daughter back into life.

The last one was the clumsiest, but it felt more honest than the others. Still, she didn't know where to go from there. She wished she could call her sister, but Pam's number in Minneapolis had been disconnected again. She tapped her pen against the paper. She probably shouldn't have let Justin go to the retirement home, as if it were a normal Friday, as if their daughter had not just killed someone else's. But even the police had allowed Kara to come home, as if Bethany Cleese were a dented signpost. The grandfather clock in the living room chimed nine, then quarter past, then half past. The phone rang again. The caller hung up on the answering machine. Eva again, probably. Leigh looked at the stationery. There was nothing to write. There was nothing she could say.

She went upstairs, each wooden step making its familiar creak beneath the soft runner. She and Gary had bought the house before Kara was born—Gary's father had helped them with the down payment. And every year they had renovated something. Now the house almost looked as stately as the other Victorians on their street. She herself had scraped paint, screwed in hardware, and dragged concrete stepping stones across the yard. The windows were still drafty, and the roof needed repair. But it was a house, a real house with a yard and a garage, and what didn't belong to the bank belonged to her and Gary. It was the only place, her whole life, that she'd ever lived in for more than a year, and she loved it as if it were a person. Sometimes, standing in her sunny kitchen, she would look out the window and see the porch swing and the tulips she'd planted by the front walk, and it would still occur to her, after all these years, how bright and pleasant her life was now, how much better than before.

She felt her way down the dark hallway to the door of Kara's room. She opened it slowly, quietly. Kara's blinds were open, and a street lamp gave off enough light so Leigh could see her daughter lying in bed, the blanket pulled up to her chin. She crept forward and placed her fingertips a few inches from Kara's nose, waiting to feel the soft exhale. She had done this so many times as a young mother, inexplicably worried that her new baby girl was not just asleep, but dead. But she felt the breath. She curled her fingers into her palm, as if trying to hold it there. A damp strand of Kara's hair was matted against her cheek, but her face looked peaceful. *She killed someone,* Leigh thought. She might think this from now on, every time she saw her daughter. She would hide it, but it would be there in her mind. It would be in everyone's mind, and knowing this made Leigh want to lean down and kiss her sleeping daughter's forehead, as if she could bless her with something, the strength to endure all that guilt and judgment. But she didn't want to wake her.

She went back downstairs and sat at the table.

I can only hope you can find it in your heart to forgive

She was still there, chewing hard on the end of the pen, when the headlights of Gary's car illuminated the driveway. She put the cap on the pen and looked at the clock. Quarter till ten. This time yesterday, Bethany Cleese was alive. She was probably asleep in her mother's house. Leigh could picture her—her dark hair smooth and straight against her pillow. Or, if she was still awake, she was doing homework, preparing for her final exams, the last day of school. She would have been excited about the coming summer. Leigh tapped her pen against the paper. The body would be at the morgue now. She shook her head and closed her eyes.

Justin came in from the garage first. He moved through the mud-room noiselessly, but Gary, just a few steps behind, stepped on one of the aluminum cans that Leigh had left on the floor that afternoon. He pressed his hand against the wall, steadying himself. Leigh stood, and Justin turned around. The three of them picked up the cans and tossed them wordlessly into the bag at Gary's feet. Gary's eyes met Leigh's.

"She went to bed right after you left," she said. "Are you sure you gave her the right dose? She's a lot smaller than you."

"She's fine. I didn't give her that much."

Leigh reached out and pulled Justin under her chin, her hands tight on his bony shoulders. The obvious lesson in all of this was that she should be grateful her own children were still with her. She was. She pressed her nose against his hair and inhaled as deeply as she could. He'd been using her shampoo again.

"How'd it go?" she asked.

"Okay." Justin thumbed through one of his music books. "Mrs. Fairway just got a hip replacement, so I had to sing the alto parts. We did 'Boogie Woogie Bugle Boy' again. That's everyone's favorite."

Leigh nodded and forced a smile. It was good that Justin had gone. Last summer, no friends had come over to see him. He'd spent most of his days by himself at the library, reading books about vampires and werewolves. She looked at Gary. "So what did you think?"

He looked at her blankly. His glasses were smudged.

She lifted her fingers from Justin's shoulders and pantomimed playing the piano. "What did you think of the music?"

"Oh. I didn't stay to listen." He pointed at his cell phone in his pocket. "I wanted to talk to Pete. I was worried they'd be in bed when we got home."

Leigh nodded. Pete was Gary's brother, a lawyer in Boston. He was a corporate lawyer for a large pharmaceutical company. She didn't see how he would be of much help.

Gary moved to the dining room. He looked as if he meant to sit at the table, but when he got close, he stopped, staring down at the scattered pieces of stationery.

"What's this?"

"Oh." Leigh walked in behind him. "I was trying to write . . . just a note or something. To Bethany's mother. I can't remember her last name, but it might be in the paper in the morning."

He exhaled slowly through puckered lips. Gary never really got angry, at least not what Leigh would consider angry. He didn't yell or throw things. He didn't threaten or call names, and then storm out without his coat. He got displeased. That was about as far as it went.

"I could look it up on the Internet," Justin said. He stood behind them on tiptoe, trying to see what his mother had written.

Gary kept his eyes on the table. Justin stepped closer to Leigh and touched her arm. "Can I go jump on the trampoline?" he whispered. "Just for a little while?"

She nodded, tousling his hair, and he reached out, his arms tight around her hips for just a moment. But she felt the kindness of the gesture even after he'd left the room.

Gary looked at her over the tops of his glasses. "You can't send a letter. Not yet. Pete said not to talk to anybody, especially her family, until we talk to lawyers, both criminal and civil. He said not to talk to anyone." He looked at the phone. "Have you called anyone back?"

She shook her head. He sounded like his brother, like his father. "Gary, it's a note that says I'm sorry. That's all. You don't need a lawyer for that."

"We have to be very careful. We can't be—"

"Human?"

"That's exactly right. That's what I was going to say. We can't be human. Thanks for finding the word for me."

She looked away. He didn't need a temper. He was good at quiet sarcasm, and that usually did the trick.

He took her elbow and pulled her to him. "I don't want to fight," he said. "I just... we have to look out for ourselves. We have to look out for Kara. And sending a note tomorrow instead of waiting a few days isn't going to make any difference for that woman."

That woman. Leigh didn't like the way that sounded, but she didn't know her name either.

Gary sighed, tilting his head back. "Whatever she's feeling, she's going to be feeling for a very, very long time."

Leigh slid into a chair. Gary sat beside her. His eyes fell to the stationery, to all the attempts she had made. He reached under the table and took her hand.

"We're going to have to be good to each other," he said. "We're in for a bad time."

She brought his hand up to her cheek. They had been married for almost twenty years; they had, of course, already been through other bad times. In the early years, the electric bill and the gas bill and even the mortgage had sometimes been paid with a credit card they were not sure they would ever pay off. And they had taken turns holding sick children through long, exhausted nights, which in the too-early mornings had made them look at each other not as lovers but as overtaxed coworkers, both of them longing and subtly vying for time off. Even after there was enough money to be comfortable, even after the children were older and more independent, just getting along, Leigh found, could still be hard. Two years before Kara's accident, Gary's back had gone out: there were weeks of pain and hurtful crabbiness, and then the surgery—Leigh, when she came home from work, was nurse and cook and waitress and physical therapy coach. Her caring and tenacity were not recognized until Gary was no longer in constant pain. And even in good times there was often bickering. They both tried to avoid it, each of them letting so many grievances go, but some battles had to be fought. Some bickering wasn't pointless. Some bickering was inevitable. Important. They were not the same people, but they shared everything big—children, a house, a bed, a checking account, a life.

The marriage had somehow survived all this. She believed, sometimes, it was their one common trait—stubbornness—that pushed them to not just endure, but to continue to try to love one another. She still called him on her lunch break to see how his day was going. He still rested one hand on her leg when they were in the car.

But they had not yet seen trouble like the accident, a girl dead. Still holding Gary's hand, Leigh took a breath, as if preparing to go underwater.

"We're going to have to get Kara through this," he said.

"And Justin."

He seemed momentarily confused. "Yeah. Of course."

The grandfather clock chimed ten. She understood what he was saying, but she felt guilty, talking with her husband about being good to each other, about getting Kara through this, when someone else's child was dead. It was the same strange disconnect she felt almost every morning when she read the paper. No matter how much sympathy she felt for the victims of earthquakes and armed robberies and wars and famines, eventually, she had to turn the page and finish her coffee, put the breakfast dishes away, and get her children and herself off to school.

"We should go to bed," he said.

She nodded, but she was thinking of Bethany, picturing her down on the asphalt. There had been blood. "Do you know ... Did she die right away? Did she suf—"

He let go of her hand. "Stop it, Leigh. Stop it. We've got to be practical. Just sitting here feeling bad won't do anyone any good." He pointed at the stationery. "It won't help her, this woman. And it won't help Kara."

She looked at the table. She couldn't argue with that. But her eyes stung with fatigue, and she had the sensation that her brain was shutting down, sputtering along, like a car running low on gas. She knew that she didn't want to be practical. She didn't want to circle the wagons, and think of only her own. "You go on," she told him. "I'll be up in a minute." She touched his hand, but she was looking at the stationery. She had to write the letter before she went to bed, even though she understood that he was right: lines were being drawn, a family on each side, and she couldn't mail anything yet.

THE SUMMER LEIGH WAS pregnant with Justin, there had been a terrible accident in Rayburn, a smaller farming town ten miles north of Danby. A nineteen-year-old grocery clerk, late for his shift, had crossed the center lane in a no-passing zone and hit the sedan of a woman driving her baby home from a doctor's visit. The clerk suffered a broken foot, and the baby, strapped in his car seat, was unharmed. But the young mother was killed instantly. When Leigh read about the accident at her dining room table, she had cried, one hand over her eyes, the other resting on her own bulging middle. Kara sat across from her, eating a bowl of Cheerios and watching her worriedly, while Gary reached over to touch her hand. She knew he would chalk her outburst up to the pregnancy and hormones, and though she'd smiled at him and squeezed his hand, the idea that he would think this made her angry. She understood that he was partly right—she had cried more easily throughout both her pregnancies. There was no denying that. But she also knew that the sadness she felt while pregnant, for strangers, for the entire world, did not feel like hormones so much as a kind of elevated consciousness, a heightened sensitivity to truth. She cried not just for the dead woman and the motherless baby, but for the nineteen-year-old, who, Leigh assumed, would be shackled to guilt for the rest of his life.

Leigh could still remember his name—Kevin Wornall. He was charged with involuntary manslaughter and tried later that fall. Leigh had followed the trial in the paper, hunched over the dining room table while nursing Justin in the mornings. The defense attorney had done all he could—he'd brought in the boy's parents and high school teachers to testify that Kevin was a good boy, kind and polite and skilled at fixing things, and that he'd been held back in school one year and had to go to summer school to finally earn his diploma. But the jury had not been moved. Kevin Wornall was found guilty and given a year in prison. The boy had put his face in his hands—this was the moment the paper's photographer captured; the picture ended up on the front page. And according to the article, when the judge allowed the dead woman's husband to speak, he stood up and told the courtroom that a year in prison was nothing, no punishment at all for killing his child's mother and a beautiful woman. He hated Kevin Wornall, he said. He didn't care about the boy's alleged troubles. He'd ruined his life, ruined his baby's life, because of carelessness and stupidity. A year in prison would never give that back.

The article included a smaller picture of the woman's husband, a big, ruddy-faced man wearing a tie that wasn't tied right. His nostrils were flared, and his mouth was tight with rage, but it was easy to see the misery and fatigue in his eyes. He was pulling double shifts, she imagined, working some hard job during the day, up with the baby at night, all of it in the midst of an aching grief. Still, Leigh felt more sympathy for the boy in the end. Her whole life, she'd tended to side with the underdog. The man had lost his wife, but he had his child, the sympathy of his community, and his own righteous indignation. Kevin Wornall had only guilt.

So Leigh wrote Kevin Wornall a letter. She waited until his sentence was to begin so she could address it to the county jail. She was back at school by then, and she wrote the letter longhand during lunch hour in her classroom. Justin had just started day care, and she was still calling every few hours to check if she had pumped enough breast milk. She was teary as she tried to find words, but it took her only two drafts.

Dear Kevin,

We don't know each other, but I felt so sorry for you after reading about the accident in the paper. I am a young mother myself, and I am heartbroken for the woman who lost her life and her time with her child. But I thought her husband was wrong to speak so harshly to you. Most people, if they are honest, would have to admit to occasionally making errors when driving. I know I made a few, especially when I was younger. I ran a stop sign once. I drove the wrong way down a one way street in an unfamiliar town. Either of these mistakes could have killed someone else, and it is only because of dumb luck that no one was hurt. So I am no better than you are. You have done nothing that I haven't done, but you are being punished so brutally, most of all, I imagine, by your own mind. I guess I just want you to know that not everyone thinks you've done something unforgivable. This year will probably be a hard one for you, and I hope you remember that Mr. Mc-Cullom was speaking out of grief for his wife, and more, I suspect, out of his rage at the general unfairness of life, not really his rage with you.

You certainly don't need to write me back, but if you'd like to, please use the P.O. box on the return address. Either way, I'll be thinking of you.

Sincerely, Leigh Churchill

She felt better after she mailed the letter. She'd done what she could; for once, she'd reached into the daily news, stuck her hand into some of the sadness in its pages, grasping for some real contact. She imagined Kevin Wornall reading her letter in his prison cell. She didn't know what he looked like—the paper had shown only the one picture of him with his face in his hands. But she pictured the face of a boy in her English class who never had clean clothes, who lowered his gaze whenever she looked at him, who answered questions in a trembling voice. In Leigh's mind, at least while writing this letter, Kevin Wornall and this boy had become one person. They both needed mothering, a gentle touch. They needed to not be alone.

But when Kevin Wornall finally wrote back, it was clear she'd been terribly misunderstood. Maybe Kevin Wornall just wasn't a good reader. His own words were difficult to read, many of them misspelled, and they looked as if they'd been written by a child, his cursive winding above and beneath the blue lines of the notebook paper he'd used. He'd thanked her for writing him and being nice. But he'd done a bad thing, he wrote, and he had to pay for it. He wouldn't write her again, because he already had a girlfriend. He thought she should know. Above his signature, he'd written "sorry."

When she showed the letter to Gary, he'd started to smile. But when he saw her face, he stopped.

So many years later, in the middle of the hot, miserable summer when her own daughter was careless, Leigh thought of Kevin Wornall and the way he'd put his face in his hands in the courtroom, and the way the dead woman's husband had used the word *hate*. But she also remembered the letter she'd written to him, the hope she'd felt before she mailed it, and also her despair when he'd written back and she realized she had not been able to adequately communicate something she'd felt so deeply.

·   ·   ·

LEIGH WOULD HAVE TROUBLE sleeping for months after the accident that killed Bethany Cleese. That first night, she didn't sleep at all. Gary lay turned away from her, and she wasn't sure if he was really sleeping or if he just didn't want to talk. She lay beside him with her eyes closed, her hands at her sides, but her mind stayed awake, moving rapidly from worry to worry. Kara might have to go to jail. She would lose her scholarship. College might be out. There would be a picture of her in the paper, her face in her hands, and some stranger reading the paper with her morning coffee would look at her with pity and compassion, thinking she needed to be mothered.

She wondered if Bethany had seen the car coming, if, in her final moment of life, she'd looked through the windshield and seen Kara's face. If Kara never saw her, if she was on the phone, she might have been laughing.

A lawsuit was certainly possible. They wouldn't be able to afford college for Kara anyway. And maybe not for Justin. They had a five-hundred-thousand-dollar insurance policy, but she didn't think that would be enough. Not for someone's child. If they lost the house, they would have to move in with Gary's brother in Boston. That would be fine. He had a big house. They had those spare rooms in their basement. Peter's sons were a little older than Justin, but they'd never gotten along with him. They would adjust. Would Kara come with them? She would have to go somewhere. She couldn't stay in Danby. It would be good for all of them to go away, maybe, to not have to face people, to go somewhere else and start over. If they didn't, they would always have to worry about running into Bethany's mother. And Danby had never been a good place for Justin. It might be easier for everyone, if they just had to slink away.

But at the thought of actually leaving Danby, a heaviness settled over her chest. She'd hated the town at first, the smallness of it, when they'd first come here for Gary's job. She'd been happy in Lawrence, a true college town with good restaurants and museums and coffee shops that stayed open all night. But Danby State had fewer than three thousand students, and the town, apparently, did not think entertaining them was its responsibility. There was only one movie theater, and it showed two films at a time, one of them always G-rated. There were no bookstores. There was no mall, just a feed and farm supply store that sold Levi's and shirts with snapping pockets, wool sweaters, and aprons hand-embroidered with verses of Scripture. Leigh had to drive to Topeka or Wichita to buy clothes.

But over time, she'd gotten used to Danby. She liked that many of her former students were adults now. She liked to see how they changed as they got older, at least the ones who stuck around. She liked that there was only one homeless man in town, and that everyone, including herself, knew that his name was Jerome. When he walked down the middle of Commerce Street with outstretched arms, wearing red sweats and the neon green ski jacket given to him every winter by the police department, people slowed and gave him the right of way as if he were an ambulance or a fire truck. Most days he wouldn't come inside, but when it was very cold, people went looking for him, gave him blankets and food, and occasionally cajoled him into their trucks and cars so they could drive him to the Methodist church, which kept a cot for him in the basement.

During the warm months, there was a farmers' market Tuesday, Thursday, and Saturday mornings in a parking lot downtown. On Saturdays, for years now, Leigh had walked there with a mesh bag and a twenty-dollar bill. She liked buying tomatoes and squash and cucumbers from the people who grew them, and she liked buying bread and pastries from the Mennonite women who covered their hair and made everything from scratch. Some of the people she bought food from were the parents of former students, and they still called her Mrs. Churchill and gave her free scones and ears of corn or bouquets of daisies, letting her know how their Ryans and Brians and Lindseys and Jennifers were doing in college or in the army or in vo-tech school or in Chicago. There were things she didn't like about the market—there was always someone trying to give away puppies or kittens that Leigh knew no one would take, and every week, a group of women with very long hair handed out Bibles and unsolicited advice about avoiding eternity in hell. But usually, someone was playing a fiddle or a guitar, and Leigh would catch sight of Jerome sitting on the back of a truck and eating something one of the Mennonite women had given him, and seeing this and hearing the music always made her feel as if she were a part of something big and good.

It would be a loss, she thought now, lying in her bed, to leave all that behind. They could move to another small town, of course. There were plenty of little towns with farmers' markets and Mennonites. Leigh had lived in several of them growing up. But that was the point—she didn't want to live in several small towns, or even two different small towns; she wanted her children to grow up in just one place, to know a certain town, a certain house, as home.

At a quarter to five, she heard the thud of the newspaper against the front door, and the receding whirl of the paperboy's bike. She slid out of bed and took her sweatshirt off the bedpost as quietly as she could. Gary didn't stir when she opened the creaking door to the hallway. She moved past Justin's room, pausing outside Kara's door. She stood there for a moment with her fingers on the doorknob. How many times had she stood in this spot, just like this, trying to decide whether or not to knock, trying to know how to react to Kara's moods, to guess what a good mother would do? She didn't know. With Kara, especially, she always felt she was just guessing.

She thought of how peaceful Kara had looked the night before, lost to sleep, and decided not to risk waking her.

Outside, the birds had started to sing. The sun was only a faint glow on the horizon, but most of her neighbors had left their lampposts and front lights on. Once her eyes adjusted, Leigh could see her newspaper lying on the grass, bundled in its translucent blue bag. She raised her gaze to her neighbors' houses. There was a newspaper on almost every lawn. It was a matter of hours until they all knew. It should be the least of her concerns, but it concerned her. Once the neighbors knew, this quiet street she loved so much, with its lilac bushes and magnolia and pear trees, wouldn't feel the same.

Across the street, Ida Pickett came out in her blue bathrobe. She saw Leigh and waved. "Up early this morning?" she called out. Leigh waved, pretending not to hear, and hurried back inside.

She turned on the light and spread the paper on the dining room table. The article was on the front page, next to a smaller article about farm subsidies.

Pedestrian Killed in Accident

Bethany Cleese, 16, of Danby, died yesterday afternoon after being hit by a 1998 Chevrolet Suburban at the corner of Seventh and Commerce Streets as she walked home from school. The Suburban was driven by Kara Anne Churchill, 18, of Danby. According to police, Cleese was crossing Seventh Street in the crosswalk when she was hit by Churchill.

"There's nothing wrong with that crosswalk," said Marta Gonzalez, who works at the bakery close to the intersection where the accident occurred. "It's marked. There's a big stop sign. But people just drive right through it without looking. I see it all the time." Gonzalez did not see the accident that killed Cleese, but she said that over the years, she has seen many close calls. "I hate to say it, but it's the college kids and the high school kids. They're going too fast and not paying attention."

The cause of the accident is still under investigation. Churchill could not be reached for comment.

Bethany Cleese was a sophomore at Danby High. She played the flute in the school band. "She was a dedicated student," said Ryan Backbo, her music instructor at Danby High. "She practiced, and she'd improved so much this year. I'm stunned, and very sad, as all of her teachers will be. My heart goes out to her family."

Cleese was also a member of her church's youth group, which was led by Jim and Cynthia Tork. "We are heartbroken," said Jim Tork. "A young person's death is always cause for great sorrow, but Bethany, especially, had such a lovely presence. We will miss her, and her mother will be in our prayers."

Cleese lived with her mother, Diane Kletchka, who could not be reached for comment.

And there was Bethany beside it all, smiling in her yearbook picture. There were the large dark eyes, and the uneven smile, so endearing. She'd worn her hair down for the picture, curled it with rollers, maybe. It fell in dark waves around her shoulders. Or maybe her mother had curled it for her. Leigh brought the newspaper close and touched her finger to the picture. Bethany's face had not changed so much in the two years since Leigh had had her in class. Leigh had a distinct but mundane memory of another girl, in the middle of a test, leaning across the aisle to ask Bethany what time it was. Bethany had looked at Leigh to silently ask permission to respond, and after Leigh nodded, Bethany had leaned toward the other girl and whispered *"Ten to two."* Leigh could still hear the three soft *t*'s. She remembered this moment for some reason. She remembered the exact way the light had hit Bethany's face.

"What does it say?"

Leigh jumped, and the newspaper crinkled in her hands. Kara was sitting on the couch in the still-dark living room, her knees curled up to her chest. She was wearing the skirt and T-shirt she'd worn the night before, and the skin around her eyes looked bruised. For a moment, Leigh thought Kara had beaten herself, maybe banged her head against a table. But it was just eye makeup from the day before. She hadn't washed her face.

"It's just... it's just the bare facts."

Kara held out her hand, and Leigh understood that she was to bring the paper across the room to her. She hadn't said "please." She hadn't asked. She'd simply held out her hand, as if Leigh were a waitress with a tray at a wedding. But now was not the time to consider such things. Leigh walked across the room and gave her the paper. She watched Kara's eyes move across each line, reach the end, and then start again with the headline.

"How long have you been awake?"

Kara didn't look up. Leigh waited.

"Kara. You still need to answer me when I ask you something. I'm sorry about all of this, but you still need..." She faltered, trying to think.

Kara looked up and held her mother's gaze for a long moment, and even though she was sitting, Leigh had that feeling of being studied from above. Leigh walked to the couch and sat. There were several feet between them, but even coming that close felt strange. She reached over and tugged the newspaper from Kara's hands. "I was thinking. It might be good for you to write down some details about the accident, what led up to it, while it's fresh..."

Kara stared at the wall. She appeared fortified, sealed off, as if she were trying to withstand a tirade. But there was no tirade, Leigh thought. She was being nice. She was always just trying to be nice. Kara didn't know what a tirade was.

"While you still remember the details, I mean. I can write them down for you."

"Why?"

"Because you might need to— you might forget something important."

"Important for what?"

"Honey." She touched her arm. "You realize...I don't want to scare you. But there's a possibility you could go to jail for this. We're going to have to call a lawyer on Monday. Or two lawyers. There'll be a criminal case, and a civil case. We could be sued. I know you feel terrible right now, but—"

"I just killed someone." Her voice was a dull monotone. "I don't care if I go to jail or not."

"You may think you don't care now, but—"

"I don't care. But I'm sorry you and Dad might be sued. I'm sorry."

"Kara. That's not what I'm most worried about. I'm trying to help you." It was true. But the words came out in an indignant gasp. She sounded like her own mother. But she was not her mother. She was a good mother, and she would try to be understanding, even when she didn't understand, even when real empathy was beyond her. And it was certainly beyond her now, considering what would have happened if, in her own youth, she had run over a pedestrian. One thing she knew—her mother would not have tried to help. She would not have been as patient with Leigh's feelings. And in the very unlikely event that she had, if her own mother had ever reached over and touched her arm to try to reassure her, Leigh would have been grateful.

She looked at Kara, who had turned away from her to stare at the floor. You don't appreciate it, she thought, and she was horrified, though the words never left her mouth. Despite all her good intentions, her self-discipline and restraint, she heard that voice as her own.

Chapter 4

LEIGH'S MOTHER WAS BARELY over five feet tall, maybe a hundred pounds, her hips so slim she could wear jeans made for children. But she was hard looking. Her arms were lean and muscular, and the backs of her hands were knobby with bone. She had wide gray eyes, and pale skin that appeared to be stretched tightly across her face, and this combination gave her the look of someone ready to burst out of themselves, an energy or sound barely contained. She moved quickly, decisively. When she cleaned the house, cabinets slammed and dishes sometimes broke, even when she wasn't angry. The only time she was still and quiet was when she allowed herself a cigarette, and even then Leigh thought of her as a coiled snake, vigilant and waiting.

She'd slapped Leigh's older sister, Pam, across the face once, but it was just once, and she had done it immediately after learning that their next-door neighbor, Mrs. Restevet, had discovered Pam, twelve years old at the time, on the couch in the dark with Aaron Restevet, who was fourteen, both of them naked from the waist up. Later that afternoon, Leigh's mother told both Leigh and Pam that she was still very upset, and that she didn't want Pam to end up pregnant. But she also said that she was wrong to have slapped Pam, and that she was sorry. She'd held her right hand in her left as she spoke, pressing it against the bone of her hip, as if she worried it would get away from her again.

They were living in Missouri then, in St. Joseph maybe, or Gladstone. Leigh got the locations of her memories mixed up—they had moved often; every year, there had been a different apartment in a different town. Leigh's mother said they were lucky they got to live in so many different places. She had grown up in just one house in just one town in southeast Ohio that she referred to as "that miserable shit hole" so often that both girls, when they were older, could not recall the actual name of their mother's birthplace. She had taken them there once, when their grandfather was sick, dying actually, but their mother didn't tell them that at the time. He'd worked in coal mines his whole life, and silicosis had finally gotten ahold of his lungs. Leigh was seven and Pam was nine, but as an adult, Leigh would only vaguely recall the house her mother had grown up in— it was painted toothpaste green in the front and not at all in the back, and there were nylon yellow curtains on the windows, a washing machine on the front porch, its door sealed with duct tape. There was one small bathroom under the stairs, and in the back, there was an outhouse with a moon-shaped hole cut into the door. That morning, before they'd left, their mother had braided both Pam's and Leigh's hair so tightly it made them both tear up, and then she'd pinned the braids in coils at the bases of their necks. She'd told them to keep their heads away from the back of the couch and the rugs.

Their grandmother, Pam and Leigh knew, had died when their mother was young. But there were aunts and uncles there, some who looked so much younger than their mother, some who looked much older, and they all called their mother Anna May, which was strange, because Pam and Leigh had grown up thinking their mother's name was just Anna. There were other children there, but most of them weren't nice to either Pam or Leigh: they said because Leigh and Pam were new, they had to use the outhouse, not the indoor bathroom, and when Leigh and Pam looked scared, the other children called them names. They sought refuge in the kitchen, where they were put to work sorting beans that one of the aunts poured on the table from a burlap sack. She told them to throw away stray pebbles or clumps of dirt.

Their grandfather stayed in his bedroom and coughed. He was small, like their mother, and he lay under a green blanket that had U.S. ARMY stamped across the back. He and their mother had the same birdlike faces, all bones, no flesh. Leigh tried to be nice to him, but he didn't smile much, and he didn't seem sad when it was time for them to leave.

When Leigh's mother pulled their car back onto the gravel road, she pointed out a beautiful yellow flowering bush in front of the house and said, "See those long branches beneath the flowers? That's what he used to whip us with." She rolled down the window, lit a cigarette, and almost smiled. "You girls don't even know what that feels like."

Leigh studied her mother's gray eyes in the rearview mirror. She couldn't tell if she wanted her to ask another question or not. Her brows were lowered as if she were trying to concentrate; this was the way she often looked when she smoked.

"That's sad," Leigh finally said. Her mother said nothing back. There was just the sound of tires rolling over gravel and the engine racing as her mother shifted gears again. Leigh and Pam, both in the backseat, glanced at each other. Their mother didn't always like for them to talk. But Leigh could see her mother's shoulder over the top of the front seat, and she thought about how people on television often touched someone's shoulder when they knew someone they loved was sad. Her mother was wearing her blue wool coat, and Leigh could imagine how it would feel under her hand, scratchy but soft, her mother's firm arm beneath it. She lifted her own hand, thinking, *This is what people do, there is nothing to be afraid of.* But when she actually placed her hand there, her mother turned quickly, looking scared, and Leigh's hand, as if frightened itself, slid off to the side.

PAM AND LEIGH HAD not seen their own father since Leigh was five and Pam was seven. Their mother said he was in Florida, selling cars, which was the perfect job for him, she said, because he was good at lying to people. But when Leigh was very young, he'd lived in the same town in Arkansas that they'd lived in, and on Sundays, Leigh remembered, she and Pam would go over to his apartment. He was tall and thin—lanky—but when he took off his shirt, you could see muscles. He had Leigh and Pam count how many pull-ups he could do from a bar in a doorway, and he had Pam sit on his feet while he did sit-ups on the floor. When they went somewhere, he wore bell-bottom jeans and shirts that were made of something shiny, not satin, but almost, and he had a big stereo that could make the windows shake. He also had a motorcycle, not a car, and so he had to drive them over from their mother's one at a time. "My little daredevils," he'd called them in his friendly, laughing voice. "My little backseat babes." Leigh had hated the motorcycle. When she had to ride it, she clung tight to her father with both hands, her face buried in the back of his shiny shirt. Once, she'd left her leg too close to the exhaust, and it gave her a circle-shaped burn on her inner calf that hurt for more than a week. It turned into a light pink scar that no one else noticed but that, even much later, felt more tender than the rest of her body.

There was one Sunday that Pam had been in trouble with their mother because she hadn't really gotten started on an art project that was due the next day, a framed hooked-rug picture of a cat. All Pam had had to do was use a special hooking tool to tie the correct colored piece of yarn to the coordinating square in the picture, but there were hundreds of squares, and though their mother had bought Pam the supplies for the project a week earlier, by that Sunday morning, Pam had not even completed the first row. She told their mother she could finish if she could stay home from her father's just this once. She would sit in her room and hook all day. But their mother said no. No way. Did they know what her week was like? she had asked, looking at Leigh as well as Pam, as if they had both done something wrong. Work and kids, work and kids, never a minute to herself except for a few hours on Sunday, and she was damned if she was going to give even that away just because Pam waited till the last minute to do an art project. Did they know what she would have given to have had somebody buy her *art materials* when she was a child? Nobody was buying her *art materials*. And when she was young, she'd done her work *on time*. She hadn't expected other people to go changing their schedules because of her own poor planning.

And so when they heard the motorcycle's engine in the drive, they had all gone outside together, Pam holding the rug frame in one hand, a plastic bag with the hook and yarn in the other. "You'll be fine," their mother said. She held the plastic bag up to Pam's face. "Here. Hold this in your teeth. Now you've got a free hand to hold on with." And so Pam, who was just a smaller, slimmer version of their small, slim mother, had climbed on and clenched the bag in her teeth, her gray eyes wide on Leigh's as she wrapped her free arm around their father's torso. He was facing forward, not saying anything, because by then, he and their mother did not look at or speak to each other unless at least one of them was yelling. For the rest of her life, Leigh would remember the sight of them driving away, her older sister's small body on the back of the motorcycle, the bag hanging from her mouth and the rug frame wedged between her arm and her leg, the wind already pressing against the material like a sail. *She'll fly away,* Leigh had thought, and she'd wished she could reach for her mother's hand, for something to keep her own body anchored. *She'll fly off the back and he'll keep going. He won't even know she's gone.*

YEARS LATER, WHEN LEIGH reminded Pam of this story, Pam, always forgiving, always ready with excuses for everyone, would point out that at the time, their mother's life really had been all work and kids, and that those Sunday afternoons must have been the only time she had to do something for herself—to take a bath, maybe, or go to a movie, or even just to clean the house without it getting messy again before she was even done. "That was when she was working at the bowling alley, at the concession stand," Pam said. "Remember? She'd bring home those little paper nacho trays with the cheese sauce in a plastic container, and it's not any good cold, but she would sit right down on the couch and start eating the chips when she came home. That was her dinner." When Leigh didn't acknowledge the recollection, Pam looked at her like she was crazy. "You don't remember her working at the bowling alley? You don't remember her eating those nachos?"

Leigh didn't remember. When she tried to think back to the years when they had lived in Arkansas and then Missouri, she had hazy memories of different apartments, one in a basement that was always dark, the windows high and some of them blocked by shrubbery. In every apartment they'd had two televisions, one in their mother's bedroom, the other one out in the living room, where she and Pam would watch cartoons. During meals in the kitchen, her mother would turn the television in the living room at an angle so she could see it from the table, but if something really caught her attention, she would go into the living room and eat on the couch, her plate balanced on the armrest. Leigh remembered that her clothes and toys were kept in cardboard boxes, and she remembered her mother sorting through them and saying, "You all just have too much. That's the problem. You have too many clothes, too many toys. You don't even know what you have."

She and Pam usually rode the same school bus. They didn't sit together because Pam was older and sat in the back, sometimes making out with boys. But they would walk home from the bus stop together, even when Pam started junior high and they rode different buses, because only Pam got to wear the apartment key around her neck. When they got home, their mother would still be at work, and Pam would make peanut butter and jelly sandwiches for both of them. They would watch cartoons together, *Scooby-Doo, Super Friends,* and sometimes they would dance in front of their mother's big mirror to Pam's little record player turned up as loud as it would go. One Easter, their mother bought them matching shirts made out of a gauzy, light material. The sleeves reached past their elbows, but the underside of the sleeves had been cut so what remained floated free. Butterfly shirts, Pam called them. After school, after cartoons, Leigh and Pam would put on the shirts and jump off their mother's bed, listening to ABBA and the soundtrack from *Xanadu,* until the man upstairs pounded on their ceiling, or until their mother came home.

And Leigh remembered that in that same apartment, she had once been so sick that her mother allowed her to stay home from school. Her mother had to go to work, and that afternoon, Leigh had woken up with her pillow and sheets covered in her own vomit. Waking up to the smell of it had made her vomit again, and then it was in her hair, on her blanket, but she was too weak to stand up and get away. She cried out, but no one came. She was thirsty. She didn't know what time it was. She crawled across the room to Pam's bed, whimpering as she slid between the clean sheets with her filthy hair and nightgown. She had a doll with her, a smiling baby with a soft middle and hard arms and legs, and even though she could smell and see vomit in the doll's pale hair, she fell asleep with her nose against its plastic cheek.

When she woke again, Pam was standing in front of the bed, still wearing her backpack.

"I'm sick," Leigh said. She heard her own voice and started to cry. "I threw up."

Pam let her backpack fall to the floor. And then Leigh could hear her in the kitchen, running water, opening a drawer. She returned with a glass of Tang. Leigh sat up against the wall and drank, watching as her sister took the blankets and sheets off the other bed.

"You want to take a bath?" she asked, her nose wrinkled, and Leigh nodded yes. Pam went to go run the water. The bathroom was at the other end of the hall, close to their mother's room, and to Leigh, it made more sense to crawl there than it did to walk. By the time she made it to the bathroom, the water was high enough to sit in. She worried she would fall asleep in the water. She worried she would drown.

"Call me if you need me," Pam said. "I have to go wash these, so yell really loud." The washer and dryer that everyone in their unit shared was in the basement, and their mother had a rule that they were never to leave laundry there unattended, because a month earlier, someone had stolen an entire load of good clothes.

And then Pam was gone, and Leigh was alone again, watching water drop from the faucet into the tub, her head woozy, her mouth still tasting of bile. She wished she would have told Pam that she didn't care about having clean sheets and blankets, that she would rather have her just stay there with her. She had been alone all day.

But only a minute later, Leigh could hear Pam back in the apartment. She knocked on the bathroom door and said she couldn't wash the sheets after all. The basement door was locked, and their mother had the key.

"SHE DIDN'T HAVE ANY choice," Pam would argue, years later, when Leigh asked her why their mother had left a sick child home alone. "It wasn't the kind of place where you could take a day off. She was providing for us, you know, and you've got to admit, she did a pretty good job. We always had food, clothes. I don't think she was getting child support then, or if she did, it wasn't much."

Leigh sometimes wished she could remember their mother the way Pam did, as someone to understand and admire, a single mother working long hours to support her daughters, hard and distant for good reasons. She had to admit that her mother's career path, in the end, was impressive. She had not finished high school. She'd given birth to both Pam and Leigh before she was nineteen. After their father moved out, she did other people's laundry, stuffed stacks of flyers into stacks of envelopes, took care of other people's children as well as her own. Later, when Pam and Leigh were old enough for school, she cleaned hotel rooms and served food at a bowling alley. She answered the phone at a nursing home. She took care of retarded people. She gave them baths, fed them, changed their diapers. By the time Leigh was ten, her mother had saved enough to attend cosmetology school in Kansas City. She learned how to perm, cut, color, and blow-dry. She learned all this by doing it for eight hours a day, first on wigs and then on real people, with an instructor who would come over every few minutes to check her work and, if she'd done something wrong, make her do it over again.

"And I've got to pay them for the pleasure," she'd explained to her daughters. She was making dinner, emptying a can of beans into a pot. She was still wearing the pink smock with a white cornered collar, someone else's name stitched onto the side. "I pay all this money so I can work my ass off. It's kind of like having kids." She'd smiled at Leigh and Pam then, to show them she was half joking.

After she got her license, things got a little better. She got a booth at a salon, and then they had more money. She was good at doing hair, she told her daughters. She'd found her calling. If she did someone's hair once, they usually called again and asked for her, and all her appointment slots were filling up. She got the air conditioner in the car fixed. She bought Pam and Leigh new school clothes, and bedspreads and curtains for their room. When their father did send child support, she put it in the bank under each of their names. She brought home shampoo samples in tiny packets, and she gave both Pam and Leigh permanent waves that made their hair smell like apples.

But she never stayed at one salon for very long. She couldn't get along with people. She fought with other stylists over missing brushes and stolen clients. She fought with the owners over whether she should have to share her tips with the receptionist, and whether or not she could smoke in the back room during her break. "They're jealous," she told her daughters. "They're mad because I'm making more than they are. I'm not giving that bitch at the desk ten percent of my tips for sitting there on her big ass. Everybody wants to share and be so nice, but that's not the way I see it. They're taking money from you all, too. Food from your mouths. And I don't fucking like it."

So they moved, the three of them, at least once a year, to new towns with new salons owned by people who hadn't yet heard that their mother could be difficult to work with. They lived in little towns around Kansas City—Ottawa, Gladstone, Lee's Summit, Bonner Springs. And every new town meant a new apartment in a new apartment complex and a new school with different kids and different teachers who couldn't pronounce their last name, who got confused because it was different from their mother's. "Just explain it," their mother said. "It's not a big deal. People get divorced." She tilted her head from side to side and laughed. "Tell them your name is Voe and mine is Hesse. Sounds like hazy, rhymes with crazy."

Leigh and Pam glanced at each other and looked away. They knew better than to say something like that in front of a room full of kids, some of them mean. They would jump on anything, some people.

IT GOT TOO DIFFICULT for Leigh after a while, trying to make new friends all the time, walking into a strange cafeteria and hoping to find someone to sit with. When she was very young, she had only to be friendly and ask questions and someone would usually take pity on her. But by seventh grade, it mattered that she didn't have the right face or the right clothes or the right shoes, and she could see it in the eyes of the girls she tried to talk to. So she developed a system. When she started at a new school, she brought a book with her to lunch and sat in a corner. If someone came and sat beside her, fine; if someone didn't, she would still be okay. She did her homework during study hall, while the other girls huddled in groups and painted one another's nails.

"It's good you take advantage of your opportunities," her mother said, looking over her report card. "Wish I could say that about your sister."

Pam also had her own system for adapting to every new school: she just got a new boyfriend. Once she chose a boy, she had friends—his friends, and his friends' girlfriends. It was as easy as that for her. She had turned out pretty. She looked the way she really was, sweet and full of concern. She'd gotten their mother's wide gray eyes, but her hair was pale blond, like their father's. Her teeth had come in straight. And though most of her body was still small like their mother's, by the time she was in eighth grade, she had the breasts of a larger woman.

"Where the hell did those come from?" their mother would ask, and her tone would be that of someone demanding an answer, someone confronting a thief. Pam had no answer, of course, so there was little for her to do but look down at her suspicious breasts. Still their mother kept asking. She asked Pam where she got her breasts in front of saleswomen at clothing stores, in front of doctors leaning forward with stethoscopes, in front of lifeguards at the city pool. "You sure as hell didn't get them from me," she would say. And then she would look down at her own proportionate chest and sigh, smiling as if it were all a joke. She never did any of this to Leigh. Leigh was taller than her mother, but she was thin all over, with no breasts at all, and this seemed to balance everything out for her mother. When Leigh was at the pool, or in a dressing room at the mall, her mother just said she looked nice.

BUT WHEN THEY WENT to school, no matter where they lived, Pam was the lucky one. At home, she showed Leigh the notes that had been pushed into her hand or stuffed into her locker. They came from ambassadors—*John R. thinks you're cute and wants to meet you*—or sometimes from the suitors themselves. Pam would have to choose carefully and quickly—if she hurt the wrong boy's feelings, he might become an enemy, she told Leigh, so it was best to have a boyfriend right away. That way she could use it as an excuse not to go out with someone else, but still not make anyone mad. She told Leigh this as if giving advice Leigh would someday need and use. But Leigh knew they weren't the same. Their faces were just different enough—her eyes were a little smaller than Pam's, her hair not as blond. She would never have such an easy time.

So it was nice, sometimes, to hear her mother say she was the smart one.

"Pam needs to put more effort in her school work," she would say, opening kitchen cabinets and slamming them shut, looking for some grocery she hadn't bought yet. Pam could be sitting right there, hunched forward with lowered eyes, but her mother would look at Leigh as she talked, as if the two of them were arriving at a decision. "You know what I mean? I'm not out there busting my ass fifty hours a week so she can hang out with some asshole wearing a jean jacket in the back of a truck at the Burger King when she should be at school. Do you ever see me going out? Ever see me having a good time? No. I work and work and work. I'm on my feet all day. I buy you girls everything you need. And then I open Pam's report card and see C's and D's and F's, like she's some big dummy. Your sister is going to end up pregnant, okay? Pregnant and dumb." She would circle the small kitchen as she talked, opening the refrigerator and closing it hard, the condiments rattling on the door. "Why won't she listen to me? I get upset because I care." Her voice would get louder, her eyes wider, and it would look as if the nameless thing that always seemed wrapped tight inside her body was finally about to burst out. "I just want things to be good for you two. Doesn't she understand? I want you both to have a good life."

When Pam did get pregnant, she was seventeen, and she was, in fact, dating a boy who wore a jean jacket, who was nice to her only some of the time. She moved in with him, into a trailer behind his parents' house, packing up her things while Leigh was at school and their mother was at work. She left a note for them on the kitchen table. Leigh read the note first, when she got home from school. When she heard her mother coming up the stairs to their apartment, she ran back to their room—or her room, it was only her room now—closed the door, and put a pillow behind her head and over each ear, preparing for the explosion. But there was only silence, and it went on for so long that Leigh finally put the pillow down and looked at the door, wondering if their mother had left, if she had gone back down the stairs, gotten into her car, and was now driving around town trying to find her sister so the right person would feel her fury.

But when she came out to the kitchen, she found her mother at the table, smoking a cigarette and looking out the sliding glass doors that led to the little balcony that overlooked the parking lot. Pam's note lay on the middle of the table, as if she had pushed it away. She looked up and smiled at Leigh.

"It's fine," she said. "Really. I don't care anymore." She reached for the note, picked it up, and let it fall lightly back to the table. "It's a relief, actually. I don't care."

But she did not look relieved. She looked, Leigh thought, deflated, as if the force that had always been wrapped up inside her had been squeezed into something small. "You're my good girl," she said, reaching up quickly, her hand coming close to Leigh's hair, almost touching it. Though Leigh missed her sister, and she knew she should be worried for her, she was, at that moment, happy for herself.

THE YEAR PAM WAS pregnant for the first time, living with her boyfriend in his parents' trailer, Leigh went out for the debate team. She'd learned that joining clubs was a good way to make friends at a new school, and even the freshmen on the debate team got to travel to tournaments in nearby towns on a bus, with occasional overnight stays in hotels. There was a fee involved, to pay for the hotels and the gas, but when Leigh asked her mother for the money, her mother looked unhappy for only a moment, and then she nodded and said that yes, her education was important, and she would see to it that the fee was paid.

The debate topic that year was water pollution. Leigh spent

many lunch hours in the library, copying charts on groundwater depletion and tracing diagrams of carbon chains onto notebook paper that she would then transfer onto poster board in neat Magic Marker, starting over if she made a mistake. She practiced saying things like "while my opponent's information seems correct, a closer look suggests...," and though it was difficult to believe that these words, these words of an adult, could ever come out of her mouth easily, after a while, they did. "You're good at this," the debate coach told her. Leigh sometimes imagined her own mother looking at her like this, saying these same words. But most of the debate tournaments were in other, bigger towns, and when they had practice sessions so the parents could watch, her mother was usually working.

Pam came to a practice once. She was eight months into the pregnancy by then, and she waddled into the auditorium with her head and shoulders tilted back, as if trying to counter the weight of her belly. People turned to look and she smiled back at them. She gave Leigh a quick wave and sat in the back row. She was still wearing her uniform from the doughnut shop, the smock stretched tight over her belly. Whenever Leigh got up to speak, she leaned forward in her chair, her eyes narrowed with concentration.

"You're so smart!" she told Leigh when it was over. She had to turn to the side when they hugged, her belly against Leigh's hip. Her hair smelled like fried grease. "I didn't know what you were talking about half the time. But you sounded smart. You sounded like someone on TV." She reached into a small white bag, pulled out a doughnut, and gave it to Leigh. The doughnut was cherry filled, Leigh's favorite. For reasons she could not identify, Leigh felt the sudden pressure of tears behind her eyes.

"How's Mom?"

"She's the same," Leigh said, though it wasn't true. Their mother had been nicer lately, more willing to talk and smile. Maybe their mother had only so much caring in her, not enough for two, but enough for one. Or maybe their mother just liked her more.

Pam leaned forward to wipe sugar from Leigh's lips. "Does she talk about me?"

Leigh nodded, though this wasn't true either.

"Well," Pam said. "Maybe after the baby comes, you all can come by."

WHEN LEIGH GOT HOME that night, her mother was in the kitchen, stirring something in a large pot on the stove, a towel clothespinned around her neck like a giant bib. "It's the best I could do for an apron," she said. She laughed at Leigh's startled face. "That's right. I'm cooking. Don't have a heart attack. I had a color and perm cancel, and I got it into my head that I was going to make us a nice dinner. We're having a stew I used to make. No sandwiches tonight."

Leigh took off her coat and her backpack, trying to show some surprise, but not so much that her mother might be insulted. She knew she should not mention the debate practice, or the fact that Pam had come. Her mother might think she was trying to make her feel bad.

When they sat down to eat, her mother ladled some of the stew into a bowl. Leigh saw beige meat and onions and green peppers, her two most hated vegetables, floating in a broth bubbly with grease. She'd eaten the entire doughnut Pam had given her. Usually she just made her own sandwich at night, if and when she was hungry. She hadn't known this was going to happen.

"Thank you!" she said. "This looks great! Wow!"

"I got all fresh ingredients, nothing frozen," her mother said. She unpinned the towel around her neck. "The supermarkets these days, they've got everything. You can get all these vegetables in the middle of winter. You don't even think about it now."

Leigh had to gag into her napkin after every swallow, and it was difficult to keep the smile on her face.

"Do you like it?" her mother asked.

"It's so good!" Leigh said. "I can't believe you did all this."

Her mother told Leigh about a man who had come in to get his beard shaped. He'd guessed her to be in her early twenties. She blushed a little, telling Leigh this. That was what he'd said anyway. Leigh nodded as if she agreed, though it wasn't true. Her mother was in her thirties, but she looked older, not younger. Her hands were red and rough and wrinkled like an old woman's—she said it was from the chemicals at work.

Finally, her mother got up to turn on the television. She stood in front of it, turning the channel dial slowly, her bowl of stew in her other hand. Leigh snatched several napkins, held them under the table, and used her hands to empty the bowl. She stuffed one napkin full, and covered it with another, and then another, and then pushed the wad into the front pocket of her sweatshirt.

Her mother stopped changing the channel on the opening credits to *One Day at a Time*. She stepped away from the television, turned around, and smiled. "Have you seen this show?" she asked. She sat on the couch, her stew balanced on the armrest. "It's good. It's really good. It's about a single mom."

Leigh followed her gaze to the screen, to the quick clips of the funny, smart, red-haired mother and her two teenage daughters. Leigh watched *One Day at a Time* every week, hungry for the life contained in it. The mother, Ann Romano, was always helping the daughters, listening to them, giving good advice. Leigh watched the show as if it were a window to her future life, when she herself would be a mother.

"One of my clients told me about it," her mother said. "It really shows what it's like, you know, trying to do it all by yourself."

Leigh stood up, her hands cradling the damp wad of napkins in her sweatshirt pocket. She was two steps away from the garbage, but she stopped in the doorway to the living room, her eyes moving from her mother's untroubled face to the television screen. The first commercial break ended, and the characters started talking. Her mother laughed and nodded at the first joke the television mother said, and something about the look on her own mother's face made Leigh hold her gaze there. *She thinks she's like Ann Romano,* Leigh thought, and it was strange, embarrassing almost, to think that her mother could watch the show and laugh at the right times, to see everything Leigh wanted so much played out on the screen, and not recognize the difference. You could be completely wrong about yourself, Leigh thought. You could not see yourself at all.

And then her mother turned to her, her smile gone. "What's in your pocket?"

Leigh looked down. The broth had seeped through the material, a dark stain spreading out. She moved toward the garbage, but her mother was quick, up and across the room in an instant. "What is it? Is it—"

She pushed Leigh's hands aside and pulled out the wad. The napkins gave way, and the remains of the stew bulged out like the entrails of a dead animal. For a moment, neither of them moved. Leigh could hear the television, the studio audience laughing.

"You're throwing it away," her mother said quietly. The broth was dripping from her hands. She threw the wad of napkins into the sink. "What I made for you. You're just throwing it away."

"I'm sorry." Leigh reached for the mess in the sink. She would eat it now, right out of the sink. She would do anything. But her mother pushed her hand away, picked up the napkins, turned, and dropped them into the garbage with a thud. When she turned back, she gave Leigh a long, appraising look, her chin lifted and turned to the side.

"You don't appreciate anything." Her mother spoke quietly, and it was clear that a firm judgment had already been made. "You've never been hungry, not one day in your life. You have no idea what that's even like. That's the problem with you, you with your extracurricular activities and your expensive tennis shoes."

"I'm sor—"

Her mother made a slicing motion with her hands, a director signaling a cut. "That's it," she said. "I've had enough."

AND THAT REALLY WAS the end, it seemed. Because just after the stew incident, that very week, her mother started going out at night, and she was sometimes still gone in the mornings. She bought new clothes for herself. She got her ears pierced. She stopped buying groceries. Leigh started picking up the things she needed from the convenience store across the street from school. She'd ride the bus home, carrying soda pop and bread and cherry-filled doughnuts in a brown paper bag on her lap. At first her mother left her money, but when summer came, Leigh got a job at the Dairy Maid, and her mother didn't leave money anymore.

In July, Leigh came home from her shift and found her mother at the kitchen table, looking at a map of Los Angeles. She glanced up and smiled.

"I think I'm going to move to California," she said. She smiled, her eyebrows high. She'd cut her hair in a curly bob by then, and it made her look younger, more girlish. She was wearing a pink sleeveless dress and earrings shaped like butterflies.

Leigh sat down across from her. She was still wearing her Dairy

Maid uniform. She still had her name tag on. She wasn't used to standing eight hours a day, and her calves hurt. Her mother had said "I," not "we." She cocked her head. "What?"

"I think I'm going to move to California. Los Angeles, maybe. Or San Diego. Somewhere where the weather is always good." She squinted out the window, blowing a stream of smoke. "I'm sick of this heat. I'm sick of this apartment. The landlord won't fix the stove. He's never going to."

"When?"

She shrugged, still looking out the window. "Pretty soon. I quit the salon today. I'm sick of that woman. I'm sick of her shit."

Leigh watched her take a drag of her cigarette, waiting for her to say more. She did not.

"By yourself?" she asked finally.

Her mother looked right at her then, wrinkling her nose, something like sympathy in her eyes. "Yeah. Rents are pretty expensive out there. I'll probably be able to afford only a studio. And not in a good school district, I bet. You'll be better off staying here."

Leigh looked at her mother's hands, at the cracked skin around her nails.

"By myself?"

"Honey. It's not like you're twelve."

Leigh could feel tears forming around her eyes. She would be sixteen in a week.

"You've got a job now. Even when school starts, you can do it part-time. And you can stay with Pam, I bet."

Leigh blinked, and there were the tears, pooling in her eyes, visible. When her mother saw them, her face went hard.

"Don't start that. Don't be such a baby. I wasn't much older than you when I was taking care of a baby and myself. I'm just asking you to take care of you."

Leigh blinked again, and there were more tears. When her mother spoke again, her voice was louder.

"You know, I've spent a good eighteen years doing nothing but working for you girls." She tapped out her cigarette on a saucer and stood up. "I've never gotten to live the way I wanted. You don't know anything about that. You've never even had to work, and now you finally have a job, and you think you should get to spend it all on junk food, let me worry about the bills. And you don't appreciate anything. You just take and take and take. You don't even think about what you have. I spoiled you girls, that's the problem." She shook her head. "Quit acting like some poor orphan. My God. You've got money in the bank. Use it for whatever. You've got almost a thousand dollars now."

Leigh wiped a hand across her face. She did feel like an orphan. She would have to live in the trailer with Pam and her boyfriend and her baby. Her mother didn't want her to come. "That's not enough for college," she said.

Her mother smiled in a way that didn't seem nice so much as it seemed she was trying not to laugh. She took a step closer, using her fingers to wipe away a tear. She did it tenderly, softly, but her fingertips were callused, and they felt rough against Leigh's cheek.

"Well." She clicked her tongue and smiled. "It's a lot more than anybody ever gave me."

Chapter 5

THE MORNING AFTER THE accident, after Kara had gone back up to her room, Willow called again. Leigh did not pick up the phone, but she listened to Willow's worried message, her plea for Kara to call. The phone kept ringing: more of Kara's friends left messages, their youthful voices full of awkward concern. Leigh recognized some of their names—Hallie, Kyra, Jen, Danielle. Kara had been friends with these girls since grade school. But she kept making new friends every year, an army of friends, it seemed to Leigh, more than anyone could keep up with. It was one of the reasons Leigh had given in and let Kara get a cell phone. But they were all calling the home line, leaving messages on the machine. Kara must have turned off her cell phone, Leigh guessed. And her daughter's army of friends, after hearing the news, were trying to reach her any way they could. Some of them, Leigh suspected, just wanted to get the story. High schools were microcosms, and, as in the real world, people liked to see celebrities fall. But Leigh dutifully wrote down every name and message. *9:30 a.m. Jane called to say she loves you. 9:42 a.m. Devonne (sp?) said to call any time. 9:50 a.m. Jo (Joe?) called. Worried about you. Feels so bad.*

When she was not listening to the answering machine and taking messages, Leigh sat at the computer they kept in the hutch, searching the Internet for "Bethany Cleese." She found other Bethany

Cleeses who were still alive and well—a poet living in Minneapolis, a mother of two advertising her home manicure business in Georgia. She finally found the right Bethany, the dead one. Her picture was in the archives of Danby's daily newspaper. The picture had run just over four years ago, and in it Bethany looked more childlike, fuller in the face than the way Leigh remembered her looking in class. She wore a red windbreaker and held a kite up to the wind. Her hair was down, blowing hard to one side, and she squinted up at a low gray sky. Another girl, younger and smaller, held the roll of string. *Flying High*, the caption read. *Bethany Cleese, 13, of Danby and her cousin, Amanda Price, 11, of Austin, TX, take advantage of strong winds and fly their kite at the track field by Greeley Elementary. Bethany's mother, Diane Kletchka, also of Danby, submitted the picture.*

The only other article about the right Bethany, the newly dead Bethany, was an electronic version of the one about the accident Leigh had already read in the paper that morning. She clicked on it, as if she would find different words there, a different end to the story. But they were the same. And once again, her eyes lingered on Bethany's yearbook picture, at the half smile and curled hair, the dark eyes looking right back at the camera.

A floorboard upstairs creaked. Leigh gazed at the ceiling above her, the floor of Kara's room.

She shut off the computer and went back upstairs. Gary was in bed with his eyes closed, but when she lay down beside him, he turned toward her and put his hand on her shoulder. She grasped his hand and held it tight. It meant everything, she considered, for him to reach out to touch her like that, for him to let her know that he was still right there with her. He'd been right when he said they would have to remember to be good to each other, to not allow the tension and misery of the coming days to eat away at what they had sustained for so long. If they were careful, they could get each other through this. She thought of the mother's name, Diane Kletchka.

Kletchka might be her maiden name, but maybe she'd remarried. Leigh wanted to think she was married, and that she had someone kind with her now.

AT ELEVEN O'CLOCK, EVA left another message. Gary and Leigh were still in their room, lying side by side in their bathrobes and looking at the ceiling, but the answering machine's volume was turned up, and they could hear her voice from upstairs. "I wish you'd pick up," she said. The word *wish* came out dramatically, full of longing and grief. But Eva did many things dramatically, Leigh considered. She didn't answer the phone.

At noon, Eva called again. Leigh was still in her bathrobe, sitting in the dining room, her forehead pressed against the table. She had tried again to write a letter to Bethany's mother, and again, she had failed. Gary was upstairs in the shower. "I'm going to just come over," Eva said into the machine. "I drove by this morning, and I see you've got your blinds down, but I think you're there. I have food." There was a long pause. "I have doughnuts."

Maybe three minutes later, she was at the front door, knocking and calling Leigh's name. Leigh sat at the table, her hands in her lap, watching Eva's slender silhouette move behind the closed blinds. She heard the clink of metal, bracelets jangling. "Come on," Eva yelled, knocking on the glass. "Are you there?" Leigh shook her head back and forth. And then, finally, there was silence, but Leigh continued to shake her head. *We are not here.* She looked around at the furniture, the square of sunlight on the hardwood floor, the throw pillows on the couch. *We will never be here again.* From where she sat, she could see the newspaper in the recycling bin. She could make out a bit of the headline, the *P* of *Pedestrian.*

It would be nice to talk with someone, maybe. She might feel more sane. But Gary was right—she shouldn't talk with Eva about this, not yet. She wished she could get ahold of her sister.

She heard the motor of the garage door opener. A moment later, the side door opened, and Justin, Eva, and Willow walked in through the mudroom. Eva was wearing a sleeveless black dress, ankle length, and it caught on one of the spikes of a rake in the corner. She smiled at Leigh before turning to free herself, picking at the material with her nails. "Sorry," she said, nodding at Justin. "Your kid blew your cover. You'll have to train him better if you want to hide. I thought it might be nice for Kara to see Willow." She walked into the kitchen and hugged Leigh, her earring pressing hard against Leigh's cheek. "Oh God. How are you holding up?"

Leigh frowned at Justin and then felt guilty. His nose looked sunburned. She hadn't even known he'd been outside.

"I'm sorry," he whispered. "I didn't know what to do." He had something on his teeth, she noticed. Chocolate. Eva had already given him a doughnut.

Willow carried in the box of doughnuts. Eva directed her into the dining room, bracelets jingling. Willow appeared to make her way across the room in just two quick strides, her flip-flops sliding on the floor. She was tall and thin like her mother, and she was wearing very short shorts and a white, billowy shirt that probably belonged to Eva. She set the box on the table. "Is Kara here? Is she upstairs?" Willow had the high, thin voice of someone not very smart. But she was smart. She was on the math team. Her grades were as good as Kara's.

"I don't think she wants to see anybody right now, honey," Leigh said. "I'm sorry," she added, meaning it. Leigh associated Willow with a bird or a lamb, some fragile, easily spooked animal that needed to be treated gently. She didn't have any of her mother's confidence, and from the start, this had made Leigh love her. She did not get upset when Willow came over and raided the refrigerator, finishing off cartons of ice cream and bags of chips, all those calories emptied into that bottomless pit, the furnace of her insane metabolism. Leigh smiled whenever she met Willow's eyes. She told herself she was just being kind, but really, she needed Willow to like her. It might prove to Kara, to everyone, that the fault between them did not lie entirely on Leigh's side. Another girl, a different girl, might like Leigh just fine.

But Willow only managed a nervous smile, her eyes moving past Leigh to the stairway. Leigh turned and saw Kara at the top of the stairs, wearing pajama bottoms and one of Gary's white undershirts. Her hair was matted to one side, and she was squinting down at them as if the light was too bright, though the blinds of every window were still down. She lifted just her hand to wave at Willow, turned it, and made a beckoning motion. Willow started up the stairs.

"Wait," Leigh called out, her voice too loud, too fearful. Willow flinched and turned quickly. Kara turned much more slowly, her gaze cool on Leigh.

"I'm not sure you should..." She stopped. It seemed cruel to keep Kara isolated in her room, away from her friends. But Gary would be so angry. And perhaps he was right. "You girls know you can't talk about what happened."

"I was in the car," Willow said. There was no sneer in her voice, no rudeness. She was always soft and quiet, difficult to hear. "I already know what happened." She shifted her weight and looked at her mother for confirmation.

Eva's eyes moved from her daughter's face to Leigh's. "We're not here to get any information," she said. She waved her hand, and the bracelets jangled. "We just came to offer support."

"It's very serious," Leigh said. Her eyes moved up to Kara. "I know you were both there, but you can't talk about it. We have to talk to a lawyer first. Maybe you should visit down here."

Kara stared at her mother. She appeared newly miserable, as if Leigh's words were more than she could bear. "Can't I just talk to my friend?" she asked.

Leigh looked up at her dumbly. This was Gary's fault. He made these rules, and somehow, she always had to enforce them. He made these rules, but he remained well loved.

Eva cleared her throat. "Willow." Her voice sounded cool, authoritative. "You understand what Mrs. Churchill is saying. You can't talk about the details. You get that, right?"

Willow nodded. Her long earrings swung back and forth, and the expression on her face implied that everyone around her was being very stupid. Leigh kept her eyes lowered. She heard Willow's flip-flops reach the top of the stairs, and then the closing door of Kara's room. She heard the shower turn off in the master bathroom. She turned and sighed, looking at Eva and Justin, at the box of dough-nuts on the table.

Eva spotted the drafts of the letter to Bethany's mother—Leigh could see her trying to read them without lowering her head. Leigh stepped in front of her, scooped up the drafts, and tucked them into a magazine.

"Speaking of lawyers." Eva took a seat at the table. "Do you have one already? I asked around. I think you should go to Sue Taft." She opened her bag and took out a notepad, the pages pink and shaped like a pair of lips. There was a phone number written on the top page, and she tore it off and put it on the table. "I hear good things about her. I met her once, at a fund-raiser. She seemed nice, but I guess she's re-ally aggressive. Competent, I mean." She leaned forward. "And I'm sure she could use the money. She got divorced last year. Her hus-band had a not so little gambling problem. Blew through their sav—"

"Stop!" Leigh clapped her hands over her ears and glanced at Justin. He'd already taken the seat next to Eva, and he smiled and clapped his hands over his ears too.

"Sorry." Eva opened the box and took out a doughnut. She held one out to Leigh with just her fingernails. "Everybody knows that already. And it's not like you're going to say anything to her about it. It doesn't matter. I really did hear she was good."

Leigh shook her head at the doughnut, slid into the chair at the opposite side of the table, and put her face in her hands. It still startled her sometimes, how much Eva knew about people. Eva was the secretary at the junior high, and she typed memos to teachers and filed official correspondence with parents and kept the appointment ledger for the school counselor. She was also not-so-secretly dating the principal, Rick Bechelmeyer, a man so kind and well intentioned that Leigh imagined he would have no suspicions when his beautiful girlfriend asked for details of his day at work, oozing concern for him and their fellow citizens.

It was more than that, though; Eva knew about people outside the school too. Her ex-husband, Willow's father, was a professor up at the college, and she was still friends with many of his friends. She still got invited to their parties. She was on the Arts Council, and she helped organize the Friends of the Library fund-raiser every year. Whenever Leigh went anywhere with her, they were constantly stopped by people who knew Eva, people who wanted to make sure she had their phone numbers or e-mail addresses, people who seemed desperate to make contact. Eva would promise to get ahold of them, taking their hands and whispering "we must talk" in a somber, dramatic way, as if she and the other person were spies or heads of state. She meant it, though—when Leigh was out by herself or with Gary, she would often see Eva huddled in the corner of a restaurant with some other friend, nodding sympathetically, and no doubt, Leigh knew, sucking in more information.

And then, for some reason, Eva liked to take all the information she'd gathered and lay it out for Leigh. Every time they were together, with no prompting from Leigh, Eva would blurt out her knowledge of extramarital affairs and property disputes and medical conditions. She seemed desperate to get the words out, as if she were an old sage, ready to expire, wanting all she knew to live on in someone else. Why she chose Leigh for this privilege was a mystery. She didn't even know why they were friends. They worked at the same school. Their daughters were friends. They were about the same age. They both liked to read. But they were very different people. Eva had more interesting clothes and a more interesting life—she had more people who wanted to spend time with her, and she had the capacity and will to arrange it. It would have exhausted Leigh, all those appointments for coffees and lunches. If she had an extra hour in a day, she might try to read or just lie down on the couch with her eyes closed.

Eva, however, had made up her mind that they would be friends, and she was diligent about seeking Leigh out. She left messages and then called again. She waited for her in the school parking lot and begged her to come get coffee, and it was hard for Leigh not to feel a little special and lucky.

"You're the only smart person around," she'd told Leigh once, "not including the ones up there." They had been in Leigh's front yard, and Eva had turned around and waved at what at first appeared to be the grain elevator on the horizon. But then Leigh saw she meant the campus. "And they're such snobs," she added, with real bitterness in her voice. "They act like they aren't, but you can see it."

Eva had been a sophomore, studying art at the University of California at Davis, when she fell in love with her sociology teacher, whom she thought at the time was a professor, but was really just a graduate teaching assistant working on his doctorate. Against school policy, he asked her out, and they started an affair that made their schoolwork suffer, and made them both—in Eva's words—"insane with passion." By the time he finished his dissertation, she was pregnant. He was offered a job at Danby State, and he told Eva that if she would marry him, he would take it. They would move to Kansas together. She wouldn't listen to her parents. At the time, she said, it sounded romantic. She'd grown up in Northern California—temperate, progressive, and beautiful—and the general ease of it had started to seem boring. To her twenty-two-year-old mind, marriage and motherhood in Kansas sounded exotic.

By the time Willow was five years old, Eva's husband was sleeping with new sophomores, and, oddly enough, according to Eva, he also got a lot more boring. "And fat," she'd added, wrinkling her mouth, as if this were the greater indignity. "His voice changed. It was weird. It got more nasal. Really. It sounded different. I didn't even care about the girls. The reason someone like him has to keep screwing young and dumb women is because only the young and dumb ones will do it."

She got a good settlement with the divorce—financially, at least. But the professor was adamant about one thing—he couldn't leave his job in Danby, and he wanted to see his daughter on a regular basis. So until Willow turned eighteen, Eva couldn't leave Danby. "I've made the best of it," she'd told Leigh once, as if she had survived a great trauma. "You can make any place interesting if you try."

And, Leigh had to admit, Eva had made Danby more interesting for her as well. Being her friend was like having hundreds of tiny microphones planted in people's homes and cars, the wires all leading to her ear. She would hear about divorces, someone's overmedicated child, someone's shoplifting arrest, someone's bipolar mother-in-law. She would tell Eva that she didn't want to know these things. They were other people's secrets, and she didn't want to gossip. But she was aware that sometimes she waited until Eva had already given her some piece of information before she asked her to stop. She told herself this wasn't completely her fault—Eva spoke quickly.

"You shouldn't feel bad," Eva told Leigh once. "I mean, you're not gossiping. You're just listening. And the only reason I tell you things is because I know you won't tell anyone else. You're good like that. I mean, I've got to talk to somebody. People tell me all this shit about themselves." She'd looked suddenly exhausted, her eyes rolling back into her head. "I don't know why they do. Something about my face, I think. But I have to, you know, *process* it. If I couldn't talk to you about things I know, I'd probably talk to somebody else less trustworthy, someone who would blab it all over the place. *That* would be gossiping. *That* would be irresponsible."

And in some ways, Leigh considered, knowing the things Eva told her made her a better person. For example, it was through Eva that Leigh had learned that one of the tellers at her bank had slit both his wrists when he was in high school. "And he meant it," Eva had whispered, her breath warm in Leigh's ear as they'd walked out of the bank. "Deep cuts. He wasn't kidding around. The only reason he's still alive is because his mother came home from work early. One of those fluky things. He's on meds now, I think." Leigh had dutifully reminded Eva that none of this was any of her business. But the next time she was at the bank and the boy who had slit his wrists waited on her, she took extra care to smile at him and say thank you. Later that year, he made some small mistake with her account, and she was very understanding. If Eva had not told her about his slit wrists, she might never have noticed him enough to think about him, or wonder why he wore long-sleeved shirts buttoned at the wrists even in the summer. She wouldn't have noticed him at all. She might have sighed loudly when he made the mistake with the deposit. She never would have studied his eyes when he wasn't looking and wondered if he was happier now.

And there had been others. It was, of course, Eva who had told Leigh that the eighth grade teacher Leigh thought she didn't like was involved in a bad custody dispute, and that she'd spent all her money on lawyers and had to take a second job as a telemarketer. This information made Leigh act more kindly not only toward the eighth grade teacher, but also toward the telemarketers who called during dinnertime. And she'd learned from Eva that the whiny lunchroom attendant who was always tired and sitting down on the job had lived in five different foster homes and was now putting herself through night school.

And Leigh learned that Eva's boyfriend, the principal of the junior high, whom Leigh had initially thought of as a nice, earnest, but somewhat dim bureaucrat, had lost his little brother to cancer when he was sixteen. He'd wanted to be a writer, but his parents had wanted him to go after something more solid, and so he had, thinking they'd suffered enough.

EVA WAS INSISTENT THAT Leigh tell her something. She wanted to know how Kara was doing. She wanted to know what the police had said. She wanted to know if Leigh had known the Cleese girl or her mother. She wanted to know if they had good insurance.

"I can't talk about any of this yet," Leigh said. She kept her eyes on the box of doughnuts.

Eva nodded but continued to watch her with the same kindly, concerned expression she gave to people they bumped into on the street, to the friends she met out at coffee shops. Leigh had seen this expression often, but never from this angle, head-on.

"Willow said the girl just came out of nowhere. I mean, they were laughing, paying attention to the dog, but Willow never saw the girl either. Not till she was on the ground."

Leigh's heart started to pound. *What dog?* she thought. She didn't know anything about a dog. "Eva," she said. "Really. I can't talk about this yet."

"Well, just so you know. Willow brought the dog home." She grimaced. "She thinks we're keeping it, but we're not."

Leigh lowered her eyes.

"What about graduation?"

Leigh looked up. She had completely forgotten about graduation. The ceremony was the next day, Sunday afternoon. They had planned to take Kara out to dinner afterward. They had gotten her a present—a pair of very small diamond earrings. The earrings had been Gary's idea, but Leigh was the one who bought them. "I don't think we're going to make it," she said. "I can't imagine that she'll want to go."

"Well. She can pick up her diploma anytime." Eva clicked her tongue. "But you must be sad about that. You must have wanted to see her graduate."

Leigh nodded, though really, it wasn't as if Kara's graduation was some long held dream. Leigh had written "*I'm so proud of you!*" on the card she bought to give Kara with the earrings, and just writing those words had felt a little fake. It just didn't seem like a huge accomplishment for Kara to finish high school. To avoid this fate, she would have had to do something rash, like run away from home, or take up cocaine. And these options, for someone like Kara, seemed as if they would require much more determination and cunning than simply going to school every day with all of her friends, and doing her homework at night at the big oak desk they'd gotten her for her fifteenth birthday. For someone like Kara, graduating was simply the path of least resistance.

"I just hope she doesn't think everyone hates her now," Eva said.

She sounded sympathetic, truly concerned, but her eyes were trained on Leigh's.

Gary came downstairs. When he saw them all at the table, he didn't try to smile. He nodded at Eva grimly, and slid his eyes toward Leigh's. His hair was still wet from the shower, and he'd cut himself shaving. She could see a smear of blood by his ear and a thumbprint on his white T-shirt.

"They just stopped by," Leigh said. "They stopped by as Justin was coming in."

"They?" Gary asked.

Leigh cleared her throat. "Willow's here. She's upstairs with Kara."

He looked at the stairs and then back at Leigh. He shook his head with disbelief.

"We told them not to talk about it," Eva said.

"I didn't know what to do," Leigh said. "Gary. She's been up there by herself all day."

He said nothing. His jaw was clenched. He didn't seem to know where to look.

"They won't talk about it," Eva said. "And if they do, it doesn't matter. Gary, we're on your side."

He nodded, more a silent plea for her to quit talking than a concession. He scratched his neck, smearing the blood from the cut. No one said anything. He looked at the empty chair beside Eva's, the other empty chair beside Justin's. He swayed forward and moved his arms to steady himself.

Leigh started to stand. "Do you want to sit down?"

"No." He did not meet her eyes. "I've got to, uh . . ." He looked at the dining room window as if he wanted to jump through it, to escape into the sunny day on the other side of the blinds. "I'm going to go downstairs and . . . watch the game," he said. His voice was stiff, formal, as if he were speaking to a large crowd. He looked at Leigh and Eva, and then his eyes rested on Justin. "You want to come?"

Justin shook his head. He was looking under the table at Eva's feet. She wore beaded sandals that showed her toenails, which were painted a deep maroon, each one studded with a tiny rhinestone.

Gary nodded and opened the door to the basement. Leigh listened to his heavy steps and waited. He didn't turn on the television. Eva reached across the table and took her hand.

"Don't worry," Eva whispered, nodding at the door to the basement. "Really, I was married. And I'll tell you this. Happy or not, I think it's always a good idea to have at least one friend your husband doesn't like."

Leigh shook her head. "We're just both really..." Her voice broke, and Eva squeezed her hand. She stared at Leigh, her eyes full of kindness and also a hard determination. *I'll sit here all day,* her eyes said. *You're going to tell me something.*

Leigh looked up past her at the blinds. "It's so nice that you came," she said, her voice flat, unconvincing. She didn't care. Eva had to go. Leigh had to get her out of the house. It was one thing to have a friend who made you feel as if you had microphones planted all over town so you could listen in on other people's pain and tell yourself it made you kinder. It was quite another, Leigh understood now, to look across your table and see that same microphone, waiting, absolutely silent, and pointed directly at you.

SUE TAFT'S LAW OFFICE was on the west side of town, where all the new houses were going up. The building looked like a large colonial home, complete with narrow pillars and a portico. But Leigh knew it was constructed out of a substance that was essentially very dense Styrofoam. She'd had a dentist's appointment across the street during the building's construction, and her dentist's receptionist had told her that all summer long, tiny white balls escaped from the preformed bricks, blowing onto her car like hail. The day Leigh was there, the stray balls swirled in the wind and landed in the trees, caught on the hedges, and piled up on the construction workers' trucks, until the whole area looked, indeed, as if it had been caught in a hail storm, which seemed so strange in late August, when the sky was almost always a bright blue.

In a different situation, Leigh might have mentioned all this to Gary and Kara. If this were a normal day, she thought, she would have told them about it, pleased to know some local trivia that might interest them. But today, pulling into the parking lot of the Styrofoam law office, she said nothing. She wondered when chatter would be okay again, how much time would have to pass.

"Nice out," Gary said when they got out of the car. Leigh nodded, and Kara looked up, squinting at the sun as if noticing it for the first time. She was wearing her soccer shorts and the same T-shirt of Gary's she'd been wearing all weekend, her hair pulled back into a knot at the nape of her neck. Leigh remembered that Kara should have started her summer job today, serving frozen yogurt at the shop downtown where she'd worked last summer, and the summer before that. Her long hair would have been blow-dried and brushed, and she would have been smiling at people, innocent and carefree, wearing a pink apron and handing back change. Leigh stayed in this alternate world for a moment, basking in its ease. Gary would have been up on campus, still giving finals. Leigh herself probably would have gone back to her classroom to take the decorations down from her bulletin boards, to get rid of the clutter in case they used her room for summer school. She might have cut out early to go for a walk. She'd always loved this time of year, the freedom of summer without the heat, the redbuds still in bloom. But this morning, walking up to the door of the law office with the warm morning breeze gentle against her face, she didn't smile. She wouldn't love June this year. She might never love it again, she thought, though maybe that wasn't right. She was still in this world, she and her living daughter, with all of its troubles and pleasures. Bethany Cleese was not.

They went inside. A receptionist led them down a carpeted hallway to a room where a woman sat behind a large oak desk, talking on the phone. She was older, in her sixties maybe, with horizontal lines on her forehead that moved as she talked. Her hair was curly and gray, cut short. She waved them in and kept talking. "Fine," she said. "But he didn't purposefully violate the restraining order. He just happened to be there. This is ridiculous. You're wasting everyone's time." She looked up and motioned for them to sit.

There were two armchairs on either side of a love seat facing the desk. Kara sank into a corner of the love seat as if she had been pushed, her arms at her sides, her hands pressed downward. It was the same way she'd sat at the table at breakfast that morning. She hadn't eaten anything.

Gary sat beside Kara on the love seat. Leigh took one of the chairs and looked around the room. There were no framed photos on the desk or on the walls, no sign of Sue Taft's gambling ex-husband. Maybe she'd taken them down after the divorce, Leigh thought. Or maybe not. She was a criminal attorney. They probably didn't put out family pictures. Gary tugged on his tie. The office was air-conditioned, cold even, but he was sweating.

"Sorry." Sue Taft hung up the phone and held out her hand to Leigh. She shook Gary's hand, and then Kara's. She told them she was sorry about what had happened. She asked them to please call her Sue. But her voice was all business and efficiency; it did not sound much different from the way it had when she was on the phone. She leaned across the desk and looked at Kara. "I read the article in the paper, but I need more information. I've got to ask you some questions. Can I just go ahead and get started?"

Kara answered the attorney's questions clearly, keeping her voice calm, though as she spoke, tears slid down her face and fell, one at a time, onto her bare legs. Leigh got a tissue out of her purse and handed it to Gary to hand to her.

"You were on the phone when the car actually struck her? You were talking to someone?"

"Lots of people do that," Gary said. "That's not illegal."

Sue Taft raised one finger to him. She kept her eyes on Kara.

"I had just called someone." Kara pursed her lips. "Richard. My friend. We'd found a dog, a stray dog, and I thought it looked like his."

Leigh frowned. She'd never heard of any Richard.

"The dog was in the car?"

"In the backseat. It was trying to get up front. My friend, Willow, was trying to keep it in back."

"Did your friend touch the steering wheel? At all? Accidentally?"

"No."

"You didn't brake until after you hit the victim, correct?"

Kara lowered her eyes and shook her head. "I didn't see her. I didn't brake until I...heard— I heard her hit, I heard the car hit something. Then I braked."

"You're eighteen?"

"Yes."

"You were ticketed at the scene?"

"Yes. Not stopping for a stop sign."

Gary opened the folder he'd brought. It was the big blue one he'd used for his upper-level class that semester. That morning, he'd emptied the pockets of student papers, pulled his attendance roster from the binder, and written ACCIDENT across the cover with a black marker. He slid the traffic ticket across the desk. Sue Taft leaned back in her chair and studied it. She was quiet for a long time, and they could hear the whirl and click of the air conditioner and the hum of cars outside. Leigh glanced at Gary. He had his head lowered, his jaw clenched, as if he were expecting a blow.

Sue Taft leaned forward in her chair again, tapping her fingers on the desk. Her nails were chewed short, and her finger pads made a soft, drumming sound. She turned and reached for a book on the shelf. "I'm guessing you'll be charged with reckless driving," she said. "That would be the worst-case scenario. They'll probably start out high, and come down from that."

Gary squinted at her behind his glasses. "Why is that worst case? What does that mean?"

Sue Taft flipped through the book's pages. "Well, it's a class C misdemeanor. At the very least, she would be sentenced to five days in jail. But that could be suspended. Maximum..." She ran a finger down a page with very small print. "Thirty days in jail, five-hundred-dollar fine. Of course, in that case as well, the jail time could be suspended."

"Thirty days and five hundred dollars?" Leigh cocked her head. "That's it?"

Gary and Kara and Sue Taft all looked at her, moving only their eyes, not their heads.

"That's good, I mean." It was true. It was good news. She was relieved. Grateful. "I'm just surprised that that's the worst-case scenario. It doesn't seem like much...considering..." Leigh held one hand flat in front of her and moved it, trying to come up with a gesture that would imply what she did not want to say. She put her hand back in her lap.

Sue Taft cleared her throat. "The facts just aren't there for anything else. We're not talking manslaughter. There were no drugs involved. You said she had a clean record. It was clearly a mistake. The only reason I think they've got a case for reckless driving is because she was driving downtown in the middle of the day. There were a lot of pedestrians, so running a stop sign and driving into a crosswalk could be considered willful or wanton disregard for the safety of others." Her eyes met Kara's, and they both looked away. "But honestly, I think there's a chance they won't even charge her with reckless. There was no bad weather. She wasn't driving down the sidewalk." She shrugged. "They might just go for inattentive driving. No jail time. It's like a speeding ticket."

A sound escaped from Leigh's mouth. It was almost like a laugh, a little gasp of disbelief. Gary looked at her again.

"The only reason they might go for a charge of reckless driving is that a death resulted." Sue Taft was looking out the window now, her fingertips moving over her chin. "It was in the newspaper. The front page. They have to think about how this looks to the public. But I'm just guessing here. We'll find out at the arraignment—if there is one—in a couple of weeks. In the meantime, my recommendation would be for you to go ahead and apply for a diversion. It's basically a contract between the defense and the state, and if they accept, no matter what, there won't be any jail time. There won't even be a trial. They'll give you a fine and community service. I can give you the application now." She turned, opened a file drawer, and produced a stapled packet of papers, which she slid across the desk to Kara.

Kara stared at the top page, her hands at her sides.

"But she has to plead guilty?" Gary asked. "If she applies for a diversion, it's the same as pleading guilty?"

Sue Taft nodded. "It's just a trick to save everyone time and money. And if they accept"—she looked at Kara—"you won't have a criminal record. So this won't follow you in the future, when you apply for jobs, for loans, for schools...if you're ever in another accident...if you ever go into politics..."

Gary picked up the packet and started looking through the

pages. Kara's eyes remained on the part of the desk where the packet had been.

Gary cleared his throat. "I know you're not a civil attorney, but we're obviously concerned about a lawsuit. Is there any...Is there anything we can do, just to protect our house, our savings? I mean, she, the girl's mother, should get some money, of course, but..."

"I don't think you'll have to worry about that—a lawsuit, I mean. If she weren't eighteen yet, that would be a concern. But she's an adult. They can't come after your assets, only hers. You have auto insurance, I assume. If you have liability, she'll get that. But nothing out of your pocket, unless they could prove some kind of culpability on your part, something wrong with the car."

Leigh shook her head. It was good news. She was just surprised. "That just seems so..." She couldn't think of the word.

"Great," Gary said. He sighed and rubbed his eyes. "Oh God. I think I can breathe again."

Sue Taft started to stand. "I'll be in touch about the arraignment. Until then, try not to talk about this with people. If the police want to talk to you again, call me right away. Don't talk to the media, of course."

"Wait," Leigh said. "I'm sorry. I wanted to ask about—" She was having trouble forming words. She looked at Gary for help, but he only looked at her blankly. "I wanted to know if it is okay for me to write a note to the mother..." She could feel Kara's eyes on her, watching. "The mother of the girl who died."

Sue Taft frowned. "Saying what?"

"Just saying I'm sorry...sorry that it happened."

"Oh. That's fine, I suppose. Obviously you don't want to admit any particular guilt, or imply Kara's, but just a general letter of condolence is fine. Did you know this girl at all? Do you know the family?"

"I had her in class, Bethany I mean." She could still feel Kara's gaze. "I met her mother only once."

Sue Taft nodded, and for a moment, Leigh thought she might comment on how sad all this was, or on how strange it must be to know the girl who had been killed and to be the mother of the girl who had done the killing. But she didn't say any of this. It wasn't her job, Leigh considered. They were paying her to do something very particular.

"Are you going to the service? It's tonight, isn't it? I saw it in the paper."

Leigh nodded and glanced at Gary. She'd already planned on going. She hadn't told him yet.

"It might be a nice show of sympathy," Sue Taft said. She caught Leigh's eye and held it as she spoke. "I imagine there'll be a lot of students there, a lot of young people." She looked at Kara. "You should all go, if you think you're up to it."

THE DAY WAS WARMER when they walked outside. Leigh put her hand up to shield her eyes from the sun. Gary had parked under the shade of a small tree, but its shadow had moved, and when they opened the doors, a wave of heat rolled up to their faces. Gary and Leigh stepped aside, fanning the warm air past them. Kara climbed into the backseat and shut the door.

No one spoke. Gary drove with the air conditioner on high, the vents aimed toward the backseat. The relief he'd expressed in the lawyer's office seemed to have already left him. He drove with both hands on the wheel, not resting one palm near Leigh's knee, as he would normally have done. Leigh understood this—he was distracted with worry and grief, and so was she. But she missed his hand there, the sureness of its weight.

At the first red light, he turned around.

"Kara, you have to wear your seat belt."

Leigh waited for sound of movement from the backseat. When she heard nothing, she turned around. Kara looked like a cornered animal, trapped there behind Gary's seat, her long legs folded up in front of her. She did not appear able to move. Leigh glanced at Gary and shook her head. He should let it go, she thought. He was, in her opinion, a bit too militant about seat belts, as he was about bike helmets and knee-pads, every invention to protect. They were a good idea, of course, but Leigh had not worn a seat belt the first twenty years of her life. She didn't think any of her mother's cars had even had seat belts in the backseats. And she had lived. Pam had lived. Surely Kara would survive a two-mile trip without injury. They were almost home. And Leigh could understand that, in these first miserable days, Kara might not be worried about her own safety.

She turned back to give Kara a look of sympathy, but her daughter's gray eyes stared back at her coldly.

"Kara," Gary said, his voice stern. If he'd seen Leigh shake her head, he didn't let on. The light changed, but he didn't move the car. Someone behind them honked. Leigh heard the pull of Kara's belt, the consenting click. They moved past the farm and food supply, past the junior high. Gary drove with his hand over his mouth.

They were on Commerce when Gary braked hard. Leigh went forward, the strap of her seat belt holding her back. "Oh Jesus," he whispered. He craned his head right and then left, trying to find somewhere to turn, but they were surrounded by traffic. Up ahead, Leigh could see what he didn't want to drive past: The chain-link fence by the northeast corner of Seventh and Commerce had several bouquets of flowers stuck into it. Someone had left a teddy bear with a yellow ribbon around its neck, and there was a poster-board sign that read, WE WILL MISS YOU BETHANY in red letters. A small wooden cross hung from a notch on a fence post.

They had to stop for the light. Gary took one hand off the wheel and reached back through the seats to pat Kara's knee. "It's okay," he said. "It's okay. It's going to be okay." Leigh turned around. Kara was staring out the window at the sign and the flowers. Her eyes were wide, her gaze steady, and Leigh had the impression she was forcing herself to take it all in. "Honey," Leigh said. She wished she would have thought to put her hand on Kara's knee, the way Gary had done. But doing it just hadn't occurred to her until he had done it. And now there was no room for her hand.

"I'm not going to apply for a diversion."

Gary and Leigh looked at each other. The light changed. Leigh turned around, surprised to find Kara looking back at her with no real animosity.

Gary turned back to face the road. "You have some time to think about it," he said. "You don't have to decide right now."

"I have decided." It was that new voice again, so flat, so strange. "I just decided."

They pulled into the driveway and then the garage, darkness falling over their faces. Gary turned off the engine and took a deep breath, ready to speak, but Kara sprang out of the car.

"I don't want to talk about it." She walked quickly to the door to the mudroom. She was just inside when she tripped on the edge of the rake, stumbling to the concrete floor. Gary got out of the car and moved toward her, but she shrank away from him.

"Just please, just, please, just leave me alone," she said.

"Honey . . . ," Gary said. He bent over her, trying to help her up. Leigh got out of the car. She had the feeling of being underwater, of only being able to move more slowly than everyone else.

"NO!" Kara made a frantic motion with her arms, and Leigh thought of how she'd been as a toddler, independent from early on, never wanting to be carried. She stood up, rubbing her arm, and looked over the hood of the car at her mother. "Will you explain it to him? Will you?"

case they had company, or in case some of them broke. When she was young, she had dreamed of eating at a table with matching plates and glasses.

"She's got to think about her future." Gary leaned over her again, reaching for the coffee. "Even if Tufts doesn't find out about all this, a... you know... a conviction might give her some trouble when she applies to grad school. What if she wants to go to law school some-day? Or medical school?"

Leigh shut the cupboard. "I guess she's not thinking about that right now."

"What?"

She turned. He had his hand cupped over his ear. "I can't hear," he said, nodding in the direction of the piano. "He's got to stop with that. It's making me crazy."

The piano fell silent. They looked at each other until Gary turned and trudged into the living room.

"Hey. I like your playing, J. I do. It's just right now—"

"It's fine." Leigh heard the piano's cover close.

"You can keep playing, just maybe something not so—"

"That's okay. I'm done anyway."

By the time Leigh got to the living room, Justin had already dis-appeared upstairs. Gary stood by the piano, gazing out the window.

"You have to be careful with him," she said. "You have to con-sider. This is all happening to him too."

"I know." He looked irritated. She reminded herself to remain calm. The first year of their marriage, his irritation would have wounded her for days. She'd taken every darkening in his eyes so personally—she'd had no model of marriage, no idea what to ex-pect, aside from what she'd seen in movies and on television. It took her years to understand that he could sometimes be bored with her or irritated with her, but that it didn't mean he didn't love her any-more, or that he was planning to leave. He knew this for himself from the start—he'd never seemed too worried about boring or irritating her. He never seemed to worry she would no longer love him. But it was different for her. Even after all these years, after they'd had a fight or even a minor disagreement, she was still surprised sometimes to wake, the very next morning, to find him turned toward her, his hand in her hair.

He was about to say something else when they heard a hissing sound from the kitchen. They rushed in to find spilled coffee on the floor, and wet clumps of coffee grounds on the counter.

"Oh Jesus." Gary touched his forehead. "I put the water in twice. That was stupid." He reached for a paper towel, but it was a new roll, and the first towel wouldn't pull free. He cursed and gave the roll a hard knock, and the entire roll popped free from the holder and fell to the floor. He made a low, growling sound and pulled up his leg as if he meant to stomp on the paper towel roll or the puddle. But then he just stood like that, one foot raised, frozen.

"I'll get it," Leigh said. She put her hand on his back. "Are you okay?"

He lowered his foot slowly, but he stayed where he was, looking down at the spilled coffee.

"Go lie down," she said. "I'll get it. Go rest, Gary. It's okay." She steered him toward the living room. He went easily, as if his feet were on wheels. "I'll get it."

He gave the puddle a backward glance. "Thanks. I'll make it up to you."

She had to laugh at that, the ridiculousness of it. He turned to hug her, and she rested her forehead against his chest. Over the years, she had done this so many times that it seemed there should be a hollow there, like an indentation on a pillow.

"I can't believe I did that," he said.

She didn't know if he was talking about the coffee or what had just happened with Justin. It didn't matter, she decided. They were both accidents, one and the same. She reached up and squeezed his shoulders. "You were just distracted," she said. "I do things like that all the time."

GARY DIDN'T GO LIE down. After Leigh mopped up the spilled coffee, she went upstairs, and she heard his voice in Kara's room. She couldn't hear what he was saying—the door was closed, and Justin was playing his stereo. She moved closer to Kara's door. Neither Gary nor Kara spoke. Leigh wondered if they knew she was out in the hallway. She turned and knocked on Justin's door.

He didn't answer. She knocked again and said his name, trying to be heard over the music he was playing, some woman singing in French. When he still didn't answer, she opened the door and saw him lying on his bed, his legs crossed at his ankles, his hands pressed flat over his eyes. He still had the Spider-Man bedspread she'd gotten for him several years ago. She'd meant to get him a new one, now that he was getting older. He hadn't said anything to her about it, but she worried it wouldn't look good if he ever had a friend over.

"Honey?"

He sat up with a start.

"I'm sorry." She smiled. She couldn't help it. His bed was just a twin, but he looked so small on it, his legs and arms pulled close to his body. "I didn't mean to scare you." She slid inside his room, closed the door, and turned down the volume of his stereo. "And you know, your dad didn't mean to snap at you like that. We love hearing you play the piano. He's just worried, you know. About Kara."

Justin bit his bottom lip, and it occurred to her then, as it had so many times, how much her son looked like Gary. He'd gotten his dark eyes, his thin lips. He really didn't look much like her at all. But there was something intangible of her in him. He held his chin the way she did, lowered a little and turned to the side. "Like a boxer," Gary sometimes said. "Like a bull."

"You okay?"

He nodded. His window was open, and she heard the crack of a bat and excited shouting. She looked around his room. Everything was in its place, his closet doors closed, his books and CDs arranged neatly on his shelves. The surface of his desk was in slight disarray—a month earlier, he'd sent away for a kit that contained two thousand toothpicks, glue, and instructions for how to use them to create an elaborate model mansion. He'd made great progress with it over the last week—he had all the walls done, and he'd started on the roof.

She sat on the foot of his bed and poked him gently on the leg. "Will you please come to the store with me? We have nothing to eat in this house." She squeezed his leg. "You can pick out a movie or something."

He nodded again and went to the closet to get his shoes. She glanced out his open window and saw a group of boys playing baseball in the park behind their backyard. She turned back to Justin and smiled. He would be fine, she told herself. She'd been unhappy at his age, and she'd turned out okay. Better, maybe. Better because of it.

USUALLY, WHEN SHE AND Justin were alone in the car, Leigh played the radio. They liked the same station, and for a while, when she had been giving him rides to school every morning, she'd let him use her cell phone to call in if there was a contest. But today, she drove with the radio off, both hands on the wheel, and Justin did not complain or try to distract her. When she got to the store's parking lot, she drove even more slowly, waving several pedestrians in front of her before she eased into a space.

"Just a second," she said, maybe to Justin, maybe to herself. She peered through the big windows at the five cashier lanes. Becker's was the only full-stock grocery store in town, and in twenty years, she had not once made it through a shopping trip without bumping into someone she knew—former students, parents of students, friends of Eva's, colleagues of Gary's. She turned off the engine and waited for Justin to get out of the car; once he did, she would have to follow.

But he didn't get out. He sat with his fingers flat on his bare knees. After a while, he looked up at her.

"You're scared," he said.

She was going to deny it. She started to shake her head. But then she turned and met his gaze. He was an odd kid. He knew things.

"A little," she said.

He frowned and looked at the doors of the store. "You didn't do anything wrong. People won't be mad at you. They won't even be mad at Kara. It was an accident. She didn't mean to do it."

"I know." Leigh took a deep breath. It might be true. But just the week before, the cashier with the lazy eye had shown Leigh and Gary a picture of her grandchild. It was the kind of friendliness Leigh appreciated—a quick interaction, full of goodwill, but with no pressure, no exchanged phone numbers or last names. That all might be lost now. The cashier must have seen Leigh in the store with Kara many times; if she read the paper, she would look at Leigh differently now. Everyone would.

"Sometimes, when I don't want to go in to school in the morning, I pretend I'm from the future."

She looked at Justin. "What?"

He nodded, reaching one sunburned arm down to scratch at a mosquito bite on his ankle. "I pretend I'm from the future, like I came in a spaceship. So my clothes are different, everything." He glanced up at her and then back at the doors. "So if people are…

you know…mean or something, the other kids, I just think, It's because I'm from the future. They're laughing because they don't know things I know. They don't know them yet."

She felt tears welling. He was above and beyond all of them, those little shits he had to go to school with. They had inadvertently made him superior. He'd been tormented so much, isolated so much, that he knew worry when he saw it on someone else's face. And of course his imagination would be well developed, like any muscle forced to work hard every day. She saw it all the time in her own classroom—the kids who were excluded and teased were often the ones who came up with the most interesting ideas for papers, who really understood the stories and poems she taught. She couldn't be blamed for liking them more.

"The future," she said. She cupped his chin in her hand and smiled. "I like that. How did you come up with that? That's great."

"Kara made it up." If he saw the surprise on his mother's face, he didn't show it. He shrugged and got out of the car. "She knows I hate school, how it is for me. So she made that up and told me to try it."

WHEN THEY WENT INTO the store, Leigh did not pretend she was from the future. She kept her eyes lowered as they moved through the aisles, her hands tight on the handle of the cart. Justin walked quietly beside her, his fingers twitching to the rhythm of the song on the store's sound system. She thought he might be tired, but she suspected he also understood that someone might be watching, and that it wouldn't be appropriate for them to joke around or laugh, even for a moment. In the produce section, she paused near the bananas, at the exact spot where she had once bumped into Bethany Cleese and her mother. She stepped carefully around the square of speckled linoleum where she thought Bethany had stood, and then stared at it, trying to comprehend, to dull the shock of it, once and for all.

"Mom?" Justin touched her arm.

"I'm fine," she said. But she stayed where she was. It was a matter of time before she would bump into Bethany's mother. She could be around the corner at that very moment. Leigh would have to get used to the idea. Every time she went to the store, or the farmers' market, or just for a walk around town, she would have to take the risk that she could walk smack into Diane Kletchka and all that misery Kara had accidentally caused. And even if Leigh was careful to never look carefree in public again, it wouldn't matter. She would feel selfish and guilty the moment she had to look into that woman's eyes. She didn't want to see her. She didn't want to go to the funeral. She didn't care if the lawyer thought it would help.

They finished their shopping without incident. The checker with the lazy eye wasn't even working—a college girl with bright blue hair rang up and bagged their groceries without so much as looking up. Leigh helped her put the bags in the cart and followed Justin to the video section. She could hear the automatic doors opening and closing, but she kept her eyes on the back of his head.

He looked back. "Can I get two?"

She nodded. He put a DVD case in her hand.

"Are you sure you want to get this one?" She looked up, but Justin wasn't there. She turned and noticed Audrey and Bob Nutter through the slats of a video shelf. She turned back quickly, ducking her head.

She might have hidden from the Nutters on any day, even before the accident. The Nutters, quite simply, wore her out. She'd met them several months earlier, at a party at Eva's where they had been wearing matching blue sweatshirts that, because of their short, round bodies, had made Leigh think of blueberries. Eva had introduced them to Leigh and then drifted back into the crowd, and Leigh had sensed that they were awkward and shy, a little older than everyone else. She was there by herself—Gary always managed to have a lot of work on the nights of Eva's parties. So Leigh spent several minutes trying to talk to the Nutters, using all her social graces. It felt as if she were interviewing them for a job they just weren't going to get. They answered her questions with enthusiasm, but then allowed long pauses to follow, both of them staring at her, Audrey Nutter's strange eyeglasses making her eyes appear far too large for a human. Audrey did accounts for a fence company. Bob processed loans for the bank. That was how they'd met Eva, but he couldn't talk about the details, of course. When Leigh told them she was a teacher, Bob Nutter had made a high-pitched, approving sound, and Audrey Nutter said something about teaching sounding fun, and they both nodded with vigor until Leigh found herself nodding too. They didn't seem to want any more information, though they both continued to give her eager smiles. So she'd struggled on for several more minutes, telling them about Justin and Kara, asking if they had children themselves. They continued to stare up at her pleasantly. Bob Nutter had very, very chapped lips that were difficult to look at without wincing. Leigh asked them about their hometowns—another dead end. They were both from a town Leigh had never heard of, which they described as "nice." Audrey thought it might be a little drier than Danby, but Bob thought the weather was about the same.

"You made quite an impression on the Nutters," Eva told her later. Leigh had stayed late to help her clean up, and they were both a little tipsy. "They thought you were *the nicest person*." She blinked quickly and smiled. "Maybe they just meant the nicest person at the party. But they might have meant in the whole world."

Leigh stood where she was, two empty wineglasses in each hand. She sensed something good was coming.

"They're swingers, you know."

"What?"

"Swingers." Eva raised her hands and made quick dancing movements, her bracelets sliding to her elbows. "They swing around. They're unrestrained. They're the Henry and June of Danby." She laughed, her mouth wide, both eyebrows high and arched. "I hope they didn't like you too much." She laughed again, almost choking on a swallow of wine.

Leigh had clicked her tongue disapprovingly. "How do you know this?"

"From the horse's mouth. I had coffee with Audrey once—once, I tell you—and she blurted it all out. I guess she thought it would make us great friends. I don't think she gets out too often. Any hoot and holler, Bob was having sex with all these women he'd met on the Internet—don't picture it, please. Audrey found out, and was very upset, blah blah blah, nothing surprising. But then she somehow ended up sleeping with *his brother* in retaliation, and Bob was devastated, and then *she* got on the Internet, and they almost got a divorce, but then they decided he was a sex addict, so now they're in therapy."

Leigh had carried the wineglasses to the sink, trying hard to act unperturbed. "One," she told Eva, "you shouldn't have told me that. Two. That doesn't make them swingers."

"I know." Eva tossed the rest of her wine in the sink. "But it's fun to say, isn't it? Those two are *swingin'.*" She put her glass down and held her arms out a little, imitating, Leigh assumed, Audrey Nutter's short-legged waddle. "They're swingin' in their blue sweatshirts, okay? They're looking Midwestern sexual norms straight in the eye, and saying, No, man, no, we're going to spread our love around."

Leigh had laughed then, despite herself, and that kept Eva going. She made up a personals ad for the Nutters. She imagined them in a bar. Leigh had put her hands over her ears and said she felt bad. She said she worried she would think of this the next time she saw them.

Eva said, "And they're going to *know* you're thinking of it, baby. They're going to see it in your *eyes*."

BUT MONTHS AFTER THAT dinner party, and only three days after Kara's accident, when Leigh, crouched furtively behind a video shelf at the grocery store, heard Audrey Nutter call out her name, she thought only of how to flee. Both Bob and Audrey Nutter, now walking toward her, were wearing Bermuda shorts, Bob's held up by a belt with a large bull's head on the buckle. He looked older than she did, Leigh realized, sadder, the skin beneath his eyes pulling down, the pink of his eyes starting to show. What she knew about them flashed through her mind.

"We read about the accident in the paper." His voice was quiet, his eyes on hers. "That was your daughter?"

Leigh nodded, taken aback. They looked so worried. Perhaps they misunderstood. "My daughter was the one driving," she said. "She wasn't the one who died."

They continued to stare at her. They didn't seem any less concerned.

"We're so sorry," Audrey said, peering at her from behind the glasses. "We thought of calling, but we didn't want to bother you."

Bob nodded, his hand on Audrey's back.

"Well, thank you." Leigh turned. She looked over their shoulders, searching for Justin. She understood they meant well, but she couldn't endure their awkwardness today. "I'm waiting for my son. We're in a rush. We've got to be at—"

And then Audrey Nutter's arms were around her, her large eyeglasses pressed against Leigh's shoulder. Leigh stepped back, surprised, but Audrey held tight.

"We're thinking about you," she whispered.

Leigh stopped struggling. She had the sensation of being caught in some viscous substance, thick and protective and warm.

"This must be so hard."

Bob Nutter nodded, his hands in the pockets of his shorts. Leigh could see he was searching for words, trying hard, his forehead creased with concentration. "Anybody could have done it," he finally said.

She tried to smile, but guilt made her mouth feel stiff. The Nutters did not know her. They didn't know she had learned about some sad, secret part of their lives and entertained herself with it. She'd thought she'd known so much.

Audrey released her, and when Leigh stepped back, Justin was at her side. He looked at the Nutters, then up at his mother, waiting to be introduced. Leigh put her hand on Justin's shoulder.

"Honey, these are my friends, the Nutters," she said. *They're from the future,* she thought.

WHEN THEY GOT HOME, Gary was at the dining room table. He must have heard them come in, but he continued to stare at the chair at the other end as if someone invisible to everyone else were sitting in it and giving him very bad news. His hands were together, fingers raised, and he kept them pressed against one side of his nose. He still wore the shirt and dress pants he'd worn to the lawyer's that morning, but the shirt was wrinkled, his sleeves rolled up. He'd taken off his tie.

"How's it going?" Leigh asked. He met her eyes and shook his head. There was a plate at the other end of the table, and on it was a piece of toast, uneaten, and also an apple with a few bites missing. The inner flesh of the apple had not yet browned.

She had just been there, Leigh thought. She'd gone back up to her room when she heard the car.

Gary pointed at the movie cases in Justin's hand. "What'd you get?" He was straining to sound friendly, enthusiastic.

Justin handed him the movie cases. He looked at the refrigerator, his mother's purse on the counter, one of the corners of the ceiling. He looked everywhere but at Gary's face.

"Haven't heard of this. What's it about?"

"Flying robots."

"Huh," Gary said. He handed the movie case back to Justin.

"It's not really science fiction," Leigh said. Gary hated science fiction, she knew. "It's supposed to be really good."

"Huh," Gary said again. He looked at the refrigerator, at the picture of Kara kicking the soccer ball.

"I'm kind of tired." Justin started walking toward the living room. He yawned and stretched. Leigh almost believed him. He was a better actor than his father.

"Okay," Gary said.

Leigh followed Justin to the stairway, reaching through the banister to touch his shoe. "I'll watch the movie with you later, okay?" She hid the dread she felt.

"Okay," Justin said. He sounded fine, but she couldn't see his face. She waited for his door to shut before she turned around.

Gary was sitting with both feet on the floor, his arms over his chest. He seemed to be watching Leigh carefully, waiting for her to speak. "Kara won't go to the funeral," he finally said. He sat back at the table and crossed his arms.

He kept watching her, saying nothing. She walked across the room, eyes lowered, and sat in the chair next to his.

"She says she wanted to go, but now she won't because the lawyer told her to. She said she isn't going to go to a funeral to be strategic. She said it was for the family, Bethany's family, not an opportunity for her to try to look good."

Leigh nodded. "I can understand that."

Gary lowered his hand to the table hard and fast. They both flinched at the sound.

"Sorry," he said quickly. She nodded and touched his hand. She understood he hadn't meant to scare her. He was just frustrated. Clearly. He was frustrated with her. "I don't think the lawyer meant she should go to the funeral to be strategic, Leigh. She never used that word."

"But that's what she meant."

"No. She meant that it would be a good idea for Kara to go to show she's ... mourning, that she's thinking about this. There's no lie there. She's devastated. She doesn't eat. She doesn't come out of her room."

Leigh looked across the table to the uneaten toast and apple. "At least not when I'm home."

She waited. Gary usually consoled her when she said something like this. But he was silent. He tapped his index finger on the table twice, his eyes steady on her face. He was looking at her strangely, as if she were his opponent, as if they were playing chess. "But she should go," he finally said. "It's the right thing for her to do."

"But she doesn't want to go."

His hand came down again. This time, neither of them jumped.

"Why are you fighting me on this?"

"Why are you fighting with me? Gary, if you want to make her go, go upstairs and make her go. I don't have any special power. She doesn't even talk to me. You know that."

His eyes narrowed. "I think you said something to her. I really do. She won't apply for the diversion. She won't go to the funeral. And she said you would understand."

"She said I would understand about the funeral?"

"No. She said you would understand about the diversion. And you say you don't know why she would say that. But then you do understand about the funeral."

Leigh blinked. "Of course I do. Don't you? It's Bethany's funeral.

It's for her family. It's not for her, for us. It's not an opportunity to make ourselves look good. And yes, the lawyer was being strategic. And yes, it's a little creepy."

"You're the one who said you were going."

"I thought I might want to go. I knew Bethany. I was her teacher."

"So are you going?"

"Are you?"

He paused. "I think we should go."

She put her hands over her face. She wished she could just stay in darkness. She couldn't face Bethany Cleese's mother. She knew that, now that the funeral was hours away. "I can't go," she said.

"Leigh..."

She took her hands down. "What? We might be intruding. Did you think of that? They might not want us there."

He shook his head. He looked so sad, she thought. Disappointed. Disappointed with her.

"What?"

"I just think it's... I just wonder why you wanted to go to the funeral until the lawyer said it might help Kara. Now that it might help Kara, you don't want to go."

Her lips parted. She had no words. She had been there the day her own mother had slapped Pam for going to the basement with the Restevet boy, and she remembered the stunned look on Pam's face, how her eyes went wide and roved around the room, trying hard to refocus. Her own eyes were doing that now. A small, pained sound moved out of her mouth.

"I'm just telling you what I see," he said. He pursed his lips, thinking. "And I know you two have always had this...thing between you—"

She stood up. She couldn't see. She had to steady herself with the table. "I'm not going to listen to—"

He grabbed her hand and held it. His grip wasn't tight, but it was firm—the gesture almost seemed romantic. Because he was sitting and she was standing, he appeared to be pleading for something. "Tell me you want the best for her." He raised his free hand and pointed at the left lens of his glasses. "Leigh. Look me in the eyes and tell me you want the best for Kara."

It took her several breaths to realize she was squeezing his thumb with all her strength, hard enough to hurt. She let go, but there was a part of her that wanted to keep hurting him, to make him understand.

It seemed right, she thought, to hurt him. After all these years, for all these years, he had misunderstood her so completely. She was sure of it. She was.

Chapter 7

THEY DECIDED TO WAIT in the car for a while, in the parking lot across the street from the church. They had made a deal. If it looked like mostly family going in, they would leave. But if enough people showed up—more than thirty, Gary said—they would go in as well. Leigh lowered herself in her seat and watched, hope fading to dread as car after car rolled into the church's parking lot. She recognized other teachers from her school, and also teachers from the high school. Some of them were already crying when they got out of their cars, and when they met, they hugged one another and shook their heads. A group of teenage boys huddled near a lilac bush. One of them was smoking, wearing a suit that looked too big.

It was a beautiful summer evening, the sun just low enough that the breeze felt cool. Leigh had her window rolled down, and she could smell charcoal burning in a grill. She'd never noticed the church before. They were less than a block away from the daycare center Justin and Kara had gone to when they were small.

"Do you see the mother?" Gary asked. He was slouched over the steering wheel, his chin resting on his sleeves. He'd worn his blazer, heavy and dark, despite the weather. "Would you recognize her?"

"I don't think so. I don't think I see her, I mean." She would recognize her, of course. *She'll be the walking dead,* Leigh thought. *She'll be the one who won't recover.*

Gary leaned back in his seat. "Did you mail the note?"

She shook her head. He waited.

"I don't know what to write." She looked back at the cars rolling into the church's parking lot. "I'm still thinking of what to write."

Eva and Willow arrived with Rick Bechelmeyer, who was wearing the same suit he wore to important school meetings. They walked hand in hand, the three of them, Eva in the middle.

"Oh good," Gary muttered. "The press is here."

"That's not fair," Leigh said. She was in the habit of defending Eva to Gary. It was the only reason she did it now.

"What's she doing here? Did she know the girl?"

"She's here with Rick," Leigh pointed out. She frowned. Rick hadn't been principal when Bethany was in junior high. "She's here with Willow."

"Willow was friends with her?"

"She was in the car, Gary. She was with Kara."

A group of teachers huddled around Eva. She hugged them each for a long time, her eyes closed, her face contorted with pain. She had been the school secretary when Bethany was in junior high, Leigh thought. It was possible that she'd known her.

"We've got to go in," Gary said.

Leigh nodded and looked at her watch. It was almost seven. Most of the crowd had moved up the steps and into the church, but the boys by the lilac bush lingered. The boy who had been smoking stepped on his cigarette and looked at each of the others, and then the four of them walked up the steps together.

Leigh and Gary got out of the car. She stood still for a minute, maybe two. Gary came around the front of the car, took her hand, and pulled her forward. She was wearing dress shoes, and she could hear the sound they made on the asphalt beneath her, but she did not feel the movement of walking. She felt as if she were floating, pushed toward the steps of the church against her will, like driftwood caught in a current.

The hearse was parked around the corner of the church, its back door left open, waiting. Leigh looked away. She'd always hated hearses—the steady, unwavering, beetlelike way they crawled along the streets. She understood they were only symbols, frightening because of association. But whenever she saw a hearse in her rearview mirror, creeping up behind her, she felt as if she were being pursued by death itself. She imagined it was this way for everyone. A hearse could show up anywhere, reminding you of the potential for grief when you least expected it, even when you thought you were happy, listening to the radio on a sunny day.

WHEN THEY GOT INSIDE, the minister was already speaking. They ducked into the space behind the last pew. It was a newer church, functional and spare. Leigh could smell sawdust and paint. The walls were white, and, with the exception of a large wooden cross on the far wall, bare. The only ornate spot in the building, it seemed, was the door they had just entered through. It was a modern door, with a handicapped-accessible push bar, but a large square had been cut out of the top half and filled in with stained glass. Even that didn't look especially beautiful—the stained glass was simply a grid of different colored squares, red, yellow, and blue. But the effect was warm, a multicolored, diffuse glow falling on the aisle just to the right of Leigh's feet. Leigh wondered how often Bethany had come here for church. She wondered if she had loved it, believing everything, or if she had been forced to go. Perhaps she had come with her mother dutifully. Perhaps she'd just been biding her time.

prehend its purpose, when it happened to a loved one who had lived a full life. But Bethany was young, just sixteen, and he admitted he wasn't sure he could adequately comfort her family.

"Jesus himself noted there was no sense in tragedy, that God sent rain on the righteous and sinners alike. He offered no answers, only compassion and love, and so that is all we have when death, seemingly senseless, falls on someone we love in the bloom of youth."

The minister nodded down toward the front pew again. Leigh craned her neck forward. She felt pressure on her hip, Gary pulling her back. When she glanced at him, he looked at her with alarm. She shook her head and leaned back. She didn't know what she was doing. She didn't know what she wanted to see. Her eyes moved to the smiling portrait of Bethany, and then over the heads of the teenage boys in the last pew. They were young blooms, she thought, their thin necks long stems, their bowed heads all folded potential. But she remembered enough of her own adolescence to know they probably didn't feel this way inside. When she was sixteen, she had certainly not thought of herself as a flower. She was living with her sister and her new baby in the trailer behind her sister's boyfriend's parents' house. She didn't remember looking forward to anything. On the contrary, she remembered secretly fantasizing about dying, or not about dying exactly, but about what would follow her death. She'd imagined her mother coming back from California to bend over her grave and weep.

Gary's arm moved away from her. He clasped his hands and lowered his head, as had everyone in the church. Leigh started to lower her own head, but she felt the warmth of light from the window move across her face, and she instinctively raised it again. The minister was still speaking, but his voice was quiet and soothing, his head bowed. She understood that what she was doing was a violation of sorts. It was a matter of common trust, agreeing to close your eyes in a room full of people who were supposed to close their eyes

In front of the casket, mounted on an easel, was a large picture of Bethany. It was the same picture that had been in the paper, and Leigh forced herself, once again, to take in Bethany's smile, the soft curve of her cheek, the dark curls falling to her shoulders. She wasn't necessarily a happy-looking girl, Leigh decided. When Leigh had had her in class, she'd been serious, thoughtful. She'd had friends, mostly other quiet girls who followed directions and never caused any trouble. But she hadn't been popular. She would have been happier, once she was out of high school, out of Danby. Leigh bit her lip and looked at the carpeted floor.

Evening sunlight bathed the pews through clear rectangular windows, but as the sun began to set, the slant of light moved toward the back of the room. Without speaking, without looking at each other, Leigh and Gary moved away from it, inching back into the shadows, a little every few minutes, until their backs were against the wall.

Leigh couldn't see Bethany's mother. But the minister, young and freckled, with red hair, nodded at someone up front when he said that those who mourned would be blessed and comforted. He paused after that, and Leigh listened, waiting for a sob or a whimper that she knew would reach her as a physical pain. But it didn't come. She could see a few people on the far right side of the first pew—she recognized the junior high's Spanish teacher and also the actor-handsome face of Jim Tork. The man sitting beside him was small, with a scraggly ponytail tucked into the back of his collar. When he turned his face to the minister, Leigh saw the curve of his cheek, his olive skin, and thought that it might be Bethany's father. She lowered her eyes, embarrassed. She'd worried about only one grieving parent. She hadn't thought he would come.

The minister spoke in a wavering voice about how he had spent the last few days struggling to find words of comfort for those who loved Bethany. It was hard enough, he said, to accept death, to com-

too. But this was the only time she could watch her fellow mourners when they couldn't see her, all of them with bowed heads, as vulnerable as if they were sleeping. It was only during the prayer that she wasn't afraid of what they would think of her, and she was able to focus on Bethany, and the grief contained in the room.

But Eva's eyes were open and staring back at Leigh. She was sitting near the aisle, her head turned, her chin resting on her bare shoulder. She had the thoughtful expression of someone watching a dramatic scene in a movie, but when she saw that Leigh had seen her, she smiled and discreetly lifted her hand to wave, holding her bracelets steady with her other hand.

With no change in expression, Leigh bowed her head. When the minister said amen, she looked up, but she kept her eyes trained on Bethany's smiling picture, her face blank, careful not to look in Eva's direction. Hypocrisy or not, she wasn't in the mood to be watched.

The minister introduced Elissa De St. Jeor as a close friend of Bethany's and asked her to come forward. To Leigh's surprise, the girl in front of Gary stood and started up the aisle. Leigh hadn't recognized her. When Elissa De St. Jeor had been in seventh grade, she'd had auburn hair that hung long and straight down her back. Now it was jet black, and cut at a severe angle above her chin. When she got to the front of the church, she turned to address the pews, and Leigh recognized the familiar features, the long thin nose, the startled-looking eyes, though her face had been powdered a ghostly white. She wore an oversized dark T-shirt over a long black skirt, and she had something that looked like a bolt pushed through one of her earlobes. In seventh grade, almost every day, Elissa had worn a pink shirt that barely covered her belly button and a denim miniskirt. She'd had to be told that it wasn't appropriate to give the boy sitting in front of her a back rub. Leigh had worried about her.

Leigh was, perhaps, the reason the two girls had become friends.

She'd paired them for some project in the middle of the school year—Leigh's thinking was that Bethany, such a good worker, always quiet, would be a positive influence on Elissa. But her plan had backfired: Bethany had started misbehaving. Leigh had even had to keep Bethany after class once, because during a test that was supposed to be silent, she had laughed hard and loud at something Elissa whispered. Leigh finally separated them, banishing Elissa to a desk by herself on the far side of the room.

Now Elissa stood in front of Bethany's casket, reading a poem she'd written, black mascara running down her powdered cheeks. Leigh braced herself for the worst—sentimental clichés that would make her cringe and also feel terrible. But the poem was good, if a little cryptic. The lines didn't rhyme, and there were references to aliens and outer space that made the young minister furrow his brow. When she finished reading, she nodded at the minister, who nodded back at her. She moved heavily to a cart with a laptop computer and a CD player that had been positioned near the pulpit. She was going to play Bethany's favorite song, she said, and show pictures, given to her by Bethany's mother. She gestured toward a projection screen behind the coffin.

The music started—a song Leigh didn't recognize—and then there was a picture of a baby on the screen. Brown eyes. A few beginning strands of dark hair on a perfectly curved head. A ruffled green dress with a yellow bow. Leigh's stomach muscles tightened, and she heard Gary take a deep breath. In the next picture, Bethany was learning to walk. Her eyes were wide, ecstatic. A woman bent behind her, grasping her hands. In the next, she was older, five maybe, looking thoughtfully up at a circus elephant, her hands clasped behind her as if she were reminding herself not to touch. She wasn't smiling in this picture; she looked more like the somber girl Leigh remembered, thoughtful and quiet, her right eye slightly larger than the left. Leigh took Gary's hand. They would endure this. They would look hard at every single picture. They would see, without blinking, every birthday party and first day of school. It might feel like torture, but what it really was, she hoped, was a sincere effort to share the grief. Bethany's mother, she believed, understood this. She had handed over her dead daughter's baby pictures to this girl who looked like a vampire because she wanted everyone to understand, as much as they could, what she had lost, so the terrible sadness would be spread out evenly among them, and maybe thinned a bit.

Leigh stared hard at the screen as the pictures changed, her teeth gritted, her fists curled tight, taking on as much as she could.

"I don't want this."

The words emerged, clear and distinct, from the front pew. There was a rush of hushed voices, and then a woman stood up. "I don't want this," she said again. She raised her palms to the projection screen as if it were a speeding car coming toward her. Leigh could see only the woman's raised hands and the back of her hair, which was cut short and bleached, a cluster of dark roots visible at the top. But she knew who it was. She'd known the moment she heard the voice. It sounded hoarse, throaty, from days of crying.

Elissa turned off the music. Even with the pale makeup and the dyed black hair and the combat boots, she appeared frightened and obliging. She touched a button on the computer, and the projection screen went blank.

Bethany's mother waved her arms in every direction, at the casket covered in flowers, at Bethany's portrait, at the mourners in the pews. "I don't want this," she said again. A gray-haired man stood and reached for her arm, but she pushed him away. She put her hands over her eyes.

"No," she said, firmly now, as if she were tired of being nagged. "Okay? No. I don't want any of this."

"Diane. We understand." The minister stepped toward her.

She turned away from him, her arm stretched toward him, trying to keep him at bay. "No you don't." She started laughing, and then stopped all at once. She was wearing a dark skirt and what looked like a man's black sweatshirt. Just the tips of her fingers were visible at the ends of the sleeves. "I appreciate the effort. But you don't." She looked across the aisle at the man with the ponytail. "And you, what are you doing here? Now you show up. A lot of good that'll do her now."

He turned away. Someone else stood and put a hand on her shoulder. She shrugged it off. "I don't want this," she said, facing the pews again.

"It's okay, Diane," someone called out. "Diane, honey."

"No. I don't want this. I don't." She turned, looked at the coffin, and then at the picture on the easel. She turned, wincing, and wrapped her arms around her head again. And then she was moving fast down the aisle. People reached out for her, but she kept going, shrinking from their hands.

Leigh felt Gary's hand on her elbow, pulling her away from the aisle. She lowered her eyes and waited for the sound of the church's door opening beside her. But it didn't open. She braced herself. They shouldn't have come. Kara was right. And now they would be told this was true. She was aware of the tightening of Gary's grip on her arm and the sudden, perfect silence around her. When she looked up, Diane Kletchka was standing in the aisle and looking back at her, her dark eyes narrowed with recognition.

"*I'm so sorry,*" Leigh whispered. She tried to hold the other woman's gaze, but she couldn't manage it, and she felt guilty for this, disgusting. She looked at her mouth, her chin. Several people from the front were moving quickly down the aisle.

"Diane," the gray-haired man said. "Come back. This is important. You have to see this through."

Diane Kletchka did not turn around. Her eyes moved past Leigh, to Gary, and then to the empty space beside him. She was looking for Kara, Leigh realized, and as she was realizing this, Diane Kletchka put her hands on the push bar of the church's door. Leigh looked away, but she heard the door swing open and hit the church's exterior. There was an explosive sound, loud enough to make Gary flinch. But Leigh was still surprised when she turned back to see stained-glass shards, red and blue and yellow, falling onto the pavement just outside.

She kept her eyes lowered. She didn't want to turn around, to see who was watching, who had seen. She didn't care. The gray-haired man ran past her, calling out to Diane Kletchka, but no one answered. He pushed the door open again, and Leigh watched his brown shoes trample over the broken glass.

The church door eased shut, slowly, with a quiet click, and Leigh, suddenly very frightened for her daughter, could still feel the evening breeze on her face.

Chapter 8

LEIGH HAD EXPECTED THAT the good citizens of Danby would write in to the newspaper about Kara's accident. People wrote in about everything, and they didn't seem to worry about repeating one another. Almost every day, there was a letter about the new and unpopular traffic roundabout at the end of Commerce for which the city council had paid a half million dollars. There were letters about property taxes, littering, and a proposed indoor smoking ban. There were letters about Iraq.

Some people wrote in regularly—Cynthia Tork, whom Leigh assumed was Jim Tork's wife or sister or daughter, often wrote in to rally likeminded readers to boycott the one movie theater in town until they stopped showing R-rated movies. ("Even if you don't see those movies, your neighbors might. Your children's friends might. They will be influenced, and in your midst. And that, my friends, could some day cause a problem for you.") A man who signed his letters Mick L. Jagger wrote in on a variety of issues—the mill levy, parking availability, and abortion. All of his letters, no matter what the issue, used the phrase "WAKE UP PEOPLE!" as a closing.

What Leigh was not prepared for was how quickly after the accident the letters about Kara would appear in the paper. The day after Bethany's funeral, there were two.

To the editor:

I was deeply saddened to read about the accident that killed a pedestrian in the crosswalk of Commerce and Seventh Streets. But I can't say I was surprised. Unfortunately, as long as irresponsible parents allow their teenage children to tool around town in enormous vehicles before they learn to drive properly, we can expect more of the same. I live across the street from the high school, and every weekday at three, I watch mere children screech out of the parking lot in Mommy's and Daddy's SUVs. They blare their music, with no consideration for other people's ears. Few of them watch for pedestrians, and most of them go too fast. For years now, I have been looking out my window and saying to myself, "Someone is going to get killed." Well now someone has. The girl who was driving was talking on her cell phone. I can only shake my head and think that if young people need to talk on the phone while in a vehicle, maybe they should take the bus!

Sincerely,

Roma P. Goodwin

To the editor:

Our society is upside down. Things that should be punished are not punished, and things that should not be punished are. Bethany Cleese's "crime" was that she tried to walk across the street in an age when people think they can drive and talk on the phone at the same time. It didn't matter that she was in the crosswalk when she was run down and killed—it's a crime to walk anywhere, apparently. And punishable by death! In a saner society, people would be able to walk across the street, and drivers wouldn't be able to talk on the phone while driving. WAKE UP PEOPLE!

Sincerely,

Mick L. Jagger

Leigh stared dully at the newsprint. Even reading the paper would be different now. She'd always had mixed feelings about reading the paper every morning—so much of what she read, even in the local section, depressed her. But it seemed important to know what was going on, especially in her own town. Gary called Danby's paper a gossipy rag, and she knew this was true. But she had always liked that about it. She'd enjoyed scanning the police blotter and letters to the editor for names she recognized. How comfortable she'd been, how smug.

She was still looking at the paper—not reading it—when Gary came downstairs. She sat up and folded it closed. He wouldn't see the letters about the accident unless she showed them to him. He got his news from *The New York Times,* and he had an online subscription to *The Boston Globe.* Leigh had to keep him apprised of local happenings and controversies. Even when the subjects were serious—intelligent design in the schools, a proposed highway that would force farmers to sell their land, the battle over whether a Wal-Mart should come to town—he sometimes listened with a little smile that annoyed her. It was as if the part of town that was not campus was a joke to him. When they first came to Danby, Leigh had thought it was sweet that he still wanted to get the news from his hometown paper. But they'd been in Danby for nineteen years.

"Morning." He kissed her on top of her head as he passed. They had been gentle with each other since the funeral, since they had walked hand in hand over the shattered glass in the church's doorway, heads lowered, moving as quickly as they could to the car. On the way home, he'd tried to comfort Leigh. Or maybe he was trying to comfort himself. He'd pointed out that the accident had just happened. The mother's grief was still raw. She wouldn't stay that angry for long, he'd said. She couldn't. Leigh had stared out the window and said nothing. She didn't think what he was saying was true. And all night long, lying awake in bed, Leigh thought about the funeral and the stained glass breaking, the way the shards had looked lying on the pavement, shiny and glittering and sharp.

The phone rang, and Leigh shook her head. "Don't answer it," she said. She went into the kitchen, and dropped the newspaper into the recycling bin. It was eight fifteen in the morning, and Eva had already called twice.

Gary looked at the phone as the machine whirled and beeped. "It's her, isn't it?"

She didn't answer.

"She loved that last night, that drama. Now she's trying to make it last."

Leigh shook her head, frowning. They listened to the outgoing message.

"Hello? Leigh? It's Eva. Look, Gary ... Kara ... I'm sorry to keep calling. But I absolutely have to talk to Leigh this morning. Right away. Leigh? Call me. It's impor—"

Leigh hit the stop button. She met Gary's eyes and looked away. He cleared his throat, but that was all. He wouldn't rub it in. He wouldn't say, *I told you she was no good, a nosy gossip. You didn't believe me, but now that she's talking about us, about our daughter, you see how disgusting she is.* It wasn't in his nature to be mean like that, and she was grateful for this.

"You've got a meeting this morning?" He almost smiled, touching her hair. She leaned toward him and closed her eyes. She liked the way he smelled in the morning, a little musty, like the house. He was a good head taller than she was, and she felt the stubble of his chin against her forehead.

"Ordering textbooks." She opened her eyes and looked at her watch. "I've got to be there at nine thirty." She lowered her voice. "And listen, Justin is downstairs watching TV. But I don't want him just sitting down there all day. Maybe you could do something with him. A project in the yard or something? Before it gets too hot."

"I've got to turn in grades tomorrow." He turned and saw her face. "I'll do a little something with him. I thought you already ordered your books."

"I did. Rick wants us all to come in, though, to make sure there's"—she used her fingers as quote marks—"a balance of views." She shrugged. "He's new. I imagine Jim Tork and his crew have complained about our radical choices, or maybe just mine. I know the science teachers have to come in this morning. And the history teachers. And the PE teachers. Sex ed."

"What was your radical choice?"

"*This Boy's Life.* 'A Good Man Is Hard to Find.'"

He laughed and shook his head. It was the first time she'd seen him laugh since the accident.

"*The Great Gatsby.*"

He looked at her over the tops of his glasses. "Are you serious?"

"The characters are amoral and they curse, according to Tork. You think it's funny? Wait until I can't teach it."

"This town . . ." He rolled his eyes. "What? They want you to just have them read C. S. Lewis every year?"

"Pretty much." She didn't mind Lewis. He was on her list for seventh graders.

"Well, it doesn't matter." He leaned past her and poured himself a cup of coffee. "The smart ones will read the others on their own. They'll read them in college."

"They won't all go to college." She was getting irritated. She sometimes suspected he didn't think much of her job. He thought she just supervised a holding pen, babysitting until the real sorting began.

But he nodded vigorously. "You're right," he said. "You're right." All at once he was smiling, an actual glimmer in his eyes. She knew this smile, and she looked away and rolled her eyes. If her husband was a snob, he was, at least, a snob who allegedly admired her concern for the underdog. He respected a value he had never shared. They'd had their first real fight after only a month of dating—KU had open admissions then, and Gary had said something dismissive about the less successful students in his composition class, the ones who couldn't put a sentence together, the ones who could barely spell. Leigh had surprised him—vehemently defending these students, telling Gary that anyone who called himself a teacher should be up for the challenge of helping students who had to struggle to learn, who had to try harder just to get by. "Any teacher *worth his salt,*" she'd added, surprised by the sureness, even anger, in her own voice. He'd looked at her for a long time without saying anything, and she remembered thinking, *this is it, we're going to break up, that's fine, I don't care, better now than later.* But then he'd smiled and said, much to her surprise, "I think I'm going to try to marry you."

He was giving her that same smile now, over twenty years later, in their kitchen. Maybe it was patronizing. Some days it felt that way. Today, after rolling her eyes and turning away, she changed her mind, looked up at him, and smiled back. They held each other's gaze, and she felt something like ease until a board creaked above their heads. They both looked up, foreheads creasing, at the ceiling beneath Kara's room. It had been a relief to talk about something else, to feel something else, to at least pretend to think about something besides the accident.

"How long has she been awake?"

Leigh shrugged. "I heard her moving around in her room when I got up. At six."

"Has she eaten?"

"No. I knocked and asked if she was hungry. She said she wasn't. Don't worry. She'll probably come down when I leave for my meeting. She'll see my car leave, and she'll know it's safe to come down and forage."

Gary said nothing, and Leigh stood still, listening to her own breath. She had been half joking, and she'd expected him to protest. She looked up at the ceiling. Kara probably was, in fact, waiting for her to leave. And she was probably hungry.

"I might leave early," she said. "I've got some errands to run." She grabbed her keys and slid past Gary. She tried to smile, but she couldn't quite meet his eyes.

SHE DIDN'T HAVE ANY errands, of course, and she had a half hour before her meeting. She drove around aimlessly for a while, listening to the radio, avoiding Seventh and Commerce. She lapped the town twice before she realized what she should do, what she had to do, right then. There was a pack of note cards in the glove compartment—an end-of-year gift from an appreciative parent. *Please accept this very small token of our appreciation for all the hard work you did with Jordan this year. No other teacher has ever taken the time you have to help him reach his full potential. You are the first teacher, he told us, who didn't make him feel dumb.* She had stamps in her purse, and probably a pen. She could get it over with now.

She gave herself five minutes, sitting in her car in the delivery lot behind the grocery store, a note card pressed against the steering wheel. She gritted her teeth and tapped the pen. *Just write something,* she sometimes told her students, when they looked up with anxious faces from blank pieces of paper. *Anything. Just make yourself do it. It doesn't have to be perfect. It doesn't even have to be good. But at least try. You must have thought something about the poem I read. Whatever it is, write it down. Just try to explain to me what you're thinking. That's all writing is, an attempt to connect, to share your mind with someone else.*

Dear Diane Kletchka,

I am Kara Churchill's mother. I am so sorry this happened. Kara is miserable. She did not go to Bethany's funeral because she is too upset. She will not even leave her room. She's not eating. I'm not telling you this to garner sympathy—I just want you to know why she didn't come to the service.

As you know, I had Bethany in my class years ago, and I believe I can almost imagine your grief. I don't know what else to say. My heart is with you.

With deepest sorrow,

Leigh Churchill

She read it over just once before she sealed the matching envelope. Nothing she wrote would be adequate, she reasoned. She just needed to get something in the mail. She'd looked up the address in the phone book the night before: 436 Bramble Street. She knew where Bramble Street was, not far from the high school. Bethany had probably been walking home when she died, when Kara hit her. Leigh pictured the accident—what she knew of it. Still sitting in the car by herself, she whimpered and covered her eyes.

She got out of the car and peeked around the corner, searching for anyone she knew. But her path looked safe. She jogged around to the front of the grocery store and slid the card in the mail drop, her head lowered, turning back toward the car as quickly as she could. It was done. Irrevocable. She got back in the car and told herself she would just drive around until it was time for the meeting. But really, even before she turned the ignition key, she knew where she would end up.

Bramble Street was in a new development—five straight streets of boxy, efficient-looking houses that had sprung up a few years ago in what had been an overgrown field. The houses looked tidy and cheap—they were all one story, built on slab foundations, and most had plastic white tubes snaking out from the rain gutters into the yards. The lawns were neatly mowed, and there were swing sets in some of the backyards. A large, hand-painted sign in one of the yards read "SLOW DOWN! WATCH FOR CHILDREN!"

She didn't have any trouble finding the house. It looked like all the others, but there was evidence of fresh grief—a covered casserole dish sat on the front step like a waiting guest, and two bouquets of flowers had been stuck into the front yard's chain-link fence. The blinds in the big front window were down, and what looked like a yellow flowered sheet covered a smaller window on the side. Still, after Leigh rolled to a stop across the street, she hunched low in her car, her sunglasses on. She imagined Bethany coming home from school, undoing the latch of the chain-link fence, walking up to the house. She imagined her waving to her mother through the window. The window with the yellow bedsheet for a curtain had probably been Bethany's, she decided. She imagined her looking out of it, waiting for life to begin. Leigh pictured her face, the way she had looked in eighth grade, her dark hair still in braids sometimes. Leigh had always been nice to her, even when she'd started making trouble with Elissa De St. Jeor. She'd always had a soft spot for girls like Bethany, shy and quiet, a little awkward. As a teacher, she wanted to encourage them. *Hang in there,* she wanted to say. *Much better things will be coming your way.*

A grim-faced fat woman approached on the sidewalk, then cut across 436's yard to the door. She looked down at the casserole dish on the step, and then just stood there, her arm raised, ready to knock, but not yet knocking. Leigh had the engine idling. The car didn't make much sound as she pulled back into the street. But the fat woman turned around, looking, it seemed to Leigh, right through the car window into her eyes. There was no accusation, no recognition. Still, Leigh left her hand cupped against her face. She didn't want to be who she was. She wanted to step hard on the accelerator, to flee from the woman's stare as quickly as possible.

But she drove away slowly, watching for children, the window that she had decided was Bethany's burned forever into her mind's eye.

BY THE TIME SHE pulled into the junior high's parking lot, she wasn't crying, but she was close. She parked behind the school and searched her purse for her cell phone. She realized she'd forgotten it, and this, oddly, was what made the first tears come. She got out of the car, hurried across the lawn, and knocked on a side door until a janitor, peering at her sorrowfully through the glass, shook his head and let her in. She still had fifteen minutes. Her plan was to find Rick Bechelmeyer and let him see her face so he would understand that she couldn't sit through a meeting about textbooks right now. Rick was kind to a fault. He would relent. She could be out of the building before the other teachers showed up. That was all she wanted.

But when she got to the office, Rick was already in the meeting room, talking to a blond woman Leigh assumed was a new teacher. She had the look—she was young and pretty, and she wore a pink sweater set with large white buttons shaped like flowers. Her skirt fit loosely and fell well below her knees, and she carried a canvas bag that read KIDS COUNT! in cheerful orange letters. The only things that didn't seem teachery were her shoes—they looked expensive. But she had a determined, earnest gleam in her eye, and Leigh felt certain she was about to meet someone she would spend years avoiding in the teachers' lounge.

"Hi." Leigh waved to Rick from the doorway, half her body remaining in the hall. She didn't even want to go in. She wanted him to come out and talk to her alone. There was a good chance this would happen. She'd been at the school for sixteen years before he was hired as principal, and he usually treated her with deference. He was younger than she was. She wouldn't have known it, but Eva had told her he was only thirty-eight. *I'm sleeping with a younger man,* she'd told Leigh, whispering as if she'd wanted to keep it a secret.

"Oh Leigh," Rick said, "I'm...glad you're here." His tone wasn't convincing. He was wearing the same jacket he'd worn to the funeral, different pants. "Come on in. This is—"

The blond woman smiled and started to raise her hand.

"Listen. Sorry." Leigh winced. "I'm not sure I'm up for this right now." She managed a half smile at the new teacher. "Sorry. I just came in to tell you..." She looked back at Rick, stepping inside the room. "I can't be here when everyone shows up. Not right now. I'll just tell you, real quick, that I still want the books I ordered." She waved her hand, dismissive. "I know some parents have complained, but it's ridiculous. It's too ridiculous to talk about. They're going to have a problem with anything I teach unless it's the Bible." She was slightly invigorated, hearing herself talk. She was too miserable to be bothered with crazy people, she was saying, and this felt true and right. The new blond teacher looked alarmed, and this was a little pleasing.

"If they have a problem, they can talk to me about it next year, or they can take their kid out of my honors class. They can homeschool him in their fallout shelter and never let him think for himself, whatever, but they're not going to dictate policy for the other ki—"

"Leigh!"

She jumped at the sternness in his voice. He stared at her with no smile. "This is Cynthia Tork." He gestured at the woman beside him. "She wanted to come to the meeting today to discuss her concerns about the reading list."

Leigh nodded. She could picture the expression on her own face—mournful, desperate. She doubted they would feel any pity.

Cynthia Tork cleared her throat. "Yes. I asked if I could come and meet you." Her voice was higher than Leigh's, but her gaze was steady, unflinching. "I assumed the people charged with educating our son would care about my point of view. I assumed we would be able to discuss our different points of view. Like adults."

"I apologize," Leigh said. She forced herself to meet the other woman's eyes. She didn't look at all the way Leigh had imagined her. Reading all those righteous letters to the editor, Leigh had pictured the author in a homemade dress, her hair pulled back in a bun, the woman from *American Gothic*. But Cynthia Tork, in the flesh, had blond highlights, manicured nails, and the elocution of a television anchor.

"Well, that's something," she said, one eyebrow arched high. "But now we know how you really feel."

"I think we should discuss this at another time," Rick said. He had one hand behind each of their backs, not touching either one of them. "Let's give everybody a chance to calm down."

Cynthia Tork ignored him, her blue eyes still on Leigh's. "My husband said he spoke with you about our concerns on the last day of the school year. He said you seemed respectful and receptive." She cocked her head and smiled.

"I'm sorry," Leigh said. She glanced at Rick Bechelmeyer, to let him know he was included in her apology. It was all she could do. She took a deep breath. "I shouldn't have said those things. I don't intend to change my book selections, but I'll be glad to speak with you and your husband. I'm sorry I can't do it today, because I'm not doing so well.... I'm..." She searched Cynthia Tork's face for any potential for sympathy. "I'm in the middle of a...bit of a...family crisis, and—"

"I know."

Leigh stared at her.

"I knew Bethany." Her voice softened, and her pretty nails

moved over the buttons on her pink sweater. She swallowed, and then there were tears in her eyes. "She was in our youth group. She was a lovely girl. Absolutely lovely."

Leigh looked down at her hands. It was impossible to know if Cynthia Tork had meant to use the accident this way—after all, Leigh had brought it up. Cynthia Tork had simply stated that she had known Bethany. There was nothing overtly cruel or calculating in that, and those were real tears in Cynthia Tork's eyes. But it was still such a powerful weapon. Once Bethany's name had been spoken, Leigh lost all interest and hope in defending herself.

"We'll have to do this later," Leigh said, moving to the door. "I'm sorry," she said again. She escaped into the hallway just as a group of teachers approached. They were her coworkers, people she saw every day, but they looked almost unfamiliar in their summer wear, shorts and T-shirts, sandals and flip-flops. They had been talking, laughing, but when they saw her face they hushed and stepped back. She focused on the floor and moved past them. There seemed no other option now. For years, she had exchanged lesson plans and pleasantries with these people, and she didn't have an enemy among them. But she didn't have a close friend, either. *I keep to myself*, she had more or less told them, with every averted glance and fleeting smile, with every lunch break she spent reading at her desk or talking to Gary on her cell phone. She couldn't say, for certain, why she had taken pains to shut them all out. It wasn't something she had planned on or even thought about—her behavior felt instinctive, somehow linked to her very survival. But now that she was literally running away from the principal's office and the mess she had made there, now that she felt misunderstood in her own home, now that she was scared and embarrassed in the streets of her town, in the aisles of the grocery store, she wished that she had tried harder to foster some sort of connection with one or two of these people she saw every day, if only to have someone know her well enough to see past the accidents—her own, Kara's—to the good intent that was there every day.

It was too late for that now. She bowed her head and turned into the dim hallway that led to the back parking lot. The janitor was still there, mopping the linoleum. When he saw her running, he warned her to be careful. She nodded and smiled, but she didn't slow her feet. She needed to get back to her car. She needed to go home and lie down.

But when she pushed her way through the double doors, she saw that her car would be no sanctuary. Eva was sitting on the hood, wearing a cream-colored dress, her legs crossed at the ankles. She waved and held up a plastic cup of what appeared to be an iced coffee.

"Mocha latte, right?"

Leigh walked to her car with her head lowered. She was crying again. There would be no hiding it. They would have to move. Probably to Boston. She would tell Gary when she got home. "Thanks," she said, taking the cup. Eva's dress was linen, and Leigh wondered if she had considered how dirty the car was before she'd hoisted herself up on the hood.

"I thought the ice might melt before you came out. I wasn't sure how long the showdown would last." Eva looked at the school and narrowed her eyes. "Cynthia. She's just a Cindy if I ever saw one. But did you see the size of her wedding ring?" She lowered her voice. "I bet she's the one who paid for it. I heard she comes from money."

Leigh lowered her cup. "You knew she was going to be there? Rick knew?"

Eva sighed and slid off the car. Some dust did catch on her dress, but she brushed it away into the wind. "I've been trying to warn you all morning." She stepped forward, her bracelets pressed tight against Leigh's neck. Her embrace was as firm as Audrey Nutter's, and her cheek was warm from the sun.

"I'm on your side," she whispered. "And I can be helpful, okay? You've got to start answering your phone."

Chapter 9

EVA NEEDED A RIDE to Leigh's house. Willow had dropped her off at the school on her way to visit Kara. "The reversal has started," Eva muttered, buckling herself into Leigh's passenger seat. "The kid is dropping me off. Pretty soon she'll be taking me to day care. And then buying my diapers. Everything turns around."

"Kara knew she was coming over?"

As soon as Leigh asked this, she regretted the way she had done it, with too much surprise and interest. She could feel Eva's gaze taking in her face as she put the car in gear.

"Yeah. Is that okay?"

"Of course. It's great." Leigh remembered to concentrate on her driving. And she would turn left where she usually turned right, taking the long way to avoid Seventh and Commerce. *We Will Miss You Bethany.*

"How's she doing?"

"Kara? She's okay. Considering." *I'm guessing at this,* she thought. *I actually have no idea. My daughter doesn't talk to me. She doesn't come out of her room when I'm home.*

"Well, I'm glad they're getting together today." Eva pulled down her sun visor and looked at her teeth in the mirror. "Maybe Willow can lift her spirits a bit."

"Maybe," Leigh said.

They drove in silence for a while. Leigh wished her sister would call. She was lonely. She was alone.

Eva cleared her throat. "And you know, this'll probably be Kara's last look at her before the biiiiig change."

"What do you mean?" Leigh turned onto her street. A neighbor out watering his lawn waved to her. She waved back and smiled. He was just being nice, she thought. He knew. Everyone knew.

"You know what I mean."

She glanced at Eva. "No I don't."

"Kara didn't tell you?"

Leigh shook her head carefully.

"Willow's getting breast implants." She smiled at Leigh's surprise. "I can't believe Kara didn't tell you. Yeah. She's really excited."

"Why?"

"Why is she excited?" Eva smiled. "Because right now she doesn't have any tits, and pretty soon she will. Big ones. Not huge, I mean. But they'll show up."

They were in Leigh's driveway now, their car shaded by the large sycamore in front of the house. Weeds grew high around the flower bed by the door. She wondered if Gary had done anything with Justin. She pressed the button for the garage door.

"You're letting her do that?"

Eva turned toward her slowly and completely. Her long earrings trembled in the air conditioner's breeze. "Yes. I'm letting her do that, Leigh. Obviously. She was very smart about it. She did all the research on the surgery, the doctor. She made a great case, so we made a deal. She's been bugging me about it for years. I told her if she graduated on the honor roll, her father and I would pay for three quarters of it. She's paying for the rest with her own money."

"Gordon? Gordon knows about this?"

"Of course."

Leigh rolled her eyes. She couldn't help it, picturing Eva's ex-husband, with his tweed jackets and his sideburns. So academic. A life of the mind. She started to turn off the engine, but then stopped. It was so hot, even in the garage—they would have to keep the air on if they stayed in the car.

"Will she care that you told me? Should I act like I don't know?"

"Why would you do that? She doesn't care who knows."

Good thing, Leigh thought.

Eva gave her a sidelong glance. "Is there a problem?"

Leigh started to shake her head. "I just... I'm sorry. I think it's ridiculous."

"Why?"

"Well, she's just a girl, Eva. She's not done growing."

"She's eighteen. And I'm her mother." Eva looked down at her own chest, her clavicle sharp and well defined. "Believe me. She's done growing."

"Well. Aside from that. Something about it just isn't right."

"And what would that be?"

"She could spend that money on college."

"She's going to college. There's no problem there."

"Or a car."

"We gave her a choice. She chose breasts."

"A car is more practical."

Eva bit her lip. The gesture was subtle, but Leigh understood. They had given Kara a car. She rested her head on the steering wheel. She was no longer in any position to judge, not Eva or anyone else. She never would be again. There was a kind of freedom in it, maybe. "It just seems...," she started, her voice softer now, less certain. "It seems like we should be teaching our daughters that beauty comes from within, and that—"

Eva clicked her tongue. "So why are you wearing lipstick?"

"What?"

"Are you wearing mascara?" She eyed Leigh's blouse. "And I bet anything that's a push-up bra."

"That's different," Leigh said. But she put a protective arm across her chest. She wouldn't have called it a push-up bra. Extra supportive, maybe. Well made.

"How is it different?" Eva leaned back against her window. She wasn't smiling, and one of her eyebrows was raised in a way that made her seem intimidating. "Didn't your dentist have Justin wear those little rubber bands around his two front teeth to close the gap? Why'd you do that? What's wrong with a little gap? Inner beauty is what matters."

"Okay." Leigh held up her hands in surrender. She'd never made Eva angry before. She'd never criticized her parenting, either. "It's not my business. I guess I just have a problem with the whole idea..."

"Guess so." Eva smoothed down her skirt.

"I just..." Leigh changed her tone, so it sounded confiding, humble. She looked at her half finished mocha in the cup holder. She wanted to make amends. "Doesn't it seem a little unfair? I mean before, if you were skinny, you got to be skinny, which I suppose was fun. And if you were bigger, if you had to worry about your weight, well, then you at least got breasts."

"A boobie prize," Eva said. She smiled, but she didn't look at Leigh.

"Sure. And now you see these skinny girls, string beans like Willow, with these huge breasts, and well, it's just not right. It upsets... the balance."

"It's not as if you're competing with her. You're married. What do you care?"

"No." Leigh shook her head. She had been misunderstood. "No that's not it. It's not about competing. It just seems you should get one or the other." She smiled. She was half-joking.

"Ahhhhh." Eva made one exaggerated nod. "Now we get to it."

"Get to what?" Leigh was looking around the garage. The recycling was still in stacks by the wall. Gary hadn't done anything with Justin.

"The heart of it." Eva smiled back, to show they were still friends, but she opened her door and stood up. "You know what you are? You're the happiness police." She knocked on the roof twice, bracelets jangling. "Really, Leigh. You should get a siren for the car."

WHEN THEY GOT INSIDE, they could see Kara and Willow through the kitchen's back window. The girls were out on the deck, their backs turned toward the house. Willow was eating potato chips out of a bag, and Kara leaned forward, her elbows balanced on the deck's railing. Eva and Leigh stood in the kitchen and gazed out at their daughters. The image was striking, and Leigh wondered if Eva was thinking the same thing she was—that it was impossible to look at the girls, at their young bodies, their lean, muscled arms, their smooth, vein-free legs, and not think of beginnings, of capacity, of energy. Kara had finally washed her hair, and it fell down her back in soft waves that glinted gold and red in the sunlight.

"Like colts," Eva said quietly, maybe to herself, maybe to Leigh.

Willow folded the bag of potato chips under her arm and put her other arm around Kara's back. She rested her head against Kara's, and then it was clear, from the way Kara's shoulders moved under Willow's arm, that she was crying.

Eva glanced at Leigh. Leigh frowned, and looked back out the window. But she could still feel Eva's stare. She turned back to Eva, waiting. She didn't know what she wanted her to do.

"I think Kara is crying," Eva said, the words coming out slowly. She cocked her head, waited another moment, then moved toward the back door. She knocked twice, as if she were waiting to be asked in, not out. The girls turned around, and though Kara's face was teary and red, they both smiled when they saw who it was.

"Hey kiddos." She said it with affection, an old inside joke, moving toward them with outstretched arms. Both girls turned into the embrace. Eva kissed Kara on the forehead, and rubbed her arm. Kara did not pull away.

Leigh watched though the window, understanding moving through her like a wave of nausea. She never knew what to do. It had simply not occurred to her to rush outside to comfort her daughter. Even if the idea had occurred to her, she wouldn't have done it— she would have worried about being intrusive. Now, of course, she could see it was the right thing to do, but only because Eva had already done it, and only now because it was too late. Eva had left the door open, and Leigh could feel humid, warm air seeping into the air-conditioned house. She walked through the door, into the heat, and closed it softly behind her.

"Hey," she said. She was wringing her hands. She put them at her sides. "You okay?" She focused on Kara, on her squinting pink eyes, but she was very aware of Eva and Willow, the audience for her impending failure.

Kara made a gesture somewhere between a nod and a shrug. She really did look older, Leigh thought. She'd already lost weight. And there was something about her eyes, how they kept moving, never settling in one place, as if she were searching for something she already knew she wasn't going to find. Leigh could picture how Kara's eyes had looked before: serene, contemplative, a little intimidating when she wore her glasses.

"Can I get you something?" Leigh shifted her weight. "Something to drink?"

Kara shook her head. She had her head on Eva's shoulder. The three of them looked like a little team, Leigh thought. She could imagine them in happier times, sitting around and talking about hopes and fears, breast implants and boyfriends. There was the proof in front of her. Somehow, Eva was in the loop. Kara trusted her—Eva, of all people—more than she trusted her own mother. And now, out in the backyard in the heat of a June morning, Eva had a front row seat to the miserable chasm between them. She had been a fool to think she could keep her problems with Kara a secret. Kara talked to Willow, and Willow, unlike Kara, apparently talked to her mother. Eva had known everything all along.

The phone rang. Leigh, who had not answered the phone in the last three days even when she was sitting right beside it, rushed inside. She turned away from the window when she picked up.

"Leigh. Hi. It's me."

She was so grateful to hear her sister's airy voice that she made a whimpering sound, something between a sigh and a whoop, just before she started yelling. "Pam! Where the hell have you been? I've been trying to call you for days. Your number was disconnected again. I told you to tell me if you needed help with the bill. I hate not being able to reach y—"

"I'm sorry. There was a fire."

"What?" It had felt good, she realized, to yell at someone. She felt the energy falling away from her.

"There was a fire in the big complex across the street. You remember it? The one with the yellow balconies? It burned it to the ground. They hosed water on it all night, and it backed up the sewers and flooded my building. There's soot and water everywhere. It ruined my futon. Nothing works. I had to move out."

Leigh blinked. She was standing in her sunny kitchen. Kara must have started the dishwasher. The motor made it difficult to hear. "Where are you now?"

"Right at this second?"

"Sure."

"I'm outside an Osco Drug."

"In Minneapolis?"

"Yeah. My minister let me use her phone card. I'm sorry I scared you."

"No. No. I'm sorry, Pam. I'm so sorry this happened. Where are you staying?"

"With people from church. Cody and Wilma—you met them when you were up here, I think. They've been so nice. Wilma gave me some of her clothes. But they don't have a phone."

Leigh looked out the window. Willow was talking, smiling about something. Eva appeared to listen intently, but Kara stared off into the backyard. "How long... what did your landlord say?"

"Oh, he's so upset. He had fire insurance, but they're not going to pay because the fire wasn't in his building. Can you believe that? I feel so bad for him."

"Pam! What about you?"

"Oh..." Pam's voice seemed to move away from the phone. Someone was yelling in the background. "I'm just grateful I'm alive. Two people died in that fire. An old married couple. I knew them. I mean I knew who they were. I waved to them sometimes, you know, if we were all outside."

Leigh grimaced. Pam had been in her apartment for less than a year. The previous summer, she had called Leigh from a women's shelter in St. Paul.

"You can stay with us," Leigh said. "Can you take the bus? Can I send you money so you can take the bus? You know it might be just as cheap to fly."

"No no. I'm okay. Cody and Wilma said I can stay here as long as I need to. I just hate not having a phone. I worry I'll miss Ellis calling."

Leigh sighed. Ellis was Pam's oldest son; he'd been in Iraq for almost a year. "You can give him our number. It would be easier for you to get to the bus station, right? I think I can buy you a ticket on the computer, and they can hold it for you there. When can you come? Can you come tomorrow? You'll have to stay on the phone so I can tell you what time."

Pam made a soft groaning sound. The person yelling in the background had gotten louder. "This is why I didn't want to call. You're always bailing me out. Gary probably thinks I'm the biggest mooch."

It wasn't true. Neither Leigh nor Gary minded the bailing. But Leigh imagined the bailing didn't feel good for Pam, always being the one with the hard luck, teetering on the edge of the abyss.

"No," she said. "You don't understand. We need you to come. There was an accident." She heard herself talking, saying the words. When she said Bethany's name, her voice broke.

For several seconds, there was only silence.

"Pam? Are you there?"

"Oh Kara. Oh. Poor Kara."

"Yes," Leigh said. *Not to mention the dead girl,* she thought. *And me too. There's me.*

"I'll come right away. I'll come tonight. Go check the computer. I'll take a bus tonight if there is one."

Leigh leaned over to open the hutch and turn on the computer, the phone still pressed against her ear. She glanced back out the window. The figures on the deck seemed blurred, and she couldn't make out Kara's face at all. Still, she already felt stronger, now that Pam was coming. She already didn't feel so alone. Her sister floundered through life, moving from one hardship to the next, hapless with men and money. But she was the closest thing Leigh had ever had to a mother, the kind she'd wanted, at least.

Chapter 10

WHEN LEIGH WAS IN high school, she worked behind the counter of the Dairy Maid in Eureka, Kansas—part-time during the school year, full-time in the summer. The Dairy Maid was like any other fast-food restaurant in town, paying low enough wages to attract only the young and inexperienced; but it was different in that, because of the feminine nature of its name, and because of the life-sized statue of a Swedish-looking and very voluptuous farm girl that doubled as a microphone for the drive-thru, hardly any males in Eureka applied to work there. The resulting fact of the Dairy Maid's workforce being made up almost entirely of high school girls was not lost on certain kinds of Eureka men. The girls' uniforms—polyester pants and white shirts with baby blue vests sewn over them—weren't exactly revealing, but that might have been part of the charm. On any given weekend afternoon, several Creepy Old Guys, or COGs, as the girls called them, would take position in the Dairy Maid's booths, trying to strike up a conversation with whichever Dairy Maid employee was unlucky enough to be charged with refilling the salt and pepper shakers, wiping down the tables, and mopping the floor. *How old are you, anyway? Yeah? You look a lot older than that. I'm trying to think of what movie star you remind me of.* They also showed up in the drive-thru, eyes moving over Dairy

Maid shirts to the Dairy Maid name tags. *I'd love some fries with that, Darcie. That's a pretty name, by the way.*

Leigh, mimicking the other girls, pretended to be disgusted and annoyed. But in truth, she looked forward to the nights she worked the drive-thru or the dining area. For one, it was more interesting than just staring down into a fry vat all night. For another, some of the Creepy Old Guys weren't really that old. Some of them could have been college boys, if there had been a college in town. There was one who couldn't have been much older than twenty, who was nice to Leigh in particular, or at least it seemed that way, most of the time. His name was Mitch. He'd told her that. He drove a pickup truck, and he did some kind of work that made him very sweaty and also very tan, so his light eyes looked like they were burning, glowing, when he looked at her through the drive-thru window. One day, he looked and looked at her without looking away, and though this was unnerving when it happened, after he'd taken his food and change and his truck had rumbled away, Leigh felt giddy. She had recently come to the hard understanding that she was not going to be beautiful. Her hair was no good, her eyes too small. But if she turned her head just right, in the right kind of light, she could almost still be pretty. She'd just read *Jane Eyre*, so she knew it was possible to be poor and plain and still have someone love you.

So it hurt her feelings when she heard the other Dairy Maids talking about Mitch, complaining about him, calling him a COG. They thought his stare was creepy. He stared at all of them, it turned out, avoiding only the real hard-luck cases—the obese, the moderately disabled, and the manager, Bonnie, who was well into her thirties. Leigh consoled herself with the idea that he'd at least found her attractive in some vague, interchangeable way. At school, she seemed to have been deemed undesirable on the basis of some strange code that she did not understand. She still read books during lunch, and in gym class, she partnered up with the pregnant girl or the girl who chewed tobacco and lined her eyes with a ballpoint pen. Out of all the places she had lived, Eureka had been the hardest place to make friends. The Dairy Maid was the closest thing she had to a social life, somewhere to go on Friday and Saturday nights. She could be funny at work, even around the Dairy Maids who were popular at school. She felt more relaxed and chatty, knowing she had a reason to be there, and something to busy herself with if another girl ignored her.

But it wasn't a good job for making money. You couldn't support yourself with it. When Leigh's mother announced she was moving to California, moving there by herself, Leigh tried to explain this. She made only minimum wage. A month of paychecks wouldn't even cover rent for the apartment.

Her mother assured her she would manage. "The lease here is up in August," she told Leigh. "And it's not like you need two bedrooms anyway. You should move in with your sister." She was distracted, packing only her warm-weather clothes into a suitcase, tossing her cold-weather clothes into a pile by Leigh's feet. "I'm sure she'll be glad to have you. She'll need some help with the baby. I can tell you right now, that Danny isn't going to be much of a dad."

Leigh didn't want to move in with Pam. She was living with Danny in his parents' trailer, parked in a little patch of yard behind their house. A month earlier, she'd given birth to Ellis, a pretty, pink-faced baby who looked so much like his mother that Danny's parents requested a paternity test. If Pam had been insulted, she didn't say so. She'd needed the parents on her side. Danny had already turned sulky and brooding, sneaking up to the house some nights to sleep in his boyhood room.

"I tell you what," her mother said. She held a sweater up to her neck and looked at the mirror before she tossed it into the no-go pile. "If you want, you can clean this place for the security deposit.

But you've got to do a good job." She spoke with marked effort, as if she were trying to explain something very simple to someone very stupid, someone who needed to be led by the hand in every aspect of life. "That alone should cover a deposit on a smaller place, with a couple months' rent left over." When she looked up and saw Leigh's face, she clicked her tongue and rolled her eyes. "I'll leave you the vacuum, okay?"

In early July, Leigh's mother gave her a tight hug in front of her car, which was already packed, facing outward, gassed up for the first leg of the trip. At sixteen, Leigh was several inches taller; she first registered her mother's tears as a dampness against her own neck. It took her a moment to understand, to believe they were really there. When she did, she was too stunned to speak.

"You're my good girl," her mother whispered. "I love you." When she stepped back, she was looking up at Leigh and really crying, her smile wide and unguarded, her mascara starting to run. For a moment, Leigh felt hopeful.

"I'm almost forty years old," she said. "Forty years old, and I've never gotten to do what I want. You won't ever know what that's like. I know you don't understand this, but that's because you have no idea what that's like."

Still wiping away her tears, her mother got into her car, and, blowing just one kiss out the window, really just drove away.

LEIGH STARTED CLEANING THAT night. She made several trips up and down the apartment building's stairway, carrying her mother's winter clothes to the Dumpster in the back. She threw away chipped plates and paper cups and folders of school work and old food from the refrigerator. It was just the beginning. Every day for more than a week, she came home from her shifts at the Dairy Maid, still smelling of french fry grease and chocolate sauce, and cleaned. She moved her little radio from room to room, depending on where she was working; the music kept her company. She took down the blinds and washed them in the tub. She scrubbed the kitchen floor. She cleaned the oven, the stove. She used a knife to pry off the pool of wax that had hardened on the edge of the tub after Pam had burned a candle there. She vacuumed.

She wasn't sure what to do with the remaining furniture. The Salvation Army agreed to come pick up the couch and the dining room table and the twin beds that were still in what had been Leigh and Pam's room, but they had no need or room for her mother's queen bed. Leigh slept there for the last few nights of July, waking in darkness when she heard strange sounds, someone moving around in the apartment downstairs. She would get up to check the locks on the door, the locks on the windows in the empty rooms.

THE NEXT TIME MITCH came through the drive-thru, Leigh leaned through the window and asked him if he ever moved furniture. "I was thinking, you know, you have a truck. I have to move a bed out of my apartment." She was conscious of calling it her apartment, as if she'd always lived there by herself.

He didn't answer at first. But he stared hard at her, as if no one else existed, as if he were completely unaware of the other girl working the drive-thru with her, who was looking at Leigh and shaking her head in tiny, almost imperceptible movements.

"I might be able to help you with that," he finally said. His voice was low, so adult sounding. She almost lost her nerve.

"Maybe you know someone who would want to buy it?" She leaned through the window, her elbows outside, so she couldn't see the other girl at all. "It's a good bed, nothing wrong with it. Queen-size. But I don't need a lot of money for it. I just need it moved out."

He nodded as if he understood not just what she was telling him, but everything she had not said. "I'll ask around," he said, taking his food and then his change.

When she turned around, Bonnie, the manager, was right behind her, glittery eye shadow settled into the wrinkles on either side of her squinted eyes. "That's not a good idea," she said. "You don't want some strange man coming to your apartment. Will your mother be there?"

Leigh nodded. She knew what she was doing.

But Bonnie frowned, looking through the drive-thru window, where now there was just empty space. "There's something wrong with that guy. Plenty of girls around here his own age. He doesn't need to be coming here and looking at you girls all the time."

Sour grapes, Leigh thought. For the rest of her shift, she could almost hear herself humming.

The next day, Mitch stopped by the front counter to tell her he'd found someone who would pay thirty dollars for the bed. He'd split it with her. She agreed, but he kept looking at her, as if he were unsure what she'd said, as if she had spoken in code.

She looked over her shoulder to make sure Bonnie wasn't around. "But you bring the beer," she said, pointing at him, her voice as offhand and playful as she could make it.

Saying that changed everything. It was like putting on a costume. Just like that, she could become someone else.

BUT WHEN MITCH WAS actually at the apartment, sitting beside her on the living room floor and drinking the beer she'd told him to bring, she was scared. He'd already been married, he told her, and his ex-wife was a psychotic bitch. He had two little boys he never got to see. He worked construction, mostly putting shingles on roofs. He was saving up money to buy a bass guitar. He finished one beer, and then another, and then another. Leigh did the best she could to keep up. But beer didn't taste the way she'd thought it would. He had nice lips, she decided, plump and pink, like a doll's. She tried to focus on them. He pointed at the pile of books in the corner. "Those yours?"

She nodded. Her lips felt rubbery, and she didn't trust herself to speak. Her radio was plugged in next to her. The Bee Gees sang "How Deep Is Your Love?"

"You read them all?"

He seemed incredulous. She looked at the books. There were three. She had just finished the big one, *Moll Flanders*.

"I never fucking read," he said. "I get bored."

"Well." She focused on his lips. "I've had a lot of free time lately."

They were quiet for a while, just the radio playing. He was looking at her when the song ended. "You're cute as hell," he said.

It was so nice, hearing that. She was wearing a T-shirt and shorts, and she looked better than she did in her uniform, her toenails painted, her legs shaved and smooth. She was getting better-looking maybe, growing into herself. She took another sip of beer. It would be nice to have a boyfriend, someone to stay the night.

But when they went into her mother's bedroom, where the queen bed sat, unclothed and enormous, the only piece of furniture left, she got nervous again. "It's so nice of you to help me," she kept saying, moving to the far side of the bed as if she meant to lift one side, as if she were strong enough to be of consequence. Then she felt dizzy, and it seemed the only thing to do was to lie down, and the bed was right there. He lay down, and she turned toward him, and then things happened quickly. His mouth was cold from the beer, and his tongue moved inside her mouth in a jerky, mechanical way, but his hands were warm against her skin, under her shirt, over her back. Everything felt the way she'd thought it would, a series of movements, a slight giving way. What really held her attention was the idea of what she was doing.

I'm not your good girl, she thought.

When it was over, she felt embarrassed, being naked with no sheets to cover herself. She went into the bathroom to dress. When she came out, he was already dressed too. He tugged the mattress down the hallway to the front door and then outside, down the concrete steps to his truck while she took a screwdriver to the frame.

He helped her carry the legs of the frame down to his truck. When it was all packed in, the tailgate up, he looked at her through narrowed eyes. "That was kind of weird," he said.

"Yeah." She nodded and looked away. She didn't know what else to do. She shifted her weight, searching for any feeling of change. She'd thought she would feel more different.

"It was kind of weird," he said again, more talking to himself. "I've kind of...uh...got a girlfriend." He pointed back up at the apartment. "I would have told you. I didn't know that was going to happen." He frowned. "It was pretty much your idea."

"Right," she said. "Can I have my money now? For the mattress?" She held out her hand. She kept her eyes lowered until he laid a five and a ten on her palm. She felt a sadness creeping up on her, something familiar and expected. She rearranged her thinking to hold it off.

"You know I'm only sixteen."

He feigned surprise, his plump lips parting.

"Oh shit," he said. "You're kidding."

"So I wouldn't tell anyone about this if I were you." It was like putting on another costume, saying these tough words, though she could hear her own voice shaking. "And don't come back to the restaurant. Ever."

"Okay," he said. He backed away from her, palms raised. His eyes were wide, and now he seemed younger than she felt. He stumbled getting into his truck, hitting his chin on the door. Before he drove away, he looked at her through the back window. "Fucking psycho," he said.

Her legs shook as she made her way back up the concrete steps, but she was fine, she decided. She didn't like him anyway. She was an adult now. And the bed was moved. It had to be done.

She took a shower, the bathroom door open so she could hear the little radio in the living room. "Hot Child in the City" came on, and as she washed her hair, she moved her hips in and out of the water, singing along. She told herself that she was the hot child in the city, a seductress using her youth and beauty to get men to do things like move heavy furniture for her. And she was mean and strong, threatening them into silence. For a while, she felt good.

But when she got out of the shower, there was no furniture to sit down on, just piles of clothes that she would have to pack and move somewhere—she didn't know where yet. She stood for a while with a towel wrapped around her. She looked at herself in the mirror that she had looked in every morning before school for almost a year and considered, the excitement already leaving her, that she looked the same. Nothing had changed. She was not hot. She was not in a city. And despite her best efforts, standing there by herself in the apartment, she still felt like a child.

SHE DIDN'T GET THE money for the security deposit. The landlord, sympathetic but firm, explained that her mother owed back rent—he showed her his records, the neat columns of numbers. He thanked Leigh for cleaning the apartment. "That shows integrity," he told her, patting her back, as if he were giving her something she could use. "You don't get the money, okay, but you can feel proud that you cleaned up after yourself." He stopped, considering. "And them."

It was a long walk to Pam's with her suitcases. The sun was out, hot. By the time she arrived, she was crying. Pam and Danny were sitting out on the front step with the baby. Leigh told them what had happened, pacing in the narrow yard between the trailer and the house. She was still crying, but it was all rage, no sadness.

"Your mom is a real bitch," Danny said. "I knew that the second I met her." Danny spoke almost exclusively in declarative sentences: *We're out of chips.... I'm tired.... My mom says I seem stressed out.... The baby's up.* He didn't like Leigh and Leigh didn't like him, but on this occasion, she appreciated his good judgment.

"I'm sure she didn't know," Pam said. "I'm sure she thought you would get the deposit." Ellis was asleep on her lap, his tiny face shaded by a tree. "Come sit down. Come inside. It'll be okay. I'll make you some lemonade."

But Leigh didn't want to go inside. She continued pacing. Her anger felt energizing, even after the long walk in the heat. She couldn't let go of it—the hours she'd spent cleaning, scrubbing on her hands and knees. She wanted to undo it. She wanted to go back and use her spare key to get into the apartment. She would track mud in, smash the polished light fixtures, and let the glass fall to the floors.

But that wouldn't help anyone, Pam pointed out. That wouldn't fix anything at all.

Danny went inside, but Pam continued to try to talk Leigh down, her voice soft, soothing. She talked to Leigh the same way she talked to the baby. "Come sit down," she said. "Come on, now. I'm sure it was just an accident."

Years later, when their lives had started to turn out so differently, Leigh would think back to that hot day in front of Danny Lipper's parents' trailer, considering the different ways she and her sister had thought about what their mother had done. At the time, she had wished she could be more like Pam. She had always admired Pam's placid nature, just as she had admired her beauty. Both assets seemed foreign and unattainable: Leigh's indignation was simply there, a pressing force, as real and as unavoidable as her smaller eyes and flatter chest.

And later, she would wonder if her very anger was what had saved her. It was hard to know what, exactly, had kept her life from melting into one more like Pam's. Some of it was luck—she could have gotten pregnant that first time with Mitch. But after that, it was something else. She made other mistakes. She was as desperate for love and affection as her older sister had been, and in some ways, more vulnerable to flattery. But unlike Pam, when it came right down to it, she always protected herself: *you've got to wear something, pull out now.* She understood that the authority in her voice was linked to her sense of justice—she had suffered enough, and she would suffer no more. She was needy and awkward and eager to please, but in the end, when it mattered, she was committed to self-preservation.

OR IT MIGHT HAVE just been that Pam went first, and Leigh got to watch and learn. She saw what it was like to have a baby but no money. Pam was a tireless mother. She didn't get frustrated when Ellis cried, even when she was going on little sleep from being woken many times in the night. She carried him around in a sling, saying *sh sh sh* in the Laundromat, in the grocery store, in the trailer, on long walks into town. Leigh watched her with awe and sympathy, and also with a growing conviction that she herself would not have children, not anytime soon, at least.

She'd read somewhere that when a pair of deer crossed a highway, the buck often stayed back and let the doe go first. Leigh thought of Pam this way sometimes, a gentle doe, the unwitting martyr to her younger sister's success. Yet it didn't seem right, to think of her sister, with all her beauty and generosity and kindness, as a bloody carcass on the highway, the white flash of a cautionary tale.

But Pam was always making bad decisions, and depending on her was hard. After Danny left, his parents said Pam and Leigh and the baby could stay in the trailer. They changed their minds when Pam started seeing Trevon. They loved their grandson, they said, but they couldn't have some black man and his friends hanging around their property. Trevon helped them find an apartment. He went back to his wife, and Pam started seeing Jeff. And then it was Gil. The boyfriends blurred together in Leigh's mind—she forgot their faces and voices and recalled only their transgressions: the one who left Pam, the one who stole from her, the one who threatened to set her on fire. She was always saying she'd had enough. "I'm done," she would tell Leigh. "I'm all done with these bad guys. I am." But she was never done. Whenever Leigh thought of her sister in those days, she pictured her with her arm outstretched, her hand open, waiting to grasp whoever came along, whoever could use a lift.

It was around that time, during her senior year, that Leigh decided she would take steps so her own life would be different.

BUT THERE WAS NO money for college. The thousand dollars her mother had given her might have covered one semester, but Leigh spent most of it her senior year, helping Pam with bills and groceries. She stayed at the Dairy Maid through the school year, fifteen hours a week. In May, she considered her options. There would be no scholarship to save her, no benefactor who knew her secret worth. She berated herself for not trying harder in school, for not always doing her homework. It had been hard to find the time to do it—there was work, and on weekends, she'd watched Ellis so Pam could waitress on the best shifts.

And then just before she graduated, she saw an ad in the back of a magazine for nannies. The agency was looking for Midwestern girls to work for families on the East Coast. The successful applicant was promised $250 a week plus room and board. Leigh went to work on the numbers. She deducted for taxes, vacation time, and still the final amount for fifty-two weeks seemed impressive. She was under no delusions. She knew caring for small children was hard work. But it had to be easier than the army. Cosmetology school was out. She would feel like her mother. The chemicals would make her think of her, the way she'd smelled.

She went to the interview conference in Kansas City. Most of the girls had already worked in a few placements, and they had horror stories—unpaid overtime, grueling housework. The mothers, they said, were bitchy or crazy or condescending; the fathers lecherous or easily provoked or both. Leigh thought of the money she would make and smiled through her interview, assuring the panel that she loved children. Within a month, she was on a flight from Wichita to Philadelphia, where she would spend the next year as a nanny for the Aubrey-Gold family, whom she imagined as the cruelest people in the world, just to prepare herself.

But for the first time in her life, she was surprised by her good fortune. The Aubrey-Golds were nice to her. They were lawyers, both of them, talkative and friendly. They worked in the same building on different floors. At first, they teased Leigh about what they thought of as her accent, but when they saw it hurt her feelings, they stopped. They asked her about Kansas, about Arkansas, about all the places she'd lived. They took her out to dinner, a few times without the children. They had a nineteen-month-old son, Max, and a four-year-old daughter, Stella, and though Leigh's days with the children were long and exhausting, she liked both children, and they seemed to like her. One of the parents was usually home by six, and Leigh could go up to her room and rest. She had her own bathroom, three evenings off a week, and one weekend day totally free. Sometimes she went out. The nanny agency had given her the phone numbers of other nannies, and there were always mixers and outings to restaurants and museums. But she didn't go to these often—she was intent on saving her money. Some Saturdays she walked to a café and made a mocha latte last two hours, sipping slowly, so she could read or watch people or listen to them talk around her. She went to see the Liberty Bell and Independence Hall.

But mostly, she stayed in her room, reading. She liked that she could hear the Aubrey-Golds through the walls, their boisterous voices as they got the children ready for bed. Mrs. Aubrey-Gold was funny and loud, easy to hear as she read Max stories about moons and gorillas. But it was Mr. Aubrey-Gold that Leigh listened for. He gave Stella a bath sometimes, and Leigh could hear him through the wall, his pleasant, gentle voice encouraging her to tell him about her day, to tell him what her favorite color was, her favorite number.

Leigh thought she was in love with him. She thought about him all the time, which was odd, because he was short and pudgy, almost fat, and probably twenty-five years older than she was. She loved his voice. She loved that he never yelled, not really, not in a frightening way. She loved how the children, when they were on the sofa watching videos, rested on his lap as easily as they rested on their mother's. Leigh couldn't tell if the marriage was a completely happy one. The Aubrey-Golds fought sometimes, but only at night, after the children had gone to bed, and they kept their voices low, so it was hard for Leigh to hear what they were saying, even with her ear pressed hard against the vent. But she decided they probably weren't that happy. They had been married a long time, and Mrs. Aubrey-Gold didn't always listen to him when he talked. The few times he and Leigh were alone together, she found herself leaning forward a little, her eyes heavy on his. If he noticed this, he didn't let on. He kept his hands in his pockets and walked away, whistling, oblivious, or maybe not.

After a while, by March, certainly, Leigh was grateful for his passive refusal. She didn't want to mess up a family, not one she admired so much. And if she really thought about it, it wasn't Mrs. Aubrey-Gold whom she envied—it was Stella. It would be such a luxury, she imagined, growing up with a father like that. Some nights, it felt like a taunt to Leigh, to lie in that bed and have to listen to the bathwater running and Stella's laughter, how bright it sounded, how sure.

IN THE END, SHE would later decide, all that envy had been good for her. It was perhaps the most valuable thing she came away with from her year in Philadelphia, more important, maybe, than the ten thousand dollars she managed to save for school. The Aubrey-Golds had given her a glimpse of the possibilities for her own future. There was no law that said she had to have her mother's life, or even Pam's. She would go to a university, and she would graduate before she got pregnant. She would be funny and warm, with a respectable job, nothing like her mother. And she would marry a man who knew how to be a father. She had a plan, and she would stick to it. Her children would thank her someday.

SHE WENT BACK TO Kansas for school. KU was the cheapest option, since she still qualified for in-state tuition, and since she wanted to go to a university, not a community college; at the time, the distinction seemed important. But even in Kansas, even with ten thousand dollars, she couldn't afford the dorm. All through college, she lived with various roommates in a small apartment off-campus.

It wasn't bad. Her favorite roommate, Deirdre, had been thrown out of the dorms for smoking pot. The week she moved in with Leigh, she found a dozen pigment-dyed sheets at a garage sale, and she and Leigh hung them on the walls and draped them from the ceiling. They were a fire hazard, certainly, especially since Deirdre still smoked, but they gave the bare, tiny rooms a bedouin feel, and although Leigh was an education major and Deirdre was undecided, they considered themselves artistic. It was helpful to think of themselves this way, young bohemians, dismissive of wealth and real furniture. Leigh slept on a mattress someone else had thrown out. Deirdre—whose parents had cut off financial support because of her falling grades—slept in a sleeping bag on the floor. They ate ramen noodles for dinner. In the mornings, they snuck into the dorm cafeteria and grabbed boxes of cereal, their heads lowered, the hoods of their coats pulled over their foreheads. They cut each other's hair and made fun of the girls in the sorority across the street. Every autumn, the sorority girls would stand on the lawn with the new pledges and sing their songs and do their special hand claps. Leigh's bedroom window faced the sorority, and she would have to play her radio loud to drown them out.

She was a serious student. She took sixteen credits every semester. She tried to take twenty credits once, thinking she might try to finish early. But she couldn't manage it, not with waiting tables on the weekends. She resigned herself to four years and tried to budget accordingly. She envied the students who had more breathing room in their schedules: she stared wistfully at pamphlets in the study abroad office, at the course catalog for the English Department. She didn't allow herself to major in English. It wasn't practical. With an education major, she would be able to find a job right out of college. *There's always a need for teachers,* her adviser had said. If she could have made herself be completely practical, she would have majored in accounting or gone to nursing school. But she was bad with numbers, clumsy with beakers. And as an education major, she still got to take a few literature courses. It was a compromise.

She didn't really date. Deirdre, and the roommates who followed her, had boyfriends, boys they met in bars and Laundromats, soldiers on leave from Fort Riley. When the boyfriends came over to the little apartment, Leigh stayed in her room, reading or studying. She felt older than everyone, and not always in a good way. She developed a horizontal crease on her forehead not long after her twenty-first birthday. She grew more intolerant of the sounds of parties and laughter and sex and television that her little radio couldn't drown out.

But as a whole, she liked college. Her classes weren't so demanding, and she let herself take one literature course every semester. Walking across campus, she would catch glimpses of her reflection in the glass of a window or a door, and she had to smile at her determined gait, at her book bag slung over her shoulder. She was breaking new ground. No Voe or Hesse had carried books around a campus before, not as far as she knew. She was the turning point in her family line, the beginning of something good.

STILL, SHE FELT SORRY for herself sometimes. At the beginning of every school year, when the sorority pledges moved into the beautiful sorority house, she would watch from her window. The girls arrived with parents who took pictures of them with their suitcases and helped them carry bicycles and stereos and plastic laundry baskets of books and pillows up to their rooms. In the evening, there was a mother-daughter mixer on the lawn—the mothers wore corsages and sang a good luck song to the girls, reading the lyrics from paper programs that eventually blew across the street. Leigh had picked up one of the programs and brought it in to show Deirdre. They made fun of the song, changing the lyrics and singing in squeaky voices. Deirdre, high at the time, had thought it was very funny. But the next year, Leigh was alone the night of the sorority's mother-daughter mixer, and there was no one to make fun of the song with, so she sat by her window, listening to the singing in her dark little room, angry and embarrassed when the first tears formed behind her eyes. By then she was a junior, and she knew that some of the sorority girls would be in her classes. Some of them would be English majors, and some of them, still riding the wave of their mothers' best wishes, would occasionally raise their hands in class, and much to Leigh's surprise and dismay, say things that sounded smart.

DURING HER SENIOR YEAR, she went to a benefit dinner for KU's Students Against Hunger. The president of the group—an earnest daughter of Mennonites from western Kansas—was Leigh's roommate at the time, and so Leigh felt obligated to buy a ticket and go, though she doubted she would get her money's worth of food: the meals served, her roommate explained, would vary in quality and quantity to represent the unequal distribution of hunger in the world. Eighty percent of ticket holders would get rice and water. Fifteen percent would get rice and beans and water. And five percent—the lucky first worlders—would get steak or salmon and a salad and a potato with a choice of beverage, including wine. "It's basically a raffle," her roommate said. "You might win big, but probably not." Leigh wasn't feeling that lucky. She had a sandwich before she went. That turned out to be smart, because when she arrived, the line for the food was already long and once she got to the front, her roommate, who was all business, not willing to pull any strings, informed her she would get the third world portion of rice. Leigh went to the assigned kettle and watched as a small beige lump was dumped on her plate. She felt guilty for eating the sandwich earlier, for not being willing to endure the banquet's real lesson for even a short time. She was given a cup of water and directed to a seat at a table where people were already eating. She wasn't allowed to choose her own seat. She found out later from her roommate that the organizers had intentionally made the haves sit by the have-nots, so people couldn't cluster according to fortune and ignore the inequities, the way they did in the real world.

The other people at her table all seemed to know each other, and they were talking seriously, picking at their plates of rice. Only one of them, a tall man in a sweatshirt sitting next to the empty chair, had a steak and salad in front of him. When Leigh sat down, he looked at her plate. "Oh good," he said. "More awkwardness. Welcome." But he looked happy to see her, and Leigh smiled back. She'd seen him before—around the English Department, at readings. He was a graduate student, she imagined—he looked to be in his late twenties, already losing his hair. She liked his face, how open and friendly it was, as if he fully expected that she, or maybe anyone, would want to talk to him. He said he'd seen her at readings and lectures, and that he'd thought she was a graduate student too. He was a doctoral student in literature, he said, from Massachusetts. His focus was Shakespeare. His name was Gary Churchill.

"What a name," she said. "Churchill, I mean." She was surprised at how comfortable she felt. Usually she was shy, especially with strangers, male and female alike. She had a book in her purse. She'd planned on reading it while eating. She wondered if she should get it out now, to show him he didn't have to talk to her if he didn't want to.

"Yeah. My dad says we're distantly related to him. My mother doesn't believe him. They named their cat Winston, though." He rolled his eyes. He had an accent that made her think of the Aubrey-Golds. It wasn't quite the same, but he sounded more like them than she did. "They love the joke. The cat's in the family Christmas picture every year." He pointed at his head. "Last year with a little Santa hat."

She swallowed some rice. She liked the way he talked, so quickly, the words just sailing out of his mouth, one after the other, no thought, no worry. She could envision his parents, still married, still sharing a cat and inside jokes. She could picture the Christmas card.

"What about your name? Voe... How do you spell that?"

She spelled it.

"What is that? English? French?"

"I don't know." She took a sip of water. It was her father's name, probably shortened from something. He was living somewhere in Georgia, with a new wife and a new baby. Pam had tried to call him on Thanksgiving.

"You want to split this?" Gary Churchill nodded down at his dinner. "It'd make me feel a whole lot better. I can't eat in front of someone not eating," he said. "Here. Have the potato."

He tried to fork it over to her plate. Leigh's roommate, standing at the front of the room, shook her head and clapped her hands. "No sharing!" she said brightly. Her eyes were hard on Leigh's.

Gary looked at the potato still perched on his fork.

"You're a socialist," Leigh said. "They have to be firm with you. Stop the revolution now." She heard the sly tone in her voice. It was so unlike her, to try to be witty. But she felt witty. It was as if his ease and confidence were rubbing off on her. It was like someone else yawning, making her yawn.

He smiled, his eyes moving over hers. "No," he said. "Not a socialist." He waited until her roommate wasn't looking and tossed the potato onto her plate. "Just a soft heart."

THEY SPENT THEIR FIRST few dates going to free readings and sneaking into the dorm cafeteria to eat dinner. He was as poor as she was then, at least on the surface. He had health insurance—his parents paid the premium. But he had no car, and his apartment was smaller and sadder-looking than hers was. The showerhead didn't work, and the water came out of the bath faucet so slowly it took more than a half hour to fill the tub. They slept on a fold-out couch in his living room. He had a bedroom, and a bed, but it was covered in a neat grid of CVs and cover letters addressed to various universities and colleges.

"My God," Leigh said, seeing them for the first time. "How many places are you applying to?"

"Twenty-four." He leaned down and straightened one of the piles. "Everybody wants to teach Shakespeare. I should have picked something else."

She glanced at one of the pages and grimaced. "Danby State?"

"It's a job."

"Yeah, but you'd have to live in Danby.... Have you ever been there?" Leigh had never been there, actually. But she knew where Danby was on the map, west of Topeka, way out there on the interstate where everything flattened out. Between the two of them, she was the native Midwesterner, and she felt it her duty to warn him.

"I wouldn't mind a smaller college, to tell you the truth." He frowned at some of the other piles. "At some of these bigger places, there's more prestige, more money, but you have to publish all the time. There's a lot of pressure. I want a more rounded life, you know? I want to teach. But I want a family. I want to be able to live."

She nodded, her eyes moving over the piles of papers on the bed, then up to his face, the slope of his temple. She was listening closely.

"I mean, I want to have kids, and I want to be able to play ball and do stuff with them every now and then. My dad is all right, but he's a doctor, a workaholic. I remember just wishing we could watch a ball game some time. We went to Fenway Park together just once, the whole time I was growing up." He looked at Leigh, embarrassed. He knew her story, her background. "I don't mean to whine," he said. "My dad is okay. Nice to my mom. Overall, we're pretty good to each other."

When he looked up, she turned away. She was worried her face would reveal all the longing she felt.

Eventually, she would be found out. They would joke about it later, looking at their wedding picture, which they would keep on the mantle in the living room of their house in Danby, Kansas. "The cat that ate the canary," Gary called it, and it was obvious, looking at the picture, that Leigh was the cat. In the picture, they stand in front of a borrowed car, the hem of Leigh's knee-length wedding dress blowing high in the wind. She is trying to hold the dress down, using both hands, but her arm is wrapped around Gary's. Her smile is enormous, all teeth, her eyes bright and full of surprise, as if it has just at that moment occurred to her that the life she'd always wanted has finally begun, that she has really pulled it off.

Chapter 11

WHEN KARA WAS FIRST born, Leigh tried to breast-feed. Nursing hurt more than she'd thought it would. The illustrations in the books she'd read during her pregnancy never showed the mother wincing, or a nipple, bloody and red. But Leigh ignored the pain and put Kara to her breast whenever she cried, because she had read that breast milk was best, and because that was the kind of mother she had decided she was going to be. But at Kara's first check-up, when she was still so small, only a week old, the nurses discovered she was losing weight. They put her writhing, naked little body on a scale before and after Leigh nursed her, and they discovered what the trouble was—Kara wasn't really nursing when she was at Leigh's breast. She was just sucking. Nonnutritive sucking, they called it. All that pain for nothing, Leigh thought.

The nurses told her to get a pump. That way Kara would still get breast milk. Leigh could give it to her in a bottle and measure how much milk Kara actually swallowed. It sounded like a good idea, but Leigh hated the pump, the humiliation of it, the now obvious correlation between herself and a dairy cow. And it was exhausting. Feeding Kara, which she did every three hours, day and night, took twice as long with the pump. Her milk started to dry up. It took her forty-five minutes to pump four ounces, and she had to do it when Kara was taking one of her fitful naps so it would be ready in a bottle when she woke. Kara would sometimes throw up the milk, and sometimes Leigh would cry, thinking how hard she had worked for each ounce now drying on the carpet, on the couch, on her robe. After three weeks, with Gary's encouragement, Leigh put the pump in the garage, switched to formula, slept more, and felt guilty about it for years.

It unnerved her, that first failure as a mother. She wondered what else she would do wrong. She consulted books and parenting magazines, but the accompanying pictures of mothers looking lovingly down at smiling babies only made her feel worse. She was always so tired, so worried. She felt sore and thin-skinned. She felt like a teenage babysitter, waiting for the real mother to come home.

"Of course you do," Gary's mother told her. "Everyone feels that way at first." She was a tall, thin woman, with Gary's kind eyes, her gray hair cut in a no-nonsense little cap that Leigh connected with being from New England. She and Gary's father had flown to Kansas when Kara was first born, and then just his mother had returned a month later. She'd been so helpful, tidying up the house while Leigh and the baby napped, doing the dishes and sterilizing the bottles, running to the store for diapers and wipes. "You should get some rest," she'd told Leigh. "Sleep when the baby sleeps." But that last visit, she was already acting strangely, laughing at odd times and forgetting Leigh's name. They didn't know it then, but she was showing the first signs of the tumor in her brain that would kill her in less than a year.

"I just don't feel like myself," she'd said, touching her temple lightly. At the airport, she'd held Kara close, touching her downy head with one finger. "I hate to leave you all like this," she said and gave Leigh a worried look. "Will your... mother... will she be visiting?"

Leigh shook her head and lowered her eyes. She felt so embarrassed around Gary's family. They didn't understand where her parents were. California and Georgia, Leigh had told them. And they had looked at Leigh as if that answer made no sense.

Leigh's mother had not completely ignored Kara's birth. She'd sent a gift—an entire box of dainty little baby clothes, brand-new, the tags still attached. She'd written, "I bet she's cute," on the back of a postcard with the San Diego skyline on the front. "Give her a kiss for me. Love Mom." It was the closing that weighed heavily on Leigh, the words *love* and *Mom* right next to each other. She tried to summon the anger that had carried her through the last few years, protecting her from the ignored birthdays and graduations, the invitations to California that had never come. But all she felt now, looking at her mother's postcard and holding her own child, was sadness. The baby had softened something in her, made it malleable again, vulnerable to hope. She kept imagining her mother would just show up one day. She would want to hold Kara and coo to her for hours, the way Gary's mother had done. Leigh understood it was a fantasy, but it was a fantasy she enjoyed. She pictured her mother looking down at Kara with a serene smile, her face almost unrecognizable, more like the smiles of the mothers in magazines than anything Leigh remembered from real life.

Pam came to see the baby. She brought Ellis, now seven; Rex, who was five; and Ryan, who had just started walking. Pam was on her own again. Ryan's father had some kind of mental illness—he was kind and funny when he took his medication, but he had stopped taking it when Ryan was born, and he'd disappeared not long after that. Pam and her boys had moved into public housing in St. Louis, all three boys sleeping in one room, garbage piled up on the stairway. Pam told the boys to quit talking about the garbage and assured Leigh and Gary she was fine. She nuzzled Kara and let her tug at her long hair. Pam had put on weight with each child, but her face was the same, lovely, and she wore the same blue eyeliner she'd worn in high school. "Hello you," she'd whispered to Kara, who seemed mesmerized by her aunt's wispy voice, or maybe her dangling earrings. "You're so lucky you got a girl," she told Leigh, whispering so the boys wouldn't hear her. But then she'd shaken her head, real fear in her eyes. "I didn't mean it like that," she said firmly, glancing upward, as if pleading to undo a curse. "I love my boys. I love them. I wouldn't trade them for anything in the world."

WHEN KARA WAS FIVE months old, she and Leigh developed acute bronchitis at the same time. Through much of the ordeal, Gary, who had only a hacking cough and a runny nose, took care of Kara so Leigh could rest. But in the afternoons, Leigh was on her own—Gary was up for tenure, and they'd agreed he shouldn't cancel any classes.

"We'll be okay," she assured him. She didn't sound convincing. She could barely lift her arm to wave good-bye. She sat at the table, wheezing, Kara crying in her arms. Her bathrobe was stained with cough syrup. On the table lay an impressive arsenal of medicine, Kara's prescriptions in one colorful pile, Leigh's in the other. There was a nebulizer and an asthma inhaler. Cough syrup. Benadryl. There was the sandwich Gary had made her for lunch, with exactly one bite missing. One bite had been all Leigh could manage.

"I'll be home by four," Gary said. He stood in the doorway, letting in the early May heat. He sniffed and coughed, maybe just to show solidarity. "I don't feel good about this. I think we should find a sitter until you're better."

She shook her head. She wasn't going to leave her sick child with a sitter. And anyway, a sitter wasn't in the budget. The new house was beautiful but full of problems, the roof already leaking. "Go on," she said. "We'll be fine."

Kara was still crying as Leigh watched the car back out of the driveway. She listened to her own wheezing breath and looked at her watch. She had to give Kara the medicine with the nebulizer again. She poured the vial of medicine into the machine and flipped on the switch, pressing the plastic mask over Kara's nose and wailing mouth. "It's okay," she whispered. "Sh sh sh." But Kara coughed and sputtered, her arms flailing. Three times, she managed to push the mask away.

Leigh dialed her pediatrician's phone number. She had it memorized. And the receptionist knew her voice. Leigh knew she annoyed them, calling so much. She didn't care. She needed to know what to do.

She asked to speak to a nurse.

"Your name please?"

"Leigh Churchill." She frowned, shifting Kara to her other arm. She hated the receptionist, eight months pregnant and glowing with health.

"Oh. Your voice sounds bad. You sound like a frog."

"Yes," Leigh said.

"Hold on."

The nurse came on in a moment. Leigh described Kara's frantic attempts to free herself from the nebulizer's mask. "I'm just worried she really can't breathe with it. How do I know if it's hurting her?"

"It's not hurting her. It's helping her. You have to do it. Three times a day for ten minutes."

"But how do I know if she can't breathe?" She was close to tears. She was having trouble breathing herself.

"You'll know, Mrs. Churchill. She'll turn blue. You'll know."

Leigh hung up the phone, turned on the nebulizer, and held the mask over Kara's nose and mouth. She looked at her watch to avoid Kara's ferocious glare. At ten minutes, to the second, Leigh lifted the mask. Kara let out a wail that Leigh believed bypassed her ears and went directly to her mind, piercing it like a small sword.

The phone rang.

"Leigh?"

"Yes." She moved the receiver to her other ear, away from Kara's mouth.

There was a pause. "Can I speak with Leigh Voe?"

"This is Leigh. I'm sick. I have bronchitis."

"Oh. Leigh. This is your mother."

Leigh cocked her head.

"Hello?"

"Yes," Leigh said. "I'm here." She ran her hand over Kara's head.

"Guess where I am?"

"California."

"Nope."

She coughed. "Then I can't guess."

"I'm in Kansas."

Now the voice sounded familiar, the coal country twang reemerged. Leigh looked out the window, at the cloudless blue sky. She'd taken a lot of medicine. And she was very tired. She might be dreaming this. But she never thought that when she was dreaming.

"I'm less than an hour away from your town. Heading in that direction!"

"Oh." It really was her mother, Leigh thought. It was her voice. But she sounded so happy, like a girl.

"Why didn't you tell me you were coming?"

"I wanted to surprise you. I've got another surprise, too. And I want to see my granddaughter. Pam says she's beautiful."

"Okay," Leigh said. Kara looked sleepy, her little fists rubbing at her eyes. She would go down for her nap soon. *Sleep when the baby sleeps.*

"Well..." Her mother laughed as if Leigh had said something funny, or maybe stupid. "I need to know how to get to your house. Can you give me directions from the interstate?"

"Yes," Leigh said. She had an odd, robotic feeling, as if she were just following commands, her destiny for the day, and maybe forever, already laid out before her. She looked at the front door. It was almost impossible to imagine her mother walking through it, into this house where she lived as an adult, where she herself was a mother. She looked out the front window and saw the front porch swing, the red tulips she had planted along the walkway. She heard herself saying the names of the roads leading to her house in the croaky voice no one recognized as hers.

Kara went down for her nap right away, and for the first time that morning, Leigh had two free hands. She still had a hard time cleaning; she just couldn't stand up for very long. She tried to vacuum sitting down, moving around on her knees. She leaned heavily against the counter as she did the dishes. She decided to prioritize: She didn't want to be wearing a stained bathrobe when her mother saw her. She changed into a shirt and jeans. They were clean—Gary had tried to keep up with the laundry.

But when Leigh looked in the mirror, she whimpered. It was almost summer, a bright sunny day, but her skin was drained of color, and her eyes looked small and tired. She hadn't showered for days. She brushed baby powder through her hair and put on lipstick. She didn't look right. She knew it, but there was nothing she could do. She made her way down the stairs slowly, holding on to the banister. The vacuum cleaner was still out where she'd left it. She leaned down to pick it up, but ended up sitting beside it. The floor felt magnetic, and soft against her cheek. She closed her eyes for just a moment.

When she opened them, the doorbell was ringing in a steady, quick beat. She got up and opened the door to find her mother and an old man staring at her as if she had frightened them.

"Well, there you are." Her mother laughed nervously, her hand at her throat. "We've been waiting out here for a while. Where were you? You knew we were coming."

Leigh blinked. It was really her. But she looked different. She was wearing a yellow sundress with a sweetheart neckline, like something a teenage girl from the fifties might have worn to a dance. She also wore an enormous white sunhat, the floppy brim falling over one of her eyes. She'd gotten heavier, a little thicker in the waist, but she also somehow seemed smaller, the brim of her hat level with Leigh's shoulders. Leigh shook her head. Of course. She herself had gotten taller. "I'm sorry," she said, resting her head against the door frame. "I fell asleep. I've been sick. Bronchitis." She looked at the old man. "Who...?"

Her mother covered her mouth and stepped back. "Bronchitis? Oh God. Are you contagious?"

"I don't think so. I don't think it works like that. Not at this point. We've had it for a while. Me and the baby."

"Well..." Her mother gave the man a nervous glance. "We'll be careful all the same." She put her hand on the man's arm and smiled up at Leigh. "This is Wayne." Her voice implied that Leigh knew all about Wayne and had been waiting for some time to meet him. Leigh extended her arm, and then, remembering that they were being careful, brought her hand up and waved. Wayne smiled. He wore wrap-around sunglasses, the lenses tinted yellow. The hair on his head was slicked back, dark brown, but the hair coming out of his ears was curly and gray. He wore khaki pants and a white Izod shirt that was stretched over his protruding belly so tightly that the little alligator on his chest appeared to be headed outward, toward Leigh.

Leigh looked at the black Cadillac in her driveway. Her mother smiled.

"Could I use your bathroom?" Wayne asked.

She ushered them in, making vague apologies as she directed

Wayne to the bathroom. She used her foot to roll the vacuum cleaner out of the way. Her mother stopped in front of the stairs, where Leigh had hung up framed photographs the way she'd seen in a magazine. There was a picture of Gary in a cap and gown, receiving his doctorate. There was another of Leigh in the delivery room, her eyes tired, her smile faint, looking down at Kara for the first time. By and large, Gary's family dominated the wall—black-and-white photos of both sets of grandparents in their younger days; his maternal grandmother in a bridal gown, smiling a crooked-toothed smile in front of a church in Ireland; his paternal grandfather looking pensively back into the camera's eye, wearing his navy uniform from World War II. And there were color shots of Gary as a child. In one, he stood between his parents and held up a small trophy—he'd told Leigh he couldn't remember exactly what the trophy was for, but in the picture, he looked ecstatic. There was another of Gary sitting with his brother on the front step of a house, both of them eating ice cream cones. His mother had stored her family's pictures in a neatly organized wicker basket that she kept under her bed in Boston. When Leigh asked if she could have some photographs, his mother had made copies and kept the originals.

"So where's my granddaughter?" Leigh's mother asked. She was still looking at the pictures. Her arms were folded, half her body turned away from the wall. She was still wearing the big hat. Leigh moved around to her side so she could see her face. It felt strange to see it so close, close enough to touch if she wanted to. She couldn't get over how small her mother looked. But she still gave off that tense, coiled feeling. And her gray eyes still seemed distant, preoccupied, never resting on one picture for too long.

"She just went down for her nap. She'll be up in an hour or so."

Her mother turned away a little, and the hat obscured her face again. "Must be a surprise for you, seeing me all of a sudden. I was working all the time up till I met Wayne. Now I'm finally going on vacations. He wants to take me to all these exciting places. I finally asked him this time if we could stop by Kansas City." She touched the frame of Leigh's wedding picture. "He said of course. Of course you want to see your girls."

Leigh said nothing, and her mother stayed turned away.

"Before that I was just working all the time, always working."

"Yes," Leigh said. She understood this was an apology, or something like it. It would be all she would get. She pointed at the picture of Gary at his hooding ceremony. "That's Gary. He'll be home by four. You could stay for dinner? You and . . . uh—"

"Wayne. We're starving now, to tell you the truth." She took off the sunhat. Her hair was blonder, and shorter, curly in front. "We almost stopped at that cute little steak house coming in on the highway, the one shaped like a big covered wagon? Wayne wants to go there for dinner. Is it any good?"

"We've never been." Leigh coughed. It was an impressive cough, full of mucus and pain. Her mother winced and stepped away.

"I could make you a little something now." Leigh put her finger to her forehead and tried to remember what was in the refrigerator. "I don't know what we've got. Gary's been doing all the cooking."

Her mother turned and raised her eyebrows. They were plucked thin, the edges drawn in with pencil. "He does the cooking? Must be nice."

"Well, just recently. I've been sick." Purposefully, she coughed again.

"Still . . ." Her mother turned away from the pictures in a slow circle, her eyes moving back over the living room. "I don't remember your father ever cooking anything." She nodded back at Gary's picture. "He's a professor?"

"Uh-huh." Leigh leaned against the wall behind her.

"So you don't even have to work."

"I work. I'm a teacher. I teach at the junior high here. I took maternity leave when Kara was born, and now it's almost summer, anyway. I'll go back in the fall."

Her mother smirked as if sharing a joke with herself. Leigh tried to think what could be funny. Something was different about her mother's face. She looked younger than Leigh remembered, though she was eight years older than when Leigh had last seen her. Her forehead was unlined, her gray eyes wide awake looking. Aside from the eyebrows, she looked pretty.

"Aren't you going to ask about Wayne?" Her mother nodded toward the hallway that led to the bathroom.

Leigh nodded, but said nothing. She couldn't stop looking at her mother's face.

"I don't want to tell you when he's in the bathroom. That's not how I planned it."

Leigh's eyes fell to the ring on her mother's left hand. "You're married?"

"Engaged." Her mother held her hand up so Leigh could see the ring. The diamond was enormous, twice the size of Leigh's. Things started to make more sense.

"He's just the nicest man," her mother said, holding the diamond up so it sparkled in the afternoon light coming in through the living room window. "We're actually on our way to Costa Rica. He has a place down there, in a sort of retirement place he likes to go to for a few months every year. There are a lot of Americans, he said. It won't be so different." Her eyes went wide, and she looked like a child. "But there are monkeys. Just running around. He showed me pictures. And oh my God, the beaches. So beautiful. Just so pure. I'm going to swim in the ocean every day."

Leigh coughed. She didn't need to cough as much as she was coughing. But when she coughed, she sounded as sick as she felt. "Kansas is on the way to Costa Rica?"

"No. That's my point, Leigh. I mentioned I wanted to see you girls, and he changed the tickets so we flew into Kansas City. Just like that. We saw Pam yesterday in St. Louis. Oh God," she said, groaning a little. "Each of those boys has a different daddy. Each one a different color."

Wayne appeared in the hallway, drying his hands on his khaki pants. He smiled at Leigh. "I've been through Kansas a million times, back when I was in sales. It's a very wide state."

"Wayne just retired from Yilon." Her mother sat lightly on the couch, fanning the skirt of her yellow dress around her. "You've seen their commercials? With the little elf? He started out in sales and worked his way up to vice president. They had a party for him last week, at a big hotel downtown. Downtown San Diego."

Wayne ducked his head, his lips in a slight curl, so that even with the wrinkled face and sagging jaw line, Leigh could see the boy in him, easily flattered, anxious to please. "Do you have anything to drink?" he asked. "We've been in the car a long time."

"Oh. Sorry. Of course. What would you like?" She considered the actual options. They had no wine, no soft drinks. They had formula, Gary's protein shakes, and orange juice.

"I'd love a Tab," her mother said. "Or anything diet. But I need caffeine."

Leigh shook her head. Her mother sighed and gazed out the window.

"I'll run get you one." Wayne was already walking toward the door, car keys jingling in his hand. He favored one leg heavily, like he had pain in his hip, or maybe his knee.

"You're a sweetheart," her mother called out. When he closed the door behind him, she rolled her eyes. "I bet he just wanted one for himself."

"He does seem nice," Leigh said. Her voice held no conviction. She was still trying to understand what was happening, to know what she was supposed to do and say.

"Oh, yes." Her mother nodded through the window at the Cadillac backing out of the driveway. "And that's just a rental. Back home he's got a Mercedes. Beautiful car. He lets me drive all the time. He doesn't really like to."

Kara wailed from her room. Her first cries after waking always sounded so plaintive, so distressed. Even if Leigh ran to her room immediately, she still felt negligent. "I'll be right down," she told her mother.

But to her surprise, her mother followed her up the stairs. When Leigh opened the door to Kara's room, her mother slid past her and reached the crib first, swooping down with outstretched arms. Kara stopped crying when she picked her up, and the two of them gazed at each other.

"She looks like me," her mother said. "She really does." She lowered her head and nuzzled Kara's tiny nose with her own.

Leigh nodded and leaned against the edge of the crib. Her mother looked around the room, at the clouds Leigh had stenciled onto the walls, at the lamp in the shape of a smiling bear, at the changing table that matched the crib. "Disposable diapers." She clicked her tongue. "What I would have given for that."

On the way down the stairs, she said something again about being hungry.

"Oh," Leigh said. "I'm sorry. I was going to make you something. If you keep holding her, I can."

"I could hold her forever," her mother said. But when they got into the kitchen, her mother said she needed a cigarette. "I'll hold it up high," she told Leigh, raising one hand. "I'll hold her down here."

"No. No, I'm sorry. You'll have to go outside."

Her mother pursed her lips. Something hard flashed in her eyes.

"It's Gary," Leigh said. "He's sensitive to smoke." This was a lie.

She was the one who hated the smell. She hadn't known it when she was young, breathing in her mother's cigarettes. Smoke had just been the air in the house—it was just what was. But now she couldn't be around it, and she certainly didn't want her baby breathing it in. "Plus we're sick," she added.

Her mother agreed to go smoke on the back deck. She handed Kara over to Leigh. As heavy as Kara felt, Leigh was glad to have her back, to look down at the little face that she loved. She turned her head when she coughed again. There was a block of cheese in the refrigerator, and some broccoli. She thought they had crackers somewhere. She hoisted Kara's weight on her hip and reached for a knife and a cutting board. She could feel sweat emerge from her hairline, and Kara felt heavier than usual. But she still had the dreamlike feeling of not making any choices, of simply doing without deciding. If this was a dream, she would have to figure out what it meant. She'd taken psychology, and she'd read a book on Freud. She would have to look at it again. She wanted to know what an unexpected visit from your mother represented, what preparing food symbolized, what sickness symbolized, what holding a baby meant.

Her mother's cheeks were pink when she came back in. "It's only May, and already so hot out there," she said, fanning her face with her hand. "It was the same way where I grew up. It never gets this way in California. Never too hot, never too cold. I just love it. Wayne says it's the same in Costa Rica."

Just then, Gary came in the side door from the garage. He had folders under one arm, a stack of books under the other, and the plastic handle of a bag of diapers clenched between his teeth. He looked as if he needed to set everything down very quickly, but he stood still in the doorway, looking at Leigh's mother, and then at Leigh, who was still holding the baby and trying to speak.

"This is my mom," Leigh finally croaked. "She surprised me." She smiled and wiped her brow with the back of her hand.

"Nice to meet you," her mother said. "Call me Anna. Oh my goodness." She put her hand to her chest. "You're a tall drink of water, aren't you?"

Gary opened his mouth, and the bag of diapers fell to the table. "Nice to meet you." He looked at her for only a moment before his gaze returned to Leigh. "What's going on here?"

Leigh gave him a blank look. He looked back at Leigh's mother. "She's sick. Did she tell you she was sick?"

Her mother nodded and took a piece of cheese off the cutting board. "She said she wasn't contagious."

He squinted down at her for several seconds before he again looked at Leigh. Whatever he saw in her face then had a decisive effect. He dumped the books and folders on the counter and held his arms out. "I'll take the baby," he said. "Go sit down." He looked at Leigh's mother and nodded toward the cutting board. "Maybe you could do that? She really isn't feeling well." He gave Leigh a hard look. "She should have told you."

"She told me." Her mother swallowed and took the knife from Leigh. If she knew he was angry, she didn't show it. If anything, she sounded a little coquettish, her head lowered, her eyes tilted up. "I was telling her how lucky she was, you doing the cooking. I remember being sick with my girls when they was little. I never got any help. I was taking care of other people's kids, in fact. Do you remember that, Leigh? I used to look after the Wansing twins." She shrugged. "I figured I was home watching you and Pam anyway. Might as well be bringing in money."

Leigh nodded. She didn't really remember the Wansing twins, but Pam had told her about them. The boy twin had found their mother's cigarette lighter and set fire to the drapes.

Her mother cut the broccoli in quick, efficient chops. "I'm just so happy to see how well little Leigh has done for herself." She looked up and glanced in every direction, referring, apparently, to the house. "I always encouraged her with her education, and now she's a teacher, you're a professor." She furrowed her brow. "I don't know why it didn't work with your sister. She's always been a train wreck, that one." She lowered her voice. "And she's let her looks go, that's for sure."

"I like Pam," Gary said. The words came out slow and deliberate. "She's nice." He shifted Kara to his other shoulder.

When Wayne came back from the store, he ended up in the living room, talking with Gary. Gary held Kara in such a way that Leigh could see her face through the open doorway. She appeared comfortable, even happy. Leigh smiled and tried to concentrate. She felt as if she'd been given a brief opportunity to photograph something her own mind had accused her of making up. Her mother was here, and so was her daughter, and so was her husband. Her mother had changed their travel plans, because she'd wanted to see Kara. Leigh looked out the window at the sunny blue sky. It would be cooler out in a few hours. If she were just feeling better, they could go on a picnic. They could go to the big park downtown where the college students played guitars and saxophones for money. She could picture it, she and her mother walking together, taking turns holding the baby, Gary and Wayne walking behind them. They'd walked like that with Gary's parents.

"There," her mother said, pushing the cutting board away from her. "You're all set for chopped broccoli and cheese." She glanced over the counter to Wayne. "But I think we'll head out for dinner ourselves."

"You're leaving?"

Both Gary and Wayne looked over, and Leigh touched her hand to her mouth. She hadn't meant to sound whiny.

"Well, we're hungry," her mother said. "Hungry hungry, for

steak. I already told you that." She lowered her voice. "And Wayne wants to eat there. I told him we would." She smiled, raising her voice again. "Why don't you come with us? We can bring the baby?"

Leigh frowned. They had taken Kara to a restaurant just twice since she was born. The first time, she'd screamed and cried, and they'd had to leave early. The second time, she'd thrown up on Leigh, and they'd had to leave early.

"Well, we'll come back," her mother said. She walked around the counter and found her hat where she had left it. "We have to be back in Kansas City by tonight. We've got an early flight to Houston in the morning, and then we're off to Costa Rica from there. But we'll stop back by here after we eat." She smiled, dropping the hat on her hair and then pushing it down. "We'll bring you something. Steak? Salad? Anything you want."

Leigh shook her head. *This is it,* she thought. *She's leaving again.*

"She hasn't been hungry," Gary said. Leigh turned to find he was just behind her, leaning against the wall. He was still holding Kara, rocking her slowly from side to side, his fingers flat against her back.

"Oh." Her mother took a pair of sunglasses out of her purse and slid them on. "Well. Would you like anything, Gary? Then you won't have to cook tonight."

He shook his head, his eyes looking hard into the dark lenses of her glasses. All at once, Leigh felt everything about the day change. Until that moment, she hadn't been able to clearly judge what was happening. Her mother was all she'd known of mothers. But looking at Gary's face, seeing the disgust in his eyes, she understood that from an objective point of view, her mother was despicable. Self-centered. Thoughtless. Not a mother at all. Gary knew because he'd had a normal one. When she had first told him about her mother, he had been disbelieving. *She just left?* he'd asked. *How could she just leave?* Leigh looked out the window again and, remembering the picnic, felt warm tears in her eyes. She was such an idiot. Always duped. Literally not knowing any better.

"Gary," she said, her voice as toneless and steady as she could make it. She sat at the table and kept her eyes on the scattered medicine in front of her. "Wayne rented a really nice car. Do you want to go out and look at it with him for a minute? It'll give me and my mother a chance to say good-bye."

"Not good-bye," her mother said. She was still smiling, unaware. "Leigh. You really are out of it, aren't you? I told you I'll come back after we eat."

But Gary was already heading to the door, waving for Wayne to follow.

Leigh summoned her energy and stood up. "I'll keep the baby with me," she said.

Everyone stared at her. Even Gary looked uncertain. She coughed twice and held her ground. "I don't want her to get too hot. It's still warm out." She stood up and walked toward Gary, arms outstretched, and simply lifted Kara out of his arms. She knew what she was about to do, and she believed that holding Kara while she did it would give her strength and courage. She was a mother. She knew what to do, what being a mother meant. Kara's small body felt warm and light. Leigh breathed in the scent of her almost hairless head and waited for Gary and Wayne to leave.

When they did, she turned around.

"Don't bother coming back here tonight. In fact, don't ever come back here again."

Her mother blinked. Her face appeared to grow smaller beneath the brim of the hat.

Leigh turned her head away from Kara's and coughed. It was a deep, wracking cough she could feel throughout her chest, everything shaking loose. When she caught her breath, she started again. "There's something wrong with you." She coughed again, struggling to make the words clear. "I don't know why you had children. You don't have a maternal bone in your body. I'm sick, you idiot. I'm sick. And the baby is sick. That's why I can't go have steak. You haven't seen me for eight years. You left for California when I was sixteen. You didn't care what happened to me. And then you finally come back to see me and your granddaughter, and you don't even... it's like it doesn't even occur to you to do what a neighbor would do, let alone a mother, a grandmother. It's like you don't even know."

Her mother shook her head. She looked confused, wounded. "I... I..." She gestured feebly at the chopped broccoli and cheese.

Leigh rolled her eyes. "And don't you ever let me hear you say anything bad about Pam again. A train wreck? She's not a train wreck. She's a decent person. She cares about other people. And she's an excellent mother to those boys. Maybe she's fallen on hard times right now, maybe she's made mistakes, but she's a better person than you are. A better mother, a better person." She felt increasingly strong, her voice gaining in volume. "She could run *circles* around you in both departments. Almost *anyone* could." She stopped to catch her breath. She was going to cough again. She needed water. She carried the baby over to the cupboard, got out a glass, and waited, almost gleefully, for her mother's attempt to retaliate. Whatever she said, she would pounce. She felt invigorated, alive, almost healthy. Kara whimpered, squirming in her arms. Leigh realized she'd been squeezing her too tightly.

But her mother said nothing. She stood completely still, her hands at her sides, still wearing the ridiculous hat. She still looked confused, bewildered, and this made Leigh more angry.

"What? You don't have anything to say for yourself? Are you dumbstruck? Are you that stupid?"

Her mother took off the hat and rubbed her head. "But I..." She looked down at her hat, or maybe her hands. Her nails were long now, polished pink. She looked up at Leigh, right into her eyes. "I gave you girls everything."

She seemed so sincere that Leigh felt briefly confused herself. She wondered, for just a moment, if she had just imagined everything—the trailer where she'd lived with Pam, the empty seats at her graduations, and even before that, when her mother was still around, the heavy silences between them.

Her mother's expression changed. She was angry now too, indignant. "I know all about being sick and taking care of babies." She shook her head quickly. "I don't know where this is coming from. I worked so hard. I gave you girls everything, everything I ever wanted for myself."

Leigh lifted Kara up to her shoulder. "Well, you must not have wanted very much."

Her mother laughed at that. She stopped abruptly, her gray eyes hard, her jaw set.

Leigh waved her hand. "Forget it. Just go to Costa Rica. Go have fun. I mean it. I don't begrudge you that. I know you've worked hard your whole life. So go have fun with Wayne, and go swimming every day and see monkeys. I don't care. Just don't pretend you're a mother. Because you really missed the boat on that one. You missed it a long time ago." She rested her chin against Kara's soft head. "And I've got my own family now. Just go."

LATER, WHEN SHE WAS calmer, when she could reflect on the day more clearly, Leigh would remember that in her final speech to her mother, she had said the word *go* several times. Her mother had no other option, or at least it must have seemed that way. They were in Leigh's house, in Leigh's kitchen, and although she was coughing and pale, her rage must have made her intimidating. She'd been holding a baby in her arms. She'd been unassailable, and right.

Still, on that day, when she had watched her mother walk out her front door to the waiting black Cadillac, Leigh hadn't felt victorious. Her mother had hardly put up a fight. She'd just walked away again.

Five years later, she died of lung cancer in a hospital in San Diego, hairless and thin, with Pam beside her, whispering about Jesus and holding her hand. Wayne had fallen asleep in a nearby chair. Leigh was in St. Louis looking after Pam's boys. She had paid for Pam's ticket. She couldn't go to California herself. She was pregnant with Justin, and by the time they knew it was really the end, her obstetrician told her she shouldn't fly. And, of course, it was too far to drive. She was grateful for the excuses, all the reasons she couldn't go. She could imagine the scene at her mother's bedside, the tearful reconciliation and last-minute apologies. It all seemed false to her, a script she would have to read from. Her mother would finally admit all that she wished she would have done and said, now that it was safe, now that she no longer had to do it or say it.

Still, Leigh was glad to know Pam had been there with her. She didn't hate her mother. She didn't want her to suffer. And she didn't feel as guilty, knowing Pam was there, giving their mother love and comfort, far more than she deserved.

Chapter 12

L EIGH WASN'T EXACTLY SURE when her sister had turned Christian. Sometime when her boys were small, Pam started wearing a little gold cross around her neck. And then each of the boys got a cross necklace too. Leigh acted like she didn't notice. In her mind, Christianity was like Amway—you didn't bring it up with a true believer unless you wanted in or were ready to ward off a serious sales pitch. Pam, much to her sister's relief, didn't bring it up either. She would occasionally mention church, but it was usually in the context of a story about why she couldn't get there— because the car broke down, because one of the boys was sick or acting up, because they were in a new town again and didn't know where to go. Leigh would offer vague sympathy, and then subtly change the subject.

But Pam's three sons were more vocal about their new faith, and their enthusiasm was hard to divert. They spoke about Moses and Abraham and Joseph with a reverence little boys usually reserved for superheroes; they told Justin and Kara stories about dark hallways at school or housing project playgrounds where God or Jesus had told them how to flee or what to say to avoid death at the very last minute. They sang songs they'd learned at Sunday school, harmonizing sometimes, until their secular cousins felt jealous. After one visit from Pam and her boys, Justin insisted he wanted to start going to church. For more than a month, Leigh dutifully dropped him off on Sunday mornings. She endured a brief phase of his cautioning her she would go to hell if she didn't start coming with him, if she kept going to the bagel shop down the street and reading the paper and drinking coffee until it was time to pick him up. But she held her tongue, as did Gary and Kara. After six or seven Sundays, he stopped asking to be driven to Sunday school. There were mean kids there too, he'd told his mother sadly. When she heard the disappointment in his voice, she'd felt guilty for her initial relief.

After that, on Sundays, she took him with her to the bagel shop, trying to make up for it all.

But Pam's children, as far as Leigh knew, never grew disillusioned. They continued to wear their crosses, even when they were handsome teenagers, even when Ryan, the youngest, just two years older than Kara, was arrested for petty theft. He and Kara had played in the sprinkler in Leigh's front yard together when they were small, and Leigh still had a clear memory of Ryan's bending down on chubby knees to kiss Kara's elbow when she'd scraped it on the cement drive. He was seventeen the first time he was arrested. Pam sent him to a boot camp run by a minister and former drill sergeant. She didn't know what else to do, she'd told Leigh, other than praying every night. It seemed neither the praying nor the boot camp worked. Days after Ryan turned eighteen, he was arrested for using someone else's checkbook to buy stereo equipment in Des Moines. He had marijuana in his pocket and more in his car. Two years later, he was still in jail. Kara had interviewed him over the phone for a story about prison life for her high school newspaper. Ryan was forthcoming and helpful—Kara had always been his favorite cousin. She'd won an award for the story, which took up three full pages of the school newspaper. Kara sent Ryan a copy in the mail.

Around that time, Leigh's sister started regularly attending a small church in Minneapolis. The church called itself the Love Church, which had worried Leigh—in her opinion, her sister, kind and floundering and overly generous, was ripe pickings for a cult. But she had been even more concerned with Pam's boyfriend at the time. Leigh had never met Kyle—he'd been living with Pam for three years, but he never came with Pam and the boys when they visited. Leigh knew the boys didn't like him. They'd each left home early, one by one, and they'd each told Pam it was because of Kyle, because they didn't like the way he treated them, and they didn't like watching the way he treated her. When Leigh called her sister, she would have to listen to tearful explanations of why Kyle was the way he was and how he could be so sweet sometimes, and how she just didn't know what to do.

"Dump him," Leigh advised. "All three of your kids hate him. Every time I call you, you're crying."

In the end, it was not Leigh's tough stance that encouraged her sister to finally unload Kyle. No, even she would have to admit it was probably the Love Church that finally gave Pam the courage. She'd been going there just four or five months when she called Leigh from the women's shelter. The apartment's lease had been in her name, and when Kyle refused to leave, she'd had to.

"So he gets your place?" Leigh had asked. "He gets your furniture?"

"Yeah," Pam said. "I guess he does."

When Leigh went up to Minneapolis to help Pam find somewhere to live, she met some of her sister's new friends from the Love Church. They came to help Pam move, and they brought housewarming gifts, potholders, plates, towels, most of them purchased—this was freely admitted—from the thrift store across the street. They brought framed Jesus quotes and crocheted blankets and homemade chili. They made nonalcoholic punch because so many

THE REST OF HER LIFE

of them were recovering. Some of them had accents that were difficult to understand. The minister looked like a grandmother in a
children's book—she had gray hair, bifocal glasses, and a packet of
tissue in her purse that she got out for someone's runny-nosed child.
When she'd talked to Pam, she'd called her "daughter" and held her
hand. "I'm so happy for you, daughter," she'd said, gesturing around
the tiny apartment as if it were something grand. "I'm just so glad to
see you doing well. And so is God. I can tell you that right now."

When Leigh went home, she tried to describe them all to Gary,
but it was hard to do, to give the details, without feeling like she was
making fun of them, which wasn't what she wanted. So she just told
him what was true—that Pam was spending time with people who
seemed to really care about her, and that she seemed to be doing
well. She seemed calmer, she told him. And she wasn't dating anyone. That, in itself, was something new.

BUT BY THE SUMMER of Kara's accident, Leigh's older sister had reason not to appear calm. Her youngest was still in jail; her
eldest was in Iraq. The middle son, Rex, was doing fine, living with
a woman in New York; but when Leigh picked up Pam at the bus
station, her first thought, upon seeing her sister, was *she has aged.*
She'd gained more weight, and her eyebrows seemed to have mi-
grated downward, giving her a permanently worried expression.
They hugged and then stepped away, taking each other in.

"Have you talked to Ellis?"

Pam nodded. "He's in Baghdad. He's fine. I gave him your number. How's Kara?"

"Hard to tell." Leigh slid her sister's duffel bag onto the backseat
of her station wagon. "She still doesn't say much to me." The words
come out of her mouth quickly, a release of painful pressure. She
didn't have time to mince words. Once they got back to the house,

everyone would want to talk to Pam. But for the car ride home, Leigh had her to herself.

Pam buckled herself into the passenger seat. She was wearing red sweatpants and a very large yellow T-shirt that read DON'T LEAVE UNTIL THE MIRACLE HAPPENS. Her hair was still long, but it had started to thin. It looked darker too, not even blond.

"I think it's pretty normal," Pam said slowly. "Isn't it? I don't think teenagers tell their moms anything."

"I don't think this is normal. And she's not really a girl anymore."

Leigh kept her gaze on the road, but as she drove, she could feel her sister's eyes move over her face. She didn't know what she'd been hoping Pam would say to her. There was nothing that would make it better. But Leigh didn't need to be advised or consoled so much as she just needed to talk to someone without fear that what she said would be judged or repeated or both. And for that, she could think of no one more reliable than Pam. Already Leigh felt a little better, or at least paid attention to, understood. Her sister could be so quiet and watchful, her furrowed brow conveying concern.

"Anyway, we're hoping she'll talk to you," Leigh said, pulling onto Commerce. "Or that she'll let you talk to her. We're trying to get her to . . . the lawyer said she should apply for a diversion. It's an agreement between the prosecutor and the—"

"I know all about diversions."

Leigh nodded. She'd forgotten about Ryan, and her sister's own journeys through the court system. "Well. The lawyer thinks she could maybe get one if she applies, which would mean no jail time, and nothing on her record. She doesn't think Kara'll get much jail time anyway, a couple of days. It's the record that's important. But Kara says she won't do it. She's gotten it into her head that it's the easy way out, and that she should"—Leigh raised one hand from the steering wheel in mock respect—"fully suffer."

"I can see why she would think that."

Leigh lowered her hand. "Actually, I can too. That's exactly what I said to Gary, and he got mad. He thinks I'm the one who talked her into it. He thinks I told her she should go to jail. But I just meant that I can understand why she would think she should to go to jail, to not just get out of it and go back to her, you know, easy life."

Pam nodded again. "But you didn't say that to her."

"No. Of course not." Leigh glanced at her sister. "Anyway. We don't have a lot of time to change her mind. Her arraignment is next week. She might not even have to go if she applies for the diversion. But she hasn't done it yet."

She slowed the car. They were approaching Seventh and Commerce, the light about to turn red. Leigh had successfully avoided the intersection for days, but today, she'd driven down Seventh on purpose. She wanted Pam to see where the accident had happened. She wasn't sure why, but it seemed crucial that her sister know exactly what had happened. Leigh wanted her to know what she knew.

She pulled the car alongside the curb. A lilac bush was so overgrown its leaves and flowers pressed against Pam's window. "See the crosswalk? That's where the girl was walking. Kara was coming that way."

Pam leaned forward to see in front of the lilac bush. Her eyes moved over the chain-link fence, where people had left more cards, more crosses, more teddy bears and roses. The WE WILL MISS YOU BETHANY sign was starting to fray around the edges. One good strong breeze and it would be gone.

"That's all stuff people have left for her. Bethany, I mean." As if that were necessary to add, Leigh thought. As if anyone would leave anything for Kara.

"That's her?" Pam pointed to where someone had tied a plastic-coated enlargement of Bethany's yearbook picture. "Can we go up and look at it?"

Leigh made a whimpering sound of protest. She didn't want to look at Bethany's picture again. She had seen it in the newspaper, on the computer, at the funeral, and now, staring out at her from a chain-link fence on the main drag of town. When she closed her eyes, the picture came to her at once, the exact tilt of Bethany's head, the glimmer of the photographer's flash reflected in dark eyes. "I can show you the same picture at home," she said. "It's on the computer."

"But I'd like to see what people have written." Pam craned her neck. "It looks like there are cards and things." She looked at Leigh. "Do you not want to?"

"I…" Leigh tried to come up with a reason they couldn't. "I'm scared," she finally said.

"Of what?"

She could think of no answer to this. *That someone might see me* seemed too shallow for the real shame she felt just looking at the fence from the car.

"I think we should go look," Pam said. She put her hand on Leigh's.

They walked lightly on the grass, tentatively. Leigh could smell the flowers on the lilac bush. She could hear a sprinkler working. She heard birds. It all seemed like trickery, bait. She couldn't escape the idea that she shouldn't be there, that she was an interloper on hallowed ground. She looked back at the street, at the crosswalk, shielding her eyes from the sun.

Pam leaned forward, her eyes moving over the crosses and flowers and notes fluttering in the wind. Leigh stood behind her, reading out of the corner of her eye. *You were my friend,* one note said. It was tied to the fence with a pink ribbon. Leigh backed away from it, toward the car.

"She's lovely."

Leigh turned back. Pam was looking at Bethany's picture.

It wasn't fair, Leigh considered, how a photograph captured someone at just one moment in time, holding them there forever. Bethany could not have known that the one second that she sat for her sophomore year portrait would come to contain her so completely, to represent everything she was and might have become.

"She was my student," Leigh said. "Two years ago. She was a bright girl." She looked over Pam's shoulder and nodded at Bethany as if they had agreed upon something. "Shy, you know, but some of that was her age. It kills me to think of what she might have..."

Pam nodded. There was nothing more to say. But for a few minutes more, they stood quietly by the fence, taking in Bethany's unchanging smile.

WHEN THEY PULLED INTO the driveway, both Justin and Kara were waiting on the front stoop. Leigh turned off the engine without pulling into the garage, though the door was already up. Justin ran toward them with flailing arms.

"You're here!" he shouted, opening Pam's door. "I have a new movie for us to watch. It's about zombies. It's really gross. But it's funny. And I taped *American Idol* for you. I taped this week's, last week's, and the one before. Have you been watching it? Do you know who's going to win? Remember last time you just watched two shows and you knew who the winner would be? If you can guess this time, you can make money. There are people who bet on it. I read about it."

Pam got out of the car to hug him. "I haven't been watching it, honey. I don't know."

"Let's give her a minute to breathe, J." Gary appeared in the garage. "She just got here."

Pam smiled up at Gary. "Hey Perfessor."

She had been calling him this since they'd met. Leigh had thought it was a joke at first, but then Pam had sent them a Christmas card, addressing it in very nice calligraphy to *Perfessor and Leigh Churchill and Family*, and it was only then that she considered her sister really might not know the word. "Shouldn't we tell her?" Gary had asked, his voice hushed, as if up in Minneapolis, Pam had something in her teeth, and they could see it from three states away. No, Leigh had said. Don't say anything. She'll figure it out on her own.

Pam was a good foot shorter than Gary. He had to bend at the waist to hug her. "Sorry to hear about the fire," he said. "That's terrible. That's some bad luck."

Leigh turned away and rolled her eyes. Gary tended to slip into a strange country accent around Pam. "You sound like you're on *Hee Haw*," Leigh told him once. He'd gotten mad.

He reached into the car for Pam's bag. "Heard from Ellis lately?"

"He's in Baghdad. And he was fine this morning. That's all I know."

"Ryan?"

"Well. I always know where he is. I can say that."

"Rex?"

"He's in New York. Still with the same girl. Not in Iraq, and not in prison. New York sounds pretty good."

Kara made her way down the front walk. She was wearing the same cutoffs she'd been wearing every day since the accident, though she'd put on a blue T-shirt that looked clean. Her hair was pulled back in a knot, but almost half of it had slipped out, so, from the front, she looked asymmetrical, off balance.

"Hey you." Pam walked around the car to hug her. It was hard to know how long they stood together, Kara leaning down, her face pressed into her aunt's shoulder. Everyone else waited, approving at first, and then uncomfortable, not sure what to do with themselves. Gary cleared his throat and carried Pam's bag into the house.

Justin stepped forward and tugged on Pam's shirt. "Don't... leave...until...the miracle...Aunt Pam, I'm trying to read the back of your shirt. *Don't leave until the miracle happens.* What does it mean? Why does it say that?"

"Justin." Leigh put a hand on his shoulder. "Let's go inside. Let Kara talk to your Aunt Pam."

"I don't want to. And they're not even talking."

Leigh frowned. Her son was usually so intuitive, so good at picking up on the moods and needs of other people. What was different now, she imagined, was that he didn't care. Summer had just started, and already he'd spent too much time by himself, ignored by his miserable sister and his distracted parents. He wasn't going to be ignored by his beloved aunt. He was getting that straight now.

Pam stepped away from Kara and tried to read the back of her own shirt. "Oh, I think it's an alcoholic thing. I'm still wearing Cody's and Wilma's clothes." She smiled, patting her wide hips. "Mostly Cody's."

Justin nodded quickly. He didn't really care about the shirt. "There's a new ice cream place downtown, and each table has its own jukebox, right there at the table, like that one place we went to in Minnesota? We have one here like that now."

Pam smiled, smoothing back his dark hair. "You're taller," she said. "You are."

"And remember how last time I was trying to do a flip on the trampoline? I can do it now. Well, I did once. My mom saw me."

Leigh nodded, holding up her palm as if to testify. Pam took advantage of the distraction to look past Justin and catch Kara's eye. "You want to go for a walk later?"

Kara nodded, smiling in a way that still looked sad, and turned back to the house. Leigh watched her daughter's slim body move away from her. It was that easy, for Pam, at least. All she'd had to do was ask.

. . .

JUST BEFORE NINE O'CLOCK, the sky glowing pink with the setting sun, Pam and Kara were still on the porch swing, where they had been sitting since they'd returned from their walk more than an hour earlier. Kara had her knees up by her chin, her arms wrapped around her legs, and she was talking. She had been talking for a long time. Standing on the other side of the door, Leigh couldn't hear a word, not with the air-conditioning on and the cicadas singing. But when she peeked through the door's little window, her daughter looked as if she were saying something important, something that required great concentration. Pam was turned fully toward her, one elbow resting on the back of the swing.

When Leigh opened the door, they both looked up with a start. Kara rolled her lips together.

"I'm just getting the mail," Leigh said, her palms raised in a gesture of innocence. She realized, too late, that that sounded defensive, mad, so she put her hands down and slowed her pace in front of the swing. "Nice out, isn't it?"

Pam and Kara nodded. Pam smiled.

Leigh went to put her hands in her pockets, but she was wearing a skirt without any, and her hands slid down her sides. "Finally cooled down."

There was no reply to this, just the creak of the swing moving back and forth. Leigh turned and moved quickly down the front path to the mailbox. She opened the mailbox and held up the envelopes, as if to prove to them she did have a purpose. When she walked back to the house, they both stared past her, out at the darkening sky. She smiled, to show it was all fine, swatting an envelope across her forearm.

"Mosquitoes, though," she said helpfully. "They'll come right after me. I better get in."

Once she was inside, the door shut safely behind her, she let her face fall in line with how she felt. She pressed her ear against the door, but she could hear only the murmur of their resumed conversation, not the actual words.

She heard Gary on the stairs and moved away from the door. She set the mail on the counter in the kitchen.

"Hi," he said. He'd just gotten out of the shower, and he was wearing the gym shorts and T-shirt he would wear to bed. He looked refreshed, reenergized. His neck smelled like the lotion he shaved with. "What are you doing?"

"I was going to make some pudding."

He laughed. She'd never been much of a cook. Instant pudding was her specialty. When the kids had been younger, she'd made it every night for dessert. Kara used to stand on a step stool beside her, measuring out the milk.

He rested his chin on the top of her head. "How are you doing?"

"Okay," she said, and though her voice wavered, he didn't hear it. He didn't see her face.

"Yeah, well, okay is good. I think okay is the best we can hope for right now. It's nice to have Pam here, huh?" He looked around. "Where..."

"I think she's still out front with Kara."

When he turned to the window, Leigh moved out of his arms and bent forward to search the lower cabinet for the mixing bowl.

"Oh yeah. They're out there talking." He looked at his watch. "They've been out there for a while, haven't they?"

"Yeah." She was looking for the big spoon. She stared into the mess of the utensil drawer.

"Good. That's great. Did you tell Pam about the diversion?"

"Yeah." She kept her eyes on the drawer. The big spoon was right in front of her. She hadn't seen it.

"Good. That's great. She's always really liked Pam, you know? Maybe Pam will be able to talk her into it."

She slammed the drawer shut. He flinched.

"What the hell is that supposed to mean?"

He needed several seconds to take it all in—her raised voice, the big spoon in her hand, the sudden tears brightening her eyes. He raised his palms to her, the way she had raised hers to Kara and Pam a few minutes earlier. But there was no defensiveness or irony in Gary's gesture, and none in his expression.

"I know she likes Pam. I know that. Okay, Gary? I know Pam is wonderful, and I know my daughter likes her, and will talk to her for hours."

"I didn't mean—" He almost smiled. He was going to tell her she was being ridiculous. He was already giving her that look.

"And I'm sick of you commenting on my relationship with Kara. I do want what's best for her, for your information. I do. It's not my fault she doesn't like me. I'm a decent person, Gary. Okay? I've tried to be good to her. I've tried hard to be a good mother. Very hard. Harder than a lot of people. I don't know what it is…about me… It's not my fault. I try."

He took a step forward, sympathy and comfort in his eyes. She almost went to him.

"I think you try sometimes…" He paused, pursing his lips. "I think you try in your own way."

"What?" She wanted to hit him with the spoon. She was that angry. She put it on the counter and crossed her arms. "I think I just said I don't want any more commentary or advice from you." She could feel the anger moving through her body, fanning out. It had to go somewhere. It would go to him. "You know, I'm not really sure you're in any position to be giving me advice. You don't have a great relationship with Justin. He doesn't exactly rush to your arms when you come home. You notice that? Maybe you should quit giving me advice and think about how you could try harder with him…." She paused, searching for words. She was too mad to think. "You know, you could try all the time, and not just in your own way. How about that?"

His breathing slowed, and he stepped back. "So we're even then," he said.

She looked away. This was how he won their arguments. He stayed calm, and so she felt and seemed more crazy. She heard Justin on the stairs, and they both turned to watch his entrance. He was wearing the MIRACLE T-shirt Pam had been wearing earlier and shorts from last summer that were too small. The outfit made him look strange, a little elfin, his pale legs long and out of proportion. Out of the corner of her eye, she watched Gary. He looked mildly distressed.

"They're still out there?" Justin sighed dramatically and looked at Leigh. "Can I go out there too?"

"No. They're talking. Wait until they come inside."

"But Kara's gotten to talk to her all night."

She opened the pantry and got out the pudding mix. "Well, they need to talk, Justin. Okay? I don't want you to bother them."

"But I wanted to show her how I can flip." He nodded in the direction of the backyard. "She said she wanted to see it."

"Then wait." She closed the pantry door and turned around.

"But it'll be dark soon."

Leigh held her hands up near her temples. He was annoying her. It was strange. He was usually so good. "Then I'll go out with you. You can show—"

"Actually, you can show me."

Leigh and Justin both turned to look at Gary. There was a beat of silence, and Justin's eyes shifted to his mother's face. She could almost see his mind churning, trying to think of a way out.

"Come on," Gary said. He put his hand on Justin's shoulder,

steering him toward the back door. "Your mother's busy. And I want to see the flip." His tone left no room for argument.

Justin glanced back at his mother as if he were being led away to a firing squad, but his feet kept moving forward. Leigh heard the back door open and close, and then the house was quiet again. She would make pudding, she thought. She would keep making the pudding. But the silence surrounding her felt like a reproach, and her arms felt heavy as she reached for the measuring cups. She had to lean against the counter for a moment, overwhelmed by self-loathing and sadness. She was within thirty feet of the four people she loved most in the world, and she'd never felt more alone.

IT WAS DARK BEFORE Pam and Kara came in. Pam was scratching her neck. "You were right about those mosquitoes," she called out. "They just love us, don't they, Leigh? But they leave Kara alone. Thicker skin, maybe." When she passed the kitchen doorway she stopped. "Ooooo. Pudding? Is that tapioca?"

Leigh forced a smile. "Yeah. It'll be ready in a second." She peeked around the corner, where Kara stood, her head lowered, her body slouched against the wall. "You want some? Justin and your dad are out back. We could have a ladies' dessert."

"Actually, I'm pretty worn out." Kara was already turning away. "I think I'm going up to bed early."

Leigh started to nod, but then stopped herself. Gary hadn't taken no for an answer. Maybe she was too quick to concede. "Have some dessert with me," she said. She'd tried to sound authoritative, but the words just came out loud and harsh. She smiled again, softening her voice. "It'll take you five minutes, and it'll mean a lot to me."

Kara stared at her for several beats.

"I said I didn't want any," she said finally. She sounded like her father, just like him, ready to face down the world, or at least Leigh, with only logic and calm reason. It was the end of the discussion. She gave her aunt an embarrassed smile, turned around, and jogged up the stairs.

Leigh turned back to the counter and started stirring the pudding. She was clenching her teeth in a way that sometimes gave her a headache. She knew she was doing it, but she couldn't stop.

"You know," Pam said carefully, "it's just hard, I think. Each one of my boys went through a time when he was sure he hated me."

"So she does hate me?" Leigh stirred hard and fast, the bowl tucked in the crook of her arm. "She admitted it?"

"No. No. She didn't say that."

"Then what did she say?"

"About..."

"About me." Leigh's voice was deadpan, her face blank. She could take it. She wanted to know.

"Oh...." Pam frowned. "She didn't say she hated you."

"But she does. What does she say about me? What is it that I do that makes her hate me?"

Pam shook her head.

"What?"

"You'll have to talk to her about that for yourself."

Leigh put the bowl down hard. "She won't talk to me! She won't! You saw what just happened. That's how it always is! That's how it's been for a long time. And I have no idea what it is that's so terrible about me. So if she told you something, just—"

Pam lowered her eyes.

"Fine." Leigh slid past her sister and put the mixing bowl in the refrigerator. "Fine. You two have your secrets."

"Leigh." Her sister sounded imploring, desperate. "What do you want me to do? You wanted me to talk with her. I did. If I report everything back to you, she won't trust me anymore. What do you want?"

Leigh frowned. Her sister, the most understanding person she knew, was sick of her. Everyone was. "Okay." She fluttered her fingers in the air between their faces. "I'm sorry. I'm yelling at everyone tonight. I'm crazy. I'm mean." She started to wipe down the counter with a dishcloth. But she couldn't manage it. She didn't care about the counter.

"Did you talk about the diversion? Can you tell me that?"

Pam nodded, her eyes still lowered.

"Is she going to take it?"

"I don't think so."

Leigh sighed, rubbing her eyes.

"She says she shouldn't get to take an easy way out." Pam furrowed her brows. "She thinks the reason she's getting off easy has to do with you all…having more money than the girl who got hit."

"What? That's ridiculous. She said that?"

Pam put her hand to her mouth. "I thought you knew that. Don't tell her I told you that. She trusts me, Leigh, and if I—"

"Fine," Leigh said, waving her hand. "But that's ridiculous. I don't know where she gets that."

"Well. It's not completely ridiculous." Pam moved the mixing bowl away from the edge of the counter. "It is true that rich people get away with things. Sometimes. And poor people don't."

Leigh hesitated. She was not sure if they were still talking about Kara. Her nephews had gotten away with very little.

"We're not rich, Pam," she finally said.

Leigh saw the slight tremor in her sister's eyes, a reference to their surroundings. Everything was relative, she supposed. She looked down at the mail she'd dumped on the counter. She was tired. Her teeth were still clenched, and she was getting a headache.

Her eyes fell to one of the envelopes, where Cynthia Tork's name and address were written in calligraphy on a small pink sticker.

Pam looked around her shoulder. "What?"

"Hold on a sec."

It was a white envelope, business size, with a breast cancer stamp neatly applied to the corner. Leigh tore out the letter. This would not be good, she warned herself. There was no way this would be good news.

Dear Leigh Churchill,

I apologize for writing you at home; however, I assumed you might not check your mail at school over the summer break, and I'd like to reach some agreement before Caleb starts your honors class in the fall. My husband and I have both given voice to our concerns over your proposed reading list, and we would now like to know if our concerns have any impact on your curriculum. We hope you can respond in a timely fashion so we will know if we need to take further steps before the school year begins.

I will be brief. Because we care about our son's education, both Jim and I have read over your selected reading materials for next year. We find the story lines depressing, and full of immorality. The Flannery O'Connor story, for example, depicts the murder of an innocent family. The killer, who equates murder with stealing tires, is shown as deep and complex, with a comical line at the end of the story to show he is also funny—though he has no real remorse. *This Boy's Life* follows the adolescence of a boy who has violent impulses toward strangers, who has no problem lying to his parents and other adults, and who, perhaps most disconcertingly, develops a worrisomely close friendship with another boy who is nurturing homosexual tendencies. Obviously, these kinds of story lines and main characters are not in line with the values of a conservative community such as Danby, and we can't help but wonder if you are pursuing a personal agenda. Jim and I believe most parents would be as concerned as we are if they only knew what kinds of values are promoted by the books you were planning to teach next year. When we have told other parents what these books are about, most of them agree they are uncomfortable with your choices.

Some parents, however, have been hesitant to find fault with your selection of *The Great Gatsby*. It's a "classic" after all—meaning someone, somewhere, has deemed it "art," and therefore, apparently, above reproach from simple folk such as ourselves. But as Jim and I are in the practice of looking to the Lord, not society, to tell us what is and what is not beautiful, we are able to see this story with fresh, objective eyes. And what we see is a story about very shallow people who seem to have no moral compass at all. They casually take the Lord's name in vain. They commit adultery. They drink and drive. But it's okay, because they're glamorous and attractive. Daisy, the love interest of the novel, kills another woman by running her over with a car. What kind of a message does a book like this send to our young people? Given your current situation with your daughter, I would think that you of all people would see the need to teach young people the importance of responsible decision making, especially while operating a car.

Your principal and supervisor, Rick Bechelmeyer, has suggested that Jim and I should simply pull Caleb from your class, as it is an elective honors class. But Caleb qualified for the honors course because of his high grades, and we think the school needs to "honor" its duty to make him comfortable in whatever class will help him reach his fullest potential. It just seems fair that we come to some sort of compromise. Jim and I certainly have no problem with literature—we're both avid readers, and we know how books can be used to instruct not only young people's minds, but also their hearts and souls. Have you ever considered teaching more uplifting, positive stories? Have you considered teaching books about boys and girls with strong morals? The members of our youth group love *Sarah's Heart,* which is about a young girl who resists the temptation to steal—and ends up becoming wealthy in ways she never expected. *The Boys of Bettleton* is a great adventure story that will not just keep children turning pages— the tale also demonstrates the importance of honoring your country. We can supply you with several similar titles. But we ask that you read these two aforementioned books in particular, as we would like to see them become part of your honors reading list.

On a personal note, I would like you to know that although I found your words at our previous meeting hurtful, I hold no personal animosity toward you. On the contrary, you have my concern and best wishes, as I know this must be a difficult time for your family. Jim has been ministering to Bethany's mother, and I have been deeply moved by her grief. But at the meeting, I could see you were grieving for your daughter, and perhaps for Bethany as well. Jim and I have been praying for Bethany's family, but you and your daughter have been in our prayers as well.

Sincerely,

Cynthia Tork

"I hate this woman," Leigh said.

Pam winced.

Leigh let the letter fall to the counter. "That's right, Pam. I hate her. I know you don't hate anybody, but I do. I hate Cynthia Tork." She walked to the dining room, sat in her chair, and set her forehead against the table.

"Why?" Pam looked around the corner. "Who is she?"

Leigh spoke with her forehead on the table. "She's a self-righteous, pushy, bigoted, know-it-all yet ignorant parent who wants my honors English class to read only books that have nothing to do with real life."

Pam said nothing.

Leigh looked at her. "What?"

"Nothing. I don't know what to say. I haven't read the books you're talking about. I can't—" She sighed. "Maybe you shouldn't worry about this right now. You might feel different about it, about this woman, later."

Leigh looked away. Pam was always trying to calm her down. They could be out in the heat in front of Danny Lipper's parents' trailer again; they were having the same conversation. Leigh was sick of it. She hadn't wanted to calm down then and she didn't want to calm down now. Her anger felt good, justified. And where had Pam's stoic passivity gotten her? She'd been their mother's whipping girl, right up to the very end.

She looked up and gazed at Pam coolly. "Well, I've read the books, okay? I know this woman, and I can tell you, I hate her." She ran her tongue over her teeth. "If you read the books, if you read any books, you'd probably hate her too."

In the silence that followed, Leigh felt as if her heart were physically sinking, plummeting to somewhere dark and silent from which it might never again rise. There was no part of her reasonable mind that wanted to be cruel to her sister. The anger that had felt so fortifying a few seconds earlier now felt uncontrollable, bigger and stronger than she was.

Pam stared back at her warily. It was a mistake, Leigh considered, to confuse placidity with stupidity, to think that because one doesn't react, one doesn't feel, or know. And it was probably a mistake to assume that because someone had put up with other people's crap her entire life, she would continue to put up with it forever.

"I'm sorry," Leigh said. "I'm sorry I said that." She shook her head quickly. Pam would forgive her—she was almost certain of that. She could already see sympathy in her sister's eyes, a tired understanding. But she had to know for certain. She wouldn't be able to fully breathe until she got a response.

"Okay." Pam pursed her lips and looked at her watch. "Want to go watch *American Idol?*"

Leigh stared at her, no response.

Pam shrugged. "Your son taped three episodes for me. I've got to get on it."

They each took a bowl of pudding downstairs. Pam used the remote to rewind the tape while Leigh flopped onto the futon that Pam would sleep on that night. Pam's duffel bag was unzipped on the floor, and Leigh could see some of her clothes, or, rather, the men's T-shirts and sweatpants that she had borrowed from her friends. Leigh tried to think of something in her own closet she could give to Pam, something that would fit.

"We should go shopping tomorrow."

Pam looked up from the remote. "For what?"

Leigh leaned forward and pulled a very large white undershirt out of Pam's bag. "For clothes. For you."

"Yeah. I guess. Oh, hey, I brought pictures." Pam leaned forward and pulled two plastic bags out of the duffel bag. "I kept all my photo albums and stuff on the top shelf of my closet, so the water didn't get them. And I was looking through them, and I saw these ones that Wayne sent me after Mom died. I don't think you've ever seen them. Mom had them with her out in California."

She handed the photographs to Leigh. The first was a Polaroid of Leigh and Pam when they very young. Everything in the background—her mother's old Impala, a magnolia tree in full bloom—was awash in the yellow-green light that Leigh associated with pictures from that era, but Leigh and Pam looked tan and healthy in matching blue sleeveless dresses. Their hair was braided, and they were both smiling. They held hands.

"We look so happy," Leigh said.

"I guess we were that day. I remember those dresses. She bought them new for us. It was a big deal. You grew out of yours in a month."

The next was a Polaroid of their mother and father. He stood behind her, his arms wrapped around her shoulders. He wore dark pants and a light button-down shirt that didn't look like anything Leigh could remember seeing him in. He couldn't have been more than nineteen, and their mother looked even younger. She wore a red dress that was too big for her—the bustline sagged, and the material hung off her hips. She looked a little apprehensive, her chin raised to the camera, her smile slight. But there were the eyes, light gray, reflecting light. Her hair had been carefully curled.

Leigh held the picture up. "Have you heard from him?"

"Not in a while. I called a couple times last year. I think he's one of those people who has trouble talking, saying what they think, you know? Maybe the phone is hard for him."

Leigh made no comment. Pam would make excuses for anyone.

The last picture was black and white, held in an old paperboard frame with tiny roses printed along the edges. There were several people in the picture, but it was the porch they stood on that Leigh recognized—the slanting slabs of wood built onto the house where her mother had grown up. There was the forsythia bush blooming in the front yard. There were the crooked front steps. She looked at the many light-eyed, pale-skinned children who stood unsmiling on the front steps. She vaguely recalled the names of some of her mother's brothers and sisters. There was a Cissy, a Bob Jack, a Jeremiah. But Leigh didn't know which was which. She had only met some of them once, and she couldn't even remember which ones.

"That's her," Pam said, pointing at one of the blond girls standing on the top step. She wasn't the tallest girl, but looking at her face, at her eyes, she was clearly the oldest. Her hands were on the shoulders of two of the boys in front of her, not resting there lightly, but firmly, as if she'd been charged with holding them in place. Beside her, just to the right of the steps, was a young, healthy version of the old man Leigh had met just as he was dying. He wore overalls under a heavy coat, and he had a cigarette in his mouth, the end pointed downward. An older woman stood next to him. She was short and round, and she wore a kerchief on her head, the front edge tight against her forehead. She had the sagging, sad face of a bulldog, serious and resolute.

"Is that her grandmother?"

"I think that's our grandmother. Her grandmother never left Ireland, remember? She told us that once."

"Maybe it's his mother, then. She looks really old."

"No. I really think that's her mom. I think they just got old faster back then. Mom said she was always sick."

Leigh picked up the frame and squinted. Her mother's youthful face stared back.

"I'm sure it was a hard life," she allowed. "None of them look like they're having a good time." She looked up at Pam. "I always wondered—did she ever say anything to you . . . when you went out there? When she was dying. Did she . . . Did she feel bad about anything?"

"You mean about us?"

Leigh nodded, shrinking back a little. She knew the answer was probably no. It was why she'd never asked.

Pam shook her head. "She didn't say much. They were giving her morphine. She wasn't that . . . focused. She couldn't concentrate. She was in a lot of pain." She looked at Leigh and shrugged, as if that were the end of it.

"Well," Leigh said, because there was nothing else. She looked back at the picture of herself and Pam in the blue dresses. "We did have it easier than she did. I'm sure we did. And I should thank her for that, I guess."

Pam nodded. She looked calm, untroubled. Leigh tapped her foot on the ottoman and glanced at her mother's photographs. "But it felt like that was all she saw when she looked at us." She leaned forward to get Pam's attention. She wanted her sister to understand, to see things the way she had. "You know? I always felt like she never saw me, me as an individual. Do you know what I'm saying? She gave us everything she ever wanted. But she never thought about what *we* wanted, that it might be different. Or that we might need something she didn't. She never saw us as separate from herself. She never saw us." She paused, nodding in agreement with herself. That was it, she decided. She'd never put words to the feeling before, but that was it. That had been the whole trouble between them.

But when she looked back at Pam, her satisfaction vanished. Her sister's mouth was pulled tight, her eyes wide. She looked away from Leigh, saying nothing, still the loyal confidante. But Leigh already knew. She knew what she couldn't guess before, what Pam wouldn't tell her, the hard answer to her earlier question. She thought of the two of them on the porch swing, Kara talking, Pam listening. Leigh didn't have to guess anymore. She could hear the words come out of her daughter's mouth as clearly as they'd just come out of her own.

Chapter 13

Pam decided not to go to Kara's arraignment. "I think I should spend some time with Justin," she told her niece, nodding as if the two of them were already of one mind. "And you'll have your mom and your dad there with you."

Leigh understood that her sister was bowing out, trying to be nice. All week long, Kara had sought out her aunt for conversation, for evening walks. But Pam would offer no competition during the arraignment, she was saying. Kara would have her mother and father to lean on, and that would have to be enough.

So on the morning of the arraignment, Leigh and Gary and Kara, just the three of them, arrived at the courthouse well before eight, as Sue Taft had advised. The courtroom looked nothing like courtrooms on television, nothing like the austere, marble settings Leigh had imagined when worrying about this day. It was in the overly air-conditioned basement of the courthouse, and there were no windows, no natural light. The carpet was blue, with a faded print. Fluorescent lights flickered from the ceiling. The chairs were the foldable kind.

They ended up waiting for hours while the judge dealt with other cases: a man with a shaved head and a happy face tattooed on the back of it was charged with driving away from a rural gas station without paying; an elderly woman who needed a walker to get to the front of the room was charged with writing bad checks throughout the county; a woman about Leigh's age was charged with biting another woman's nose during a fight in a bar; a man with swollen eyes and facial hair that had been trimmed so only a thin dark line completely encircled his mouth was charged with indecent exposure. They had come with lawyers and family, these people, just as Kara had done. Leigh found their presence comforting. When she had worried about this day, she had pictured an audience of innocent voyeurs. She had imagined her family being observed by people who had no reason to feel guilty or embarrassed, people who could shake their heads and click their tongues, and maybe feel sympathy at best. But none of those people had shown up, and she felt a kinship with the elderly check writer and the shaved-headed gas thief and especially his father sitting sadly beside him. They had their own troubles; they were preoccupied, and Leigh liked them for that.

Sue Taft, sitting to Leigh's right, used the wait to check her e-mail and look over her calendar. Kara, on Leigh's left, kept her eyes lowered, her hands in her lap. But Gary, sitting on the other side of Kara, listened to the other cases carefully, his eyes glazed and dull, his mouth wrinkled with discomfort, distaste, or both.

Kara's name was finally called, and she rose without looking at either of her parents. Leigh watched her move to the front of the room. In some ways, she looked better than she had in weeks—her hair was brushed and neatly pulled back. She wore the cream blazer and skirt she'd bought last spring for college interviews. The skirt was too big for her now. It hung low on her waist, shapeless, and as she walked, the small slit that was supposed to be in back worked its way around to her left side. Standing in front of the judge, she kept her head perfectly level, her shoulders back. But she still looked frail, vulnerable, especially standing next to Sue Taft, who was wearing an attorney power suit, pinstriped gray stretched tightly across her broad shoulders.

There were no theatrics. The man from the district attorney's office read the charge of reckless driving. The judge asked Kara if she understood the charge and the possible penalty. He asked her how she wanted to plead. Sue Taft had already explained to her that she had to plead not guilty, at least for now. The arraignment was just a formality. This wasn't even the judge who would make a decision on the case.

Still, when Kara finally said "not guilty," she spoke so quietly that the judge made her say it again. After that, things went smoothly. She was given a date in late July for her trial setting; at that time, she would be given a court date. Sue Taft said something to the judge and the man from the district attorney's office that Leigh couldn't hear. They both nodded, and that was the end of it. The whole thing took four minutes, maybe five. Sue Taft turned and made her way back down the aisle that was really just a three-foot break in the rows of folding chairs. Kara followed, her head still level, her gray eyes staring blankly at the back of the room. Leigh and Gary rose and followed them down the rest of the aisle toward the door. Kara did not slow her pace, but Gary jogged ahead and put his arm around her, blocking her view of the right side of the court-room. So only Leigh, who was walking behind them all with the dazed expression of someone simultaneously relieved that one thing was over but newly worried about whatever lay ahead, noticed Bethany Cleese's mother sitting by herself in a chair in the back row. She sat with her legs crossed at the knee, her arms crossed tightly at her chest, the way someone might sit if she were very cold. She turned her head to watch Kara move through the door, but her body—her arms and legs still tightly crossed—didn't move.

Leigh slowed and then stopped. She had no idea what she would say, but her hand was already moving up, reaching out. *Diane.* It came to her at once, what she needed to say. *Diane. I am Kara's mother. We met once, in the grocery store. I'm so sorry. I'm so sorry.* The words were in her mouth, already formed, but then Diane Kletchka started to rise, her face still turned back to the door that Kara and Gary had just walked through. Leigh could see only her profile, but something about her eyes—at least the eye Leigh could see—made her pull her hand back. The woman's gaze was so focused, it looked predatory.

Again, Leigh's body took over. She moved to the door quickly, facing forward. She opened it, slipped through, and closed it carefully behind her.

"Mrs. Churchill."

A young man with a vaguely familiar face was standing beside her. He wore a tie, and his round face was somber. The name came to her: Vic Ramirez. He'd been an excellent student, a careful reader. He'd written a very good paper on *Lord of the Flies.* It had been years since she'd had him in class.

"Mrs. Churchill. It's good to see you, though I'm sorry for the circumstance."

She nodded. She still had her hand against the door behind her, holding it shut, Bethany Cleese's mother on the other side. She'd always liked Vic. His parents, she remembered, hadn't spoken English, and he'd had to translate for them at parent-teacher conferences. He would get so embarrassed, having to describe himself to his parents with the Spanish equivalents of the glowing phrases Leigh used. Leigh didn't know Spanish, but she'd suspected he'd toned down her words. This, perhaps, was what made her like him a little more than her other good students. She had other strong writers that year, but Vic was humble, and English was his second language. He had to try harder than most.

"You're back? You went to ... Did you go to KU?" It was amazing. She was having the former-student conversation. She could have it in her sleep. Even now, standing outside a courtroom, scared and exhausted, she felt compelled to ask all the right questions.

"Yes. I graduated last winter." Vic smiled curtly. "I'm with the *Chronicle* now, actually. I was hoping I could ask you a few questions."

It was only then she saw he had a small notepad. He'd held it low by his hip, like a gun in a holster. She glanced back at the courtroom door.

"It won't take long. If you could just tell me how you think this has affected your daugh—"

And then Sue Taft was there, stepping between them, her pinstriped back almost touching Leigh's face.

"As I already said, we have no comment at this time." Her voice was low, full of authority. "No one in the Churchill family has any comment at this time." She stared at Vic Ramirez until he turned away. When Sue Taft moved away from her, she noticed Gary and Kara standing against a wall, a photographer taking their picture. Gary stared over the heads of the photographer, his face blank, as if he were completely unaware of him. But Kara looked right into the lens, blinking with every flash.

"You really shouldn't talk to the media," Sue Taft said quietly. She was frowning, angry. They had been over this.

"I wasn't," Leigh said.

Sue continued to frown. Leigh glanced back over her shoulder. The courtroom door was still closed. Vic Ramirez pointed at the door with his thumb.

"Did she come out already?" Vic glanced at his watch. "Did you see her go in?"

The photographer shook his head. Leigh looked back at the courtroom door.

Finally, Vic and the photographer started up the stairway. Sue Taft waited until they were gone before she spoke.

"I can't stress enough that you need to be very careful what you say to the media." She was looking at all of them, but, they all knew, reprimanding Leigh in particular. "It really could have an eff—"

Leigh cleared her throat. "I need to talk to Sue alone." She kept her eyes on Gary. "Would you go outside with Kara?" She didn't look at Kara. She tried to think of where they had parked. "Would you wait in the car?"

Gary squinted.

"Will you go now please?" Leigh motioned toward the stairway. He must have seen it all then—the fear in her eyes, the alarm. He still looked confused, but he put his arm around Kara and steered her toward the stairway. When they finally disappeared, Leigh turned to see Sue staring at her over the tops of her bifocals, one eyebrow raised. She looked mildly concerned.

"Sorry," Leigh whispered. She looked back at the courtroom door. "The mother of the ... girl ... the victim ... Bethany Cleese, I mean. She was in there. I thought she would come out when Kara was here. I didn't want ... you know ..." She was having trouble explaining, and it had everything to do with the way Sue Taft was looking at her. Leigh recognized the expression—it conveyed mild annoyance, a long-suffering amusement. It was the way she often looked at Eva.

"Did you need to talk to me about something?" Sue Taft adjusted her glasses. She did not sound friendly or unfriendly. She sounded neutral. She sounded like someone being paid for her time.

"Yes." Leigh decided this was true as she said it. She cleared her throat and lifted her chin. "I wanted to ask you about ... Well. I'm sure Kara has told you that she doesn't plan on applying for the diversion."

Sue Taft sighed and held out both palms, the handle of her briefcase balanced on one. "I can only give a client advice. I can't make her take it."

Leigh glanced over her shoulder. The courtroom door was still closed. Perhaps there was another exit, one she hadn't seen. She looked back at Sue. "But do you think you could talk to her about it again? I mean, it's completely ridiculous for her to go to trial, right? She'll be found guilty, right?"

"Not nec-es-*sar*-ily." All at once, Sue Taft seemed fully engaged, interested in the conversation. She pushed her glasses back up, squinting at Leigh. "I mean, yes, my advice would be to apply for the diversion to avoid the possibility of jail time. That's what the D.A. wants. They'll work something out with us. They don't want to take her to trial. But if she does go to trial, there's a chance she won't be convicted. Of reckless driving, I mean." She switched her briefcase to her other hand. "I was looking over a State Supreme Court case the other night." She pointed at a card table against the far wall. "Come over here with me. I'll show you my notes."

The door to the courtroom opened. Leigh turned to see Diane Kletchka coming out, rubbing the back of her neck and looking up at the low ceiling, though she did not appear to really see anything. She walked with her arms at her sides, her palms turned forward. She wore a gray cotton dress, something Leigh might wear to the pool over a swimsuit. She wore clogs that made a heavy, dragging sound as she moved past the stairway to the elevator.

Leigh followed Sue to the table, nodding as if she understood what she was saying. But her mind was focused on the sound of the elevator doors opening, shutting, sealing Diane Kletchka inside.

"So really, according to this precedent, the difference between recklessness and negligence is the concept of conscious disregard. See? It says right here." Sue Taft held a piece of paper up to her own eyes. *"The negligent actor fails to perceive a risk that he ought to perceive. The reckless actor perceives or is conscious of the risk, but disregards it."* She looked back at Leigh. "So that's the legal distinction. It's whether you know or not. If she should have known she could hit someone, it's just negligence. If she knew it and barreled through anyway, it's reckless."

Leigh turned away from the elevator. "So which one is it?"

"Well, that's what we don't know yet." Sue Taft sounded annoyed again. "As I said, she drove past a stop sign into a crosswalk in a crowded area. But did she just fail to perceive the risk? Did she just not see the consequences of her actions? I might be able to prove that she just didn't see, that she just didn't know. Even if she should have. But what I'm telling you, in the end, is no, the trial is not a complete lost cause."

"But you said she should apply for the diversion. You said she shouldn't go to tri—"

"And that's still my advice. I said I might be able to get her a lesser conviction of negligence, but I'm not certain. And since the punishment for reckless, with a diversion, is so light, there's really no point in going through the expense and stress of a trial. But if she won't apply for the diversion, we'll have to go to trial."

Leigh frowned. "What if she goes to trial and pleads guilty?"

"Without a diversion? That's ridiculous. That might actually make the judge angry. It's a waste of money, and everyone's time. If she's going to plead guilty, she should do it now and take the diversion."

"I think she wants to go to jail."

Sue Taft stared at her blankly.

"Can't you talk to her?" Leigh asked.

"I gave her my advice. You heard me."

"No, I mean, can you talk to her? Can you maybe talk to her about...the ridiculousness of it, going to jail? She might listen to you, if you tell her, you know, accidents happen, and—"

Fluorescent lights reflected off Sue Taft's glasses. Leigh couldn't see her eyes.

"I think that's probably your job," she finally said.

Leigh looked away and silently added Sue Taft to the list of people she hated. Her mind reeled, trying to find some way to wound her cold, staring lawyer, to say anything cutting, and it was then she remembered what Eva had told her about Sue Taft's divorce. Leigh reconsidered. Sue Taft's ex-husband had gambled away their savings. Leigh felt her hands unclench, and she rolled her shoulders back. So there was the truth, if she could believe Eva. Despite the way her lawyer was looking at her, as if only Leigh were the failure, there was a good chance both of them knew very well what it was like to try to get someone you love to stop hurting themselves and everyone else.

I'm on to you, Leigh wanted to say. *You're a hypocrite, and no better than me.*

But by then, standing at her full height with good posture, she was able to look down and see Sue Taft's naked eyes over the rims of her glasses.

"Yes," she said, reaching down to gently pat her lawyer's arm. "I understand. Thank you for your time."

THE CAR WAS STILL parked where they had left it, across the street from the courthouse. Neither Kara nor Gary was inside. Leigh turned in a slow circle, a hand over her eyes to block out the searing sun. There was no sign of Bethany's mother, no sign of Vic Ramirez or the photographers. There was no sound of conflict in any direction. It was just quiet and bright and hot. She took out her phone and dialed Gary's number.

"Hey. We're at the market." His voice was loud. She could hear a fiddle playing in the background.

"What?" She looked at her watch. It was twenty to noon. Tuesday. The farmers' market.

"Well, we couldn't stay there. Not with the reporter guy around. And I didn't know how long you were going to be. Come on over."

"What? No. Gary, I want to go home." This came out as a whine, but she didn't care. She didn't want to see anyone.

"Come on," he said. He wasn't really asking. His tone was not unlike the one she had used earlier, when she'd wanted him to get Kara out of the courthouse. "Just walk over. It's two blocks away."

She started to argue, but he'd hung up.

She drove the two blocks, which was a little dumb—by the time the air-conditioning really kicked in, she was already in front of the church parking lot where the market was held on Tuesdays. But she wanted to stay in the car, with the relative security and concealment it offered. She left the engine running, her eyes moving over the trucks and vans full of fresh eggs and tamales and wildflowers and hand-sewn baby clothes. She could see Eva's little convertible parked on the other side of the lot. She ducked her head and dialed Gary's number.

"I can see the car," he said. He was laughing about something. "Do you see us? Look up."

He waved at her from behind the rope that lined the perimeter of the market. Gary held both his suit jacket and Kara's blazer over one arm. Kara held a wriggling black puppy.

As soon as she saw the puppy, Leigh knew she would have to get out of the car. Both Kara and Gary loved dogs. Before Kara was born, when Leigh and Gary first moved to Danby, Gary had campaigned heavily for a dog. They finally had their own house, he argued, a yard. He'd always wanted a dog, the whole time he was a kid, but his dad, who was simply not a dog person, had refused. They'd had the cat, of course, Winston, but it wasn't the same. Leigh was pretty neutral on the subject, so Gary had gone out and gotten a lab puppy and named him Hal. "He'll be great to have around when we have kids," he'd said. "They'll love him." When Kara was born, that appeared to be true—she'd grown up riding on Hal's broad back and getting her face licked. When she was four, she started asking for a puppy of her own. She'd also wanted a kitten. And a bunny. And a guinea pig. Fortunately, Gary and Leigh held off on these requests: not long after Justin was born, they discovered he was allergic to almost every kind of animal hair. They'd had to give Hal to one of Gary's students. Gary was pretty good about it, and so was Kara. They tried not to make Justin feel bad. They swooned over puppies and dogs only when he wasn't around.

"Look at these guys," Gary yelled, waving Leigh over. The puppy was stretching up, trying to bite Kara's ear. "There are two of them. She found them in a drain ditch. Come feel this one's coat."

As she came closer, Leigh noticed how thin Kara looked with her blazer off. She'd always been healthy and strong, but now her arms looked sticklike, too long for her body. They looked like Justin's arms. Leigh was so disturbed that it took her a moment to register that Kara was actually smiling.

"I'll give you both of them for free." A sunburned woman sat on the tailgate of a truck that was covered with potted geraniums. Another puppy wriggled in a cage by her feet. "I can't take on any more. My dog's mean. He'll kill these two. They need someplace to go."

Gary sighed. Leigh said nothing, but she stepped closer, so she could be under the shade of the tent pitched over the truck.

"Sorry," Kara said. She was speaking to the sunburned woman, not to Leigh. "I wish we could. They're so sweet." She gently lowered the puppy back down to the cage.

Gary leaned over, working his fingers through the wires to give it one last scratch behind the ears. Leigh turned, thinking they would go back to the car, but he held her shoulder. "Hey," he said. "They've got homemade ice cream over there." He squinted to see the sign. "Homemade strawberry ice cream. I've got to have some of that. Come on."

Leigh and Kara exchanged looks of apprehension. For once, they were united against him.

"Oh, come on." Gary held out his arms to Leigh. She was the one he had to convince. If he got her on board, Kara would have to follow. "I don't get the puppy. At least give me the ice cream. My God."

She nodded, just once. The next moment he was tugging both of them through the crowd. She saw familiar faces and braced herself—for what, she didn't know. They were going right into the thick of it, the public square, with all its judgment and scorn. But no one bothered them. No one pointed or gave them dirty looks. They passed Cynthia Tork, who was wearing a red-checked apron and selling apple pies from the back of a church van. She either didn't notice them or pretended not to. They passed one of Kara's teachers from grade school. She was waiting to buy tomatoes—it would have been easy enough for her to ignore them—but she turned to smile and wave.

Still, when Gary finally pulled Leigh and Kara into the line for ice cream, they both tried to use him as something to hide behind. Unfortunately, that put them on the sunny side of Gary—within minutes, they were both sweating, woozy from the heat.

Gary turned and frowned down at them. He was sweating too, and turning a little pink, but he did that whenever the temperature got above seventy degrees. "You two go sit down," he said, pointing at a portable icebox someone had left in the shade. Leigh hung back, uncertain. Gary nodded at Kara, and Leigh noticed how pale she looked. She handed her a water bottle from her purse.

"Come on," she said, taking Kara's arm. Her skin was cool to the touch, and Leigh didn't let go of her until they were both safely seated on the icebox. Kara tried to hand the water back, but Leigh shook her head. "Drink it all. You don't look good."

Kara placed the bottle between her knees. Leigh waited ten seconds, counting slowly in her head.

"Kara. Please drink more of that. Now."

Kara raised the bottle to her lips. Her face appeared stoic, impenetrable, as if she believed her mother were trying to torment her, and she had made up her mind not to give her any satisfaction, not to show any pain. Leigh looked away and rubbed her eyes. She couldn't say anything the right way. If Gary had told her to drink the water, there wouldn't have been a problem. But because the words had come out of her mouth, Kara perceived them as hostile. It didn't matter what she said or how she said it. It was so unfair. She'd tried so much harder to be a good mother. She'd tried to do everything exactly the opposite.

"Leigh? Is that you?"

She looked up to see Heather Crill walking toward her. Heather was the treasurer for the PTA. She was friendly and good with numbers, but Leigh liked her mostly because she always looked a little disheveled, her clothes wrinkled, her hair frizzy or pulled back into a bun. She had four sons, the youngest Justin's age.

"How crazy is Tanner Marik's mother?" Heather turned her index finger near her temple, smiling down at Kara. Maybe she didn't know, Leigh thought. Not everyone read the paper.

"What do you mean?"

Heather looked at her watch. "Well, every soon-to-be seventh-grade boy in town woke up in her backyard or in her house. I mean, I saw the house—I know it's big, and I know most of them camped outside, but no way would I take that on. Jared told me that we weren't supposed to go pick them up until noon, and I hope he wasn't lying. He wasn't, right? Did Justin tell you that?"

Leigh nodded slowly. It took her a moment to understand. Every soon-to-be seventh-grade boy. Except for hers.

"He did tell you that, right?" Heather was still joking around.

"Yeah." Leigh started to smile, but couldn't quite manage it.

"Okay, well... See you later." Heather looked hurt, confused.

Leigh didn't care. She barely raised her hand in a limp wave, watching Heather walk away. They needed to move, she decided. Too bad about Gary's job. He would have to do something else.

"He's a little jerk, that Tanner."

Leigh turned to Kara, surprised. "You know him?"

"I know who he is. He was on our bus route for a while. Even when he was a little kid, he was mean." She looked more sad than angry. "But his parents are wrong too, if they knew he invited everyone but Justin. They should have checked."

Leigh nodded. She wondered if Justin had known about the party.

"My God, you two look alike sometimes."

Gary stood over them, holding three ice cream cones. "Sorry. There was a three for one special," he said, handing one to Leigh, one to Kara. "I couldn't resist."

"I really don't need to eat th—" Leigh started, and then literally bit her tongue. She remembered, all at once, that Gary didn't like strawberries or ice cream. Kara did, or at least she had, back when she let herself eat. When she felt certain Kara wasn't looking, she stole a glance. Kara held her cone close to her face, her brow furrowed. She appeared to be pondering something carefully. Gary started to whistle. Leigh turned away and bit into her own cone.

Kara's first few bites were timid, uncertain. But soon, she was really eating, taking big bites, crunching into the cone. Leigh tried to think of something chatty she could say to provide a distraction. But she couldn't focus on anything. Kara did not appear to be tasting the food, or even eating it, so much as breathing it in. It was as if she were running out of time, as if someone were threatening to take it away from her. She did not pretend to be interested in conversation or anything else. In some ways, Leigh considered, her daughter had been imprisoned, denied sustenance. She was her own jailer, and she'd been a good one. But now, finally, the life force in her was winning out. She'd wanted to deny herself, to punish herself, but in the end, her body just wouldn't just let go. It was more rational than Kara's mind. It didn't care about guilt. Or if it did, it wouldn't forever. Kara's body—all that young, lean muscle and taut skin—was just more pragmatic than its owner. Leigh had to admire it for that.

At the exact moment Kara finished her cone, Gary handed her his. He did this casually, with no eye contact.

"Those pups made me think of a dog I had when I was little," he said.

Kara looked up, her cheeks full. "I thought you didn't get to have a dog."

"I did once." He wiped his hands on a napkin. "For about a week."

Leigh smiled. She knew this story. As a boy, Gary had found a stray dog. After much pleading and whining, his parents finally relented and said he could keep it as long as it stayed in the backyard and didn't cause any problems. The dog didn't stay in the yard, and it kept causing problems. Gary would come home from school or wake in the morning to find it gone, and then he would have to search his suburban streets until he invariably found it rooting through someone's garbage or tormenting other dogs held in check by fences or chains. Gary and his brother inspected their backyard fence carefully. But it was a good fence, no holes, and there was no sign of digging. The latch worked well. So there was nothing for Gary to do but to feign illness one day so he wouldn't have to go to school. When his mother wasn't in his room, bringing him chicken noodle soup or taking his temperature, he was at his window, keeping watch over the escape artist dog. That was how he discovered the dog could let himself out of the backyard. Gary saw him actually stand on his hind legs and work the latch with his paws until the door swung open.

"It was like he had a thumb," Gary said, handing both Kara and

Leigh extra napkins from his pocket. "I swear. You smile, Leigh, okay. You don't believe me. But I tell you, Kara, this dog had a thumb. It was a tricky latch. You had to pull both up and out." He mimed the action with his hands. Leigh smiled again, and people in the line for ice cream turned to look, their faces friendly and open. He still had enough of an East Coast accent to amuse strangers with just his voice.

"So this was some genius stray dog, apparently." He kept his eyes on Kara. "And the thing is, the interesting thing, *he looked so stupid.* He was cross-eyed, had his mouth open all the time. But there was something going on in there. In his brain. Who knows what he would have figured out if we let him into the house? He would have cracked the safe in my father's office. He would have been baking things in the oven. He had the latch figured out in about a day. I didn't even think he was watching when I did it."

Here, Gary turned and looked back at Kara out of the corner of his eye. Both Leigh and Kara laughed. Kara's laugh was quiet, more of a low chuckle, and Leigh silenced herself to better hear it. Kara really did have a nice laugh, low and earnest, nothing coquettish or phony about it.

At this same moment, Leigh might have also registered a hollow, clomping sound, steady and increasing in volume. If she had been paying attention, she might have heard the sound and thought of a pair of clogs, and how they would sound on hot asphalt. But she wasn't paying attention. She was thinking about her daughter's laugh, and how, for the first time since the accident, the world almost felt normal.

"Are you enjoying yourself?"

The voice was so friendly that Gary, Leigh, and Kara each looked up with a smile. Only Leigh's faded quickly. Diane Kletchka stood maybe five feet away, looking down at Kara with a kindly, curious expression, her eyebrows high, her smile wide. Her curls had gone wild in the humidity and heat, and her plastic headband was askew.

"Are you? Are you having a good time? How's your ice cream?"

Leigh stood and took a step forward. Diane stepped around her.

"Do you know who I am?"

Kara leaned away a bit. She had some strawberry ice cream on her lip. She shook her head, her eyes moving to her father's, and then, more reluctantly, her mother's.

"I'll give you a hint, honey. You killed my daughter." Her voice grew louder with every word, and the smile faded. "My reason for getting up in the morning. My world. You ran her over with your big car because you were talking on the phone and screwing around—"

Kara dropped her ice cream on the ground. She put her hand to her mouth.

"Please." Gary held both hands up.

"But Mommy and Daddy hired an expensive lawyer, and you don't think you're guilty, apparently. Not guilty, right? And after you sit there in your nice little outfit and look so sad, your acting job is done for the day and you can just hop across the street here and have some ice cream! 'Cause it's a sunny day! And you don't really feel that bad, do you? Not—"

"She feels terrible," Leigh said. "Did you get my note?"

Diane Kletchka dismissed this with a wave of her hand. Kara looked at her mother.

"Listen," Gary said. It was his teaching tone, his tone of logic, his tone of arguing with Leigh. "This is inappropriate. This will have to stop. We understand you've suffered a great loss. But as I see it, you'll have the chance to write your... statement of impact. You'll have your day in cour—"

"Don't hand me that shit." Diane Kletchka's face was suddenly close to his. Her nostrils trembled, and her eyes were wide. "They don't care about me. The D.A.'s making deals with your lawyer. I know that. It's all who knows who, who golfs with who, let's protect the princess."

"We don't golf," Gary said. He looked confused. He looked as if he were trying to speak a language he didn't really know. Leigh touched his arm.

"Impact statement?" Diane Kletchka had tears in her eyes. "I told them my impact. Me not wanting to live anymore. How's that for my impact? And they pretty much said, in very nice polite language, that I could FUCK MYSELF, okay? They're going to give the princess a deal."

Gary swallowed. Leigh could not remember ever before seeing him at a total loss. He opened his mouth, but said nothing. People were looking. She could feel this, like a building of pressure, without even looking around.

"They don't give a fuck about me, and they don't give a fuck about Bethany, who was an AMAZING PERSON." She stepped around Gary, leaning into Kara's cower. "WHO WAS WORTH MORE THAN YOU, MORE THAN YOU COULD EVER BE WORTH, YOU STUPID, SPOILED LIT—"

"That's enough."

Leigh didn't yell. She had taught junior high long enough to know how to reach down into the lower levels of her vocal range to produce a sound that was both startling and firm. But she also felt as if she were calling on some deeper resource, going further back. She knew Diane Kletchka. She didn't know all of her, but something about her felt familiar.

Diane was quiet for several moments, her eyes studying Leigh's face.

"How can you say she doesn't feel bad?" Leigh heard her own voice shaking. "How can you look at her and say she doesn't feel bad? She feels terrible. That"—she pointed at the cone and melted ice cream at Kara's feet—"that was the most we've gotten her to eat in weeks." She took a step forward. She and Diane Kletchka looked at each other, both of them breathing hard. "You talk as if she meant to do this. It was an accident. She is not a spoiled princess. She is a good person, a decent, thoughtful person who made a mistake. She is sorry. If you look at her, if you just look, you'll know she's sorry. She is as full of remorse as a person can be."

But Diane Kletchka no longer seemed interested in looking at Kara. She turned her head away, maybe just out of defiance. Leigh looked back over her shoulder at Kara. She didn't appear remorseful so much as disoriented, bewildered. But she wasn't looking at Diane Kletchka. She was looking up at Leigh.

Diane's eyes narrowed, though she still wasn't looking at anyone. "She isn't sorry. She's going to go off to college in the fall, isn't she? La la la, like it never hap—"

"I said that's enough." Leigh handed Gary the keys and motioned with her hand toward the car. Diane Kletchka's eyes were hard on hers, bright with tears and rage. *She could attack me,* Leigh thought. *It could come to that.* She thought of the woman in the courtroom, biting another woman's nose in a bar. But she didn't move. She held the other woman's gaze until she was sure it was just the two of them.

"I want you to know..." She took a step back and lowered her eyes. "What I said in my note is true. Kara feels terrible. She really does."

Diane Kletchka rolled her eyes.

"And I am thinking of you." Leigh was crying too now, trying not to, failing. This woman wouldn't believe her crying, but she could barely get the words out. "Please know. I am thinking of your daughter, and of your loss, all the time."

For a moment, the bright sun shining down hot on their faces, it looked as if some connection had been forged. The other woman's eyes dulled, and her mouth hung a bit slack, as if something inside had been softened. But it didn't last. Before Leigh could say anything more, the other woman's teary cheeks lifted in a rueful smile.

"Give me a break." She almost seemed amused, looking at just Leigh's torso now, not her face. "I see right through you. You're selfish. You're a selfish, selfish woman. Those tears are for you and your daughter. The whole time you've been standing here, you've been thinking only about yourself."

Chapter 14

S HE WAS STILL SHAKING when she got to the car. Kara was in the backseat, her face in her hands. Gary had the engine running, the doors locked. Leigh had to knock on the window. As soon as she was in her seat, he pulled away from the curb—slowly, safely; though no tires screeched, she still felt as if she were being whisked away like a criminal witness or a hounded celebrity, someone needing protection from a crowd. Only there was no crowd. No one had followed her from the market. Even Bethany's mother had remained where she was, standing still while Leigh walked away. It hardly mattered. She might as well have been in the car with them, or hanging on outside and banging on the windows. Leigh could still see her face very clearly, the tears sliding down, collecting in the grooves around her mouth. She could still hear the voice, all that hatred in it. *You don't even feel bad.*

"You okay?" Gary asked.

"Yeah," Leigh said. It wasn't true. She felt everything but okay. She felt adrenaline pumping through her body. She felt a wave of nausea as the air-conditioning cooled her goose-pimpled skin. She felt the now-familiar weight of Bethany's death against her chest. She turned around. Kara stared out the window, her arms wrapped tightly around her chest. She wasn't crying, but her eyes suggested a complete unhappiness that seemed more despondent than tears.

"How're you doing?" Leigh asked. She regretted it at once. It had been poorly put, not what she meant. She steeled herself, waiting.

"Okay."

Leigh swallowed. There had been no ice in her daughter's voice, no glare in her eyes. Tentatively, Leigh reached through the seats. She felt awkward, a little embarrassed, as if she were trying to act like someone else, but she placed her hand on Kara's knee. Kara didn't look up, but Leigh counted to three before she lifted her hand and let her arm retreat back through the seats to her own body. Gary said nothing, and she was grateful for that. They were almost home, and she needed time to think. Kara was, perhaps, just too shaken from Diane Kletchka's words, too full of self-loathing and hopelessness to remember that she usually hated her mother, but there was also a chance, Leigh understood, that a window between them had opened. If this was even true, the window could close again at any moment; she would have to try to slip through it now, while she could still feel Diane Kletchka's breath against her face, while she was still invigorated by fear and anger, her teeth still chattering, sweat still cooling on her brow.

They pulled into the driveway. Leigh gazed at the garage door with wide, unseeing eyes. She would come up with a plan. *We need to talk,* she would say, and she would say it in a confident but loving voice, something between Sue Taft's and Pam's. She could imagine the voice. What she couldn't imagine was what she would actually say. Already, even as she got out of the car, slowly, heavily, she could picture Kara's unhappy eyes staring back at her, waiting.

They went inside. Gary cruised through the kitchen, moving toward the stairway without pause. "I need to take a shower," he said. He didn't make eye contact, and Leigh couldn't tell if he knew what was going on, what needed to happen at that precise moment, or if he really just needed a shower. The back of his shirt was damp with sweat, and his dress pants clung to his legs. He walked upstairs without another word.

Leigh looked down at the gray and white kitchen tiles, the checkered pattern of squares around her feet. The adrenaline was already leaving her. She didn't know what to say. Someone else would. Some other mother.

Kara opened a cupboard. "You want some water?"

Leigh nodded. Kara filled the glass and handed it to her.

"I didn't know you sent a note." Kara got out another glass for herself. "I mean, I knew you were thinking about it. I didn't know you'd already sent it."

Leigh looked up. "Yeah. I did. I just wanted to...express my condolences." She frowned at the words, how empty they sounded. "I wanted her to know you felt bad, and that you're not, you know, this terrible person."

"I heard you say that to her." Kara held her water glass just beneath her lips. "Thanks for that."

"Sure. Well, it's all true. It's what I think."

Kara looked at her carefully.

"It is what I think. You've always been a kind, thoughtful person. Anybody who knows you would say that."

Kara didn't move.

"I've always thought that. I know you don't think it's true. But it is. I don't know..." She held up her hands. She didn't know what to say. "I don't know why we don't get along."

"Because you don't like me." Kara lifted her chin. The way she did it made Leigh think of Justin.

"That's not true."

Kara said nothing. Her gray eyes stayed steady on Leigh.

"Kara. I honestly don't know why you would think that. I don't know..."

Kara took a sip of water, moving it from cheek to cheek before she swallowed. She'd done that as a child, Leigh remembered. *I'm warming it,* she'd told Leigh once. *I don't like it cold in my throat.* Even now, Leigh could remember her little-girl voice, the butterfly weight of her fingers.

"Maybe the way you look at me?" Her voice was low now, her gaze direct.

"What? How do I look at you?"

Kara's eyes settled on the refrigerator door, on the photos and the magnets. "You look at me like I'm annoying and stupid. You look at me like I'm tap dancing on the table if I so much as open my mouth."

Leigh worked to keep her face very still. It was probably for the best, she considered, that she hadn't known what to say earlier. For once, she had not organized the conversation.

"You sure haven't looked at me like that lately, though." Kara eyed her mother warily. "You don't seem to be annoyed with me at all these days." She paused, pursing her lips, and Leigh was at once reminded of Gary, the way he looked when deciding whether to say something both true and hurtful. "I won't say you're glad that it happened, the accident. But I will say you've been a lot nicer to me lately." She smiled, but her eyes were cold. "You should have told me this was all it would take for you to like me. I would have just killed someone a long time ago."

Leigh started to shake her head, but then stopped. Perhaps it was true. Perhaps there was something ugly inside her, something that loved only misery and bad luck. Her eyes moved over her daughter's face.

"I never disliked you." She said the words as she thought them. "I just didn't know... I couldn't think of how to... I didn't know what it was like to be someone like you."

"Like what? What is that supposed to mean?"

Leigh looked at the ceiling. She thought of all those evenings in

Philadelphia, listening to little Stella Aubrey-Gold laughing in the bathtub. "Fortunate," she said, her voice quiet, difficult to hear. It didn't matter if Kara heard or not, she thought. She wouldn't understand.

But Kara nodded as if this were the answer she'd expected. "I know you and Aunt Pam had a hard time growing up."

Leigh frowned. So her sister had betrayed confidences on both sides. Or maybe it was Gary. It was one or the other. Leigh herself had never said anything bad about growing up with her mother and without her father, not in front of her children. She didn't want to be like her mother, going on and on about how hard things had been, how much worse she'd had it, and so on. But now Kara was looking at her as if she were waiting, even begging for more information. Maybe, Leigh considered, children just want whatever it is they don't get. And then they grow up and give their children what they wanted, be it silence or information, affection or independence—so that child, in turn, craves something else. With every generation, the pendulum swings from opposite to opposite, stillness and peace so elusive.

But she couldn't stop it now, even as she saw it all clearly. Kara, for her part, was already losing patience, her eyes dulled with disappointment.

"And now I guess you do know? Now you do know what it's like to be me? Now that I'm not so fortunate?"

Leigh shook her head. She didn't know. She had no idea what it felt like to accidentally kill another much-loved human being, to suffer under that weight. She might have started this little competition in misery, but Kara had won it, hands down. A memory came to her all at once, linked by only a feeling, and because Leigh could feel the window between them sliding slowly closed, she opened her mouth, frantic for any delay.

"You know, when I was a girl..." She saw the interest in Kara's eyes and worried she had misled her. She would not tell a Poor Leigh story. She looked out the window, out over the porch swing and the lawn and described the moment as she recalled it: She had been eleven, maybe twelve. She and Pam had been playing at a fountain in some park. She didn't know what town they were in, where they'd been living then, maybe Arkansas. It was hot. She and Pam had been splashing each other, trying to cool off. There were a bunch of little kids there, milling around, and one of the mothers told Leigh and Pam to be careful. They were for a while. They were nice girls, reared by their mother to be respectful, but it was so hot out, the water of the fountain so cool, and after a while they started horsing around again, and then somehow Leigh stumbled back onto a little boy. He was two or maybe three, still unsteady on his feet, and he fell hard onto the pavement beneath her. He was more scared than anything. But he did scrape his knee, and it bled. Even now, Leigh remembered the shame she'd felt when the boy was crying, how aware she'd been that everyone was looking at her and thinking she should have been more careful. The boy only wanted his mother, so there was nothing for Leigh to do but stand there and say she was sorry, feeling big and clumsy and dumb.

She stopped talking. She was a mother herself again, looking at her miserable daughter.

"I'm not saying it's the same," she said hastily. "That's my point. That's the closest I can come to knowing what you feel like." She looked at her hands. "And it's not close at all."

"Frustrating, isn't it?"

Leigh looked up, surprised. But she understood. We all have our trifling comparisons, she considered, our weak attempts to feel each other's burdens. She forced herself to stop talking. She was trying harder now. She was trying to see, and hear. "Yes. It is," she said carefully. "So. How does it feel?"

Kara laughed. For a moment, she looked truly happy, her smile wide, all teeth. But the sound she was making was high-pitched and sharp. "How does it feel to kill someone?" She stopped smiling and closed her eyes. "It feels like..." When she opened her eyes again, there were tears, but the rest of her face seemed dissociated, with no expression, as if she were sleeping. "It feels like nothing is ever going to be the same, and it shouldn't be. I'm never going to be the person I was. I'm never, ever going to be as happy as I used to be. I'm never going to be as happy as I would have been if I just hadn't gone out that day, if I hadn't stopped for the dog, or for the drinks. Never. Because as long as I live, she'll always be dead."

Leigh said nothing. She had the impression Kara did not expect, or even desire, consolation. A small, fine crease had formed high on her daughter's brow. It was maybe a few inches below her hairline. Leigh wondered how long it had been there. She'd never noticed it before.

Kara raised her eyes to her mother's. "I thought I was miserable last year"—she rolled her eyes, still crying—"when Eric broke up with me. I guess I was, relatively speaking. That seemed pretty bad at the time. I remember I didn't want to get up in the morning. I didn't want to go to school. But even then, deep down, I knew I'd be okay again. And this time, I know I won't. I'm never going to get over this." She closed her eyes tightly, as if trying not to see something, and the pressure produced more tears. "Because even if I start to feel better, I shouldn't, and I'll know it. Every time I smile, every time I laugh, a part of me will feel like I don't deserve it, because I'm laughing and smiling while she's dead, and she's dead because of me. I'll have to think about how old she would be, what she might be doing...."

Leigh nodded, trying to think. She couldn't disagree with any of it. And though it was, perhaps, an insignificant point, she hadn't known that Eric had broken up with Kara. She'd assumed it was the other way around. She couldn't remember why she had assumed this. She tried to think back to the previous year. She didn't remember Kara's being sad.

"I wanted to do good things with my life." Kara wiped her cheeks with the back of her hand. Her fingernails, Leigh saw now, had all been chewed down to the quick. "I was going to help people. I knew I'd been given so much, that I'd had it easier than ... other people."

Leigh nodded again. She was new at this, and it was hard to know when good listening became too much listening, not enough arguing back.

"Kara," she said finally, firmly. "You can still do all the things you wanted to do."

"It doesn't matter what I do now. Nothing will ever make up for it."

"Yeah." Leigh nodded at the truth of it.

Kara looked up, surprised.

"You've got to quit trying for that, I mean. Nothing will ever make up for it." She waited, thinking. "But if you're bent on paying some kind of penance, you should try to be ... constructive about it. I know that sounds pragmatic, and maybe cold. But not applying for the diversion—that's not constructive. That's not going to help anybody. It's just a big waste of energy and time. Not just yours, but everyone's."

"It's what she wants." Kara nodded in the direction of the garage; in that general direction, more than a mile away, was the farmers' market. Leigh knew who she meant.

"No it isn't. How will it help her? How will it help her for you to go to jail for five days? To permanently mark your record? It's bad for you, but it won't help her. How will a trial help her? It's not going to bring her daughter back. It's not going to help her at all."

Kara turned away, her hands in front of her face, protective. "She wants me to go to jail." She was more upset than she had been before Leigh started talking. "You heard her. She doesn't want me to take the diversion."

"She wants her daughter back. That's what she wants. And your going to jail, your suffering, won't help that. She may think it will, but even if you spend your life in jail, even if you die, Kara, even if you stop eating again and starve to death, she's not going to feel what she's waiting to feel. She's not going to feel any better. I guarantee it. She's only going to be disappointed."

Even as Leigh spoke these words, she was surprised by the confidence she heard in her own voice. Part of her wondered if this confidence was perhaps misplaced, if she even had any idea what she was talking about. After all, she had never lost a child. She had no way of knowing the intensity of Diane Kletchka's dreams of vengeance, or what a permanent mark against Kara's future might mean for her and her grief. Perhaps punishing Kara, darkening her bright future, really would ease the woman's pain. Leigh could only guess it would not, based on her own, lesser losses and a lifetime of futile and misguided attempts at finding any restitution.

LATER THAT AFTERNOON, PAM walked into the house with slow, heavy steps. Justin, wearing her sunglasses and laughing about something, moved in quick circles around her. She handed Leigh her car keys and fell onto the couch with a groan. "Never get into an ice cream–eating contest with a twelve-year-old boy."

"I could still eat." Justin perched on the arm of the couch, one long pale leg crossed over the other. "I'm serious. I could eat right now. I could have another one of those big waffle cone things with the chocolate on the bottom and the—"

"Please stop." Pam held up her hand.

Leigh leaned over Justin from behind, lifted his shirt, and patted his protruding belly. "I'm sure you could eat more, darling, but I have a feeling you don't need to. And it's Friday. You've got to be at the nursing home in an hour." She sniffed his shirt. "You should take a shower first. And change clothes."

"Are you saying I smell?"

She squinted. He could keep such a straight face. It was hard, even for her, to know when he was kidding sometimes.

"Yes, Justin. That's what I'm saying. I'm saying that you smell."

"Okay. Okay." He kept his eyes on hers. "I'm hearing that. It's hard, but I'm hearing it."

She smiled. He was imitating his guidance counselor from grade school. "Great. Then go." She lifted her foot to his butt and stopped just short of a gentle kick. He was so bony, so thin. She might hurt him, just playing around. She sat on the arm of the couch and watched him bound up the stairs.

"An ice cream–eating contest?" Leigh poked her sister's side. "What were you thinking?"

"Sorry." Pam rolled over and lowered her voice. "I was desperate to cheer him up. Some kid had a big slumber party last night, invited every boy in his class but him."

Leigh turned back to the stairs. She heard his bedroom door close. "Why didn't he say anything?"

"He's embarrassed, I think. And he doesn't want you and Gary to worry. He's worried about you two, about Kara."

Leigh nodded. But her mind hovered over the idea that Justin had confided in his aunt about the slumber party. He had not confided in her. He was almost a teenager. Perhaps he would quit talking to her and telling her things. She'd never worried that would happen. She'd assumed he would always need her, at least more than Kara had. But perhaps he would go to Pam for understanding as well.

"How'd the arraignment go?"

Leigh shrugged. "The way we thought it would. But we had a run-in with the mother afterward."

"Who?"

"The mother. Bethany's mother."

"Oh," Pam said. It was all she said, that one word, but her voice held so much ache and sympathy that it seemed to Leigh her sister might have actually been there at the market and seen Diane Kletchka's misery and insanity for herself. Leigh relayed the entire confrontation, and her sister's face grew more distressed. It was hard to tell who she was feeling sorry for—Bethany's mother, or Kara, or Gary, or Leigh herself. And that made sense. Leigh knew this even as she was talking, even as she felt a resurgence of fear just describing the scene. There were, after all, no underdogs in the scene, no winners or losers to root for. It was a miserable situation for everyone involved. An objective bystander could only wish they would all get through it.

THAT EVENING, LEIGH WAS in bed reading when she became aware of a steady, repeated thudding. She listened for a moment, and then got up and went out to the hallway. From the window on the other end, she could see the driveway, the front door, the cloud of insects swarming around the floodlight over the garage. Kara moved in and out of the light, bouncing a basketball with one hand. Her hair was pulled back into a knot at the base of her neck, and she had on gym shorts and one of Gary's old T-shirts. She dribbled twice and released the ball with a sharp grunt. Leigh couldn't see the hoop from the window, but she heard the ball bounce off the backboard. Kara lunged for it and tried again. By then, Leigh's eyes had adjusted to the semidarkness, and she could see the strained expression on her daughter's face, the furrowed brows, the bared teeth. The ball got away from her and rolled into the yard. Kara ran after it. She swooped and turned quickly, tossing it up toward the hoop. Leigh heard the ball bounce off the backboard again. She looked at her watch. It was eleven o'clock. If this had been the previous summer, or the summer before that, she might have knocked on the glass and told Kara to come in. *Consider the neighbors,* she might have said. *Consider someone besides yourself.*

"Is that Kara out there?" Gary appeared in the hallway, wearing just pajama bottoms. He held his toothbrush in one hand, a tube of toothpaste in the other. By the time she met his eyes, they were both smiling. He'd put on weight in the last year—back surgery had kept him sedentary all winter. He was self-conscious about it; he'd always been long and lean, and now his belly protruded enough to be visible under shirts. But she liked the softness of his new belly. She liked how it felt against her, and the contrast with the rest of his body, which was still firm, strong. He moved beside her and leaned down, his arm around her shoulders. Their central air hardly cooled the upstairs—they used window units in the bedrooms and bathrooms, but the hallway always felt stuffy. Still, his arm felt warm against her back, warmer than the air around her.

"That seems like a good sign," he whispered. When she looked back out the window, Kara had her arms raised high over her head. The ball moved toward the light, and for a moment, there was no sound. Kara did not smile, but she looked momentarily satisfied. Leigh could imagine the ball moving cleanly through the hoop, not touching the sides at all.

She might partially recover, Leigh considered. She might start going out to play basketball every night; eventually, Gary would go out there with her, and it would be like all those evenings before, when Leigh had stayed inside by herself. Kara would think of

Bethany for the rest of her life—Leigh was sure of that—but after a while, her daughter might start smiling again. She might go back to the way she was, doing well in school, winning everyone over.

"Is Pam out there with her?" Gary pressed his cheek against the glass, trying to see the porch. "Is she on the swing?"

Leigh shrugged. She realized, all at once, that it had not occurred to her to wonder. This, also, seemed like a very good sign. She kept watching through the window. Her fingers tightened their grip on Gary's hand every time Kara let go of the ball, and she held her breath, wishing as hard as she'd ever wished for anything that the ball would sail through the hoop every time her daughter took a shot.

THE NEXT DAY, LEIGH came downstairs to find Kara at the dining room table, eating a piece of toast with peanut butter and reading Gary's *New York Times*. She was already dressed, wearing a clean T-shirt and her denim skirt. Her hair was still wet from the shower.

"Morning." She barely glanced up at her mother. She was wearing her glasses. A piece of wet hair was caught around the hinges of one of the frames. Leigh's hand lifted to brush it away, but she held it back, uncertain.

"Morning." Leigh went into the kitchen to make coffee, but Kara had already made it. She poured herself a cup and went back to the dining room, careful not to look at the half-eaten toast on Kara's plate. Her eyes fell on the *Danby Chronicle* in the middle of the table.

Woman Talking on Cell Phone Charged with Reckless Driving in Pedestrian Death.

And there was a picture of Kara, the picture Leigh had seen the photographer take in the lobby of the courthouse. She hadn't looked so bad in real life, Leigh thought. She hadn't looked so washed out and sickly in the cream suit, her head bowed, her eyes looking up at the camera as if she were silently pleading for death. They'd edited Gary out of the picture, but in the margin, Leigh could see most of his hand, his fingers reaching for Kara's arm. The actual article, written by Leigh's talented former student, seemed to say nothing—the arraignment had been held; everyone had said what was expected; no one had given any comment. But people would be interested in the picture, Leigh imagined. People would want to see that.

"You're done with this?" Leigh sat and moved her hand toward the *Chronicle*. She tried not to point at the picture.

Kara nodded without looking up. Leigh looked over the *Times'* front page and tried to guess what could be holding her daughter's attention so raptly: There was an article on rising gas prices, and another on party positioning for the next election. There was a feature on poverty in India, and boxed off on the side, an article stating four more servicemen had been killed in Iraq.

"Does it give their names?"

"What?" Kara looked up. She seemed startled.

"I'm sorry. I was looking..." Leigh pointed at the headline. "Does it say who died in Iraq?"

"No. But Ellis is in Baghdad, right? That's not where—that's not where it happened."

Leigh looked at both newspapers and frowned. "Okay. But let's put these away before Pam gets up. It'll make her crazy, and there's nothing she can do."

Kara nodded and went back to reading. Leigh sipped her coffee, staring dully at the table. She should leave Kara alone. She herself didn't like to be bothered when she was reading. But she could hear Gary moving around upstairs. Justin might sleep until ten, but Gary would come down for breakfast soon, and there was a good chance—Leigh braced herself—that Kara would stop reading and give him eye contact and have a conversation with him, and Leigh would have to sit there and look unbothered, all the while knowing with a crushing certainty that nothing between her and Kara would ever change.

Kara folded the paper. "I was wondering if you would give me a ride to Willow's. Her mom's, I mean. She's at her mom's this week."

Leigh blinked. She could not remember the last time Kara had needed a ride anywhere. Rides had once been their bond. All those years before Kara got her license, Leigh had spent at least an hour a day driving her to and from soccer practice and Spanish Club fundraisers and student council meetings and the humane society, and it had been hard not to resent it sometimes—the very idea that she spent much of her free time chauffeuring someone, someone who would not talk to her unless absolutely necessary, from one fun event to another. But when Kara got her license, Leigh had felt a little nostalgic for the old days, when her daughter actually needed her.

And now she needed a ride to Willow's. She couldn't drive now. Of course she couldn't.

"I mean, I can go whenever." Kara pushed her hair behind her ears, pulling free the tangle on the earpiece. "But she's uh...she can't come over here. She's...not feeling well, and—"

"She just got breast implants?"

Kara watched her mother's eyes.

"Eva told me. Yeah, I'll take you. Is nine too early? I've got some errands to run, and I want to go before it gets too hot."

"No. Nine's fine. I mean, I'll call her and make sure."

They both looked back at their newspapers. Leigh wondered if she should say something more. Or ask something, rather. She was so tired of trying to guess what to say, to ask. She tried to think of what she wanted to know.

"What do you think of that?" She turned a page of the newspaper as she spoke, and she kept her eyes lowered. "Of Willow getting implants, I mean."

A long silence followed. Leigh clenched her teeth and kept her eyes on the newspaper. She'd sounded like an idiot. She wasn't Eva. She wasn't the cool mom. She sounded like an imposter to herself.

"I think it's fine." Kara picked up her toast and took another bite. She chewed and swallowed, looking out the window. "She's wanted to do it for a long time. She's been talking about it since, like, ninth grade."

Leigh nodded slowly. *Wait,* she told herself. *Listen.*

Kara looked at her again. "She doesn't think it's going to make her a different person. She doesn't want to be a different person. She just wants them, the implants, I mean. I don't know."

Leigh kept her expression as neutral as she could. But she could see that old hostility creeping back into her daughter's eyes. Or it wasn't hostility, maybe. She looked carefully at her daughter, her gaze focused and intense, as if she were trying to peer through something opaque. No, it wasn't hostility that twisted her daughter's mouth into a tight circle. It was protectiveness. It was worry.

Kara looked away. "What do you think about it?"

"I think..." Leigh hesitated. "I'm not sure what I think. I think Willow can do what she wants to do. But I also think she was really beautiful the way she was."

Kara nodded. Leigh watched her lips go slack.

"Both you girls were. Are, I mean." She put her coffee down. "I just worry, you know, that now everyone thinks they have to do this. It'll set some impossible standard, or some standard only possible through surgery. I mean, are you, you're not thinking of...?"

"Am I thinking of getting breast implants?" Kara's eyebrows rose above her glasses.

Leigh stopped talking. She'd said the wrong thing.

"Are you saying you think I nee—"

"No!"

But Kara was smiling, or not really smiling, but clearly trying hard not to. She couldn't keep a straight face the way Justin could. But she had a good sense of humor, Leigh considered. She hadn't thought that about her daughter before. She didn't know why. Kara just hadn't seemed like the type of person who would be funny. It was like hearing a dog meow, a cat bark.

"Good." Kara's voice was suddenly low and somber. Her eyes moved across the table to her photograph in the paper, the almost-smile completely gone. "'Cause it's, you know, not really on the agenda right now."

Gary came downstairs when Kara was on the phone. Before he did anything, before he poured himself a cup of coffee or said hello to Leigh, before he even looked down at the table and noticed the sad picture of his daughter on the front page of the newspaper, he paused by the kitchen window, squinting.

"I'm going to mow the lawn," he said. He spoke gravely, as if he were looking up at a mountain he intended to climb.

He was a man of his word. An hour later, when Leigh and Kara backed out of the driveway, he was out in the front, pouring gasoline into the mower. He looked up and waved, sweat already beading down his forearm. If he was envious of their togetherness, or of their place in the air-conditioned car, he made no show of it. He simply smiled as if the vision pleased him, then turned his attention back to the lawn.

EVA LIVED ON THE other side of town, in a townhouse surrounded by identical townhouses that were solely inhabited, as far as Leigh could tell, by people over seventy years of age. Eva had been living there for years, ever since the divorce. But it still surprised Leigh sometimes, to think of someone as youthful and glamorous as Eva living in what appeared to be a retirement community. "Oh, but I love it," she'd told Leigh. "It's great. The lawn is all taken care of. There's a pool. I don't have to worry about anyone breaking in—somebody's always walking by. Rick left after I did one morning, and two different people called to let me know there was a strange man leaving my house. One of them took a picture of him with her phone."

"And you like that?" Leigh had asked.

"They're just looking after me. And they keep an eye on Willow when she's here, that's for sure. I'd like to see her try to sneak out or sneak a boy over."

Truly, Eva's neighbors—even the women—did seem to like her, which also surprised Leigh. Most of the older women she saw gardening or speed-walking around the neighborhood were typical Danby stock: they wore no-nonsense pantsuits or sweatshirts even in the dead of summer; they had the kind of hairstyles that were set once a week at the beauty salon and not washed on the days in between; their front doors were adorned with dried flowers or ceramic plates of Sunbonnet Sue or American flags, and they drove American cars with no bumper stickers; Leigh would think these women would be annoyed with Eva, with her little convertible, with her California clothes and her bracelets and her boyfriend spending the night and the parties she was always having. But they weren't annoyed. When Eva had a party, the neighborhood women showed up, at least for the early hours. They brought potato salads and deviled eggs, and once, something really delicious called corn fantasy casserole. These old women sat on Eva's big sectional couch and laughed at her jokes. When they left, they stood up on their tiptoes to hug her good-bye. They called her "dear" and "honey" and "kiddo." They told her they would come back later for their dishes or bowls, that they didn't mind at all. It would give them an excuse to come over and chat.

Not that they needed an excuse. In fact, when Leigh and Kara pulled into the driveway of her townhouse, the morning was already uncomfortably warm, but Eva was outside by the cluster of mailboxes, standing unshielded from the sun and listening to a white-haired woman speak animatedly about something. When Leigh got out of the car, she waved, but Eva kept her eyes focused on the woman, nodding every so often, her hand flat like a visor over her eyes.

A window opened above, and Willow's face appeared on the other side of the screen. "Come on up!" She was grinning down at Kara. "It's open."

Leigh looked up. Willow had the curtain draped around her shoulders. "Hi, Mrs. Churchill." Leigh smiled, registering her own disappointment. She'd wanted to see the fake breasts.

"Thanks for the ride." Kara was already moving up to the front door. "Willow said her mom would take me home later."

Leigh nodded and waved. After Kara disappeared inside, she moved under the shade of the townhouse and sat on the hood of her cooling car. Eva was still listening to the older woman talk. Leigh had to laugh to herself. Whatever juicy scandal or secret or suspicion the woman was imparting, she would get to know it soon. And she had to admit, she was looking forward to it. She was in the mood for some levity, some distraction. She felt strangely light, relaxed. When Eva and the older woman finally said their good-byes, Leigh stood up and cocked her head toward the townhouse, smiling.

Eva walked past her without a word.

"Hey..."

Eva turned around as if startled, and the effect was like the opening credits of soap operas, where character after character faces the camera with a sultry or wounded expression. Leigh thought she was kidding around.

Eva nodded back toward her house, no smile. "Kara's here? Great. Willow's been lonely." She started walking again. "Well, thanks. Thanks for dropping her off. You need her home by a certain time?"

"No." Leigh followed her to her door. "Is something wrong? Are you okay?"

"I'm fine. Are you fine?"

"I guess." Leigh was confused. There was some subtext she wasn't getting. Eva was wearing a black halter top that showed most of her back, and her shoulder blades looked hard and immobile.

"Okay. Great." She opened her door.

"Wait. Can I...Are you..." Leigh turned back to search the street for Rick Bechelmeyer's truck. "Are you busy right now? Can I..." She pointed inside.

Eva shrugged. "If you want."

Leigh followed her inside with a shiver. She was wearing an old T-shirt, and she wished she'd brought a sweater. Eva kept her house so cold in the summer. Leigh set her bag down on the big couch and looked around. The place looked good. The carpets were vacuumed, the glass table spot-free. A xylophone and drums played on a stereo somewhere. Eva moved into the kitchen.

"So who were you talking to out there?" she called out. "She looked like she had a lot to say."

"That was Betty Curry. You've met her a million times."

Leigh sank into the corner of the sectional couch. She loved the couch. It sucked her in. "I get them all mixed up, you know, the bridge brigade around here."

"Hmm. I'm not sure why. They're all pretty different."

"Sure. I'm sure they are. It's me, you know, bad memory." Leigh stared at the place on the wall where Eva had nailed one very beautiful and very high-heeled shoe. She'd done it on a whim, tipsy during one of her parties. She'd raised the hammer and explained to everyone that it had been an expensive shoe, but it was too painful to wear, and that she wanted to put it on display somehow. Everyone had laughed. After the party, she'd left the shoe there and put a frame around it. It looked surprisingly good.

After a few minutes, Leigh realized she was still sitting in the living room by herself. She stood up and walked to the kitchen, where she found Eva wearing a very old-looking apron that said I CHILD-PROOFED THE HOUSE, BUT THEY KEEP GETTING IN! She was using an ice cream scoop to extract balls of flesh from a watermelon. Maybe thirty melon balls already sat in a large glass bowl. Leigh slid herself onto a barstool.

"What's all this for?" Leigh wrapped her feet around the legs of her barstool. She'd always liked barstools. She felt like a little kid, waiting for Eva to make her lunch.

"A party."

"Whose?" Leigh swiveled her barstool from side to side.

"Mine."

"Oh." Leigh stopped swiveling.

"I didn't invite you."

"Okay."

Leigh waited. Eva dropped three more watermelon balls into the bowl.

"I didn't invite you because I'm sick of you. I've had it with you." She set down the ice cream scoop and looked at her nails. Despite the words she was saying, she really did appear more concerned with her nails than with Leigh. "I'm not going to call you anymore. I'm not going to bother you. You don't call me back. Ever. I always call you. I'm always the one trying to get you to spend time with me. I'm sick of getting my feelings hurt."

Leigh sensed a delay between her hearing of these words and her understanding of them. She was starting to malfunction, perhaps, like an old answering machine with a full tape, a computer with an overtaxed memory. She was too full of people's complaints against her. She simply couldn't hear this now.

She could leave, she considered. She could just stand up and walk out the door. But she found herself looking down at her hands, spread flat against the counter. They were still soft, her hands. Her nails were okay. She didn't get manicures, but she kept them neat. *I am not that kind of person*, she thought. *I'm different. I don't just leave.*

"Well gee," she finally said. "Sorry. I've been a little sidetracked lately." She glanced toward the stairway. At the top, she could see the closed door to Willow's room. "In case you've forgotten. I've been a little distracted."

Eva crossed her arms, one eyebrow high. "Don't use that. Don't use Kara's accident as an excuse. This is how you've always been. But it's just started to really bug me lately. You know, ever since the accident, I have gone way, way, way out of my way to try to show you and Kara that I am still with you, that no matter what, I'm still your friend. And I feel like I've gotten zip in acknowledgment from you. You've pretty much made it clear that you want me to leave you alone. Well, you know what? You want me to leave you alone? I'll leave you alone." She made a slicing movement with her hand.

Leigh felt a sudden, inexplicable fear. It seemed physical, as if she were about to be pushed off something, arms flailing, trying to hold on. She shook her head. "No, Eva. No. I've just... I've been really busy."

"With what? It's summer break." She went back to her melon balls. "And you know what? I wouldn't be mad if I thought you just didn't like me. Maybe I'm just not your cup of tea. I could handle that. I'm not everyone's cup of tea. That's not a big deal." She stepped away from the counter, eyes narrowed, head cocked, as if she were looking at a painting she didn't like and trying to figure out why. "But what's really sad is I'm pretty sure I'm your closest friend in Danby. I might be your *only* friend in Danby. And you never even call me. That's weird, Leigh. And it's annoying." She waved the ice cream scoop over the counter. "It's weird that you don't have any women friends."

"Eva." Leigh heard her own voice. She sounded like Gary: rational, slightly annoyed. "I do too have women friends."

"Name one."

Leigh laughed. Eva didn't.

"I have friends from college. Friends from before I knew you. You don't know them."

"Talk to them often?"

Leigh rolled her eyes. She'd lost track of Deirdre after she met Gary. "I talk to you."

Eva tilted her head to the side.

"My sister. I'm close with my sister. What the hell is this?"

"How often do you talk with her?"

"What? I don't know. Is there a quota? How often should I talk to her? You let me know."

"Every day? Every week?"

"Sometimes, Eva. I talk to her sometimes. She's visiting right now." She raised her chin.

"She's visited before, right?"

"She visits all the time."

"Then how come I've never met her?"

"Are you implying my sister doesn't really exist?"

"No. I'm saying that as far as I know, I'm your only girlfriend in this town, in this state, maybe in this country, and I've known you for well over ten years, and I've never once met your sister. And I know from talking to Kara that she's visited several times. That's weird, Leigh. Okay? That's weird."

"If you want to meet her, you can meet h—"

"I'd like to. I've often wondered what's so magical about your sister that she actually fulfills whatever secret requirements you have for friends. I don't know, is she insanely clever? Rich? An excellent cook? Well connected?"

"I trust her."

Leigh said the words quickly, without thinking, as if drawing a weapon in self-defense. They looked at each other for a long moment.

"You don't trust me?"

Leigh laughed. It was a genuine laugh, not aimed to hurt. Eva stared at her stonily.

"I'm sorry, but no. Not exactly."

"Why not?"

"Eva. You're a huge gossip."

"No I'm not."

Leigh stood by the counter with her mouth open, too stunned to even shake her head. People didn't see themselves, she considered. They really didn't. It was almost eerie when you saw it face-to-face. "Yes," she said evenly. "You are. And as I've told you, with this thing with Kara, we have to be careful of what we tell people, and—"

"Why? It's in the newspaper, Leigh. Everybody already knows everything."

"They don't know . . ." She tried to think of what it was she didn't want people to know. "They don't know the details. They don't know how it's . . . personally affecting us."

"And what would be so bad about th—"

"Oh. Okay. I'll tell you what, Eva." She was getting louder now, her voice starting to shake. "You try this sometime. You try being on the other side of your mouth. You try going through something hard and horrible like this, knowing that everyone you see knows all about it. You love to talk about people and tell secrets, but have you ever had to feel like everyone is talking about you? It might make you think twice before you take such pleasure in other people's—"

Eva scratched her chin and looked at the ceiling. "You know, I think I did try it. Yeah. I'm pretty sure that when my husband was having sex with his graduate student while I was home taking care of our baby in a town where I knew nobody—I'm pretty sure people were mentioning that to one another, you know, after it all came out. I'm pretty sure it was on people's minds when they bumped into me at the grocery store." She lowered her eyes to Leigh's. "But I'm not so *full of myself* that I had to think it was a big deal. So people were talking about me. Didn't hurt me. I didn't care. People talk about people."

"Good for you. You're so enlightened. But I do care. I don't want people talking about me."

"I don't know why." She held her hands in blades on either side of her face. Her bracelets slid down to her elbows. "I'm always telling Willow that if you worry about what people are saying about you, you're giving them power. If you don't worry, you keep it."

Leigh turned on the bar stool. She wasn't in the mood for Eva's philosophy, to even wonder if it made any sense. "That's great."

"I'm just interested in people." Eva set down the ice cream scoop. "I'm not out to ruin anyone. I like to talk about people because I like to know what's going on with people. I don't think I'm better than anyone. In fact, I think I like to know things about other people because then I don't feel like such a loser. The more I know, the more I know we're all in the same boat."

Leigh shook her head. Casuistry, Gary would call this. Or sophistry? She got them mixed up. "But you make fun of people. You made fun of the Nutters."

Eva frowned. "The Blueberries?"

"The Nutters, Eva. Bob and Audrey. They're people. And what happened in their marriage is private, and if Audrey told you things, you shouldn't have told everybody—"

"I only told you. If Audrey really didn't want me to tell anyone, she could have told me not to, and I wouldn't have even told you."

"Uh-huh."

"It's true, Leigh. If somebody tells me not to tell something, I don't." She paused. "Ask your daughter."

They were silent after that. Leigh sat with her arms crossed, her hands pinching her own skin. Eva placed several fingers flat against her mouth, leaning against the counter. She'd evened the score. She seemed to feel bad about it.

"At least I invited them."

"Who?"

"The Blueberries."

"The Nutters."

"The Nutters. At least I invited them. I introduced them to people. You don't do that. You don't even have parties. Imagine if everyone were you and Gary. People would just stay home all the time. Nobody would talk about anybody. Nobody would talk, period."

"So...you gossip as a public service?"

Eva looked up and caught Leigh's eye. "Think what you want, but it's true. I care about my neighbors. I want to know what's happening to the people who live where I live and shop where I shop and have kids in school where I work. And I think that's true for a lot of people. Yes, you're right—everyone in town is talking about your family right now. But what you need to remember is that not everyone is saying something mean. Most people are sad for you all. They think it was a terrible accident, and they're worried about Bethany's mother, and they're worried about Kara. That's what they're saying when they talk."

Leigh sighed. She was hunched over on the bar stool, her elbows on the counter. "I guess," she said. She was too tired to say anything else.

"Guess nothing. I know what people are saying. Right? I'm the big gossip, right? So a few assholes wrote in to the newspaper? They don't represent everyone. Almost everyone I've talked to feels bad for Kara. Terrible for her. And for you and Gary. And Justin too."

Leigh looked out the window. "Yeah, well. I still want to...move."

Eva cocked her head. "Really?"

"Yeah. Don't you want to leave? I mean, now that Willow's leaving for school..."

Eva squinted. "Ahh. I don't know. I'll travel more. But I have to admit, Danby has sort of grown on me."

Leigh almost smiled. "Well. It grew on me a long time ago. But I think we should maybe go someplace else. If we stay here, I'm going to have to worry about running into Bethany's mother every day. And that's never going to get any better. It makes it harder for her too, I think, seeing us. We bumped into her at the farmers' market yesterday, and—"

Eva winced. "I heard."

"Right. Of course you did. Anyway, I can't just decide not to worry about Diane Kletchka and how much she hates us. I can't just blow it off like...gossip."

"No." Eva wiped her hands on her apron, her face somber. "It won't work for something like that."

"And just, aside from that, I'm sick of this town. It's narrow-minded, cliquey. You know this kid in Justin's class had a party and invited everyone except—"

Eva waved her hand. "Tanner Marik is a little shit. And his parents, too, for letting him do that."

"Why do you bother asking me about my life? Why don't you just tell me what's going on with me? This town. It's telepathic."

"Oh, stop. Heather Crill is a friend of mine. She told me she'd accidentally told you about the party. She told me because she knew she'd hurt you. She felt terrible. She felt really bad."

Leigh stared at what was left of the watermelon. "Does she know about Kara? About the accident? Heather, I mean. I'm just curious."

"Of course. Everyone knows."

"She acted like she didn't know."

"Well, what did you want her to do, Leigh? Hug Kara? She doesn't know her. Say, 'I'm so sorry,' and then stand there like an idiot? People don't know what to say, not to your face, at least. They feel awkward and bad, that's all."

Leigh shook her head. She wanted to hate the town. She didn't want to hear any counterarguments. "And that Cynthia Tork sent me the most annoying letter, telling me I need to stop teaching Flannery O'Connor and Fitzgerald and just teach books that are—"

"Positive and uplifting?" Eva put her hands to her throat and made a gagging sound. "And she's praying for you, right? You and Kara?"

"So . . . you've read my mail?"

"Rick got the same letter, or he got your letter, cc'd to him. Because he's, you know . . . 'your supervisor.'"

"What did he say about it?"

Eva turned away. "I don't want to gossip."

"Eva."

"I don't want to spill secrets, you know, just because my boyfriend is the principal. I'm sorry. Your supervisor."

"Stop. Come on. What did he say about it?"

Eva went back to work on the melon. "He thinks she's a bully. He thinks she and her husband are crazy. He's going to support you a hundred percent."

"Support me? On what?"

"On fighting her." Eva popped a watermelon ball into her mouth. "On teaching what you want to teach."

Leigh lowered her eyes.

"What?"

"I don't know."

"Are you kidding me?"

Leigh shook her head. "I just don't have much fight in me right now. I've been feeling sort of...overwhelmed. The Torks knew Bethany, you know."

"Yes." Eva's voice was flat. "She mentioned that in her letter. What the hell does that have to do with anything?"

Leigh looked up the stairway and lowered her voice. "It has everything to do with everything. It will have everything to do with everything forever."

Eva looked as if she were agreeing for a moment, nodding a little, and Leigh felt as if she had spoken a great truth. But then Eva leaned over the counter, resting on her elbows. All at once, her face was very close.

"You are talking like a crazy person. You may not like me, but I am here to tell you, what you're saying doesn't make sense. Those are two separate things. Kara's accident was terrible. Bethany Cleese is gone, and that's terrible, but there is no connection between that loss and what's happening now with the Torks. Those things have nothing to do with each other. You have to separate things. You can't be thinking about the accident all the time. You have to concentrate on what's in front of you. Just by itself."

The door to Willow's room opened. Eva and Leigh turned quickly, straightening their postures. Willow descended the stairs quickly, her shoulders back, her head held high. She was wearing shorts and a very fitted, low-cut black T-shirt that showed off two new, perfectly positioned and very abundant breasts. But what held Leigh's attention was Kara. She sat on the top step, her chin in her hands, watching her friend jog down the stairs. She looked happy, completely and unabashedly happy, at least at that very moment.

"Just need a glass of water." Willow smiled at Leigh as she passed. "How's it going, Mrs. Churchill?"

"Good, thanks." Leigh couldn't help but smile back. The breasts did look good, she had to admit. She wouldn't have guessed they were fake. "You look great," Leigh said. She turned to catch Eva's eye, but Eva was watching her daughter move back up the stairs.

When Willow reached the top, Kara stood up. Both girls burst out laughing and disappeared back into Willow's room.

"She does look good," Leigh said. She gave Eva a hesitant glance.

"They're still a little swollen. They'll go down a bit more, the doctor said." Eva handed her the ice cream scoop. "Will you do this for a while? I've got to work on the cantaloupe." She glanced up at Leigh. "You can come tonight if you want. To the party, I mean. I know you probably won't."

Leigh took the scoop and went to work on the melon. "I probably won't. I don't know if I'm in the mood for a party just yet. But thanks." She took a breath, closed her eyes. She had never been effusive. It didn't come naturally, and she knew why.

"I'm glad you're my friend, Eva. I mean, if you still are. I'd like for you to hang in there with me. If you could. I don't want you to go away."

They worked without speaking for a while. There was just the sound of the stereo and the slip of melon balls into the big bowl. Leigh kept her eyes lowered, wishing Eva would say something. It was a hard thing, telling someone you didn't want her to go away when she might go ahead and do it anyway.

When they were done, the melons gutted, the bowl covered with plastic wrap, Eva took off her apron. "Well. Thanks for the help."

"Sure." Leigh stood up and rinsed her hands at the sink. This was it, she thought. The end. You could push people away, past their limits, even accidentally, and then it was just too late to get them back.

But Eva gave her a long, discerning look. She knew things about people, Leigh understood, and not all of what she knew was trivial.

Leigh shifted her weight. "What?"

"Well. I was thinking. I'm ready now, for the party, and I've got some free time. You want me to help you write that letter?"

"What letter?"

"To Cynthia Tork. Your response." Eva walked across the hall-way, to the spare bedroom where she kept her computer. "Come on. We don't have to send it. We'll just get it ready. I'm going to have some wine. You want a glass?"

They played around for a while, writing letters they could never send. Once they got serious, or slightly serious, they had the real let-ter done in fifteen minutes. Leigh was happy with the final draft, but she made Eva print her out a copy and erase what was on the com-puter. It was not a good idea, she imagined, to mail out an important letter written while drinking wine and laughing with your friend, without giving yourself at least a day to think it over. And she would have to talk with Rick Bechelmeyer herself first. But it felt good just to write out the words, to think about the here and now and not the accident even for a few minutes, and to have Eva sitting beside her, cheering her on.

Dear Cynthia Tork,

I have received your letter detailing your concerns about various books I plan to teach in the English honors class next year. Please know I do not intend to change my reading selections, especially since the honors class is an elective. You are, of course, free to take this matter up with the school board.

Sincerely,

Leigh Churchill

P.S. Thank you for your concern for my family. I'll see you in your prayers.

Chapter 15

SOMETIME IN JULY, KARA applied for the diversion.
She did this without informing either of her parents—she simply took the form from the file in Gary's office, filled it out, and mailed it in herself. Leigh couldn't be sure when her daughter had done this, or what, exactly, had pushed her into making the decision. She found out only weeks later, when Sue Taft called to let them know the district attorney's office had agreed to divert.

"What does that mean?" Leigh was out of breath, flustered. She had been vacuuming when the phone rang. She almost didn't hear it.

"It means we won't go to court. She has to do the community service, but once she does that, the case is closed." There was a long pause. "We went over this, remember?"

Leigh gave the receiver a dirty look. "So ... Kara ... she applied? She agreed to this?"

"Obviously. She didn't tell you?"

"Obviously not."

"Oh. Well. Either she did, or somebody forged her signature. I'm sitting here looking at a copy of it right now." Sue Taft lowered her voice to a mutter. "She asked for the maximum hours of community service, you know. Two hundred. The D.A. agreed, so now she has to do it. She could have gotten away with half that, easy."

"What kind of community service?"

"I don't know. Her diversion officer will call her in a couple of days. They'll figure something out, based on what she wants to do and what needs to get done. But the good news is, once she completes her service, the case is pretty much closed."

Leigh found Gary in his study. He was reading a book about King James, his bare feet up on his desk, Vivaldi playing on his little CD player. As soon as she started to speak, he leaned across his desk and turned off the music. He listened the way he read, she considered, with complete attention and focus.

"Two hundred hours?" He frowned and looked at the bank calendar pinned to a corkboard above his desk. "That's not going to work. It's almost August."

Leigh looked at the calendar as if needing confirmation. She did not want him to see her face, the joy in her expression, or her surprise that he did not seem joyful as well. But she wasn't crazy. A girl had been killed. Two hundred hours of community service did not seem like a heavy burden. She wasn't a bad mother for thinking that.

"She's supposed to leave for Massachusetts in three weeks." He closed his book and sat up straight. "Classes start on the twenty-fifth, and there's new student orientation a week earlier. She won't have time for two hundred hours." He drummed his fingers on the desk. "Do you think they might let her do some of it when she comes home at Christmas? You know, maybe a week now, a week at Christmas, a week over spring break and then maybe..." He looked at Leigh and rubbed his lips together.

"I don't know," Leigh said. He was being crazy, she thought. He was being the crazy one.

He squinted and furrowed his brow. "And why two hundred? Some arbitrary number? Maybe they don't know that it's going to cancel out college this year. Did Sue make that clear to them? Surely if they knew—"

Leigh looked down at the floor, at a crooked groove between two pieces of hardwood. It was her job, perhaps, to help him see his blind spots, as he had done so many times for her. "Kara knows when school starts," she said quietly. "She knows about new student orientation, Gary. She asked for two hundred hours."

"Well, that's ridiculous." He opened his book and looked down at the page. Leigh suspected it wasn't the same page he'd been reading earlier—he hadn't used a marker. "She made a bad decision," he growled. "That's what we're here for, Leigh. To talk her out of things like that."

BUT THAT EVENING, IT became clear very quickly that Kara wasn't going to be talked out of anything. She sat in the middle of the couch, looking at the carpet and not at her father as he paced in front of her and listed off the reasons that she needed to start college within the month. Even when his voice turned pleading, a tremble in his throat, Kara's face remained surprisingly serene, her hands flat and unmoving on her lap. She nodded as he spoke, at least pretending that she heard and understood everything he said. But when he paused to let her speak, she calmly explained she had applied for the diversion, and that had been a concession on her part. She wouldn't make any more.

"I understand you don't want me to go to jail." Her eyes followed him across the room, though she didn't move her head at all. "Even for a little while. And that's fine. There's no point in that." She glanced at her mother. "But *you* have to understand, I can't go off to school right now. I can't move into the dorms, and go to orientation, and mixers, and act like I'm a normal person, because I'm not. Maybe I'll go later. Probably." She looked down at her lap, touching a tear in the knee of her jeans. "I'm not going this year. I'm sorry that hurts you. But I'm not."

Leigh sat in the rocker by the window, her gaze moving from her husband's face to her daughter's. Kara's voice, she noticed, had changed again. It had none of the lightness of before the accident, but it wasn't the spooky monotone Leigh had almost gotten used to, either. There was a firmness about her voice now, a low steadiness. She sounded about thirty-five.

"So..." Gary shook his head. "After the two hundred hours are up, what are you going to do? You're just going to get a job around here somewhere? Scoop ice cream or something?"

"I'm going to volunteer in Mexico."

Both Leigh and Gary tilted their heads to the same exact angle.

"There's a Catholic Worker House in Juárez. They need volunteers who can speak Spanish."

"Juárez?" Gary cupped his hands around his eyes. "Volunteer to do what?"

"Take care of people. Mostly kids, I think. Old people. It's a homeless shelter. They don't care that I'm not Catholic. I already talked to the woman in charge. She's a nun."

"A nun." Gary nodded bitterly, as if he'd expected, all along, that a nun would be involved. "What do you know about this place? Where did you even find out about it?"

Kara said nothing, but her eyes moved over Gary's shoulder, and when Leigh and Gary turned, they saw Pam turn quickly in the hallway. Gary cleared his throat.

"Would you care to join the discussion?" He waved her forward, closing his eyes. "Pam? Apparently you have knowledge that we, as of yet, do not."

Pam shuffled into the room. She was wearing Leigh's apron, which was fine, since Leigh never wore it. That afternoon, for reasons Leigh did not fully understand, her sister and Justin had baked three or four batches of rock candy. They used food coloring, a very bright blue, and tried to spell out each of their names.

"It's not her fault," Kara said. "I told her not to tell you about it. And she's the one who talked me into Mexico. I wanted to go…" She made a vague flapping gesture with her hand.

Pam cleared her throat. "She was talking Calcutta."

Leigh tilted her head again. Kara looked at the floor.

"And this place in Mexico, it's good." Pam sat on the arm of the couch. "It's just over the border from El Paso. The woman who runs it, the nun, I met her once. She travels all over, raising funds, and she came to our church. She had all these pictures of the shelter, of the people she was helping, and they always need volunteers. I took her number because I was thinking of trying to go down there."

"But you're not, right?" Gary looked down at her with narrowed eyes.

"Well, I can't go now. I need to get a job and save some money." Pam sighed, puffing her cheeks out. "And I don't speak Spanish."

Gary turned away. Pam was a long-term guest, but a guest nonetheless, and he could glare at her for only so long.

"Let's look at this logically." Leigh used her firm voice, her teacher voice. She wished she could make them all stop talking. She needed time to consider, to think. "Let's just talk this through."

"She's not going to *Juárez*." Gary said the city's name as if it had once done him a personal wrong. "Leigh. She's not going. Forget it."

"I'm eighteen," Kara spoke quietly. "And I am going."

"Do you have any idea how dangerous that city is? It was just in the news—"

"The volunteers stay and sleep in the shelter. And if you want to talk dangerous…" She looked up at her father, her jaw set, her gray eyes wide and bright. "Dad. This is dangerous for me. Here. Danby. This is the most dangerous place on earth." She pointed at the patch of beige carpet in front of her feet. "It's dangerous for me here. Understand what I'm telling you. What you think I mean is what I mean."

Gary sat on the other end of the couch, deflated, his elbows resting on his knees.

"I have to go somewhere, and I have to do something. Soon. I'm telling you that. Listen to me. I have to get out of here. One way or another, right now, I have to get out of my life."

Gary nodded and held up his hand, but he kept his eyes lowered. Leigh could see he was concentrating, trying to solve the problem, to come up with a solution he could bear.

"Honey," he said finally, and his voice was gentle again, the way it usually was when he talked to her. He'd never needed to be any other way. "I understand you want to do something productive. I understand you might want to leave Danby for a while. That's fine. But there are people who need help right here in Kansas, I'm sure. There are homeless shelters in Kansas City. There are homeless shelters everywhere. What about Boston? You could stay with your Uncle Pete and Aunt Joelle."

"I'm going to Juárez."

Leigh cleared her throat. "Kara. When you say Danby is dangerous"—she paused to give her daughter a look she hoped would convey the love and worry she felt at that moment, which she could in fact feel as a physical pain, a chill through her body—"do you mean…do you mean because of you, or because of Bethany's mother?"

Kara was silent. But she had tried, Leigh thought, forgiving herself. It wasn't a terrible question. She was trying. It was all she could do.

Kara looked up, her eyes meeting her mother's. "Both," she said. "Right now I have to leave because of me. I have to get out of here and go far away and do something hard that isn't pointless." She glanced at her father, and all at once, her eyes were hard and dull. "But even later, even after that, I won't be able to come back here. Not while she's here. I can't." She moved her hand across her cheek. "You saw her. You heard what she said. She hates me. She always will."

Leigh didn't realize she was nodding, agreeing really, until Gary shot her a look. She looked back at him with a shrug. He wanted to protect his daughter from harm, and even obvious truths.

Pam cleared her throat but said nothing. For a while after that, all four of them looked at the carpet, at the empty spaces between their feet.

"Well. We'll need to speak to the nun." Leigh glanced up at her sister. "You have a number where I can reach her? And there's got to be a consulate or a Web site or something where we can check this place out." She avoided Gary's face. She understood he would feel betrayed, at least for now, and that he would be angry with her for a while. But she felt oddly certain of herself, operating on pure instinct. Kara had, after all, come up with a plan. She was taking steps to save herself. The least they could do, as far as Leigh could see, was get out of her way. And she could see the logic of going to Juárez. She wasn't sure unpaid labor in another country would bring Kara any lasting peace, but it would get her away from what scared her the most. And at least some real work would get done.

She glanced at Gary, who was indeed looking at her with an easy-to-read blend of irritation and shock.

"I'll get you all that," Kara said. She took a hair elastic off her wrist and gathered her hair back. "They have a Web site, letters from former volunteers. And some bishop. I'll show you." She leaned forward and touched her father's hand, but she kept her eyes on Leigh's, confused and startled to see what wasn't familiar: her mother looking back at her with not just love but a pure and grudgeless respect.

KARA AND HER DIVERSION officer decided she would pick up trash for her community service. When Kara told her father this, he bit his lip in a way that made him look as if he were physically trying to prevent himself from reacting. Leigh could see his irritation, his worry. To his credit, he remained quiet until he and Leigh were alone.

"That means along the roads, right? Along the highways?" He looked at Leigh and then out the window, out at the bright summer day. "The people you see out there with big plastic bags and orange vests so they don't get run over?" He seemed to hear his last words just after he'd said them. He looked at Leigh and frowned.

"And parks," Leigh said. "I think she'll be cleaning parks."

"In the middle of the day, of course," he said. "The hottest part of the day."

Her shifts were Monday through Friday, seven to four. Leigh woke early to pack her a lunch and drive her to the courthouse. The building was still closed at seven. Kara went directly to an idling van in the parking lot, giving her name to a man with a clipboard before she climbed inside. Leigh always waited until the van actually left the parking lot before she drove away. She wasn't sure why, what she was waiting for—but every morning, even after Kara was in the van and out of view, Leigh would sit in her station wagon and watch the driver and the other workers stand outside and smoke. She recognized a couple of them—a former student, and the bar-fighting woman who had been in court the day of Kara's arraignment. She'd dyed her hair black since then, but Leigh still recognized her large eyes, her thin mouth, the spiderweb tattoo on her calf.

"You don't talk to her, right?" Leigh asked Kara one morning in the car. She nodded toward the smoking woman. "The nose-biter?"

Kara followed her mother's eyes. "Lana's okay," she said, a hint of reprimand in her voice. "She's embarrassed about it, what she did. She was pretty drunk." She shrugged, opening the door. "I talk to her over lunch sometimes. She's had a crazy life."

· · ·

GARY PICKED KARA UP in the afternoons. Before he left the house, he filled a thermos with a sports drink and another with crushed ice, his face somber, serious, as if he were preparing a chemical compound, something that might explode. When Kara came home sunburned, he chastised Leigh for not putting sunscreen on her that morning.

"You mean under her diaper, too?" Leigh asked. Her teeth were clenched; she couldn't help it. She'd thought they'd moved beyond these battles. "She's eighteen, Gary. I reminded her to put it on. That's all I can do."

Gary did not respond. He looked past Leigh to the window, his eyes moving over the dead summer lawn. It hadn't rained in more than a week, and the city was letting people water only every other day. "I'm sick of the yard," he said, maybe still talking to Leigh, maybe just to himself. "It's too much work, and for nothing. We should just cover it over with rocks, maybe. Gravel. I'm sick of fighting the weather."

The next morning, Kara applied sunscreen under Leigh's supervision. Leigh helped her get the backs of her arms; she had Kara lift up her ponytail so she could rub sunscreen into the back of her neck. Kara's skin was still pink, warm to the touch, and already peeling in some places. Leigh rubbed the sunscreen in lightly, as carefully as she could. She told Kara to bring the bottle with her and apply more on her lunch break. She didn't want to nag, she said, but it was important that she take care of herself, her health, her skin. It was the only body she had. A painful burn would fade in time, but underneath, her mother warned in a gentle voice, she could be doing herself permanent damage.

IN LATE JULY, PAM got a job at the movie theater. She was tired of being bored, she said, sitting around and worrying, watching the news from Iraq. And she thought it was time she started paying rent. Both Leigh and Gary told her she was being silly. She should save her money, they said. She was just sleeping on the futon in the basement; they wished they could give her a proper bed and room. And they liked having her around. They appreciated the time she spent with Justin, who didn't seem quite as lonely and bored as he had last summer. Indeed, when Pam wrote out her new work schedule and posted it on the refrigerator door, Leigh looked it over with apprehension, wondering what Justin would do on the long afternoons when Pam was working. She tried to think what she could schedule, how she could fill his time.

"I want him on Thursdays," Gary said. Leigh stood silent, staring down, until he lifted his eyes from the paper. "We're going to do stuff together. You know, guy stuff. Little excursions. I've got it all worked out."

Leigh worried. Gary had tried this kind of thing before. The previous summer, he'd taken Justin into Kansas City to see the Royals play, and they'd both come home silent and sullen, their faces sunburned, all of Gary's excitement and goodwill gone. And there was, of course, the disastrous camping trip Gary and Justin had gone on with Gary's brother and his two sons when they had come out from Boston for a visit. Gary had thought everyone was getting along. Peter's boys were maybe a little rougher than Justin, a little more crass, but they were okay boys; Gary hadn't noticed any hazing. And then all at once, in the middle of the wilderness, Justin vanished. He simply disappeared from the campsite. An hour before nightfall, coyotes yipping unseen, Gary used his cell phone to call the police, who contacted the park guard, who sent three rangers out into the park. They called Justin's name with bullhorns and shone flashlights into the dusking woods. One ranger found Justin maybe three hundred yards away from Gary's tent. He was sitting on a rock by a turn in the river that babbled just loud enough to render him deaf to all the worried people calling his name. Gary yelled at him in front of everyone, but Justin showed no remorse. "I just wanted to go for a walk," he'd explained. "I just wanted to be by my-self for a while." He'd given his cousins a long, steady look, but never said anything more.

So Leigh had reason for concern, trying to guess what Gary might be planning for father-son outings every Thursday. "Are you going to take him to like a ... sports thing?" She sat next to Gary at the table, smiling, no judgment in her voice or eyes. There was al-ways a basketball event going on up on campus; in the summer, peo-ple could pay to go and watch the new recruits practice. They would be in a gym, at least, nice and cool. Justin would be able to en-dure it.

Gary kept his eyes on the paper. "I've got it all worked out," he said again. His voice was friendly, casual, but his clipped words made Leigh understand that if she persisted, she would irritate him, and, either way, he wasn't going to tell her more.

THE FIRST THURSDAY, GARY took Justin to the Nelson-Atkins Museum of Art in Kansas City. Justin came back with a Thomas Hart Benton calendar from the gift shop. "I like how he does the colors," he told Leigh, holding up the January print for her. "It's kind of like a cartoon. And it looks like here. Out in the country, I mean."

Gary was at the sink, preparing Kara's thermoses. They'd just gotten back, but he insisted he could still pick up Kara from the courthouse at four. "You know, Curry painted the dome of the capi-tol in Topeka, but it kind of looks like that. We could go look at that next week if you want."

Justin shrugged. He had the refrigerator door open, and he stared into it as if he expected something exciting to appear suddenly on the shelves. Leigh pulled him back, shut the door, and gave him a light, almost unconscious push toward his father.

"Or we can take an art class, maybe." Gary dropped cubes of ice into a thermos. "They have these mini-courses at the museum, I noticed. You know, not doing art, just learning about it. How to talk about it. They're not on Thursdays, though. Saturdays, I think. I bet we could still sign up."

Justin looked up at his father with apprehension. Saturday, Leigh knew, was Pam's day off. She and Justin already had a routine of going to the afternoon matinee together. She got free tickets now. Leigh gave them money for popcorn.

"Yeah," Justin said vaguely. He reached past Gary for the calendar, which had already gotten a little wet where he'd left it on the counter by the sink.

The next week, Gary took him to the William Allen White House in Emporia. Justin appeared neither tormented nor excited. The week after that, they went to a class on basic car maintenance sponsored by the Danby Police Department. Justin learned how to check oil and tire pressure. He was, of course, the only twelve-year-old in the class.

"He's going to need to learn that stuff eventually," Gary said, already defensive, though Leigh had tried not to smile when she'd asked him how it went. "He helped change a tire. They already had it up on a jack, but he was working the wrench. He knew what he was doing." He sighed and took off his glasses. "What is that saying? The definition of insanity is doing the same thing over and over and expecting different results? I'm just trying not to be insane. Okay? Leigh? I'm just trying to do something different."

BUT BY AUGUST, HE was running out of ideas. The temperature reached a hundred most days, and Justin, for reasons he would not give, refused to go to the city pool. Gary took him to an electronics trade show. He arranged a guided tour of Danby's water treatment plant. Justin trudged along on these trips without complaint. He brought books to read in the car. Every Thursday morning, without being asked, he packed lunches for both himself and his father.

"Are these Thursdays any fun for you?" Leigh asked him once. Gary was upstairs showering, but she kept her voice low, almost a whisper. She thought Justin should have a confidant, someone he could trust with the truth.

For a long while, Justin said nothing at all. Leigh wondered if he had even heard her. He was making Gary's sandwich, spreading peanut butter over both slices of bread with complete care and focus.

"Well," he said finally. "You know. He's trying to..." He set the knife on top of the open jar of peanut butter, as if he needed both hands free to think about what it was he wanted to say. Leigh watched her son's feathery brows shift and slant, his dark eyes moving around the room. And then he picked up the knife and went back to work on the sandwich. He said nothing more, and Leigh was left to wonder if he'd simply given up, his still-developing mind drifting away from a difficult subject; or if, conversely, his still-developing mind already understood a few things she didn't, and that he knew he'd already said enough.

SO EVERY THURSDAY AFTERNOON for the rest of August, Leigh was alone in the house. No one asked what she would do with her time; her family probably assumed she would spend her unmonitored summer days the way she did when they were around—cleaning and organizing, getting the house in order. The three best things about being a teacher, the old joke went, were June, July, and August; but for Leigh, summer vacation meant she finally had time to try to beat back the kudzu of clutter that filled every closet and cupboard of her home by the end of every school year. She was not a natural housekeeper. During the school year, when-ever she was confronted with Justin's outgrown clothes, or a broken appliance, or any other nonemergency household debris, her tactic was to push the offending article into whatever closet would hide it from view, promising herself to deal with it all properly in June. Gary had pointed out to her many times that she perhaps took this strategy to the extreme: from September to May, she threw lint from the dryer's screen into a pile on the floor of the laundry room. She left moldy casseroles in the back of the refrigerator; out of sight, out of mind. Gary often took it upon himself to spend a winter Sun-day scrubbing out the bottom of the produce drawers or sorting through silverware while she lounged upstairs, reading. He didn't get mad about it anymore; they had been married long enough for him to know that once summer came, she would more than make up for the deficit.

But the summer of the accident, she was, of course, distracted. Vacation was almost over before she really went to work on the linen closet, the kitchen cabinets, the winter coats still hanging in the mudroom. Once she got started, however, she worked quickly and efficiently. She packed labeled boxes and carried them up to the attic. She made daily runs to Goodwill.

"My office is off limits," Gary reminded her one Thursday morning. He stood by the door, holding both lunch sacks. Justin was already in the car. "I'll go through my clothes myself. I mean it. I know that shirt you don't like, and I know exactly where it is. Don't touch it." He could smile at her in a way that conveyed both con-cern and annoyance. "Why don't you just take the day off?"

"Maybe I will," Leigh said. She smiled. Saying the words made her feel better. Technically, she wasn't lying.

But she didn't stay in the house on Thursdays. Once his car was out of sight, she put on her sandals, went out to her own car, and drove to the strip mall that was only a ten-minute walk from her house. The strip mall, newly built and mostly vacant, boasted only a coat outlet and a tanning salon, and so at the height of summer, there were always plenty of parking spaces close to the building. But every Thursday, Leigh turned her station wagon into one of the distant spaces facing the street. From there, if she squinted, she could see across the street and past an empty field into the treeless new subdivision of squat, small houses, including several on Bramble Street.

Diane Kletchka's van was pale pink, THE CLEANING LADY written in white cursive above a phone number on every side, so it was easy enough to spot and keep sight of. Most Thursdays, Leigh followed it to an apartment complex, where Diane picked up another woman. The two of them drove to a stately Victorian not far from where Leigh lived. Diane Kletchka and the other woman entered the house through a side door, carrying in mops and buckets. Diane wore a scarf over her hair, her curls pulled back from her face. From a block away, parked under the shade of a sycamore, Leigh couldn't make out her expression.

She had been surprised to learn that Diane Kletchka was still cleaning other people's houses, still scrubbing toilets and dusting bookcases as she suffered through the first white-hot months of pain after Bethany's death. Leigh preferred to think Diane Kletchka wanted to work. Maybe all that scrubbing and vacuuming provided a distraction from her misery. But imagining one of her own children gone—and even this, just the imagining, was terrifying, a bottomless pit to fall into—Leigh was almost certain that Diane Kletchka was still going to work because, even with the insurance settlement, she couldn't afford not to. She either needed the income, or she couldn't risk losing her clients.

In Leigh's fantasy world—that imaginary existence where

everyone thought the way she did and understood immediately that she only meant them well—she could march up to the door of the house Diane was cleaning and offer her immediate services. She could take the yellow gloves off Diane's hands and pull them onto her own. She could tell Diane to go home and grieve, to lie in bed all day if that was what she needed. But all that was just a dream. In the more difficult world Leigh and everyone else actually lived in, she knew that if she approached Diane Kletchka in any way, even with the best intentions, she would get only more rage and indignation. She would not be allowed to help carry the other woman's burden, and thus relieve her own.

SO WHILE DIANE KLETCHKA scrubbed and toiled, Leigh sat in her car and read, mostly Flannery O'Connor. She had other books, lighter reads, that she could have remembered to bring along on subsequent missions, but Thursday after Thursday she stayed with O'Connor, even though the stories were upsetting, and she was, of course, already upset enough. In fact, as she hid in her car with the engine idling, the air-conditioning on because she was too nervous to roll her window down, she could feel herself grow more anxious with every comic or creepy line, every sinister or crazy character perfectly rendered. She was creepy herself, she decided, glancing up to make sure the cleaning van was still parked where she could see it. And for a variety of reasons. She hated to admit it, but Cynthia Tork had been right: Flannery O'Connor *was* depressing. And if she really thought about it, almost all the stories she had chosen for her students to read were as well. There was something wrong with her, maybe. She wanted to make her students sad.

She didn't always have a lot of time to read. Diane and the other woman would be done cleaning the Victorian in just over an hour, the side door of the house locked, the mop cart supplies loaded back into the side doors of the van. The other woman would have to be dropped off at her apartment complex again—by the third Thursday, Leigh knew the route Diane took by heart: a right onto Commerce and a left on Veer, which involved turning through one of the treacherous new roundabouts that most people in Danby still didn't know how to use. But Diane Kletchka was a good driver, attentive and defensive. She braked for people who should have braked for her; she signaled to show her intentions.

Leigh usually hung back one or two cars. Eva had once made fun of her station wagon: she'd pointed out that Leigh had chosen the exact color, make, and model so popular among the mothers-of-school-aged-children set that she doubted Leigh would be able to find her own car in a soccer field parking lot if it weren't for flashing lights and keyless entry. But it was helpful now, being invisible.

And Leigh reasoned that she herself probably wouldn't ever realize if someone was following her one or two cars back. A good driver, moving forward, would not be staring into her rearview mirror; she would be looking at what was immediately in front of her, and, of course, what lay farther ahead.

DIANE CLEANED ONLY THE one house on Thursdays. After she dropped the other woman off, she would run errands: she stopped by the grocery store and the post office; once, she went to her lawyer's. Then there was the daily stop, the routine that never changed. Each and every Thursday—and probably, Leigh imagined, all the other days of the week—Diane Kletchka went to the cemetery, the new one out by the long road to the western subdivisions. Bethany's grave was in a shaded spot close to the road, the turned earth still uncovered by grass. Leigh could usually see it from where she parked. There was no headstone yet.

Diane brought her daughter flowers—peonies, sometimes lilies.

Leigh watched her bend to place them on the mound. She would stand again, tilt her head, then crouch back down to rearrange them.

She usually stayed for at least a half hour, an hour at the most, though Leigh would have thought it was much longer if it hadn't been for the digital clock on her station wagon's dashboard. She didn't allow herself to read during the cemetery visits. She didn't even keep the air-conditioning on. The road alongside the cemetery was never busy, and she could safely sit with her window down without anyone noticing her there. And seeing what she was seeing, she believed she should be physically miserable, sticky and suffering in the heat.

SHE STARTED FOLLOWING THE van in the evenings too. It was more difficult to get out of the house alone; she had to create fatuous lies, claiming summer work in the classroom or a coffee date with an unknown friend—she didn't want to bring Eva into it. She'd tried purposefully forgetting an item at the grocery store, but a second grocery run bought her only so much time, and anyway, her family often unknowingly sabotaged her plan. She was safe from Kara, who was too exhausted from being out in the heat all day to do anything but come home and sleep. But sometimes Gary or Justin would volunteer to ride along, and Leigh would have to forfeit her mission for the night.

Even when she got away by herself, there was only a slim chance that Diane Kletchka's van would pull out of her driveway. On Monday nights, she cleaned a real estate office. On Thursdays, she went to something at her church. The other evenings of the week, there were only sporadic excursions to the drugstore or a revisit to the cemetery before it closed at dusk.

Leigh was bolder after the sun went down, nothing visible but her headlights. Sometimes she trailed directly behind the van, braking early and gently, always hanging back. She got foolhardy perhaps, attenuated to the risk. On the dark quick road out to the cemetery, she could fall into a sort of trance, her eyes steady on the van's taillights. After a mile or so, she would feel as if they—she and Diane—moved as one unit, their vehicles connected by invisible cables, pushing and pulling each other along.

AND THEN ONE EVENING, when the August air was almost cool after a late-afternoon thunderstorm, they almost crashed. They were downtown. Diane's van had just turned off Third Street onto Commerce. It was the only intersection in Danby that regularly sported anything close to what could be considered bad traffic. The problem, as everyone knew, was that the relatively fast-moving Third Street, which funneled its travelers onto Commerce by way of a very sharp right turn, gave drivers very little time to prepare for the stop-and-go parade of cars trolling for parking spaces along the town's main drag. The spaces on Commerce were angled toward the street—not having to learn to parallel park is a much-loved perk of small town living—so that whenever someone looking for a space decided to wait for someone else to back out, traffic behind the waiting car effectively came to a halt.

Leigh, having driven through downtown Danby thousands of times in her life, was well aware of the possibility that Diane's van might have to stop suddenly on Commerce, and that she would have to be ready to do so, too. But it seemed to her she glanced away for only a moment, looking up to check the dimming western horizon for any sign of more rain. The gold-edged clouds were still moving quickly, and they were light and airy looking, small enough to make the sky itself seem large and powerful, something to behold. So perhaps Leigh, always easily distracted by beauty and unusual light, looked away from the road for more than a moment. And she had her window rolled down partway—the rain-soaked breeze was that nice. Whatever the case, when she regained her focus, the van was stopped in front of her, and her foot, somehow knowing what she did not, had already moved fast to brake.

She blinked and moved her head, taking in the situation. There was an escape route, an empty parking space up ahead to her right. As if bowing to her wishes, the van moved a little farther ahead, giving Leigh just enough room to slide her station wagon into the space. Once she was parked, and, she believed, safe, she cupped her hand around her eyes and waited for her heartbeat to slow. It was only when she lifted her head to the rearview mirror that she saw the van roll back behind her, the side door almost touching her own taillights.

Diane Kletchka had pulled in far enough to the right to allow traffic to slide around her. But Leigh's station wagon was blocked in.

Leigh willed her shaking hands to unbuckle her seatbelt. She believed she could still escape on foot. She was in front of the movie theater, and the doors were opening, the early show just getting out. She could lose herself in the crowd. She could run inside and find Pam behind the concession stand. Pam would help her. Pam would know what to do. But when she looked in her rearview mirror, she saw the cleaning van's lights go dark, and she heard the engine cut off. She had no time to run to anyone. She rolled up her window and locked her door.

"Hey! HEY, I said. What the hell are you up to?"

Diane Kletchka's voice was only slightly muffled by the glass between them, but she stepped back and gave the door a hard kick, as if there were a chance she did not have Leigh's full attention. Leigh turned slowly, leaning away from the window. She could not bear to look directly into Diane Kletchka's eyes, so she looked at her rain-damp hair, the pale strands coiled on her pulsing neck. The dark roots were longer now—she hadn't colored it, Leigh guessed, since her daughter's death, and the difference between the two hues, between light and dark, was drastic and abrupt.

"I know who you are! I see you! Come out here!" Her nostrils were flared, and her hands were up by the glass. "You've been following me. Come out or I'll call the police!"

At first, Leigh believed she was afraid for her physical safety. But if that were the case, if the other woman's palpable rage was really what was making her shake so much she could barely get her keys out of the ignition, she might have just stayed in the car. It would have been safer for everyone, probably, if the police had been called. Leigh might have called them herself. But she wasn't really afraid of being hit, of being spit on. Physical assault might have felt good in its own strange way; it would have evened up the balance a bit, lessening her guilt and increasing Diane Kletchka's in the most basic and primitive way. No. What was far more frightening was the idea of cowering in her car under an onslaught of well-deserved venom. She could picture how she looked huddled in her station wagon, her eyes frightened, her mouth open but unmoving, incapable of any defense. That was the problem. That had been the problem all along. She could see herself—she could see everything—from Diane Kletchka's perspective.

She opened her door and stepped out slowly. Her hands were still shaking, and she didn't trust herself to speak; but she could smell the wet earth in a nearby planter, that lovely, loamy smell that always calmed her. She looked at Diane Kletchka's rough hands, curled tight around a smiley-face key chain.

"I'll get a restraining order."

Diane moved into her gaze, her eyes wild and searching. Leigh looked away, and she moved again.

"Why are you following me? What do you want?"

Leigh looked over Diane's shoulder, to a streetlamp flickering on in the distance. She could think only, it seemed, if she didn't look directly at the other woman. She looked too much like Bethany, maybe. She looked like everything sad and wrong, everything that had been lost.

"WHAT DO YOU WANT? YOU LUNATIC! WHY ARE YOU BOTHERING ME?"

Leigh looked at her.

"ANSWER ME!" Diane kicked the car door behind Leigh's shaking legs, but the sound of the impact was a muffled thud, clearly not what had been intended. She stepped back, twisting her foot behind her other leg, rubbing her toe against her calf. She was wearing flip-flops. She'd hurt herself. Leigh could see tears in her eyes.

Leigh held up her hands and shook her head. "I don't want to bother you. I'm just... I wanted to see you." She lowered her eyes, trying to think. "I've been so worried about you. I wanted to see something that would make me think you would be okay."

The lines between Diane's brows deepened. "I'm not going to be okay. My daughter is dead. Because of yours."

"I know." Leigh forced herself to look up again.

Diane Kletchka stepped back, alarm, even fear, in her eyes. "Go away."

"I've seen you at the cemetery. I know you're in so much pain."

"What's the matter with you?" Her voice was higher now, breathless and pleading. "Why are you bothering me? Do you know how hard it is just to get up every morning? To breathe? To eat? And now you're bothering me?"

Leigh kept her eyes on Diane's. She had the same feeling she'd had at Bethany's service, the sensation of physically taking in grief. "I have been thinking about that," she said carefully. "I have been thinking about how hard it must be for you to get up in the morning. Kara, I can assure you, has been thinking about that as well."

"Go away!"

Leigh heard the sob rise in the other woman's throat and instinctively clutched her own neck. "I am sorry to bother you. But I have to ask you. I have to ask one thing. Is this what Bethany would have wanted? I never knew her the way you did. So you tell me. Is this what she would have wanted her life to mean?"

"Shut up!" Diane raised her palm horizontal to Leigh's mouth. "Don't you talk to me about what she wanted! She'll never have anything she wanted!"

"Is this what she would have wanted for you? For you to hate Kara so much?"

Diane appeared cornered, frantic. She turned to the right, and then the left, her eyes moving up to the darkened sky. "What do you want?" Her eyes searched Leigh's. *I will do whatever you want*, they seemed to say. *I will give you anything else. Just please, please, don't take this.*

"I want you to stop hurting Kara. I want her to feel safe in this town again. This is her home. If she's scared of you, if she has to worry about seeing you, she's going to leave and never come back here. And where does that leave us? This is our home. This is where we live."

"Well. I want my daughter back."

"But she isn't coming back. It doesn't matter what you do to Kara. She's not coming back."

"I know that!" She flapped an arm forward, her car keys just missing Leigh's cheek. She almost looked sorry, realizing. She lowered her voice. "I know that."

"Then why punish Kara? What good does it do? Does it even help you at all?"

It was a good question, Leigh's trump card. If the conversation had been a debate, she would have won right then. She could see this, watching Diane Kletchka suffer and squirm, trying to come up with an answer. But she lost interest. At that very moment, for reasons she could not immediately define, Leigh thought of the Flannery O'Connor story she would teach next year in the fall, with the old, annoying woman who reaches out to her killer in the seconds before her death, touching his skin just long enough to dissolve the differences between them. Cynthia Tork was right—the story did blur the line between killer and victim, between wrongdoer and wronged. That was its intent—Leigh had always known that. She'd been teaching the story for years. What occurred to her now, however, standing between her car and Diane Kletchka, was that the story was not just creepy and depressing—it was instructive for the real world, as useful as a screwdriver, if truly taken to heart. There was a very real point—sustaining and nourishing—to all that fictional gloom.

She reached up and touched Diane Kletchka's arm. "I'm sorry," she said. She had said this before, but the words felt different, were different, with Diane's warm skin in contact with her own. "I almost know. I almost understand what you've gone through, what you've lost."

She swallowed and waited. Saying "almost" was important. She knew there were many different shades of suffering, and that she had been spared the blackest of the black, at least so far, in her life. She wanted to be careful with her words, to say only what she was certain was true.

Diane started to pull away, but Leigh held tight. "I'm sorry," she said again. "I'm so sorry." This was the truest thing she had to say, and so it seemed okay to repeat it. She was sorry in the universal sense. She had not been the one driving, but she could have been. She had not lost her daughter, but she could have. She could yet. They were both subject, as everyone was, to this world and its whims of fate—to bad drivers, to bad parents, to bad decisions, to leveling earthquakes and every other terror in the world.

"I know," Leigh said now, leaving out the "almost," hoping Diane Kletchka would understand. For though she could only imagine what it felt like to be completely enveloped in grief, she completely recognized and understood what it was costing Diane Kletchka to decide not to pull her arm away from Leigh's hand. Rage was fortifying and protective, and so much more energizing than sadness, than powerlessness, than regret. She hated to think she was asking this grieving woman to let go of what she might still need, her last remaining comfort.

When Diane Kletchka finally did move her arm, she did not pull it away so much as she simply let it fall to her side, her hand slapping against her thigh as if it were a weight she could no longer manage. Leigh opened her mouth and tried to think of what more she could say. But before she could come up with anything, she looked carefully at Diane Kletchka's face, which seemed to beg for silence, for time. Leigh nodded to show she understood, and watched her walk back to her car.

Chapter 16

KARA WENT TO JUÁREZ in September. Sister Margarita Delores, her accent lovely but difficult to understand over a crackling phone line, assured Leigh and Gary that the worker house would provide for all of their daughter's needs. In exchange for her daily labor, Kara would receive room and board at the shelter. She would eat what the guests ate, beans and rice and tortillas, three times a day, almost without fail. Sometimes there was milk. She would spend much of her time taking care of children while their parents worked or looked for work. She would cook beans. She would clean. She would sleep in a room with three other female volunteers. The room was on the third floor, and the door had a good lock. The shelter had no air-conditioning, of course, but electric fans were available, and the other volunteers reported that if they went to bed with wet hair they could get the sleep they needed.

Kara should not bring shorts, Sister Margarita said. People would mistake her for a tourist, someone with money. Her skirts should be knee length, modest. Jewelry was, of course, discouraged. The worker house had an arrangement with a health clinic in El Paso; if Kara had a minor illness, a doctor would see her, but if she came down with anything serious or expensive, she would have to be sent home. She would need to take care of herself, to keep up her nutrition and strength. She would have one day off a week, and even on those days off, she was not to use any alcohol or drugs. El Paso, with its air-conditioned theaters and shopping malls, was a twenty-minute walk away.

Volunteers couldn't carry cell phones. The shelter had a land line that Gary and Leigh could call in an emergency. They should mail letters and packages to an address in El Paso. Someone would pick them up and walk them over the border every few days.

THE DAY AFTER KARA left, Leigh and Pam went to the grocery store and bought peanut butter and protein bars and hand lotion. They bought baby formula and Band-Aids and tampons and aspirin and cold medicine. At home, they picked through cupboards and closets, checked expiration dates on cans. They had to keep finding bigger boxes for mailing, repacking, moving things around.

"This is silly," Leigh said, though she continued trying to stuff one more disposable diaper into the side of the newest, largest cardboard box. "I'm sure you can buy all this stuff there."

Pam shrugged. The truth was, they weren't sure of anything, least of all what Kara or the people around her might need. They knew Juárez was a very big city, very close to the United States; it no doubt had its share of stores with stocked shelves and credit card machines. But Leigh pictured the shelter where her daughter now lived as a sort of island, crowded in with malnourished children and overworked parents and electric fans blowing hot air around. The idea that she could mail a jar of peanut butter and expect it to actually get to Kara or to anyone else who might need it seemed magical, too good to be true, a testament to civilization and progress. But she also felt as if they were packing up all their good intentions and throwing them into an abyss. Kara would e-mail just once a week, from the library in El Paso. They would have to wait to hear from her to know if what they sent was right.

This was perhaps what it was like to mother anyone, Leigh decided, far away or close. You could only try your best, then wait to see if what you sent was needed or even wanted. If it wasn't, then you packed a new box, and tried again.

THEY GOT THEIR FIRST e-mail on a Monday. Kara assured them of her health and thanked her mother and aunt for the package. It was so thoughtful of them, she wrote. She'd needed good hand lotion, and the other things had been quickly distributed. But if they were going to buy things at the store, they might as well just send money. It would save on mailing costs. She would be able to buy more things for more people. *They have it so hard here, so many people. To them it's just normal, the way things are.*

She liked her roommates. One was in her sixties, from California, very funny; another was a mother of two grown children who had just gotten a divorce; the third was a somber woman from Philadelphia who rarely spoke but who worked very hard. At first Kara had been afraid of her, but she'd smiled at her once, late at night, when the woman from California was snoring. Their room, Kara wrote, was hot but pretty, with wooden shutters and a high, tin ceiling that made a beautiful sound under rain. The walls were decorated with postcards and drawings the children had made. The four of them shared one bathroom, with only a small cracked mirror over the sink, but they were the lucky ones, as the male volunteers, sleeping downstairs, shared three bathrooms with the shelter's forty guests. All of the volunteers had to be up at five every morning, stumbling around the kitchen to make breakfast before the adult residents had to leave for work. They took turns napping in the heat of the day, the wooden shutters pulled closed.

I sleep okay, Kara wrote. *It's a little cooler now than it was when I first got here. And I could sleep in any weather, I think. I'm so tired at the end of the day.*

Eight hundred miles away, Gary stared at the computer and rubbed the hand Leigh had placed on his shoulder. "Tired is probably good," he said, though his voice sounded uncertain. "Maybe the best thing for her now."

THE FOLLOWING MONDAY, KARA e-mailed to thank Leigh for sending money. There was a drugstore just down the street from the shelter that readily accepted U.S. dollars. She'd gotten medicine, and presents for some of the children. She'd bought a disposable camera to take their pictures. She would get copies and send some. She was doing fine, she wrote, though she was getting a little tired of eating beans.

And she wanted both her mother and father to know that almost as soon as she'd arrived, she had mailed a letter to Diane Kletchka. The idea of it had seemed less frightening, now that she was so far away. She hadn't mentioned it in her earlier e-mails, because she didn't think there was any point. But much to her surprise, just two weeks later, Diane Kletchka had written back.

Kara did not say what was contained in their correspondence. But she assured her parents she would come home for Thanksgiving. She would stay, she wrote, at least a week.

LEIGH WAS SURPRISED AT how good it felt to go back to work that fall. She'd always loved the first few weeks of the school year. Her classroom felt crisp and ready like a newly sharpened pencil, her supply closet neat and fully stocked. Looking out over her rows of fresh-faced eighth-graders, none of them yet sullen with her over a bad grade or an assigned detention, she always felt so much hope and goodwill.

Usually, she felt tired and cynical by October. But the autumn after the accident, the vigor was still with her when she decorated her bulletin board for Halloween. She was teaching her honors class *Gatsby*, and during her introductory lecture, she spoke without notes for almost the full hour, her eyes moving across the rows to rest on the face of each and every student. They could all understand—*would* understand, she decided—the beauty of the language, the genius of the details; the slow, sad tragedy of a character consumed with the past. She used her hands as she spoke, holding them in front of her as if they contained something she wanted her students to see; and her students—all of them, it seemed—perhaps responding to the real passion in her voice, or perhaps understanding that she was speaking to all of them and not just a chosen few, kept their eyes, undistracted, on hers.

PAM TOOK KARA'S ROOM. She kept it exactly the way her niece had left it—the pillows and sham arranged neatly on the bed each morning, the desk uncluttered and free of dust. "Maybe it'll rub off on me," she told Leigh. "You know, that studying thing." She continued to work at the movie theater in the evenings and on weekends, but she spent much of her days studying for her GED course and looking through one of Leigh's old handbooks on writing. She was thinking of going to college, for social work, maybe. Or nursing, possibly nursing—she'd been good at science, she remembered. If she did go back to school, she said, she wouldn't stay in Danby. She would go back up to St. Paul once she saved some money. That was where Ellis would be after he came back from Iraq.

Pam always used *after*, never *if*, when anticipating her son's safe return from the war. She spoke as if making plans for the following morning, or the following winter, something inevitable and almost mundane. But Leigh saw her sister's nervous eyes move over the front page of the paper every morning. One evening, when she and

Pam and Eva were in the kitchen making cookies to send to their re-spective children, bad news from Iraq floated in over the radio. The announcer's words settled like a choking dust over the mixer, the cracked eggshells on the counter, and the three women's faces as they looked at one another and then at the gray-and-white-tile floor. A roadside bomb. Casualties. Families that had not yet been notified. Pam rinsed her hands at the sink and walked to the win-dow, her head tilted up toward the newly gilded leaves at the top of the big sycamore. The announcer gave the stock market report, the weather forecast. Unseasonably warm. Bright and sunny.

Leigh turned off the radio and walked to the window. She took her sister's still-damp hand, and said everything she could think of that was both comforting and true. Ellis was probably fine. Statisti-cally, there was no real reason to worry. And worrying would do no one any good. Pam nodded, but she did not move her gaze from the top of the tree, and she looked tormented by what she saw there. Leigh touched her shoulder and went back to the sink to help Eva clean up. By the time they had the dishwasher loaded, they could smell the cookies in the oven, the first batch almost done. But Pam was still by the window. Leigh didn't know what to say or do.

"Let's watch a movie," Eva said. She nodded at the bowl of re-maining dough. "We can do the rest later, put that in the fridge. I'll just take out this batch and turn off the oven. And you know what? We should test these, make sure they're okay before we mail them off." She gave Leigh a meaningful look. "We should watch a movie, not television. No news. What do you have?"

Leigh frowned and tried to think. They wouldn't have anything but Shakespeare. Gary and Justin had been on a Shakespeare kick ever since they'd gone to a free performance of *Richard III* in a park in Kansas City. It had been their most successful outing together—*Richard* was one of Gary's favorite plays, and Justin had been transfixed by the actor who'd played the lead, who, according to Justin's impersonations, had apparently done much ranting and raving about the stage in a glorious red cape. The next morning, Gary had gotten out his Oxford edition and found the soliloquy Justin had liked the best. Gary went over the words with him, pointing out the double meanings and implications. Justin was clearly more interested in the red cape and the ranting, but by the next morning, he had several lines memorized. He'd put on Leigh's long maroon raincoat and marched around the house, shouting them out, and Gary had told him, with no detectable condescension, that he might be a natural actor.

And so they'd found their bridge. In the last month, he and Gary had rented and watched Kenneth Branagh's *Hamlet*, Laurence Fishburne's *Othello*—not exactly pleasant diversions from news of war.

But if her sister needed a movie now, Shakespeare would have to do. Leigh poured three glasses of milk, nestling them into the crook of one arm so she could use her free hand to gently tug her sister to the basement door. Eva was already halfway down the stairs, the plate of cookies balanced high over her head as if she were a waitress in a crowded diner. Pam did not actually resist moving down the stairs, but Leigh felt as if she were guiding someone who could not see.

Eva set the cookies on top of the television. She already had one in her mouth. "Oh, this is good," she mumbled. She held the case for *Shakespeare in Love*, which Gary or Justin had left open like a half-read book on the DVD player. "I've seen it, but I'd see it again. Have you seen it? Pam?"

Pam, who was sitting on the futon, her old bed, looked up like a startled student. She glanced at the movie case and shook her head.

"Well, it's good." Eva put her hand over her mouth and swallowed. "She won an Oscar for it—Gwyneth, I mean. She's always good, but she's especially good in this." She set down the case and held out the plate of cookies to both Pam and Leigh. "You know she sings too? Like really sings. I don't mean like an actress who can sing and not sound terrible, I mean she sounds great. I was in the car with Willow, and this song came on, and I said, 'Willow, who *is* that woman singing? She has a beautiful voice!' Can you imagine? Someone so talented at two completely different things?"

Leigh nodded, her enthusiasm only a little forced. The DVD player whirled and clicked, and she bit into her still-warm cookie, impatient. She couldn't wait for the movie to start, for the beautiful, multitalented actress to light up the screen and maybe, for a little while at least, distract her sister from her fear. But Pam wasn't even looking at the television. Her cookie sat untouched on the knee of her jeans, and she stared at a crack in the basement wall with the same haunted expression she'd had upstairs. Eva and Leigh looked at each other. Leigh used the remote to pause the movie.

Eva sat on the futon next to Pam and put her arm around her shoulders. Her bracelets caught on the back of Pam's hair, and it took them a moment to disentangle. "I'm sorry," she said softly, looking at Pam. "I know I'm chattering like an idiot. I can hear myself. But whenever I'm worried about Willow, I just have to find something to take my mind off it. Maybe it doesn't help you, though. I'm sorry."

"No," Pam said, and all at once, her eyes appeared to see her surroundings, Eva, the television, her sister, the cookie balanced on her knee. "It's nice of you. I'll be okay. I'll be okay in a minute."

Eva nodded and squeezed her elbow. It was strange, Leigh thought, seeing the two of them together, two very different people from very different parts of her life. But they got along fine. And she felt only a little of that old loneliness, and even that went away when Eva reached up, took her hand, and yanked her down beside them.

"We'll just be three worried mothers together," she said. She had an arm around each sister's neck, and she gently pulled them both in toward her. "We'll just sit here together and worry about our far-away children until they come home."

Leigh turned away and grimaced. The comparison didn't seem accurate or tactful. Willow was at Northwestern, probably in her dorm room, or maybe studying at the library, or out on a date with her perfect breasts. Leigh didn't doubt Eva missed her daughter, but worrying over a daughter in college wasn't the same as worrying over a son in Iraq. It wasn't the same as worrying over a daughter in Juárez, even. She turned the locations over in her mind, comparing the statistics of danger. Northwestern was not Juárez. And Juárez was not Iraq.

Yet here the three of them sat, worried and pensive, statistics no help at all. For any parent understands that the world is not safe. A child can be taken away forever while just walking home from school. Leigh looked up through the basement's small window and caught a glimpse of the lavender sky. Diane Kletchka, if she'd stuck with her schedule, was probably out at the cemetery, telling her much-missed daughter good night.

Worrying was painful, Leigh supposed, but compared to the alternative, a privilege. She took Eva's hand, closed her eyes, and silently sent her best wishes to Willow, who might be walking home alone from the library, or out on a date gone wrong. She thought of her nephew in Iraq. He was probably just waking up, the barracks alight with the first rays of the same sun which had just disappeared from the Kansas horizon. She wondered how he was faring, and if he still wore the gold cross around his neck. She read the paper every morning, and she knew her hope might do him little good, but she hoped all the same that he would come home soon, and that his mother's amazing, enormous heart would not be further tested.

And she thought of her own daughter, who was probably already in bed for the evening, her hair wet to ward off the heat, an electric fan whirring beside her. She wished her a restful, dreamless sleep, free of longing for the other turns she could have made, and all the ways things might have been different. She pictured Kara in the morning, rising with the other volunteers, putting on her glasses and squinting at herself in the small, cracked mirror of the shared bathroom. Leigh wondered what her daughter would see in the tired face looking back at her before her day of hard work began. She hoped Kara might see the real beauty there, the sad wisdom, and all the potential. Perhaps it was too soon for that. But she would be home for Thanksgiving. By then, her mother sincerely hoped, she might at least learn to look at herself with mercy.

Acknowledgments

I WROTE THIS NOVEL during what began as a rocky time in my life, and I am indebted to the people who helped pull me through, both professionally and personally, to better times. Jennifer Rudolph Walsh, my agent, proved herself as encouraging and caring as she is smart. I am similarly grateful for the support and flexibility I found in the good people at Hyperion: Ellen Archer's optimism and foresight were particularly helpful. My editor, Leslie Wells, read drafts as I wrote, and I am convinced her guidance and criticism made this a much better book than it would have been otherwise.

As talented as my editor in New York is, I must also mention my unpaid editor in Utah—my sister, Mollye Moriarty, who time and again muddled through the roughest of drafts, responding with insight and intelligence. Mary Wharff, David Charlson, and Aimee Peeples also read drafts and made helpful comments. John Frydman did his best to explain traffic laws and the legal issues raised in this book.

On the home front, Gretchen Goodman-Jansen and Marilyn Woodward were the kind of friends you can call for help when you are sick, your child is sick, and you are pretty sure everyone is a little sick of you and your child being sick. My mother, Joyce Melton, drove in to Lawrence to babysit during the Last Big Flu of '05.

Acknowledgments

Michelle Ward, Jill Cannon, and Melissa Bronnenberg provided me (and, more importantly, Viv) with endless hours of distraction and amusement.

Most of all, however, I want to thank my daughter, the magnificent and indomitable Vivian. She came into my life just under three years ago, and already she has cracked me up more often than anyone else I've ever known. Here's to easier breathing for both of us, Viv, and the continued joy of watching you bloom.

.